PRAISE FOR MI

CW00481419

"Thrilling entertainment."

— *PUBLISHERS WEEKLY* ON MUTATION

"McBride writes with the perfect mixture of suspense and horror that keeps the reader on edge."

— EXAMINER

"McBride's style brings to mind both James Rollins and Michael Crichton."

— SCI-FI & SCARY

"Highly recommended for fans of creature horror and the thrillers of Michael Crichton."

— *THE HORROR REVIEW*

"Michael McBride literally stunned me with his enigmatic talent and kept me hanging on right up until the end."

— *MIDWEST BOOK REVIEW*

ALSO BY MICHAEL MCBRIDE

THE UNIT 51 TRILOGY

*Subhuman * Forsaken * Mutation*

THE VIRAL APOCALYPSE SERIES

*Contagion * Ruination * Extinction*

STANDALONE SCI-FI/HORROR

*Ancient Enemy * Burial Ground * Chimera * Extant * Fearful Symmetry * Innocents Lost *
Predatory Instinct * Remains * Subterrestrial * Sunblind * Unidentified * Vector Borne*

THE SNOWBLIND SERIES

*Snowblind * Snowblind: The Killing Grounds*

STANDALONE SUSPENSE THRILLERS

*Bloodletting * Condemned * Immun3 * The Coyote * The Event*

THE EXTINCTION AGENDA SERIES

(Written as Michael Laurence)

*The Extinction Agenda * The Annihilation Protocol * The Elimination Threat*

BOOK ONE OF THE VIRAL APOCALYPSE SERIES

CONTAGION

MICHAEL MCBRIDE

PRETERNATURAL PRESS
DENVER, COLORADO

First paperback edition published by Preternatural Press

www.michaelmcbride.net

Cover Design by Deranged Doctor Design

ISBN 979-8-799-17437-8 (hardcover)

ISBN 979-8-775-08222-2 (trade paperback)

First Edition: March 2022

10 9 8 7 6 5 4 3 2 1

For my friends on the front lines

1

Brooks Range, Alaska

D r. Riley Middleton cupped her hands around her coffee mug and reveled in the sun's warmth on her face. It was already a balmy 36 degrees, despite the gusting arctic breeze, for which she was exceedingly grateful. While it might have dried out her freckled skin, tangled her auburn hair, and chapped her lips, it kept the mosquitoes from swarming. She only wished the tundra provided better cover so that the infernal insects didn't feel the need to use her as a windbreak, aggregating on the back of her jacket like a living cape.

A seemingly infinite cottongrass meadow spreads out before her, stretching all the way to a horizon bumpy with overgrown mesas. Bitterly cold creeks meandered through the willows and dwarf shrubs spotting the floodplain, where a herd of caribou grazed amid the cloudberry bushes. She closed her eyes and imagined how this area must have looked at the end of the Younger Dryas, the last major abrupt climatic event, with the glaciers melting and Beringia once more vanishing beneath the rising waters of the Beaufort, Chukchi, and Bering Seas, stranding nomadic Paleo-Indians on a new continent ripe for exploration. All around her were signs of habitation — from bifacial stone projectiles and primitive chiseling tools carved from the chert beneath her feet to the carbon scoring of ancient campfires immortalized in the permafrost — dating back nearly twelve thousand years, to a time when mastodons, wooly rhinos, and muskoxen roamed the plains, the last vestiges of the once great herds of megafauna.

It was an age critical to the survival of the human species, a tipping point that could very well have led to extinction instead of expansion, one shaped by the environment as much as perseverance, not to mention a heaping helping of luck. Unfortunately, without written records, modern researchers could only try to piece together the few remaining clues, like attempting to recreate the night sky from a handful of stars, and continually revise that picture until it defined itself, although if everything went according to plan today, Riley and her team just might gain the critical insight they needed.

She heard footsteps and turned to find Dr. Dale Edgerton walking quickly toward her. His sun-leathered face was red from the exertion, his dark eyes alight with excitement. There was only one thing Riley could think of that would cause the ordinarily stoic evolutionary anthropologist to exhibit anything resembling human emotion. Her heart leapt at the prospect.

"We broke through?" she said.

The ghost of a smile crossed Edgerton's lips.

"We're just waiting for you," he said.

Riley struck off toward the camp, spilling the last of her coffee onto the back of her hand in her hurry. The ground seemed to tilt beneath her feet as they passed through a circle of yellow tents, rounded the Quonset huts housing their tools and supplies, and headed straight toward the Grand Mesa, where their excavation was concealed beneath a framework of metal scaffolding and tarps.

She'd been the lead archeologist on the site for nearly three years, achieving the dream she'd envisioned when she'd first seen it from the helicopter that had ferried her from Ivotuk Airstrip. It had been a profound moment, one she equated with the call of destiny. While the site had been active at various times since the Nineties, they hadn't begun making significant advances until she brought her technical acumen to the leadership role. They no longer scoured the ground for artifacts, but rather mapped it using LiDar-equipped satellites capable of recreating the topography, right down to the smallest pebble, and charted the subsurface features with state-of-the-art magnetometers and ground-penetrating radars, all of which had come at significant cost, chief among them what many of her colleagues considered to be a deal with the devil. Combined, however, those tools had been responsible for what could very well be the discovery of a lifetime, one that could potentially rewrite the history of the world.

Drs. Hays Montgomery and Niles Williams crouched over the rugged hole in the sedimentary rock, surrounded by their graduate students, who covertly referred to them as Simon and Garfunkel for their uncanny resemblance to the eponymous duo. They rose to greet her, their expressions those of children waiting to run downstairs on Christmas morning to see what Santa had brought them.

"Has anyone been inside yet?" Riley asked.

"We all agreed that you should have the honor of going first," Montgomery said. He cast a sideways glance at Edgerton. "Well, almost all."

"But then you'd better move out of the way and make room for the rest of us," Williams said. His cracked lips bled when he smiled, but he didn't seem to notice. He held out a caving helmet with a headlamp affixed on one side and a digital video camera on the other. "I should point out that this decision has nothing to do with the fact that you sign our grants."

Riley donned the helmet without a word, knelt, and stared into the hole. It had been nearly two years since they'd discovered the subterranean void from the top of the mesa, using sonic waves of such low frequency that they were able to penetrate the bedrock to previously uncharted depths. Of course, they'd sacrificed resolution in the process, so all they'd been able to tell was that there was a hollow space of indeterminate size and shape within the formation. And if there was a cave, then there just might be artifacts and primitive artwork that offered them insights into the minds of the men and women who'd seeded the indigenous populations of the North and South American continents. The dry, sealed conditions and the arctic temperatures were better suited to their preservation than even the Franco-Cantabrian and Maros-Pangkep caves in Western Europe and Indonesia, respectively, which had miraculously safeguarded Upper Paleolithic paintings dating back over forty thousand years.

With the flip of a switch, the beam shot from her forehead into the darkness, illuminating the passage it had taken them nearly two full summers to excavate from the loose talus and remove the stones clogging it, most of which had been so lodged in the frozen, sandy loam that they'd been forced to chisel them free by hand. It couldn't have been more perfectly sealed had someone deliberately done so.

She glanced back at her colleagues one last time, started the recording, and crawled into the earth. The stone walls were remarkably smooth and constricted to such an extent that they forced her to lower her chest all the way to the ground. Using her elbows and knees, she squirmed deeper, her heavy breathing harsh and loud in the confines. She dictated for the camera to distract herself from thoughts of suffocation and entombment beneath thousands of tons of rock.

"I'm approximately ten feet into what appears to be a natural formation, and already the temperature has dropped a good twenty degrees. The rock is so cold that it hurts my palms, even through my gloves."

The beam outlined the end of the tunnel and diffused into the open space beyond. Another twenty feet and she reached the mouth of a cave that extended beyond her light's reach. A stone roughly the same size and shape as the opening rested on the ground inside, its surface adorned with petroglyphs of a style reminiscent of a cross between ancient Sumerian, Egyptian, and Native American. She felt a distinct coldness around her, like the breath of the dead upon the fine hairs on the back of her neck, causing her to shiver. The crown of her helmet grazed the jagged outcroppings of the rocky roof as she crawled into the cavern and rose to a crouch. It had to be at least thirty degrees colder in here. The sounds of her breathing echoed from the seemingly infinite darkness. She turned her head slowly from one side to the other, exploring the vast space with her headlamp.

"The cave is formed from Katakturuk dolomite, representing carbonate sedimentation from the Late Proterozoic Period. The limited presence of flowstone and speleothems suggests largely dry and still conditions, as evidenced by sporadic aggregates of dogtooth spar and a handful of small gours."

She stepped over one of the fragile, craterlike formations and stopped dead in her tracks. Her light focused upon human skeletal remains so old they'd nearly turned to stone. She could hardly find the voice to speak.

"I've discovered a concentration of disarticulated remains, abandonment context. The body is positioned on its back, its incomplete torso flexed, the bones of its extremities scattered. Its intact calvaria rests nearby."

A light swept across her from behind, throwing her shadow onto the rocky ground as though it were attempting to escape. She turned and shielded her eyes from the glare.

"Don't let me interrupt," Edgerton said, striking off to the right.

Riley shook her head. There was something about the presentation of the remains that didn't sit right with her, but she couldn't quite put her finger on it.

"There are no grave goods or artifacts of any kind." She crouched to get a closer look at the condition of the bones, which were hardened and deformed by a combination of putrefaction and petrification. She traced her fingertips over scratch-like striations in the cortices she would have recognized anywhere as she'd spent her summers as an undergraduate excavating Anasazi ruins in Southwestern Colorado. "This can't be right."

She pressed deeper into the cave as more and more lights emerged from the tunnel behind her. The carvings on the walls were ornate, elaborate, and appeared to tell a story in panels, much like a comic strip in a newspaper, although their meaning was lost on her. Frigid air lanced through her skin and resonated in her bones. The muscles in the back of her neck tightened, raising the hackles. Her pulse accelerated and each breath came faster than the last.

"Another concentration of disarticulated remains," she said, spotlighting them with her beam. "Abandonment context. On stomach, sprawled, torso twisted to the right."

She again crouched and traced the contours of the outer layer of the bones, which demonstrated the same telltale grooves as the last set.

"We hit the jackpot," Edgerton said. "There are more remains over here."

"What's their condition?" Riley asked, her voice high and tight.

"Disarticulated, abandonment context, largely scattered."

"What about the cortices of the bones themselves?"

"They're more stone than calcific matter by now, but there are distinct crescent-shaped ridges . . . " Edgerton's words trailed off. "Are you reading this the same way I am?"

Riley nodded to herself. She didn't want to use the word out loud, not while she was recording, but there was no doubt in her mind that the remains exhibited evidence of cannibalism.

There was a rock wall ahead of her, at the very top of which was a jagged crevice barely tall enough to squeeze through. The temperature plummeted as she crawled closer, the air growing so heavy she labored to breathe. She shone her light through the opening and into a terminal branch reminiscent of a bear's den, not least of which because of the bones scattered across the ground and piled against the walls. She raised her beam and found herself staring at a mummified corpse, contorted and pressed into the corner, its back to her, wearing the horned skull of a steppe bison on its head. It was so ancient that it hardly appeared human, its crisp, brownish skin clinging to its bony framework, and yet she almost felt as though it were the source of the coldness emanating from the depths of the mesa.

"What in the name of God happened here?" she whispered.

THE FRIGID WIND howled across the tundra, battering everything in its way. The walls of Edgerton's tent bowed inward and snapped with every gust, which, despite the heat generated by his propane stove, seemed to pass straight through the polypropylene fabric, his sleeping bag, and all of the layers of clothing underneath. He wrapped his arms tightly around his chest and tried to keep his teeth from chattering. Never, in his eight years at this site, had he experienced a windstorm remotely like this, let alone the kinds of temperatures that prevented them from working here all year long. There was a reason their archeological season lasted only three months, the same reason that had driven the primitive humans that once inhabited this region ever southward as the climate changed. It was way too bloody cold for anything shy of caribou and bears to survive for any length of time. And the infernal mosquitoes, of course. He was convinced those blasted creatures would outlast them all.

A vicious gust buffeted his tent with enough force to pry one of the pegs from the frozen earth. He poked his head out of his sleeping bag and watched the shadow of the guyline lash the opaque siding. There was no way on this planet he was going out there right now, not unless —

Another gust slammed against the wall, nearly lifting the bottom of the tent from the ground.

He didn't have a choice in the matter now. Either he drove those stakes back into the ground or he found himself tumbling downhill through the cottongrass and into the creek. And if he got wet in cold like this, he could very well freeze to death before the sun rose.

Edgerton grumbled under his breath and kicked at his sleeping bag until he was able to cast it aside. He was already wearing nearly everything he owned, and yet it felt as though he were wearing nothing at all. With as little propane as he had left, once he crawled outside, he was consigning himself to a long, sleepless night of uncontrollable shivering.

None of this would have been a problem had it not been for Little Miss Ambition, Dr. Riley Middleton. They'd all been doing just fine without the expensive equipment, let alone their new benefactor and its financial interests, about which he could only speculate. It should have been him sleeping peacefully inside the tent in the lee of the Quonset hut, not her. He'd been working this site every summer for nearly a decade. He had seniority, not to mention more experience, a better publication record, and a higher standing in academic circles. Plus, he was a bloody professor in residence at Stanford, for Christ's sake. How had he allowed himself to be relegated to the support staff?

He growled in frustration, stuffed his feet into his boots, and rummaged around until he found a flashlight and a hammer. Maybe if he dialed up the propane on the stove, he'd be able to warm up at least a little bit. Forget rationing. It wasn't his problem their stockpiles were running low and their next supply drop wasn't for another three days.

"Screw them," he said, cranking up the dial.

He'd held his tongue when he was passed over for promotion, but he wasn't about to suffer needlessly for anyone.

Edgerton unzipped the flap and ducked out into the night. The wind screamed and knocked him off balance, driving him to his knees with a whip from the untethered cord. He shielded his face and crawled around the side to where the wind had pried one of the aluminum poles from the grommet strip. It took all of his strength to bend it back into place and stretch the strap far enough away from the old hole to create a new one.

A ferocious, screaming wind knocked him against his tent. He heard something beneath the gale, an undercurrent of sound, little more than the whisper of a distant stream, only it almost sounded like someone calling his name.

He struggled to his knees, captured the guyline, and pounded the peg back into the hard ground. One more corner and he'd be right back inside, with the thermostat cranked up and a contented smile on his face as he drifted off into a blissful—

Daaaaale.

He froze and cocked his head toward the sound. He'd heard it clearly that time. The Quonset huts and the other tents in the ring were dark and silent, without a hint of movement inside. He listened for several seconds more before he resumed his task, refitting the tapered end of the pole into the grommet and hammering the stake—

Daaaaale.

He gave the peg a final tap and rose to his feet.

"Who's there?" he shouted, but the wind stole the words from his lips.

The remaining loose cord flapped behind him as he struck off toward the dark mesa, a black shape eclipsing half of the cloud-covered sky, like a wave preparing to crash down on them. He passed the tents belonging to Montgomery and Williams and had just reached the one shared by the graduate students when he heard it again.

Daaaaale.

Suddenly, he realized exactly where it was coming from and why it sounded like it did. Someone had gone into the cave and had gotten either hurt or stuck, someone who needed not just help, but *his* help specifically. Someone who could count on good old Dale to keep his mouth shut and not ruffle any feathers, someone who knew she could walk all over him and there was nothing he could do about it, at least not without being evicted from the site and losing every bit of headway he'd made with his research.

Well, not this time. He'd crawl in there and get Dr. Middleton out of whatever mess she'd made for herself while trying to find a way to take all of the credit for their shared discovery. And while everyone else was sleeping, no less! There had to be a way to turn the situation to his advantage. It was high time Dr. Dale Edgerton took charge of his own destiny and finally got what he deserved.

He shielded his eyes from the wind and staggered toward the active dig, where the tarps attached to the framework of their makeshift windbreak had torn loose and flew tattered, like the sails of a ghost ship concealing the earthen maw. A cold darkness radiated from the tunnel. He crouched before it and felt the stale breath of the mesa upon his face, as old and lifeless as time itself. In that moment, he understood exactly what had happened and allowed himself a smile that caused his chapped lips to bleed.

Dr. Riley Middleton — genius extraordinaire, master of technology, and unapologetic suck-up — had forgotten the first and most important rule of spelunking: always take a backup light. Her flashlight must have died while she was inside and she'd gotten herself turned around, unable to find her way back to the lone egress.

Daaaaale.

The voice was louder, more insistent, and unmistakably coming from the depths of the mountain.

Leaving her stranded in there all night, a victim of her own panic, would serve her right, but waking up the entire camp as he paraded her past colleagues who wouldn't find her late-night adventures at all amusing, would be infinitely more gratifying.

Dale switched on his flashlight and crawled into the tunnel. The wind roared as he scurried out of its reach, deeper into darkness somehow even colder. His exhalations echoed in the confines, metered by the thrum of his pulse in his ears. He heard the buzz of the mosquitoes that had sought shelter from the elements, felt their tiny legs on his bare cheeks and wrists. Exposing Middleton's subterfuge wasn't enough by itself; there had to be a way to turn the situation to his advantage. After all, he couldn't possibly be passed over twice. He wouldn't even need to hurt her, just scare her a little. Let her reach the decision to leave on her own, or maybe the two of them could come to an accommodation. All he really needed to do was publish his findings first, and he'd be able to write his own ticket.

He shut off his beam and continued onward until he felt open air beyond the end of the tunnel. The only sound was the hollow echo of his breathing. He totally understood how she could have gotten lost in the pitch-black cave. Had he not brought his flashlight, he never would have considered crawling from the hole and advancing into the emptiness as he did now. A glance over his shoulder confirmed he could neither see the orifice nor feel the flow of air on his face.

Daaaaale.

He turned toward the origin of the sound, which somehow seemed as far away as it had from the surface, a phenomenon he chalked up to the strange acoustics of the cave. The ground was hard and jagged and hurt his knees, but he didn't dare risk walking and injuring himself, or worse, damaging the remains. He found the bones in the darkness, tracing their hard contours as he inched around them. Had the Paleo-Indians to whom they belonged crawled through this cave, just as he did now, twelve thousand years and countless generations ago?

Already he'd lost his bearings and was just about to turn on his light when he heard the voice again.

Dale.

A single syllable whispered seemingly from all around him at once.

He pressed on and bumped into a stone outcropping. Ran his palms over the surface until he found the upper edge of the formation and recognized where he was. Just on the other side was the chamber where they'd discovered the mummified remains. Riley must have squeezed inside before her light abandoned her to the darkness. He could only imagine the expression on her face when he surprised her by shining his beam directly into her eyes.

Edgerton rose to his knees, braced his elbows on the rocky ledge, and aimed his flashlight toward the back wall. He took a moment to savor his victory before thumbing the switch.

The light struck the mummified corpse, its desiccated skin crawling with mosquitoes beneath the clear plastic tarp they'd draped over it.

In that momentary flash of illumination, it was a living, breathing entity, a tan-skinned being looking back at him over its shoulder through the hollow sockets of the steppe bison's skull. The bones scattered around it took on flesh and the bare stone became a killing room floor.

The flashlight flickered and the remains in the corner were no longer those of an ancient being, but rather Edgerton himself, naked and covered with blood, the bodies lying at his feet those of his colleagues.

His light died and the frigid darkness smothered him.

He heard the voice again, only this time directly in his ear.

"Dale."

His screams echoed into the depths of the earth.

RILEY AWAKENED WITH THE DAWN. The way the red sunlight hit the golden fabric of her tent turned it a deep shade of orange, reminiscent of the tender flesh around a peach pit. She took a moment to appreciate the beauty and savor the prospects of the coming day before casting aside her sleeping back and hurriedly dressing to keep the morning chill from settling in.

The others were obviously just as excited as she was. It was a rare occasion to crawl from her tent and find a fire already burning and the graduate students not just awake, but boiling water for coffee and oatmeal. She understood exactly how they felt; there was a big difference between starting the day knowing you're going to spend the next eight hours participating in grueling physical labor, moving stones and toting equipment, and finding yourself at the epicenter of a groundbreaking discovery with the potential to change everything the world knew about the history of humankind.

Skeletal remains were one thing, but an actual intact specimen with an unprecedented level of preservation was the find of a lifetime. Prior to this, the oldest known naturally mummified remains had been found in the Atacama Desert of Chile and dated to nine thousand years ago. This discovery potentially predated it by more than three thousand years, which could easily have been the amount of time required to travel all the way down to South America and seed that very population.

Even more exciting was the physical condition, which more closely resembled that of Ötzi the Iceman, whose five-thousand-year-old corpse had been recovered in the Austrian Alps, protruding from a melting glacier. The ice and colder temperatures had proved to be more conducive to preservation than the arid desert, so much so that researchers had been able to collect pollen and grains from the dead man's teeth and analyze the contents of his stomach and bowels with high enough accuracy to determine not just what he'd eaten, but where he'd consumed his final meal. They'd been able to divine his origin by the bacteria in his intestinal tract, a strain of *Helicobacter pylori* genetically similar to a modern strain common in Northern India. Best of all, his red blood cells hadn't deteriorated in the slightest and his DNA had been so pristine they'd been able to sequence his entire genome, which they'd subsequently traced to the Mediterranean Islands, and nineteen living descendants in the Tyrolean region of Eastern Austria and Northern Italy, who shared the same uncommon genetic mutation as their remote ancestor.

Riley couldn't wait to find out what secrets the man they were calling the Brooks Caveman was hiding. They couldn't afford to rush the process and risk damaging his remains, though. Even exposure to the outside air after so much time in static conditions could be hugely detrimental. They'd covered the body with plastic and limited the amount of time they subjected it to artificial light, but that wasn't nearly enough. They needed to find a way to contain it under carefully controlled environmental conditions and remove it from the mesa, which was where their benefactors came in. She'd already uploaded the video imagery, submitted her formal request, and set the wheels in motion. Unfortunately, satellite connectivity was sporadic at best, which meant there was no way of knowing when NeXgen would receive her communication or how long it might take to get a reply.

NeXgen Biotechnology and Pharmaceuticals might have sounded like a strange bedfellow, especially considering its high-profile defense contracts, but the fact remained that climate change, whether natural or anthropogenic, posed a significant danger to human populations, and not just from rising temperatures and sea levels. Lord only knew what kinds of diseases were frozen in these arctic wastelands — which provided the perfect conditions for the preservation of life forms requiring neither light nor oxygen for metabolic activity — just waiting to be thawed and unleashed upon a species that no longer possessed the immunities its forebears had developed. Without the presence of those antibodies, something as simple as an ancient cold virus could easily mow down the global population with such speed and severity that it would make the Spanish Flu — which killed an estimated fifty to a hundred million people in the early twentieth century — pale by comparison, a prospect of no small consequence for any company on the front lines of combating that nightmare scenario.

The moment NeXgen had learned of the budgetary shortfalls at Grand Mesa — a site already known for its distinct evidence of protohuman habitation and extreme levels of preservation — and recognized the potential for the discovery of hominin remains, it had reached out to her via the Johan Brandt Institute for Evolutionary Anthropology. Even a single phalanx, like the finger bone that had been unearthed from a Russian cave and led to the classification of a discrete subspecies of proto-human known as *Homo sapiens denisova*, could be used to generate at least a partial genome from which they could identify residual viral DNA that had been incorporated into the specimen's genetic code. If they could isolate that DNA and work backward to recreate the virus, they could manufacture treatments that could very well save the entire species from a pandemic of historic proportions, one that could start at any moment and in a place where no one expected, much like the Siberian thaw that released ancient anthrax spores and caused the evacuation of an entire isolated village.

While her colleagues might not have cared for their benefactor's cozy relationship with the military-industrial complex, Riley was a realist. Not only had they desperately needed the funding NeXgen had provided with a single stroke of its pen, but the pentagon would have been alerted to any discoveries with national security implications by the National Science Foundation or the Alaska Department of Natural Resources, anyway. The Department of Defense would have swooped in and assumed control of their excavation and all of their research without the slightest notice. At least by partnering with NeXgen, they'd be able to exert a measure of control over the usurpation. After all, it was amazing what powerful entities could accomplish behind closed doors.

But politics was the furthest thing from her mind this morning as she drank her coffee with a smile on her face, enjoying the excited conversation, if not actively participating. In her mind, she was already back inside the cave, painstakingly sketching the locations of the bones, which would provide the foundation for the research that would ultimately become a book. Her only concern, slight though it might be, was the condition of the cortices of the bones. If the scratches matched the dentition of the mummified subject or his stomach contained any amount of human flesh, there would be pressure to suppress the discovery unless she could determine conclusively that he'd been forced to eat the others in an ultimately futile attempt to survive. As it was, she was having a hard time not thinking about the enormous stone, roughly the same size and shape as the mouth of the tunnel, which could have easily been used to seal the people inside while they were still alive.

"The pictures came out perfectly," Dr. Montgomery said. "I commend you all for your skill and professionalism."

The graduate students beamed at their professor. They'd spent the entire previous day gridding off the eastern half of the cave with chalk lines and documenting the remains with rulers and directional markers to establish scale and positioning. It was a frustratingly slow process that would likely take two more full days to do the same for the western half and the adjacent chamber with the intact body, and that was before they could even touch the remains, let alone explore the full extent of the cave, at the back of which was a honeycomb of passages, some of which appeared to lead deeper into the earth, while others were plugged with stacked rocks, just like the main entrance had been. The full size and scope of the project was daunting, especially considering they had only ten more weeks before winter set in. The mere thought of spending nine whole months obsessing about a site she wouldn't be able to see until next summer was excruciating.

"Dr. Middleton?" Williams said, gently placing his hand on her shoulder.

"Hmm?" Riley said.

"I said, I don't suppose you've seen Dr. Edgerton this morning."

"Dale?" She turned and looked around the camp. "I can't imagine he would have chosen this, of all days, to sleep in."

Riley set down her mug and struck off toward his tent. It wasn't until she was nearly upon it that she noticed the front flap was unzipped and hung limply over the entrance.

"Wake up in there," she said. "We're burning daylight."

She ducked inside and recoiled from the intense heat. It was like a sauna, the heating element on his propane stove glowing cherry red. The sleeping bag was bunched against the side, and it looked like someone had rummaged through the supplies, yet the evolutionary anthropologist himself was nowhere to be seen.

"I should have known," she whispered.

Riley turned off the heater and retreated into the open air, which suddenly felt a whole lot colder. Waiting for her to enter the cave first must have been eating him alive all night. Beating her inside today would teach her a lesson. She rolled her eyes. After suffering through unending days of his less-than-subtle criticism and passive-aggressive posturing, this morning he'd actually done her a favor by allowing her to ease into this wonderful day without his constant needling.

"He already went in, didn't he?" Montgomery asked.

"You don't sound at all surprised," Riley replied.

"I should have recognized as much from the get-go, but I suppose my subconscious mind didn't want to jinx the peace and quiet."

"Well, someone needs to tell him he's about to miss breakfast."

Riley playfully elbowed her colleague and headed toward the excavation, stopping at her tent only long enough to grab her flashlight. Even though she'd already spent a full day inside, she felt the same flutter of nerves in her stomach as she switched on the beam and crawled inside. It was staggering to think that she was squirming across ground that had hardly been touched since the end of the last ice age, and by hands that would subsequently shape the future of the entire species. It smelled of unwritten history, of secrets yet to be revealed.

Her light spilled into the cave, revealing the chalk grids off to her right and the vast space ahead of her.

"You'd better grab something to eat before it's all gone," she said. "You've seen how those kids wolf it down."

She climbed over the boulder with the elaborate designs, rose to a crouch, and swept her beam across the interior.

There was no sign of Edgerton.

She pressed deeper into darkness that fled from her light. Her breath seeped from between her lips and trailed over her shoulder.

"Dale?"

Riley caught a flash of red from the periphery of her beam. She focused on it and recognized Edgerton's parka. At first, it almost looked like it had been draped over a rock, but then she saw the heels of his boots and his frightened eyes looking back over his shoulder from where he crouched against the wall, almost exactly as they'd found the mummified body in the adjacent chamber. The bare skin of his face was positively covered with mosquitoes. He didn't even blink when they crawled over his eyelashes. His lips formed whispered words, the same phrase repeated over and over, barely loud enough to be heard.

"All going to die. All going to die. All going to die."

2

Redmond, Washington

Ciara Winters awakened to a shrill howling sound. Her heart was beating as fast as a hummingbird's and her sheets were damp with sweat, which sapped her oversize t-shirt to her skin, trickled beneath her golden hair, and beaded on her brow. She sat up and felt the cool breeze billowing through the curtains, prickling her flesh with goosebumps. The air passing through her open bedroom window smelled of ozone and freshly turned soil. A flash of lightning limned the branches of the cedar and fir trees ascending the hillside and reflected from the eyes of a coyote crouching among the ferns. It was watching her. She could feel it. As if to confirm her suspicions, it yipped and howled again.

Raindrops clamored overhead like the talons of so many invisible creatures scurrying across the roof.

A crash of thunder caused the pane to shiver, only it was too loud, too close. She turned toward the source of the sound, which had definitely originated from somewhere inside the house. By the time she looked back, the coyote was gone.

She heard footsteps in the hallway, moving fast. Her mother burst through the door and ran straight to Ciara's bedside. Her hair was a mess, her eyes wide, her cheeks red and glistening with tears. She threw back the covers and dragged Ciara out of bed.

"Mom—?"

"Shh!"

Her mother took her hand, pulled her toward the door, and peeked around the corner. The hallway ended at the top of the staircase, beyond which Ciara could see into the living room, its hardwood floor awash with moonlight. And something else. Some sort of liquid that looked like it had been flung from a wet mop. A shadow passed across it a heartbeat before a silhouette, composed seemingly of the night itself, appeared at the foot of the stairs.

"Oh, God," Mom whispered, jerking her in the opposite direction.

Ciara glanced back as the man mounted the stairs, each footstep producing a hollow thudding sound. He carried a shotgun across his chest, one hand near the trigger, the other on the pump, which he slammed back and forth to chamber another load.

Shuck-shuck.

An empty shell flipped over his shoulder and a smile slashed across his face.

Ciara started to cry. Her mother led her past the master bedroom and ducked around the corner.

"It's going to be all right," Mom whispered, over and over, her breath hitching between words.

There were three doorways at the end of the hallway. Ciara's younger brother, Alexei, appeared from the one on the left, rubbing his eyes and swaying as though still half-asleep.

"The storm woke me—" he started to say, but Mom dragged him into the corridor and shoved him ahead of her.

The three of them veered into Dad's study, where bookcases overflowing with notebooks covered the walls and his computer sat, cold and lifeless, on his desk. Mom rushed to the window, threw up the sash, and frantically elbowed the screen until it popped off.

Ciara was halfway out before she realized what was happening. She screamed and clung to her mother, who brought their foreheads together and looked her directly in the eyes.

"Run as far away as you can and hide where no one will ever find you," she whispered. "Don't make a sound, do you hear me? No matter what you see, don't make a sound."

Her mother lowered her from the window and dropped her into the ornamental shrubbery. By the time she found her feet, her brother was already out the window, crying and clutching at their mother.

"You have to go!"

Mom sobbed and shoved him away from her. He crashed into the bushes and nearly knocked Ciara to the ground. She grabbed him by the hand and pulled—

A flash of discharge from the window and the glass exploded outward on a fiery spray of blood and steel. The thunderous report produced a ringing sound in Ciara's ears.

"Mommy!" Alexei screamed.

Ciara tugged on his hand and ran away from the house. She glanced back and saw the shadow man through the shattered pane. He cocked his head and raised the shotgun.

Shuck-shuck.

She tripped and fell, lost her brother's hand. He scampered ahead of her and disappeared into the forest. She pushed herself up from the wet grass and ran after him. The dead sticks and pinecones hurt her bare feet. Mud sluiced between her toes. She heard the tinkle of glass and a crunching sound as the shadow man lowered himself from the window.

The trees smothered the moonlight, stranding her in darkness so complete that she couldn't see where she was going, let alone where her brother had gone. She barreled blindly through the branches, evergreen needles raking her forearms as she attempted to shield her face.

A siren erupted in the distance, followed in short measure by another.

Her shoulder clipped the trunk of a tree, knocking her off-balance and sending her careening to the forest floor. She bit her lip to keep from crying out and crawled into the nearest shrubs, so deeply that the branches and slender trunks bit into her flesh and pinned her in place.

Don't make a sound, do you hear me? No matter what you see, don't make a sound.

The sirens grew louder by the second, but beneath them she heard something else: the crackling of detritus under a heavy tread, the snapping of branches parting before an irresistible force.

"No, please . . ." Alexei whimpered.

A flash of discharge momentarily outlined the forest downhill from her and, with a deafening boom, her brother was gone.

Ciara closed her eyes, squeezing tears from the corners. Her chest shuddered as she desperately tried to contain the sobs attempting to break free.

Shuck. Shuck.

Her eyes snapped open. It sounded like the shadow man was right on top of her, so close she could hear the spent shell clatter to the ground over the wail of sirens. An alternating red and blue glow materialized from the thicket, causing the shadows of the trees to writhe as though with a life of their own. The man picked his way through the forest toward her, less a shadow than a shape composed of nothingness, prodding the bushes with the stock of his weapon, kicking through the thick ferns.

Searching for her.

Ciara's pulse sounded like water rushing in her ears. It was so loud she feared it would give her away.

Police cruisers sped into the driveway and screeched to a halt in front of the house. In the chaos of flashing lights, she truly saw the shadow man for the first time. He wore hiking boots, jeans, and a black sweatshirt, the hood of which concealed his face. His movements were frenetic as he tore apart the thicket looking for her, glancing repeatedly over his shoulder as more and more vehicles arrived and police officers with flashlights fanned out into the backyard.

Ciara willed them to look uphill, to find her before the man did.

"There's another one over here," an officer called. "Jesus. It's just a kid."

The shadow man froze. He was maybe ten feet away, limned by the alternating lights, which illuminated the thicket in such a way that for the most fleeting of moments he almost appeared to have antlers. His shoulders sagged and he lowered his head. He turned back toward her and fell to his knees. If he looked up, he'd be staring right at her.

Flashlights sliced through the night behind him, bringing with them the crunching sounds of approaching footsteps and staccato bursts of radio communications.

He braced the butt of his shotgun against the ground, nuzzled the barrel underneath his chin, and slid his thumb through the trigger guard.

The officers pinned him with their beams.

He looked up and Ciara saw his face. She gasped in recognition as his eyes found hers. They were her father's eyes, only completely unlike them at the same time. The irises were the color of fire, as though flames burned within them, and yet she detected a coldness that she'd never seen there before, a malevolence, a presence of something other than her father. And even as she saw it, it, in turn, saw her.

And smiled.

A twitch of its thumb and it vanished with a clap of thunder.

CIARA SAT in the back of the ambulance, its lights flashing across her side yard and uphill into the forest, where men in white forensics suits passed like ghosts through the trees. They carried spotlights and numbered placards, which they placed on the loam among the ferns whenever they found a footprint or a spent shotgun shell. Shadows passed behind the shattered window of her father's study and stretched across grass sparkling with dampness and bits of broken glass.

She drew her knees to her chest and wrapped the blanket more tightly around herself. The man standing in front of her wore the blue uniform of a paramedic and shone a light into first her left eye, and then her right. He said something to her, although his words sounded foreign to her ears. She just continued to stare past him, watching the pink stain of dawn spread through treetops she instinctively knew she would never see again, much like the house itself, the front door of which was marred with a muddy boot print, the trim beside it broken. It opened and two men wearing navy blue jackets with reflective silver stripes and baseball caps with the logo of the King County Medical Examiner's Office emerged, pushing a gurney between them.

The paramedic pulled the back door of the ambulance partway closed to block her view, but she'd already seen the gray bag on top of it, and the shape of the body it held. His partner, a tiny woman with a pixie cut, held up a lollipop, unwrapped it, and offered it to Ciara, who plugged it unconsciously into her mouth. It had no taste whatsoever, but it seemed to make the woman happy, so she left it alone while the man drew her arm from beneath the blanket and slid it into a blood pressure cuff. The woman pushed back Ciara's bangs and used wipes that smelled of chemicals to clean her forehead and cheeks. She flinched when one passed over her eyebrow.

The woman whispered something Ciara couldn't make out and used a pair of tiny butterfly bandages to close the laceration. They felt like they were pulling on her eyelid, forcing her to witness the police officers materializing from the forest, carrying another gray bag between them on an orange backboard. It appeared empty at first, until she noticed the small shape inside and realized what it contained.

A ringing sound filled her ears and her vision blurred.

The female paramedic stepped in front of her, a sympathetic expression on her face, and wiped the tears from Ciara's cheeks with her gloved thumbs. She spoke words Ciara understood, words like "You're safe now" and "Everything's going to be all right," although they made little sense because she wasn't safe, and nothing would be all right ever again.

A shiver rippled through her slight frame. The woman briskly rubbed Ciara's arms and said something about going into shock, but Ciara experienced a sensation like sunlight cutting through the clouds, a moment of lucidity that brought the entire situation crashing down on her. Her shoulders heaved with uncontrollable sobbing.

The female paramedic sat down beside her and wrapped her arm around Ciara, who buried her face in the woman's chest and clutched her uniform shirt.

A bright glare appeared from the corner of Ciara's eye. She turned and saw a white van idling on the other side of the police car parked diagonally across the driveway. The officer walked around the hood and spoke to the driver, little more than a vague silhouette behind the headlights.

A man stepped between them, his shadow falling heavily upon her. He crouched before her and tipped up her chin so she could see him. He was older than the other officers and wore a suit instead of a uniform, only it wasn't a fancy suit like those worn by her father, the thought of whom caused her to retreat into herself. She remembered his eyes, the irises of which had seemed to glow in the split-second before the shotgun vaporized them.

"My name is Detective Patrick," he said. His features were soft, his expression even softer, and yet his discomfort was clear, from the tightening of his jaw muscles to the way his stare moved restlessly as he spoke. "I need to ask you a few questions, if that's okay."

"Now's not the time," the female paramedic said. "She's been through too much already."

"That's the thing. We're having a hard time putting together what happened here, and we were hoping she might be able to help us while everything's still fresh in her mind."

"It'll still be fresh tomorrow."

"Maybe, maybe not. You know how kids' minds work. They see something like this, and their brains wall off the memories to keep them from remembering, burying them where no one can find them. Until some therapist twenty years down the line digs them up, but by then there's nothing we can do about it."

"She's just a child."

"She's fifteen years old and the lone survivor of an event we can't seem to wrap our heads around. You see, a man walked right up to the front door and kicked it in. The homeowner responded by grabbing a shotgun and confronting the intruder in the living room, where he shot him at point-blank range. And then, for reasons we can't explain, used that same gun to hunt down and kill his own family. Now tell me that makes any kind of sense to you."

The officer in the driveway moved his car just far enough for the van to squeeze past. Its headlights focused on the detective's back as it headed straight toward them.

"I just want to show her a picture," Patrick said. "One picture and then I'll leave her alone. At least for tonight."

He held up his cellphone so Ciara could see it. The picture on the screen was a close-up of a man's face. He had wild black hair and bushy eyebrows. A broad, heavily stubbled jawline. Freckles of blood on the left side of his face. She shook her head. She'd never seen this man before in her life.

"Does the name Delvin Moore mean anything to you?" Patrick asked.

She'd only just begun to shake her head when the van screeched to a halt mere feet away. The driver jumped out and ran right up to them.

Patrick stood and turned to face the rapidly approaching woman, but she was upon him before he could even straighten his tie.

"Get away from her," she snapped, shouldering aside the detective and kneeling in front of Ciara. The woman had wide brown eyes magnified by thick glasses and a braid that looked like the old rope of a tire swing. "My name is Amanda Carter, honey. You can call me Miss Amanda. Child Protective Services — that's the organization that looks out for kids like you when bad things happen — asked me to come out here and make sure you're all right. You've had a really rough night, so I was hoping you wouldn't mind if I rode along with you in this ambulance, with these nice people, who look like they're taking very good care of you. We need to have a doctor get a look at you to make sure you aren't hurt, because sometimes you don't feel the pain until later. Is that okay with you?"

Ciara offered a subtle nod, which was all the woman needed. She rounded on the detective and spoke in a low voice.

"You know how this works from here. You file whatever paperwork you need to file, and we'll make her available once she's been formally cleared to talk with you by a physician and a mental-health professional. In the meantime, consider *me* her court-appointed advocate and *her* off-limits until I tell you otherwise. Am I in any way unclear?"

Patrick glanced at Ciara over Amanda's shoulder and gave her a faint smile.

"Take good care of her," he said. "I can't even imagine what must be going through her head right now."

Miss Amanda's posture softened, as did her tone.

"Of course," she said. "Once she's been discharged from the ER, I'll be taking her to the Snoqualmie Center for Children. We'll give her the best possible care, I assure you."

She gave the detective her card and turned back to Ciara.

"Let's get you to that doctor, honey."

Ciara tuned her out as she stared, for the final time, at the forest behind the only home she'd ever known. She caught a flash of eyeshine uphill from the investigators documenting the site where her father had taken his own life. The coyote watched her clear up until the paramedics closed the door.

And then it was gone.

CIARA FELT as though she were trapped in a dream from which she couldn't wake up. She was both a part of the moment and separate from it, an observer as much as a participant. Deep down, she knew that all of this was really happening to her, that this was her life, and yet she seemed entirely unable to rationalize it.

Miss Amanda must have sensed her inner turmoil. She took Ciara by the hand, which caused the tiny cuts on her palm to burn, but she was grateful for the physical contact, even if she didn't necessarily want it or understand why. The doctors and nurses at the hospital had been nice enough, if somewhat distracted. They'd constantly spoken in whispers outside her curtained area, with Miss Amanda and with each other, and been sticky sweet when they finally entered. They'd been kind and gentle while cleaning the dirt from her wounds and applying bandages and stitches to cuts she couldn't even feel, and yet their thoughts had played upon their faces as plain as day. They couldn't have been more relieved that they weren't her, the girl who'd survived the scenes splashed all over the TVs mounted to the walls, footage of flashing emergency vehicle lights staining the front of a house she'd never set foot in again.

"And this is the dayroom," Miss Amanda said. She guided Ciara from a sterile white corridor lined with the offices of counselors and doctors into a large room with a tiled floor that reflected the tube lights overhead. "This is a safe space, where you're free to be and do whatever you want, as long as you're respectful of the other children, most of whom have been through traumatic events, just like you, so sometimes they need a little extra patience."

The arrangement of furniture divided the vast open space into quadrants. One corner featured upholstered couches and chairs facing a flatscreen TV, upon which *Sponge-Bob SquarePants* played for a girl roughly her age, who'd drawn her legs up inside her baggy sweatshirt and tucked the better part of her face under the stretched collar. The adjacent corner featured circular tables upon which were arrayed puzzles in varying stages of completion. A shelving unit housed countless more, along with board games and stacks of well-read books. On the opposite end of the room was a multi-purpose game table. A water dispenser and prepackaged snacks sat on the counter behind it. And in the farthest corner, bean bags and puffy chairs were arranged around easels draped with butcher paper. One of the walls was painted with an elaborate seascape full of fish and octopi and brightly colored coral, all in various styles and crafted by different hands, most of them with minimal artistic talent.

Miss Amanda guided her in that direction. A boy maybe a few years older than her emerged from the doorway beside the mural, donning a leather jacket over his hooded sweatshirt. He glanced up at her with startlingly blue eyes, swept aside his long bangs, and offered a faint smile. There was something about the way he looked at her that made her instinctively uncomfortable.

"We encourage the children in our care to express themselves through art," Miss Amanda said. "Not only is it therapeutic — and by that, I mean it helps our unconscious minds work through emotions and memories that it's hard for us to consciously deal with — it's also a great way to tap into our creativity and develop skills we might not have otherwise known we had.

This painting might not look like much, but I assure you it was a labor of love and all of the artists who contributed to it still come back from time to time to see it. One of them, who now works as an animator for Nickelodeon — if you can believe that — even brings her children."

They passed through the doorway beside the painting and entered a bright hallway with cartoon characters professionally painted on the walls between the open doorways on either side. The room on the left looked like a classroom, only rather than desks there were two long tables, where several kids sat with an adult who taught them from workbooks.

"We offer instruction that follows district guidelines to make sure that our children don't fall behind while they're in our care," Miss Amanda said. "Most of our teachers are retired educators who volunteer their time because they know how difficult this transition can be for kids like you."

The students looked up at them from their books. Their expressions suggested that they'd seen so many kids come and go that they were only mildly curious about the newcomer in their midst. Ciara felt much the same way. She couldn't understand why Miss Amanda was telling her all of this when she wasn't going to be here for very long . . . was she?

"Over here is the cafeteria, and down the hall is the residential wing."

And with those words, the reality of the situation suddenly hit home. Every bruise, every cut, every sprain Ciara had sustained during the night broke through the numbness and she nearly doubled over in pain. Tears crept down her cheeks, and she had to release Miss Amanda's hand to wipe them away. The older woman stopped, crouched in front of her, and looked her directly in the eyes.

"I know this is all a lot to take in at once, especially considering what you went through last night. We're here to help you through this transition, at whatever pace you require. You're not always expected to wear your brave face, and everyone will understand when you don't. Counselors like me are always available to talk. Or just listen, if that's what you need. And the other kids? We like to think they're something special because they've been through some hard times, too. Maybe not exactly like yours, but just as hard, only in other ways. We all support each other here, in every way possible, and that starts with giving you as much time as you need to adjust to your new surroundings and as much space as you need to do so. All we ask in return is that you give us a chance to help you when you're ready and that you help the others when you can tell they're feeling down. Does that sound okay to you?"

Ciara tried to nod, but she couldn't seem to make her head move. Everything was crashing down around her with sounds like glass shattering inside her brain and she wanted her mom, although every time she so much as thought of her she saw the shotgun blast explode through the study window and heard her terrified voice, whispering in her ear.

No matter what you see, don't make a sound.

"It's all right," Miss Amanda said. She smiled and wiped the tears from Ciara's cheeks. "We're here, day and night, to help you through this. I know it doesn't feel like it now, but things will get better. You'll see."

She took Ciara's hand and led her past doorways through which she could see single beds, desks, and freestanding bureaus, until they reached the next to the last room in line. Ciara recognized the comforter and pillow from her bedroom at home. They'd been washed and folded and sealed in a plastic bag that rested on the bed beside similar bags filled with clothes from her closet.

"I know nothing will ever be able to replace your home, but we want you to feel comfortable here, to make this place your own for as long as you're here."

Ciara didn't want to contemplate what that meant. It wasn't like she had any aunts or uncles or grandparents who were going to rush right down and claim her. For now, it was all she could do to make her legs guide her into the strange, bare room.

"Why don't I help you organize your belongings," Miss Amanda said. "And I'll stay with you for as long as you need me."

The walls had a faint turquoise tint, barely detectable, much like the scent of whoever had lived here last. The window above the writing desk overlooked a yard with playground equipment, a garden, and shade trees that nearly concealed the twelve-foot retaining wall. A grating sound emanated from the swing set, where the boy she'd seen earlier swung back and forth, staring at the screen of his cellphone, seemingly oblivious to the man standing in the deep shadows behind him, his head framed by the branches of the trees in such a way that it looked like he had antlers. She caught a flash of silver from the stripe on the man's jacket as he turned and headed straight for the boy. He must have been one of the counselors, but the way he was dressed reminded her of the men she'd last seen pushing the body bag out of her house on a gurney.

Ciara sat down at the desk and stared out across the treetops, toward the distant mountains where her true home hid among the forested hills. There was an artist's pad full of blank paper and an assortment of writing utensils in a jar. Before she even knew what she intended to do, she'd opened the pad, grabbed a pencil, and started to draw.

3

Bethesda, Maryland

"Can you get one-millimeter coronal slices through the temporal lobes?" Davis Patterson asked. The doctoral candidate brushed his shaggy bangs from his hazel eyes, slid his glasses up his nose, and leaned closer to the monitor. "I want to get a good look at those amygdalae."

He watched the MRI technologist align the proposed cuts through the gray-scale image of the patient's brain in all three planes. The National Institute of Biomedical Imaging and Bioengineering employed cutting-edge technology and gifted imaging personnel in its quest to improve global health by developing and accelerating the application of biomedical technologies, the pursuit of which offered all kinds of opportunities for interdisciplinary graduate research, especially for riskier projects, like Davis's, which might not have otherwise received funding. Of course, as he'd learned early on, the mere mention of having survived the school shooting in Sacramento, as the scars where the shotgun pellets had passed through his cheek would attest, tended to loosen even the most cash-strapped institution's grip on its pocketbook, especially when he explained what he hoped to prove, and the implications of being right.

As he'd expected, the sagittal images had demonstrated significant thinning of the outer cortices of the amygdalae — the parts of the brain responsible for memory, decision making, and emotional responses, including fear, anxiety, and aggression. It was a physical trait common in patients diagnosed with severe antisocial personality disorder, colloquially known as psychopaths. Throw in the diminished volume of the middle and orbital gyri of the frontal lobe, and you were looking at the neurological foundation of the mind of a mass murderer, and the basis of Davis's doctoral dissertation.

"This next sequence will be a little longer," the technologist said into the microphone. His voice echoed from the other side of the observation window, within the suite, where the patient's socked feet protruded from the gantry of the scanner, which thumped with an almost techno beat. "Just hang in there a little while longer."

The patient gave them a thumbs-up, a simple gesture made more difficult by the non-ferrous wrist restraints strapped to the belt around the waist of his orange jumpsuit.

"I want to go right into the functional sequences when we're done with the structural scans," Davis said.

"What are those?" the corrections officer asked. He stood in the hallway, right outside the doors to the control room and the adjacent copper-lined examination suite, prepared to make a move if the prisoner inside suddenly got any bright ideas. His nerves were already fried at having to relinquish all of the ferromagnetic tools of his trade, most notably his sidearm, taser, and cuffs. "Don't think for a second I'm taking those restraints off of him."

"Believe me," the tech said. "We don't want that any more than you do."

"They're just a different kind of scan that allows us to trace the neural pathways associated with thoughts and emotions by following the flow of blood, which mirrors neuronal activation," Davis said.

"You can tell what he's thinking?" the officer said.

"We can't read his mind, if that's what you mean, but we can tell which areas of the brain are stimulated by his thought processes, which allows us to infer the general content of his thoughts with a fairly high degree of accuracy."

"I can't believe anyone would want to know what's going on inside that brain of his."

Davis stared at the diminutive prisoner on the monitor displaying the black-and-white, coronal slices of his face, from the crown of his head to the tip of his chin, as though he were looking back at them from the screen. He felt a chill that had nothing to do with the temperature inside the control room. The man on the other side of the glass, Richard Wesley Taylor, had been responsible for the deaths of eleven people. Or at least that was the official number for which he'd been convicted and sentenced to serve multiple consecutive life sentences at the New Jersey State Prison in Trenton. The actual number could have easily been five times as many based on the total number of elderly patients who'd died while under his care. When asked about it, he'd just sat there with his eyes turned inward and a wistful smile on his acne-scarred face, reflecting upon memories none of them cared to see and reveling in the fact that he would take the truth with him to the grave.

Considering neither the governor nor the warden had offered him any concessions, he'd likely agreed to participate in Davis's study out of some kind of twisted clinical curiosity. After all, he was a skilled nurse, even if he'd used those skills to take the lives of men and women he believed, as he'd stated repeatedly at his trial, "already had one foot out the door."

Mere hours ago, Davis had wired Taylor to an electroencephalogram, which monitored the electrical activity of his brain, recorded his brain wave patterns, and subjected him to a battery of questions. He'd painstakingly described the details of the murders for which Taylor had been convicted, which had elicited no electrical response whatsoever, effectively forming a baseline against which Davis could compare the experiential statements. By merely changing the descriptions to "I" statements — "I injected the potassium into the victim's IV line" or "I administered the fatal overdose" — he'd been able to show activity in the parts of the brain responsible for specific memory recall, thus establishing what was known as "experiential knowledge," a legal standard capable of earning a conviction in several other countries.

The only question that had made Davis doubt the validity of the Brain Electrical Oscillations Signature Test was the activity in response to the statement "I am responsible for the deaths of more than fifty people," which is why he wanted to see the fMRI scan. He needed to know if he was dealing with a true monster or merely a garden-variety psychopath who'd figured out how to game the system.

"Can you generate a tractographic reconstruction from the diffusion scan?" Davis asked.

"Absolutely," the tech said. "What are you specifically looking for?"

"I want to evaluate the white matter tracts between the ventromedial prefrontal cortex and the amygdalae to see if there's any sort of physiological disruption."

"Give me a second."

The vmPFC was responsible for feelings of empathy and guilt, while the amygdalae controlled responses like fear and anxiety. It stood to reason that their developmental retardation could very well extend to the neural pathways connecting them, potentially preventing the patient from being able to distinguish right from wrong, and making him impossible to reform, the implications of which were staggering. And terrifying. If such a simple imaging study could identify psychopathy — or, even better, sociopathy in individuals who might otherwise seem completely normal, even to themselves — at an early age, then the afflicted individual could be removed from society before committing his first crime. Of course, there was no way of knowing if that individual would ever commit that crime, which created a moral dilemma of unprecedented proportions: was it fair to take away the rights of an innocent individual — or, worse, implement a eugenic solution — because that individual *might* one day do terrible things? Or could a combination of pharmaceutical and psychological treatments be used to treat the affected patient from an early age?

A feathery, rainbow-colored image appeared on the screen. It had the same general shape as the brain, only it lacked the outer contours and convolutions. The scan used the diffusion qualities of water within the myelin sheaths to display the nerve tracts, essentially highlighting the electrical wiring of the brain, which connected idea to impulse, and impulse to action.

"You can definitely see the reduced structural integrity of the white matter fibers bridging the two areas," the tech said.

Taylor was only Davis's fourth test subject, and the prior three had shown mixed results. If he could actually pinpoint the physical mechanism of psychopathy, then could he not ultimately create a cure?

The scan finished and the buzzing and thudding of the scanner became a rhythmic thumping.

"Can you hear me out there?"

The voice coming from inside the room sounded tinny through the speaker beside the control console. They were the first words Taylor had spoken since his arrival in the imaging department.

"We can hear you just fine," the technologist said into the microphone. "Is everything all right?"

"Yeah, yeah. Everything's fine. I just wanted to ask a question, if that's okay."

"Go ahead."

"It's just that in my former life I was a nurse and I always hated coming down to MRI from the floor because I had to switch all of our portable bedside monitors and oxygen tanks to non-ferrous models, which took forever, and then I still had to fill out a screening form and take off my watch and necklace and ID badge before I could even enter the room. And we couldn't bring down patients with pacemakers or cochlear implants or a lot of cardiac and cerebral stents and clips. I guess I was just wondering what would happen if you accidentally brought that kind of thing in here."

The tech looked at Davis and raised his eyebrows. The way Taylor phrased the question made them wonder if it stemmed from genuine curiosity or if, even now, five years into the first of multiple life sentences, he was still dreaming up ways of murdering his patients.

"That's a three-Tesla magnet surrounding you," the tech said. "Its magnetic field is roughly sixty thousand times as strong as the Earth's. If you were to bring a ferrous oxygen tank in there, it would literally turn into a missile and fire straight toward the heart of that donut, going through everyone and everything in its way. Aneurysm clips would tear off the vessels they clamped, wire mesh would bend and twist, and a pacemaker would stop working."

"What if you had like a piece of metal embedded under your skin?"

"Nearly all joint replacements and surgical fixation devices are made of titanium—"

"I mean like shrapnel," Taylor said. "What if you had a piece of metal embedded just under your skin? Is this thing strong enough to pull it out?"

The prisoner restlessly crossed and uncrossed his ankles. There was a dark splotch on the bottom of his right foot that Davis hadn't noticed before, as though he'd stepped in something on his way into the exam room.

"I guess it depends upon the nature and metallic composition of the fragment, which is why we provide screening forms so that nothing like that ever happens."

"What if someone lied on their form and got into the machine anyway?"

Davis felt a sinking sensation in the pit of his stomach. He didn't like the direction this conversation was taking.

"Regrettably, there's a certain amount of trust involved," the tech said.

"What if someone didn't know they had that metal inside of them, like a Vietnam vet or something? What would happen?"

"He'd feel a distinct warming sensation as the piece of shrapnel heated up inside him and hit the panic button so I could pull him out of the machine."

"What if he could endure the pain as the shrapnel heated up? How long would it take to rip that piece of metal right out of him?"

The dark splotch on Taylor's sock expanded.

"Get him out of there," Davis whispered.

"I haven't even programmed the functional—"

"Get him out there!"

The prisoner laughed. It was a horrible, cackling sound bereft of all humor, one that stopped as abruptly as it started.

"I told them there wasn't a prison that could hold me," Taylor said. Davis jumped to his feet, but by then it was already too late. "Don't worry, though. You and I aren't through just yet. I'll be seeing you again soon."

Blood exploded from the top of Taylor's foot, spattering the giant white ring surrounding him. A silver blur streaked through the crimson mist as the object accelerated toward the isocenter of the magnet, where the prisoner's head was positioned inside a helmetlike coil.

A wet *thuck* erupted from the speaker, followed by sputtering and gurgling sounds.

"Unlock the door!" Davis shouted.

He ran out of the control room to the outer door of the patient suite. Shouldered it open, rushed to the side of the narrow conveyor bed, and pressed the button to retract the table. Blood pattered onto the floor as Taylor's body slid out, his orange jumpsuit dotted with red.

An alarm sounded from the hallway and emergency lights flashed.

The technologist caught up with him and started prying off the patient's helmet-like head coil as soon as it was within reach.

"What the hell happened in here?" the corrections officer asked.

Davis looked from the straight laceration on the top of the prisoner's foot to the torn skin underneath his chin, and finally to the corner of the razor blade, which protruded from the top of the helmet.

Taylor had known exactly what he was doing. His last words replayed inside Davis's skull as he stared at the vertex of the dead man's skull, where gray matter bloomed from a bony crater fringed with tatters of hairy scalp.

Don't worry, though. You and I aren't through just yet. I'll be seeing you again soon.

DAVIS COULDN'T TRUST his own legs to bear his weight and had to lean against the wall. His entire body had gone strangely numb, and a cold sensation had settled into his bones. The outer edges of his vision throbbed in time with his pulse. He'd gone into shock enough times to recognize the symptoms and yet there was nothing he could do to stop it.

All of his hard work, everything he'd worked so hard to achieve . . . gone in an instant.

He'd watched the flashes of the forensic investigators' cameras strobe from inside the patient suite as though from a million miles away, while officers from seemingly every branch of law enforcement grilled him about what had happened. *Flash.* Did he have a personal connection to Taylor? *Flash.* Did he know the prisoner had smuggled a razorblade into the room? *Flash.* Did he have a relationship with any of the decedent's victims? *Flash.* Had Taylor tipped them off with enough time to have saved him? *Flash.* What were the odds of a man who'd survived one mass murderer's bloody rampage being ostensibly in charge when another died? *Flash.* Was he happy that a monster like Taylor was dead?

Davis couldn't remember how he'd answered the questions, or even if he'd done so at all. In his mind, he was again fifteen years old and sitting with investigators of all stripes, every single one of them asking the same questions, searching for answers they'd never find.

Flash.

The men from the medical examiner's office waited for the forensics team to finish documenting the scene before entering. They rolled Taylor onto an orange backboard and carried him back into the hallway, where the gurney waited outside the magnetic field, a body bag primed and ready. A dozen officials from the National Institutes of Health and the New Jersey Department of Corrections waited to see the body with their own eyes in anticipation of the blame game to come. Someone was going to have to take the fall once the media caught wind of what had happened. Unfortunately, the easiest target to hit was the one that couldn't defend itself, which was undoubtedly why they all scrutinized Davis from the corners of their eyes.

An elderly man wearing a suit and tie and clutching a fedora to his chest separated from the crowd. He was tall and cadaverous, with long bony fingers and liver-spotted skin that appeared brittle to the touch. The lanyard hanging from his neck identified him as Ronald Francis, Commissioner of the New Jersey Department of Corrections. He nodded to a man wearing a jacket with the logo of the Office of the Chief Medical Examiner for the State of Maryland on his breast. The doctor removed a stethoscope from his jacket pocket, used it — as a mere formality — to listen for a pulse, and shook his head for Francis's benefit. He proceeded to pry back Taylor's eyelids and shine a penlight directly into the prisoner's eyes. Francis leaned over the doctor's shoulder and watched for the parasympathetic pupillary response. Seemingly satisfied, the old man nodded to the medical examiner and merged back into the crowd.

The men from the ME's office zipped up the bag and pushed the gurney down the hallway.

In his mind, Davis was transported to a different corridor with a different body bag being wheeled away from him. In this other time, there were lockers and spatters of blood on walls pocked with buckshot. He could still hear his classmates sobbing over the high-pitched hum in his ears. The world moved in slow motion around him as one group of investigators transformed into another, the body bag containing Richard Wesley Taylor becoming the one inside of which his best friend had just been sealed.

Davis closed his eyes as tightly as he could.

"Three . . . two . . . one," he whispered.

When he opened his eyes again, the gurney was gone and the men from the NIH and NJDOC had begun to disperse. Francis stood at the end of the hallway, staring directly at him as people passed between them. He donned his fedora, carefully straightened it, and offered a smile filled with disproportionately large teeth.

A paramedic stepped between them and looked Davis squarely in the eyes.

"Why don't you come with me?" he said, obviously recognizing the onset of shock. "Let's make sure you're okay."

By the time he moved aside, the old man had disappeared.

Davis nodded and let the paramedic lead him down the corridor toward the waiting ambulance.

―――――――

THE RECEPTIONIST GLANCED up from her desk with an expression of impatience. Davis offered an apologetic smile and physically pressed down on his knee to keep his foot from tapping. He hadn't slept for more than fifteen minutes at a time all night, and the copious amount of coffee he'd consumed was roiling in his gut. The institute had to know that none of what had happened inside the MRI suite at the National Institute of Biomedical Imaging and Bioengineering had been his fault. Unfortunately, he knew how bureaucracies worked: someone was going to have to be sacrificed to the gods of accountability, and it made perfect sense to offer up a grad student instead of permanent personnel. The fallout would likely derail not only his research, but his doctorate and any prospects for future employment in his field. And, worst of all, potentially expose him to lawsuits from the federal penitentiary system and the dead man's family. His entire life was unraveling around him and there was absolutely nothing—

"The director will see you now," the receptionist said. She inclined her chin toward the twin doors to her left before answering another call.

Davis rose on stilted legs and approached the entrance, beside which was a freshly polished gold placard engraved with the occupant's title: Dr. William S. Hightower, M.D., Ph.D. — Director of the National Institutes of Health. He swallowed hard and focused on the words he'd been rehearsing since receiving his summons, but they were all an incoherent jumble.

"Dr. Hightower isn't accustomed to being made to wait," the receptionist said.

Davis wiped his palms on his slacks, knocked softly, and entered the most imposing office he'd ever seen. The floor was hardwood, the antique desk and bookcases mahogany, velvet drapes drawn over the windows flanking them. The American and NSF flags stood in the corner. Two men sat at a circular table to his right, file folders set before them. They rose as one and straightened their ties. With his thick-rimmed glasses and bushy gray hair and mustache, Davis would have recognized Dr. Hightower anywhere, but he couldn't immediately place the younger man beside him. His hair was impeccable, his eyebrows tweezed to perfection. He wore a tailored suit and carried himself with an air of self-importance. Davis could only assume he was one of the NIH's lawyers.

"Please," Hightower said, gesturing to an empty seat with a folder in front of it. Davis took the proffered seat, but couldn't bring himself to open the folder, which undoubtedly contained paperwork detailing the termination of his grant and credentials, a non-disclosure agreement, and a form indemnifying the NIH from lawsuits. "Allow me to introduce Dr. Lewis Pennington, Scientific Director of the NHGRI."

The second man offered a firm shake, settled back into his seat, and cocked his head. He smiled at the confused expression Davis could feel forming on his face as he tried to figure out why the scientific director of the National Human Genome Research Institute was taking part in what he assumed would be a rubber-stamp disciplinary hearing.

"I trust you know why we called you here," Hightower said.

"Oh, for Christ's sake, Bill," Pennington said. "Let the poor kid off the hook. He looks like he's about to throw an aneurysm."

Hightower nodded, reached across the table, and opened Davis's folder for him. The top page was stamped CLASSIFIED and featured the names of both men seated across the table from him, along with a handful of support staff members, beneath the heading PROJECT TRIDENT. Davis stared at it for several seconds before flipping through the pages underneath, none of which used the words termination or indemnification or required his signature. In fact, it all looked like scientific data, most of which was beyond his scope of practice, not to mention his comprehension.

"I don't get it," he finally said.

"What don't you get?" Pennington asked.

The smile never left his face, nor his eyes from Davis's.

"I assumed you called me down here to admonish me for what happened yesterday and to give me my walking papers."

"There is a long list of people who bear some level of culpability in the tragic series of events culminating in Mr. Taylor's death," Hightower said. "Not least of whom is the warden, who allowed a razor blade to be smuggled to one of his highest-profile prisoners, and the guards who failed to notice that he'd shoved it into his foot between his first and second metatarsals. As you can probably imagine, none of them is any more eager to generate a maelstrom of negative publicity than we are, especially given Mr. Taylor's background."

"What he's trying to say in the most roundabout manner possible is that it sucks the guy died, but no one wants to make a martyr out of a monster," Pennington said.

"So why *am* I here?" Davis asked.

"To be completely honest, none of us knew who you were or what you were doing here. At least not until Mr. Taylor died and Bill here looked into your work and immediately called me."

"I have over twenty thousand employees and countless graduate students, volunteers, and visiting researchers on this campus at any given time," Hightower said. "I'm lucky if I can remember the names of my department heads, although given there are hundreds, I'm sure I can be forgiven."

Davis thumbed through the pages as they spoke. He recognized PCR — polymerase chain reaction — results comparing the lengths of various strands of DNA, genomic assays and chromosomal analyses, and countless comparisons between samples listed by codename and number. He couldn't see how any of this was related to his work, unless . . .

He looked up at Pennington, his heart racing in his chest.

"Are you telling me you've identified the gene responsible for the physical anomalies in the vmPFC and the amygdala?"

"While that conclusion might be a tad premature, I think that if we were to combine our research, we might be able to draw a correlative, if not causative, relationship. You see, we have access to some of the most sensitive collections of biological samples in the world, in this case tissues collected from mass-murderers killed during the commission of their crimes — everyone from international to domestic terrorists, jihadis to school shooters — from which we've been able to sequence their complete genomes for comparison against each other, common criminals, and the general population, the results of which are in that folder."

"We've only begun to qualify the genetic distinctions and haven't progressed to evaluating their physical expression," Hightower said, "while you seem to have started at the opposite end of the study and commenced working your way backward from a physiological and behavioral standpoint."

"And our two studies intersect at the gene you discovered," Davis said, "which might theoretically be responsible for the physical alterations in the criminal mind and the origin of psychopathy."

Pennington glanced at Hightower, who gave him a subtle nod to proceed.

"We're a long way from reaching that conclusion, but your research, in conjunction with our own, brings us a whole lot closer," he said. "And if we can prove it, then we can begin formulating a therapeutic protocol for eradicating that specific gene at an early enough age to prevent its expression. Think of how many lives we could save."

Davis recognized where the conversation was going and realized just how badly they needed him.

"Not to mention how much money we could make," he said.

"Don't be so pessimistic," Hightower said. "The financial compensation only matters to us here in so far as it allows us to continue our research on any number of fronts. Surely you understand that a government thirty-some trillion dollars in debt will ultimately have to cut funding to programs that don't demonstrate a measure of self-sufficiency. No one at the NIH, including the two of us, makes a fraction of what we could command in the private sector. Here, it's all about the research and our continuing commitment to the mission of enhancing health, lengthening life, and reducing illness and disability."

"Of course, we'd be lying if we said that deep down we weren't hoping to get a peek behind the curtain of divinity," Pennington said. "Or perhaps a glimpse inside Pandora's box."

Davis allowed himself a hopeful smile.

"So what do you need from me?"

"For starters, we're going to need access to your raw data, and we're going to need to bring you onto our team, which, regrettably, will complicate your educational plans in the short term, but enhance them over the long term. And we're going to need you to assimilate an entire higher education's worth of genetic knowledge as quickly as humanly possible."

"We'll also need you to continue your own work, only at an expedited pace," Hightower said. "Four subjects are hardly enough to form a pattern, let alone a conclusive one, but with the institutes' resources, we can requisition a mobile MRI unit and arrange for the participation of violent offenders previously beyond your reach. And you'll have to write protocols for scanning non-violent criminals and a control group, so that we can outsource the acquisition of that data."

Davis's mind was reeling. He needed to take a step back and get his metaphorical legs underneath him.

"Why do you call it Project Trident?" he asked. "Have you discovered three distinct genes?"

"There's really only one gene, although it has three subtle variants. Lewis's department initially discovered the pattern among the junk — the ninety-eight-point-five percent of our genome for which we can't ascribe specific functions, non-coding sequences left over from millions of years of evolution."

"We theorize that among these uncharted sequences are the combinations of base pairings that initially allowed for the development of advances like opposable thumbs and the modern uterus," Pennington said. "Only now those genes are just kind of there, like programs running in the background on your computer. Among them you'll also find the satellite DNA essential for survival, the residua of ancient viruses that helped build our immune systems, and sequences we're beginning to suspect might also code for the physical anomalies responsible for personality and behavioral traits."

"And you theorize that this Trident Gene is one of them," Davis said.

"Exactly, which is why we want you to join us, Davis. Like Bill said, there are three variations of this gene. The first affects a full ninety-seven-point-eight percent of the population — which we can state with complete confidence, thanks to everyone in the world submitting DNA samples to companies like Ancestry and Twenty-three and Me — while just over one percent, and every single mass-murderer in our database, share the second variant."

"What about the third?"

"We have a theory, but at this point it's little more than a supposition," Hightower said. "We need to identify the corresponding differences in physical expression, which presumably affect the cerebrum, as you've already documented with the violent offenders, only in what we suspect to be an entirely different manner."

"This is where you come in," Pennington said. "We need you to help qualify physiological distinctions that we can use to generate psychological profiles for each of the three variants. Thanks to you, the scope of our research has expanded exponentially. We're talking Nobel Prize contention here."

Hightower leaned onto the table and raised his eyebrows.

"So, my young friend, can we count on you?"

Davis looked from Hightower to Pennington and back again, all the while thinking about the countless children who, thanks to the work they were doing here, would never have to hide under a desk while their classmates were being slaughtered in the hallway or afraid to go to a movie or a concert because of a gunman or a suicide bomber. This was the opportunity of a lifetime, the chance to fulfill his professional aspirations before he even earned his doctorate. He could only imagine what doors this study would open and what he could accomplish in the future.

Davis beamed and held out his hand.

"When do I start?"

4

Detroit, Michigan

Special Agent Delilah Banks crept along the facade of the soot-stained, crumbling building, careful not to break cover. She wore an FBI windbreaker and ball cap over her short, curly hair. A night-vision apparatus projected from underneath the brim like an ebon horn from her espresso skin. All of the doors and windows on the main floor had been boarded over, although several had been pried loose and now simply leaned against the openings they'd once concealed. Inside were nearly fifteen thousand square feet of space, which had at various times housed the brotherhood hall of a fraternal organization, a private school, and a church, spread out over three floors that had been abandoned for as long as she could remember, levels ravaged by time and the elements, now as much of a hazard to them as the man inside.

It had taken them more than six months to track him here, six excruciatingly long months during which he'd added another two victims to his growing list of serial murders, each different than the last, which was why they'd struggled for a full year to recognize that his previous four killings had been related. Of course, it had only taken the media a single day to nickname him The Executioner.

"Ready on my mark," Banks whispered into her transceiver.

SWAT officers moved silently through the shadows in her peripheral vision, securing every potential egress and the perimeter of the overgrown industrial lot. The penetration teams were already in position, prepared to enter on all four sides of the main floor, work their way upward, and pray their target was still inside. They couldn't afford to let him slip through their fingers.

As it was, they'd been lucky to find this place. The Executioner had been careful not to leave evidence at any of the crime scenes. Not a single hair, fiber, or strand of DNA. Had it not been for Banks's intuition, which told her to collect the topsoil from a partial footprint she'd found in the alley behind the house where he'd killed his last victim and have forensics run it through the gas chromatograph-mass spectrometer, they never would have detected the presence of trace amounts of asbestos and marble, quartz, and granite grit of the same type and in the same relative percentages as were used in high-quality, early twentieth-century terrazzo — a unique composite flooring material composed of decorative stone chips and a bonding agent, which, when smoothed and polished, produced a uniformly textured surface like that of the Hollywood Walk of Fame. A mere handful of the buildings that had used it still stood and, of them, only one was in a condition suggesting the flooring was no longer sealed, let alone that the structure hadn't been brought up to code and purged of the carcinogenic insulation material.

She drew her pistol and nudged the rotting plywood sheet with the toe of her boot, releasing a swell of dust from inside. The soft earth was riddled with footprints where countless people had sneaked inside. She concentrated on steadying her pulse and attuned her senses to her surroundings. Time slowed to a crawl around her.

"Now."

Banks ducked underneath the board and dropped into a massive auditorium with a vaulted ceiling supported by bare timber beams. An elevated walkway formed a horseshoe around the chamber. The twin staircases servicing it framed the main entrance to her right, opposite the raised stage to her left. The crumbling plaster walls were covered with graffiti, the terrazzo floor buried beneath shattered glass and dust, which retained years of accumulated footprints. Water-damaged wood beams and chairs with rusted metal legs were piled in the middle of the room.

She picked her way through the rubble and rendezvoused with her partner, Special Agent Jerry Johnston, underneath the walkway. A pair of SWAT officers appeared from the main entrance, as planned, and ascended the staircase on the left, while Banks and Johnston climbed the one on the right. They rounded the balcony, passed through a doorway, and entered a room where once the open central area had been framed by ornate banisters offering a glimpse of the opulent lobby below them, but was now merely a hole in the floor through which she could see officers in black fatigues sweeping the darkness down the barrels of their M4 carbines.

Johnston veered left and headed for a row of offices with missing doors and gaps between the exposed studs in the walls where the copper wiring had been harvested, while Banks headed to the right, toward a narrow room filled with church pews. Everything inside was white from the sheer volume of plaster that had fallen from the low ceiling. The doorway at the far end was barricaded behind crates and broken furniture that obviously hadn't been disturbed in a long time.

She ducked back out into the corridor, navigated the warped hardwood flooring, and met up with her partner at a broad threshold that opened onto another landing. A broad staircase led down to the main level, where an officer had assumed position near the building's western entrance. A narrow staircase branched from either side of the room, leading to the uppermost level. They each took one and ascended slowly, cautiously, picking their way up steps that hardly seemed capable of supporting their weight.

"Main level clear," a voice whispered through her earpiece.

Banks's heart rate accelerated. She readjusted her two-handed grip on her Glock. They were running out of real estate. If The Executioner wasn't in here, he'd be able to tell at a glance that they had violated his sanctum, assuming he wasn't spooked by the footprints everywhere outside and the boards pried from the broken windows.

She crouched at the top of the stairs, pressed her shoulder against the wall, and surveyed what appeared to be a storage area. There were crates and boxes, gray with dust, against the outer walls and holes where others had fallen through the rotting floorboards into the rooms below. They dictated a wending course across the third level, toward the lone room at the far end. It looked almost like a greenhouse, only instead of glass, the framework supported corrugated fiberglass panels that had been painted black and then adorned with graffiti of a style she'd never seen before, symbols instead of words, almost like primitive cave artwork. Characters reminiscent of cuneiform and anthropomorphic creatures with elongated bodies and horns.

Johnston appeared at her side and together they advanced upon the lone entrance, a triangular maw where a panel had been broken and pulled back. They'd be completely exposed as they crawled through the gap, but there didn't appear to be another way into the structure.

Banks gestured for her partner to cover her and pressed her back against the false wall. Johnston raised his weapon and stepped sideways until he had a clear shot through the orifice. He nodded his readiness, and she slid down into a crouch. Aimed her pistol into the darkness and scurried toward the gap. Took a deep breath. Swallowed hard. Ducked inside and cleared the room down her barrel as fast as she could.

The fiberglass panels in the peaked roof were cracked, broken, or boarded over, the walls lined with ornamental cages almost like prison cells, their bars more rust than metal. Dead trees stood from planters, their trunks wrapped in the embrace of the skeletal vines that had strangled them. It appeared to be an aviary, although it was readily apparent that the only birds that had been in here recently were the pigeons and swallows nesting in the rafters.

A narrow walkway led deeper into the structure, toward a bottleneck formed by mounds of rubble, beyond which she saw a sliver of the adjacent room, slashed by columns of moonlight sparkling with motes of dust. She smelled chemicals and slowed her pace. Formaldehyde. She would have recognized it anywhere.

Johnston rose to his feet behind her, walking backward and swiveling from one side to the other as he inspected the cages, all of them stuffed with broken timber and moldering boxes.

Banks skirted a sagging, waterlogged section of flooring and studied the room on the far side of the rubble down her sightline. The outer panels had been painted black and decorated with the same symbols she'd seen on the entrance.

A pigeon burst from the shadows overhead, clapping its wings as it vanished through a jagged crack in the roof.

She paused to calm her nerves, her heart hammering in her chest.

"Second level clear," a voice said through her earpiece.

Either The Executioner was in the room ahead of her or more innocent people would have to die before they'd be able to find him again.

Banks walked in a shooter's stance, her shoulder grazing the rusted bars, until she reached the artificial chokepoint, which had undoubtedly been created by the killer, who could very well be waiting for them on the other side, mere feet away.

She thought about Dominique Silva, the twenty-three-year-old barista they'd found flayed in an abandoned house in Brightmoor, and Emma Hendricks, the nineteen-year-old undergrad whose skull had been flattened by a homemade medieval head crusher in a condemned home in Ravendale. She thought about Kimberly Simmons, the twenty-four-year-old law clerk they'd found in Westwood Park, impaled on an eight-foot iron post. And she thought about Juana Stillwell, whose body had been so badly decomposed by the time they found it in Chaldean Town that it had been nearly impossible to tell that she'd been hanged upside down by her ankles and sawed from her groin to her chin.

If she let The Executioner get away, whatever he did next would be on her, the suffering he inflicted her cross to bear for the rest of her life.

Banks tightened her finger on the trigger and squeezed through the narrowing.

There was no one hiding behind the barricade or lurking on either side. No sign of movement. There was a mattress with rumpled, dirty linens in the corner. A rocking chair draped with a jacket, its fabric crusted with an amoeboid bloodstain. Open crates bulging with women's clothing, presumably belonging to his victims. There was a table in the middle of the room, its surface plastered with photographs of the young women he'd stalked before killing, their eyes cut out with a hobby knife, just as they had been in real life. Antique curio cabinets lined the outer walls, their shelves overflowing with dusty tomes, strange creatures reassembled from the bones of other small animals, and jars filled with formaldehyde, inside of which floated paired orbs that left no doubt as to what they were.

"Jesus Christ," Johnston whispered from behind her.

Banks turned around and caught a blur of motion near the ceiling. A man suspended upside down from the rafters, like a child from the monkey bars. In his hand, a gleaming triangular blade, already pressed to her partner's throat. A pool of darkness, impenetrable even to her night-vision apparatus, concealed his face within the hood of his sweatshirt.

"Drop the knife!" she shouted.

The Executioner cocked his head like a predatory bird. She could feel the weight of his unseen eyes upon her, caressing her skin as though with invisible ice cubes. A rivulet of blood trickled down the side of Johnston's neck from where the tip of the scalpel pierced his skin.

"We have this place surrounded," she said. "There's no way we're letting you walk out of here. It's over."

"No," he said. His voice sounded like a rake drawn through gravel. "This is only the beginning."

The Executioner's hand moved with lightning speed.

Banks pulled the trigger, the flash of discharge reflecting like firelight from his eyes and revealing his contorted features. The bullet punched through his nose, collapsing flesh and bone as though turning his face inside out. His legs cartwheeled and he struck the ground on his chest at her partner's feet.

Johnston stared at her in utter, wide-eyed surprise for several heartbeats as a crimson line formed across his throat and a torrent of blood spilled down the front of his jacket. He dropped to his knees, clutching the wound, and collapsed onto his back.

"No, no, no," Banks said.

She rushed to her partner's side and closed her hands around his neck in a desperate attempt to hold the laceration closed.

Johnston stared blankly up at her, his lips moving with unvoiced words, as the light faded from his eyes and his lifeblood sluiced between her fingers.

BANKS HAD WAITED all morning for the forensics unit to finish documenting the crime scene. While she wanted nothing more than to shove her way inside, she knew how crucial it was that everything was done by the book, and not just because a federal agent had been killed and another had been responsible for the corpse she'd watched the medical examiner's office wheel out of the building on a gurney and load into the back of its van. This was by no means a run-of-the-mill serial killer they were dealing with. Judging by the sheer number of formaldehyde-filled jars, there were considerably more victims than they'd ever suspected. They needed to learn from this man, if only to make sure that no one like him ever walked the earth again.

This is only the beginning.

The Executioner's final words haunted her. She couldn't seem to get them out of her head. They'd played on a continuous loop while she washed her partner's blood from her hands, changed out of her ruined clothes, and delivered the news of Johnston's death to his fiancée. She'd heard them while watching the media line the front sidewalk with their bright lights and cameras, vying for a shot of the abandoned building in the background, and pounding down Maalox to settle her stomach long enough to survive the obscene amounts of caffeine it was going to take to get her through the coming day.

A uniformed DPD officer jogged across the overgrown field behind the building, toward where she sat on the hood of her Charger, parked in the middle of all of the emergency vehicles. She hopped down and struck off to meet him.

"Tell me they're ready," she said.

"Yes, ma'am."

"It's about time."

They'd set up a formal access point on the side of the building so as not to have their every move documented by the reporters out front, whom they wanted to keep in the dark a little while longer, at least until they had an official story to tell. She signed the crime log, donned paper booties and neoprene gloves, and ducked under the police tape covering the hole through which she'd entered mere hours earlier. The interior looked different under the light of day, at least what little passed through the seams around the boarded windows, which was more than enough to reveal the maze-like piles of junk and debris she'd navigated in the darkness.

The lead forensic investigator, Dr. Desmond Duvall, was waiting for her on the balcony. He was even smaller than she was, a fact exaggerated by his white jumpsuit, which, from a distance, made him look like a kid trapped inside a marshmallow. Up close, however, his age showed in his thick glasses, thinning hairline, and hazel eyes that had seen things that would have broken looser men.

"Sixteen," he called down to her.

"Eyes?" she said, as she mounted the rickety stairs.

"Pairs, Special Agent. We're talking sixteen victims when we only have four bodies, but that's not the strangest thing about it."

He turned the moment Banks reached the balcony. She fell into stride beside him as he headed deeper into the structure.

"Have you been able to match any of them to our known victims?" she asked.

"We have preliminary identification on all four."

"What about the rest? You figure they belong to earlier victims from before he developed his signature?"

"Hold that thought. I need to show you some things first."

Banks nodded. She hated the idea of the monster using the town in which she'd been raised as his own personal hunting ground. It was bad enough that these people — her people — had been forced to suffer through disastrous economic policies that had cost them their jobs and the collapse of the housing bubble that had left their neighborhoods on the verge of becoming ghost towns; they should have never had to endure this kind of misery.

Banks passed the hole that offered a view of the main floor, where the remains of the banisters were piled like so many broken bones, and headed toward the staircase leading to the third level.

"What about The Executioner?" she asked.

"We're still working on identifying him."

"What's the holdup? You have his body. That means fingerprints and DNA. What more could you possibly want?"

"Like I said, there are things you need to see."

Duvall led Banks onto the uppermost level and guided her through the debris to the framework of the greenhouse. He and his unit had arrived barely eight hours ago, but already he was exhausted. Working the murder of a law-enforcement officer he'd known on a personal level sucked the life out of him. It reminded him of his mortality, or perhaps, more accurately, of the tenuous grip each of them held on his or her life. One day, he'd be gone and another person would fill his shoes. Hopefully, that transition would happen gradually over time, and not so abruptly that his replacement received his or her promotion while standing over Duvall's lifeless body.

His team had pried off the broken panel to clear the entrance and carefully documented the symbols painted on the outside, which appeared to reflect a Native American motif unlike any he'd seen before, yet another curious dichotomy of The Executioner's character.

"This building was originally built in 1915 as a Danish brotherhood hall," he said. "They used this area to house flora and fauna native to their homeland, presumably as some sort of mini Scandinavian zoo, but it's been a long time since anything's been alive in here, probably dating back before the turn of the century."

Banks glanced into each of the cages as they walked past.

"He could have easily brought his victims here and taken his time with them," she said. "Had he done so, we never would have found their bodies, let alone him."

"I don't believe he thought anyone would ever find him, regardless."

"What makes you say that?"

They'd moved the rubble from the bottleneck at the entry to the killer's lair and erected portable lights in the corners, illuminating the wretched interior. The floors were grimy, the fiberglass walls discolored by mold and fungal growth. The spider webs near the peaked roof were so thick they appeared to be the only thing holding the broken panels together. A narrow walkway had been taped off between the bloodstains where Special Agent Johnston and The Executioner had died. His criminalists worked at folding tables, their laptops and evidence kits open before them. They were so engrossed in their work that they didn't notice the newcomers in their midst.

"Let me show you something," Duvall said. He approached an unattended station and turned the monitor so Banks could see the fingerprint analysis, which featured a grid with letters ascending the Y-axis and numbers running along the X-axis. There was a vaguely oval-shaped smudge in the center, marked by several red and blue dots. "Believe it or not, this is the best print we could get."

"It's completely worthless," Banks said. "You can't see a single ridge or whorl."

"That's because the decedent doesn't have any. All of those vague markings are scar tissue, and do you see that faint vertical stripe down the middle of the lower portion? That's his flexor digitorum profundus tendon, which helps close the finger into a fist. He not only cut off his fingerprint, he carved off all of the soft tissue underneath it, nearly down to the bone itself, so it wouldn't be able to grow back. And even then, it would have taken considerable effort — not to mention constant, excruciating pain — to keep it that way."

"So you couldn't find a match?"

"I didn't say that."

"What's that supposed to mean?"

"That's why I brought you up here," Duvall said. "You have to see it to believe it."

He manipulated several drop-down menus, and a second fingerprint appeared next to the first. They looked identical.

"If he's in the system, then we can ID him," Banks said.

"This print was uploaded to the Automated Fingerprint Identification System in 1994. It was collected from a rock quarry in New Mexico, where the bodies of six young women were found. In 1985."

"That couldn't have been the same guy."

"Trust me, I know. The guy I printed couldn't have been more than a toddler back then, but that's not what makes it so strange." He closed the image of the second fingerprint and replaced it with a third that looked just like it, only it wasn't a digital image, but rather a scan of an old fingerprint card. A very old one, judging by the discoloration. "This print belonged to a man named Henry Laurent Monroe, but he went by 'Pappy.' He was killed by a Vermilion Parish detective investigating the disappearance of six missing black girls, whose bodies they found buried underneath his house in 1948."

"Surely three different people could figure out a way to change their fingerprints in the same way."

"I'm sure you're right, but what are the odds of each of them being tied to a similar number of victims, all of them females in their teens and twenties, each of whom was killed in a horribly sadistic manner. The girls in Arizona were disemboweled while they were still alive and the ones in Louisiana were doused with kerosene and immolated."

"Again, we're looking at three distinct signatures."

"Except for the eyes. All of them had their eyes removed — every single one of them — and none of those belonging to the previous twelve victims were ever recovered."

Banks turned to face the curio cabinets behind her. She obviously understood the implications of what he was suggesting.

"These could belong to victims we simply haven't found yet," she said.

"Take a closer look," Duvall said.

Banks walked right up to the cabinets. The spines of the old tomes had deteriorated to such an extent that either the titles were unreadable or the sewn edges of the pages showed through. Candles had melted all the way down, sealing their holders in mounds of wax. She took a deep breath before studying the jars of eyes.

"Formaldehyde is a remarkable preserving agent," Duvall said, "but some small amount of deterioration occurs, nonetheless. Not so much that you'd immediately notice in each sample on its own, but when compared side by side . . . "

He directed the special agent's attention from one jar to the next. The eyes in the four jars stored in the first case were so perfectly preserved that he almost felt as though they were watching him. There was even a faint pink tint to the fluid from the victims' blood. The six in the second cabinet were older, the sclera of the orbs subtly yellowed, the corneas slightly filmed. The final six, arranged on the shelves of the third unit, were in visibly worse shape, and all of their irises were brown, which potentially supported the theory that they'd been African American.

"You can't possibly think . . . ?" she said.

Duvall brought over the laptop and held it up so she could see the monitor at the same time as the eyes in the middle case. The screen displayed the faces of the six young women whose bodies had been found in the rock quarry in New Mexico. They had the kinds of big hairstyles he associated with the Eighties. Three brunettes, two blonds, and a redhead. Three sets of blue eyes, two brown, and one hazel.

Just like those in the jars in the second case.

5

E dgerton felt like he was on fire. His core smoldered and invisible
flames crackled from his skin. On an unconscious level, he knew he
was in big trouble, but there was absolutely nothing he could do
about it. He was a prisoner in his physical form, an observer only peripherally aware of everything transpiring around him. The world seemed to skip,
like an eight-millimeter film missing entire scenes, time jumps interspersed
with periods of blackness. It was impossible to think clearly, to focus on any
single thought other than the sheer terror of knowing, without a doubt, that
he was going to die.

"We need to bring down his fever in a hurry," Riley said.

Her disembodied voice originated from somewhere above his head. He
rolled his eyes upward, but it was too dark to see anything.

"What in God's name happened to him?" Montgomery said. "I can feel
the heat radiating from him through his clothes."

What *had* happened to him? Edgerton only vaguely recalled hearing his
name called from a great distance. Struggling against the brutal wind and
slithering into the tunnel—

*The memory is eclipsed by another, one more forceful and intense, simultaneously
independent of his personal experience and somehow even more real. He recognizes
the flickering glow of firelight, its source beyond his range of sight. Living shadows
writhe overhead, sifting through the smoke trapped against the earthen roof. Arms
constrict around him, dragging him to the cold ground. He hears the screeching
sound of stone grinding against stone and feels a swell of panic. A rush of air and the*

flames extinguish. An anguished cry in a voice not his own erupts from his lips and echoes from the insensate darkness.

"Help me get him to the stream!" Riley shouted.

Edgerton opened his eyes and was momentarily blinded. The gray sky resolved from the blurry whiteness. He caught intermittent glimpses of the rocky mesa, storm clouds, and Riley leaning over him, her eyes wide and her face pale, as she dragged him from the tunnel by the hood of his parka.

The darkness once more rises from inside him and swallows him whole. He can't see his hand in front of his face, let alone the source of the trickling sound. There's a metallic taste in his mouth, warmth running down his throat. Blood, only it isn't his own. Flesh between his teeth, beneath his fingernails. The lacerated tissue pressing against his nose muffles his desperate exhalations.

"Are those blisters all over his face?" Williams asked.

"Insect bites," Riley said. "He was covered with mosquitoes when I found him."

"I've never seen anything remotely like this. Look at those collections of fluid. They almost look like boils."

Edgerton felt the ground fall away from beneath him, the pressure of arms around his chest, underneath his armpits. Someone held his legs, pinning them together.

Again, he finds himself in darkness, arms wrapped around him, only this time they're his own, and yet not his own. His flesh is cold and prickled with goosebumps, his body so thin he can feel the bones protruding from it. The stench of decomposition is beyond anything he's ever experienced, a physical entity trapped inside the cave with him. He retches, but there's nothing left in his stomach. A dribble of acid rises from his throat and lingers on his tongue. He dons the heavy animal skull, presses his face against the stone wall, and uses it to force his nostrils closed. His body shivers so hard —

"Get him out of his clothes," Riley said.

Edgerton shouted when they set him down. The pressure of the ground was more than he could bear. He felt tugging on his arms and legs, his joints seemingly stretching beyond their limits. Someone pulled his shirt over his head, exposing his bare skin to air so cold it felt like tiny icicles driven into all of his pores at once.

"Hold him still!" Williams snapped.

"I'm not touching him," one of the grad students said. Dark braids spilling out from beneath her Sherpa hat, freckles on her cheekbones and the tip of her nose. Maria Sanchez. "What if he's contagious?"

"They're just mosquito bites—"

"Mosquito bites don't cause a fever like that unless they're carrying something nasty."

"Then get out of the bloody way."

The blades of grass felt like nails against Edgerton's back, the grip of the hands upon him like vises.

"Keep his head above the water," Montgomery said.

Edgerton heard a splash and saw Williams wade into the clear stream, the smooth stones like gemstones beneath his feet. He didn't realize what was about to happen until his ankles and feet were in the water and they were lowering him—

He cried out from the shock of the cold water. The sound echoed around him, only he wasn't looking into Riley's face, but rather that of the mummified corpse in the cave, its desiccated flesh crawling with mosquitoes. It opened its eyes with a sound like tearing burlap, revealing sockets filled with blood. Its cheeks ripped and its rotted teeth parted, a single syllable passing between them—

"Dale."

He returned to consciousness with a scream trapped in his chest. The undersides of his lids felt like sandpaper as he struggled to open his eyes. Even the dim light caused the pressure inside his head to increase exponentially.

"Don't try to move," Riley whispered. She tipped a cup of water to his lips. It burned like Drano against the membranes of his parched throat, but he swallowed it as fast as he could until he aspirated it and started coughing. "Slow down, okay?"

He recognized the dome of his tent, the discoloration of the sun through the fabric. The camp stove glowed orange, heat radiating from it in waves.

"Hang in there, Dale," she said. "We were able to contact NeXgen on the satellite phone and they arranged for emergency transport. The helicopter will be here in the morning. We just need to keep that fever under control until it gets here."

He recognized the expression of concern on her face before the darkness once more drew him into its depths, only this time there were no memories, his or otherwise. There was only the darkness and a sensation like scratching inside of him, something clawing at the inside of his skin as though trying to burrow its way out.

RILEY WATCHED Montgomery wring water from the towel and place it on Edgerton's forehead. She prayed the constant application of cold compresses would be enough to keep his fever from spiking again. They'd managed to stabilize his temperature, but Lord only knew how high it had climbed. With permanent brain damage setting in at 107.6, there wasn't a lot of room for error, and yet that wasn't what worried her most about the situation. She'd seen the mosquitoes seething all over his face and the fluid-filled wheals that had developed where they'd stung him. Such histamine reactions were both normal and immediate; what wasn't, however, was the development of a high-grade fever within a matter of hours. They'd all been stung countless times since their arrival — Edgerton included — and yet none of them had experienced any unusual symptoms. Something about these mosquitoes was different, and it scared her every bit as much as the prospect of losing one of her colleagues.

With his limited training in field medicine, Montgomery was the most qualified among them to keep an eye on Edgerton. According to her contact at NeXgen, it was important that someone watch carefully in case he exhibited confusion, irritability, localized weakness, seizures, or if his fever climbed again — signs of encephalitis, an acute infection causing inflammation of the brain itself — in which case they'd have to find a way to more aggressively force-feed him fluids, reduce his core temperature, and pray to God they were able to manage the cerebral swelling with nothing more powerful than over-the-counter NSAIDs.

Riley ducked out of the tent and headed toward where the others had gathered around the fire. She took a seat in the chair Montgomery had vacated, facing a phalanx of graduate students who suddenly looked a lot younger than their years. No one spoke, but she could feel the weight of their eyes upon her. They needed her to say something reassuring, to offer guidance of some kind. The problem was that never in a million years had she dreamed that something like this could happen and she wasn't remotely prepared. Everyone was counting on her and she didn't want to lie and tell them that everything was going to be okay when every fiber of her being, whether rational or not, cried out that everything was falling apart.

Williams offered her a mug of coffee, which she declined with a shake of her head. It already felt like the acid was eating through the lining of her stomach. The last thing she needed was to add caffeine to the mix.

"We all knew the risks of signing on for field work in such a remote location," he said.

Riley smiled gratefully. His words were meant to make her feel better, but they had the opposite effect. She'd failed in the most important task bestowed upon her: ensuring the safety of her team. Maybe Edgerton had been right, and she never should have been given this responsibility. She was too young and inexperienced, and one of her colleagues had paid the price for her hubris.

She composed her thoughts, took a deep breath, and tried to sound more confident than she felt.

"While we're working under the assumption that Dr. Edgerton likely had an anaphylactic reaction to the sheer number of stings, we can't entirely rule out the possibility that he contracted a vector-borne virus like malaria or West Nile."

"This far above the Arctic Circle?" Judson Moore said. The grad student from the University of Colorado was older than the others, due in large part to his military service. "We've all been bitten and haven't developed anything more than a little swelling. If we're dealing with something worse than that, then maybe we should all consider getting on that chopper when it arrives."

"You're more than welcome to do so and — believe me — I wouldn't hold it against you if you did, but we shouldn't let fear inform our decisions with the discovery of a lifetime mere feet away," Riley said. "I've requisitioned every kind of insect repellant available to us, from citronella candles to sprays probably as toxic to us as to the mosquitoes, all of which should arrive on our next supply drop. In the meantime, I suggest wearing your gloves and ski masks and not skimping on the bug spray."

"While that sounds completely sane and rational, we all saw Dr. Edgerton when you dragged him out of the tunnel. That wasn't any kind of anaphylaxis. He was sweating and delirious and looked like he might have died had we not gotten him into the stream as quickly as we did. And he wasn't exhibiting any symptoms when we turned in last night, so whatever infection took hold of him did so in less than eight hours and we've barely been able to manage his fever, let alone whatever else is going on inside of him."

"Can we arrange for a quick medical examination of each of us when the helicopter gets here?" Williams asked.

"I don't see why not," Riley said.

"What if we're already infected?" Sadie Rogers asked. The doctoral candidate from the University of Pennsylvania was the quietest among them, in many ways acting more like an observer of their interpersonal interactions than an actual participant. She waved the smoke from her face but didn't appear to be in a hurry to relocate, as it spared her from the insects. The back of her hand was smeared with blood from where she'd relentlessly scratched at a mosquito bite with her fingernails, as though trying to scrape out the fluid. "We could already be incubating the virus."

"We can't afford to panic," Riley said. "Like Judson said, we've all been bitten before, but none of us experienced anything like what happened to Dale. It would be more surprising if he *didn't* develop a fever with even a normal immune response to such an overwhelming number of bites. He'll probably feel better in the morning and give us all an earful for calling for his evacuation."

Everyone chuckled at the thought.

"I can see him now," April Samuelsson said. She mussed her hair, scrunched up her face, and gave her best Edgerton impression. "Which one of you bloody imbeciles called for my extraction? Hmm? Trying to take credit for my discovery, I assume. Well, think again. Wait . . . dear Lord, what have you done with my clothes?"

"I don't think any of us woke up this morning thinking that today would be the day we saw our professor naked," Sadie said.

Riley did her best to keep a straight face while they had their fun. They needed the release. It had been a stressful day and they were still kids in many ways, only a few years removed from dorm life and frat parties.

"All right," Williams said. "We've all had a good laugh, but we should probably call it a night. As always, we have a big day ahead of us tomorrow and today's events have undoubtedly exacted a far greater toll than others."

"I'd like you all to keep close tabs on how you're feeling," Riley said. "Report anything out of the ordinary to me the moment you so much as suspect it, especially if you think you might have a fever. And I want to be notified of any insect bites so we can monitor them. While I'm inclined to think Dr. Edgerton's reaction was an aberration, I don't want to take any chances. Are we clear?"

She looked from one face to the next, soliciting the requisite nod or grunt of approval, and watched them head off toward their tent.

"Nate and Maria went to bed early," Williams said, his voice barely audible over the crackle of the fire. "Do you think we should check on them?"

"Let's give it a few minutes," Riley said. "I don't want it to appear as though I'm overly concerned."

"But you are, aren't you?"

The tone of his voice suggested he already knew the answer, and that he was in complete agreement.

"We're way out of our depth on this one, Niles. If it turns out we are dealing with an aggressive virus, it could spread like wildfire through the camp."

"Especially if it has an incubation period measured in hours."

"That's the thing. We can't say for sure when or where Dale contracted it. There's supposed to be an intermediary, isn't there? A bird or a horse or something. All we have this far north are the grouse, warblers, and caribou. If they'd come into contact with the virus, we should have noticed it long before now. You were out there near the herd a few days ago, weren't you?"

Williams nodded, opened the leather pouch he carried with him everywhere he went, and carefully packed the enclosed pipe with fragrant tobacco.

"Did you see any dead animals?" she asked.

"Not a single one." He spoke from the corner of his mouth as he puffed the pipe until the bowl glowed red. "Of course, a virus doesn't necessarily affect all species the same way and can mutate from one to the next. That's not your real concern though, is it?"

She glanced up at him from beneath her snow cap. While she had yet to admit as much, even to herself, she had to consider the prospect that the virus could have survived inside that cave in a state of dormancy and the sudden influx of relatively warm, fresh air could have awakened it from its eons-long slumber. There were undoubtedly far worse microbes than anthrax trapped in the permafrost, relics of a bygone era their ancestors had only narrowly survived, unlike the thirteen individuals who'd died in the cave. Was it possible they'd been infected and deliberately sealed inside to prevent the disease from spreading to the rest of the population? By opening the tunnel, had they inadvertently released it?

"We'll get a handle on this," Riley said. She offered Williams a weak smile and a squeeze on the shoulder. "I should go check on the kids."

She left him beside the fire in a vanilla-scented cloud of smoke and struck off toward the communal tent the grad students shared. The cold assailed her with a vengeance, absolving her of any residual warmth. Goosebumps rose along the backs of her arms and her teeth started to chatter. It was more than the cold, she knew. Perhaps she needed to make an executive decision and evacuate them all when the chopper arrived. She had no right to gamble with their lives. Another ten months wouldn't kill anyone. It would buy them time to identify and counteract any potential viral agent, assuming direct exposure to the elements didn't take care of it for them. The cave would still be here when they returned, along with whatever secrets it contained.

Riley unzipped the entrance of the tent and ducked inside. The camp stove glowed faintly, but barely produced enough heat to prevent her breath from freezing. The grad students' sleeping bags formed a pentagon around it, their rucksacks leaning against the walls in an effort to insulate them. Judson rolled over and looked up at her from the holes of his ski mask.

"Just checking to make sure everyone's all right," she said, offering an apologetic smile.

He nodded and closed his eyes again.

She hoped he hadn't noticed her smile falter. While it was dramatically warmer in here than it was outside, it wasn't nearly hot enough to justify the fact that the students who'd gone to bed early — Maria Sanchez and Nate Paulson — had kicked off their sleeping bags.

Or the perspiration on their pale faces.

---

*P*LAT.

Plat.

Judson floated at the edge of consciousness, in the twilight realm that existed between dreams and reality, unable to distinguish between the two. He envisioned the leaking faucet in his studio apartment back home;

however, he understood on a rational level that he was thousands of miles away from it.

So what was making that infernal dripping sound?

The sudden onset of an acute migraine wrenched him back to reality. It felt like someone had driven spikes through his temples and the base of his skull, their point of convergence in the center of his brain. Trying to open his eyes only exacerbated the intense pressure.

Plip.

Plat.

He'd never experienced such excruciating pain in his entire life, but if there was one thing he'd learned during his time as a Marine, it was that there was no physical limitation that couldn't be overcome through sheer force of will. He clenched his fists, gritted his teeth, and opened his eyes. It took several seconds for his sight to adjust to the dim glow of the camp stove, the coils of which were barely orange and yet seemed to gush waves of heat. His drenched clothes clung to his skin. Coupled with the dripping sound, he worried it must have started raining and the tent had sprung a leak, but the cold would have roused him, and right now he was burning up.

And just like that, everything came into focus.

The pain and pressure in his head. The absurd amount of sweat in his sleeping bag. He'd spiked a fever and needed to get it down before he ended up like Dr. Edgerton, who'd done this to him in the first place.

Plat.

Judson tried to sit up, but the ground tilted and the tent spun. He collapsed and rolled onto his side. His only option was to wake one of the others—

Maria lay on her back across from him, her tortured features limned by the orange light. She stared blankly up at the dome of the tent, her mouth hanging open. A tear drained down her cheek, rolled around the conch of her ear, and dripped to her pillow with a soft *plat*. She'd cast aside her sleeping bag, removed her outer layers, and still she'd sweated through her undergarments. Her chest rose so subtly that had he blinked, he would have missed it.

"Help," he tried to shout, but the word emerged from his parched throat as little more than a whisper.

He fought through the pain and crawled toward her. It felt like his muscles had atrophied and someone had lubricated his joints with acid while he slept. Despite his own fever, he could positively feel the heat radiating from her.

Plat.

"Maria?" he said.

He gently shook her, which merely caused her flesh to jiggle and her teeth to click together. The pulse in her wrist was faint and thready, nearly undetectable, her exhalations so weak against his cheek that he could barely feel them. Her pupils had expanded nearly as wide as her irises, leaving only a thin halo of blue. A single droplet of blood emerged from her nostril and dribbled past the corner of her purple lips.

"Wake up," he said, shaking her harder. She remained unresponsive. He slid his arm underneath her shoulders and tried to raise her head, but her neck folded limply back over his forearm. Her skin felt like it was on fire. "Oh, God."

Judson heard movement behind him, the rumpling of a sleeping bag, the subtle shifting of weight.

"Hold on, Maria," he whispered. He glanced over his shoulder and saw Nate rise from the ground, little more than a silhouette against the wall of the tent. "Help me, for Christ's sake!"

Judson lowered Maria's head to her pillow and was just about to seek a better grip when the tiny vessels in her eyes ruptured and flooded the whites with blood. He jerked his hands away—

A sharp blow to the back of his head.

Judson collapsed onto Maria, his vision sparkling with stars, a coppery taste leaking from his sinuses. He tried to push himself up again. Failed. Reached behind him and pressed his trembling hand against the base of his skull. Drew it away bloody.

A fist knitted into his hair, jerked back his head. He felt the sudden and unmistakable pain of teeth biting down on the muscle beside his neck, grinding, ripping from side to side.

Blood spattered onto Maria's wet top. She blinked slowly, crimson tears overflowing her lashes. Her pupils dilated, her facial muscles constricted, and she looked up at him, a complete lack of recognition in her eyes. She grabbed him by the shirt, pulled him toward her, and bit down on his windpipe. The pressure increased exponentially until, with a crunch, it abruptly abated and warmth coursed down his chest.

Judson's lips framed soundless words as the last of his breath burbled from the wound.

———

FIFTY FEET TO THE SOUTH, Montgomery slept sitting up against the wall of Edgerton's tent, tormented by the roiling in his gut and the burgeoning pain in his head. He was completely unaware of the blood dripping from his nose or the cold, dark sentience unfurling inside of Edgerton, who stared up at him from eyes devoid of all humanity.

6

_____

New York City, New York

M ilana Boswell awakened to the sound of screaming. She opened her eyes and jumped to her feet, knocking her psych textbook to the ground.

Children in swimsuits splashed in the fountain at the heart of Washington Square, flinging the cold water at each other and into the air. A little girl with pigtails and water wings squealed and tried to wave away the arc firing straight at her from the spout. One of their mothers filmed them on her cellphone while unconsciously nudging a stroller back and forth with her foot. Another thumbed through her email or social media feeds, completely disengaged from both her child and the homeless man rummaging through the trash bin behind her.

Milana picked up her book, sat back down in the shade of a zelkova tree, and finished the last of her coffee, which had grown cold while she'd nodded off.

Students from NYU cut through the park on their way to and from campus. Businesspeople in professional attire finished the remnants of their rushed lunches as they hustled back to work. Tourists snapped pictures of the Washington Arch and artists scribbled with colored chalk on the paving stones. Everywhere around her were signs of life, but she felt somehow separate from them, a ghost in their midst. Were it not for the passing men, whose stares lingered upon her caramel skin, light eyes, and hair as dark as a raven's feathers, it would have been as though she didn't exist at all.

A glance at her watch confirmed she'd already wasted twenty minutes that she simply didn't have. Her exam was in less than an hour and she still needed to eat something and track down another coffee. She was burning the candle at both ends, but there was nothing she could do about it. Between juggling two part-time jobs, taking care of her elderly *pūridaia*, Vadema, and trying to stay on top of her course load, she was hardly getting any sleep and felt as though she were failing on all fronts. The scholarship money was something — and she was hugely grateful for it — but it only defrayed a portion of her tuition, and while she could finance the rest at rates that assured she'd never be able to repay the principal in her lifetime, she was on her own for books and living expenses, which grew by the day as her grandmother's health deteriorated and the cost of her prescriptions skyrocketed.

At least she had Mrs. Lovato — whom Milana had known since she was four years old, making it impossible for her to call the older woman by her first name — from the townhouse next door to take her grandmother to appointments and bring her lunch while Milana was at school, but she couldn't afford to place any more demands upon her. As it was, her grandmother was straining the woman's Christian charity, and it was only a matter of time before she threw up her hands in frustration and walked away. Mrs. Lovato just needed to get them through the summer term. Milana had nearly three weeks off before the fall semester, which ought to be enough time to find someone willing to help out for a little while. Or maybe by then . . .

Maybe by then, what? Her grandmother would be dead?

Milana hated herself for even thinking it, but she'd found herself doing so more and more with each passing day. It was selfish and she knew it, and yet it was also beginning to feel like the only way out of the nightmare her life had become.

She didn't understand how so many of her classmates could have it so easy. Their parents just cut them a check or the university withdrew directly from their trust funds, while she had to scrimp and scrounge and wear the same coffee-stained jeans she'd worn to her morning job and smuggle out expired pastries for lunch. Granted, their parents were doctors and lawyers and hedge fund managers who could hardly spare enough time to attend their children's recitals or games or even their graduations, but that was still a lot better than the hand she'd been dealt. Her father had been killed in Iraq before she was even born and her mother had never recovered, so it hadn't been overly surprising when she'd finally up and split.

It didn't take a genius to figure out why that singular event had attracted Milana to the field of psychology; it was only natural to want to understand why the one person who was supposed to love her unconditionally had abandoned her, but there was more to it than that. Her grandmother had taken her in without reservation and had been a better mother than her own had ever been. She'd also exposed her to traditions, for lack of a better word, about which she otherwise never would have known.

Her grandmother's family had immigrated from Serbia in the late Forties, when she'd been a young girl. As traditional Romani, they'd immediately stood apart, even in the melting pot that was New York City. Having endured true oppression throughout their history, in the form of slavery and ethnic cleansing, not to mention their personal experience of being rounded up with their Jewish neighbors during the Holocaust, they'd decided that rather than trying to hide their heritage, the path to acceptance lay in embracing the stereotypes people associated with "gypsies." After all, being an almost mythical novelty did have its benefits.

It had been Milana's great-grandmother who'd first recognized the market for a fortune teller. Considering everyone in the neighborhood already believed gypsies had a connection to the spiritual world and came to her for advice on all things yet to happen, it seemed almost fated that she'd eventually hang out her shingle. She hadn't been gifted with supernatural powers. In fact, quite the opposite. She'd been an acute observer of her surroundings, a lay scientist of human behavior who'd taught herself to read her clients in much the same way that poker players studied their opponents for tells. She'd been able to intuit the nature of her clients' work during a palm reading by checking their hands for calluses and whether they had dirt or oil in the creases of their skin or underneath their fingernails; their social standing by their clothing and their bearing; even the reason they'd sought her out in the first place by the emotions and behavior they displayed. Of course, mostly they'd just needed someone to tell them that everything was going to be all right, that they'd come through the hard times they were enduring, which made her something of a psychologist in her own way.

She'd passed those skills on to her daughter — Milana's grandmother — who, in turn, had added many of her own, and made a solid living as a psychic. Her clientele had expanded from neighbors who often paid in barter to stock market traders and professionals of all stripes, who raised their collars and lowered their hats before entering her building so that no one would recognize them. She'd even assisted the police with several high-profile cases — not that they gave her any credit, mind you — including leading them to the body of a missing teenage girl and tipping them off to the crimes of a nurse who was ultimately convicted of murdering eleven patients in his care. And while she'd never grown rich by anyone's standards, she'd supplemented her husband's construction income well enough for them to buy a townhouse on the east side and raise their daughter — Milana's mother — among children who'd never heard the stigma associated with the word "gypsy," let alone held the prejudices of their forebears.

Her mother had learned everything her grandmother had to teach, but had shunned the notion of telling people's fortunes, which she considered a carnival trick, at best. She'd gone to SUNY, where she'd planned to do something in the healthcare field, whether as a doctor or a nurse, only instead she'd met a young Marine, who'd stolen her heart and left her pregnant, with no hope for the future. She'd tried her best, but she hadn't been able to hold down a job, keep up with her classwork, and take care of a newborn at the same time. Her only option had been to move back in with her parents, who'd looked after the baby while she was at school and let her handle some of the client load so she'd have a little spending money. Eventually, though, she'd given up on the schooling and figured that if she was going to "run a con," as she liked to say, she might as well make some real money doing it, so she'd taken her skills to Atlantic City, where she'd made as much as she could without popping up on the radar of any of the casinos. She'd also found a new circle of friends, who'd obviously meant more to her than the daughter she'd left behind.

Milana had been instinctively curious and had learned all of her grandmother's lessons at a young age, which was a blessing because she used them every day to keep the business going and put food on the table. The plan had always been for fortune-telling to be a temporary solution, a supplement to the social security checks while her grandmother battled through her health issues, but it quickly became apparent that she'd always been destined to lose. Now, Milana's income as a psychic, much like the paychecks and tips from her job as a barista, was just another means of slowing the bleeding until the money was gone and she was left alone.

She just needed to make it to grad school first, where not only did NYU's School of Psychology cover its students' tuition; it offered a generous stipend, which would allow her to focus on her chosen field and chase her dream of combining the skills her grandmother had taught her with everything she'd learned about human behavior to become a behavioral analyst for the FBI, a real-life profiler.

Unfortunately, none of that would come to pass if she didn't ace this infernal exam in — she again checked her watch — 48 minutes.

Milana opened her book on her lap once more and read the same chapter for the tenth time, hoping that repetition would help forge the neural pathways of at least temporary recall, especially for material as dry as this. She enjoyed case studies far more than theory, which, as it had already done once today, lulled her to sleep when she was already struggling to stay awake.

The words blurred until they went out of focus altogether. A warm sensation settled into her core. She allowed her eyelids to close, if only for one blessed moment, just long enough to tune out the screaming—

—of children fades beneath the patter of water striking the surface of the pool. The constant drumroll of footsteps metamorphoses into the scratching sound of litter and

debris blowing across the plaza. The drone of traffic dissipates, leaving only the rustling of branches overhead.

She looks up and realizes that she's the only one seated at the benches surrounding the fountain. A pall of smoke clings to the night sky, tinting the entire world a depressing shade of gray. A cold wind gusts through the trees, tossing the branches and casting serpentine shadows on the scattering of trash, which drifts like snow against the dead bodies littering the paving stones—

Milana screamed and again knocked her book to the ground.

The children stopped splashing each other and stared at her. Their mothers studied her with open suspicion. The eyes of passersby converged upon her. Even the homeless man raised his head over his bag of cans to see why she'd cried out.

"Sorry," she said. "I must have . . . just a dream."

She scooped up her book, stuffed it into her tote bag, and hurried out of the park, simultaneously embarrassed and deeply shaken by just how real the dream had felt.

MILANA RAN DOWN THE SIDEWALK, bounded up the concrete stairs of the old townhouse, and burst into the entryway. Her grandfather had converted the basement into a separate rental apartment and installed an inner door off the hallway for the main apartment. She took a moment to compose herself before sliding the key into the lock, turning the knob slowly, quietly, and entering on the feet of a mouse. No matter how prepared she thought herself, the smell never failed to catch her off guard. Gone were the days of coming home to the tantalizing aromas of stuffed peppers and goulash, replaced by the scents of dead skin, ammonia, and — dare she even think it? — death. There was no sugarcoating it: her grandmother was dying. And once she passed, there would be no one left to tether Milana to this world.

She heaved her tote bag onto the antique, claw-footed couch, spilling out her homework in the process. Her textbook on deviant behavior hit the floor with a thud that reverberated throughout the apartment. She closed her eyes and hung her head.

"Milana?" her grandmother called from upstairs. She spoke with a thick Serbian accent often mistaken for Russian, which offended her to no end. "Are you only now getting home?"

Milana took a deep breath, forced a smile, and headed into the kitchen to warm up some dinner.

"Sorry, Pūridaia. Class ran long and I missed my train again."

She opened the refrigerator and cringed at the sight of the nearly empty shelves. If she didn't squeeze in a shopping trip this weekend, she was going to have to get creative with some iffy-looking cabbage and packets of ketchup and relish. She grabbed the container of soup she'd made the night before, poured it into a smaller bowl, and put it in the microwave while she tracked down a spoon. It was a good thing her grandmother could no longer get up and about on her own; if she saw the condition of her kitchen, she'd undoubtedly revert to the old language, which was often punctuated by swats to the back of Milana's head.

"You know how I worry about a pretty young girl like you on the streets of this city."

"And you know I can take care of myself."

"As could my Rosella, and you've seen what happened to her."

Milana nodded to herself. She didn't need to be reminded about her mother, whose face she saw every time she looked in the mirror. She might as well have been cloned from the woman who'd abandoned her. While she didn't hold the decision against her mother — Lord only knew how she would have handled the situation had their roles been reversed — she didn't much like to think about it, either, if only because it made her sad in ways that lingered for days at a time.

The microwave dinged. She gave the broth a few twirls of the spoon and carried it down the hallway, hastening her pace as the rim started to burn her fingertips. She ascended the stairs to the second floor, shouldered open the bedroom door, and flipped on the light switch with her elbow. Her grandmother appeared even smaller than she had this morning, as though performing a subtle disappearing act beneath her handmade quilt. The hollows of her eyes looked almost bruised, her cheekbones more prominent, her teeth darker. There was just enough room on the TV tray to set down the soup between a box of tissues and the remains of the casserole Mrs. Lovato had brought for lunch.

Milana eased onto the bed beside her grandmother's bony hip and gently blew on the first spoonful.

Frayed tapestries hung on the walls amid framed black-and-white photographs of Boswells going back more than a hundred years, men and women with severe faces and hard eyes, who'd survived even harder times. *Wheel of Fortune* played on the television, although the sound had been turned down so far that the clapping of contestants as they spun the wheel sounded like the crinkle of cellophane.

"You are losing too much weight," her grandmother said.

"You're one to talk."

Her grandmother's eyes sparkled from beneath the folds of her eyelids.

"Just because I am dying does not mean I cannot take a smart-mouthed child over my knee."

"Don't talk like that, Pūridaia." Milana held the spoon to her grandmother's lips and waited for her to slurp the mouthful of soup. "You're not dying."

The old woman seemed to struggle to get it all the way down.

"We are all dying, child. From the moment we draw our first breaths until we breathe our last. It is part of the cycle of life, the completion of a circle with neither beginning nor end."

Milana tipped another spoonful past her grandmother's lips. She noted that the urinary catheter slithering across the bed beside her was clear, the bag empty.

"We need to get you some more fluids."

"You should be out there in the world, living your life, not taking care of an old woman like me."

"Like you should have been living your life and not raising the granddaughter who got dumped on you?"

Her grandmother reached a trembling hand out from underneath the quilt, supinated Milana's hand, and traced the lines on her palm. Their eyes met and Milana realized not only how much time had passed, but how little they had left.

"Raising you was always meant to be my fate, one no less important than the destiny that awaits you out there when I am gone. We all have a role to play, and it gives me great pride to see how well I have played mine. I only hope I have prepared you well enough for yours, for I see a long journey in your future. And darkness . . . so much darkness."

"You can't fool me, Pūridaia. You've already taught me all of your tricks."

"You are a smart girl, Milana. Sometimes, I fear, too smart for your own good. There is more to seeing the future than telling people what they want to hear. You must be mindful of the world around you, especially when it shows you sights you do not necessarily wish to see."

Milana tried not to think about the dream she'd had at the park. Or the memory of the dead bodies lying on the ground around the fountain.

"Well, I've caught you in a bleak mood tonight, haven't I?"

She smiled and offered her grandmother another spoonful, but the old woman shook her head and tucked her arm back underneath the covers. Her eyes were barely visible beneath her heavy lids.

"It is the times that are bleak, child. And they grow bleaker by the day."

"And on that cheery note . . . "

Milana kissed her grandmother on the forehead. She rose from the bed, collected the dishes, and headed for the door.

"You must heed the signs, child, for you are the only one who can read them. The path to salvation leads through darkness."

"Speaking of reading, I'd better turn on the sign and get ready to work." She paused in the doorway. "Light on or off?"

"Off, dear. I am so very, very tired."

Milana switched off the light and closed the door softly behind her. Each day was becoming more difficult than the last as her grandmother seemed to switch at random from the woman Milana had known all her life to her role as a soothsayer, the part she played for the gullible men and women who paid her to tell them what they wanted to hear.

And it terrified Milana.

She set the dishes in the sink and glanced at the clock. It was already almost eight and she had to be up again by four to have enough coffee brewed to withstand the morning rush. Missing that infernal train had cost her half of her night, not to mention at least fifty dollars. She pulled back her hair, threw on her shawl and hoop earrings, and drew the curtains across the kitchen and hallway thresholds. All that was left to do was to light the candles and a few sticks of incense to cover up the smell, turn on the neon sign in the front window, and dim the lights. She figured she'd study while she waited for her first walk-in client, but she'd barely cracked her book when the buzzer sounded from the speaker box beside the door.

The monitor on the wall displayed the feed from the security camera above the porch light, which cast a shadow from the brim of the man's fedora over his face. He wore an overcoat and scuffed shoes in desperate need of polishing. She could tell by the liver-spotted skin and knobby joints of his hands that he had to be in his seventies, at least. Men his age could be some of the most difficult clients, at least emotionally, as they generally wanted to know either that a recently deceased loved one was truly in a better place, that their families would be all right when they were gone, or that more than an insensate darkness awaited them on the other side.

She tucked her book back into her bag, hid it behind the couch, and leaned across it to get a good look out the window. The man had to be at least six feet tall and as thin as a rail. He appeared even older than she'd initially suspected in the red and blue neon glow. He looked up at her, removed his hat, and held it against his chest. His white hair was wispy, his teeth, when he smiled, too large for his mouth.

Milana ducked away from the window, pressed the button to unlock the outer door, and spoke in her best Serbian accent.

"Please come in."

She left the inner door cracked, assumed her place at a table draped with a crimson cloth patterned with golden designs, and waited patiently, listening to the sound of the man's footsteps in the outer corridor. She cleared her mind of preconceptions and prepared to read him the moment he opened the door, when he left himself completely unguarded for just a fraction of a second, which was all she needed.

A shadow eclipsed the gap, followed by a soft knock. The hinges creaked and the door opened. Slowly, tentatively. The scented smoke swirled and eddied around the elderly man as he entered, his movements stiff and labored. Up close, his skin appeared as thin as parchment, nearly translucent, revealing purplish vessels reminiscent of fat worms squirming over his bones. His suit was old and of a style she recognized from the pictures hanging in her grandmother's bedroom. The overall impression was of a corpse that had somehow been separated from his casket and was simply looking to find his way back to it. He seemed almost confused as he looked around the room until he found the coat rack, upon which he hung his hat, and then turned to face her with a faint smile on his cadaverous face.

With a flourish, Milana gestured to the chair opposite her.

The old man closed the door and approached her, his posture stooped, his hands clasped behind his back. In many ways, he was opaque to her. She didn't detect a hint of skepticism in his eyes, like she did in nearly all of her other new clients, who "didn't believe in this kind of thing," but allowed their desperation to overrule their misgivings. He looked past her, toward the curtain concealing the hallway leading into her home.

"I was hoping to see Vadema," he said in a reedy voice. "I've been looking forward to meeting her in person for a long time."

"I'm afraid my grandmother is no longer performing readings, but I assure you she personally taught me everything she knows," Milana said.

"Everything?"

His stare never left hers as he lowered himself into the chair, placed a fifty-dollar bill on the table, and laced his long fingers on top of it. She smelled the cloying scent of death and nearly apologized to the old man, until she realized it was coming from him. He cocked his head from one side to the other, appraising her like a carrion bird. She instinctively checked to make sure the Colt .22 pistol was in the holster bolted to the bottom of the table.

The man's grin grew even wider.

"So how does this work?" he asked.

Milana smiled patiently and held out her hands.

"I want you to close your eyes and think about the questions that brought you here. Focus on them. Concentrate all of your energies upon them. Open yourself to the universe, allow it to reveal the secret knowledge it has hidden deep inside of you."

He closed his eyes, although his eyelids were so thin that she almost felt as though he could still see her. His forehead was beaded with fine droplets of perspiration, his collar so tight it seemed to bite into his neck. The lanyard hanging from it featured his picture and the logo of the New Jersey Department of Corrections.

"Now turn over your hand, palm up, and place it in mine," she said.

The old man did as she asked, his flesh cold and dry. His hand trembled ever so slightly. She extended her index finger and traced the tip of her nail along his lifeline.

"Tell me . . . " he said, opening his eyes. His irises had taken on the color of the candlelight, as though the flames had somehow become trapped inside. "What do you see?"

A series of images flashes before Milana's eyes. Teeth tearing flesh. Buildings turned to rubble, nearly concealed by clouds of roiling smoke. Ashes falling from the sky like snow. A long-haired man standing on a mountaintop among cacti and stunted pine trees, silhouetted against the setting sun. A woman she's never seen before, screaming for her to run. Violent floodwaters roaring through a canyon. And then complete darkness, within which she senses more than sees a tall man. Horns protrude from his head and mosquitoes funnel from his mouth. His laughter sounds like shattering glass.

Milana released the old man's hand and attempted to distance herself from him, but he caught her by the wrists, his yellowed fingernails biting into her skin.

"Your *pūridaia* can no longer protect you," he said.

"Let go of me!"

She jerked her arms, but only succeeded in drawing the old man closer, his breath the source of the vile smell. The fine lines in the skin of his hands were dark, as though he'd tried and failed to wash what she instinctively knew to be blood from them.

"No one can save you from what is coming," he said, releasing his grip.

Milana stumbled backward, toppling over the chair and colliding with the wall in her hurry to distance herself from him. A framed Tibetan mandala fell and shattered on the floor beside her.

"Get out!" she screamed.

The old man stood, straightened his suit jacket and tie, and closed his eyes. When he opened them again, his irises had faded to a dirty brown. He walked across the room, removed his hat from the hook, and glanced back at her.

"I'll be seeing you again soon," he said.

He again flashed that awful smile, donned his fedora, and exited the apartment.

Milana ran to the door, slammed it closed, and locked the deadbolt. Pressing her eye to the peephole, she watched him walk down the hallway until he passed through the front door and then hurried to the window. He descended the stairs and glanced up at her. With a tip of his hat, he strolled down the sidewalk and vanished into the shadows.

"Pūridaia," she whispered.

She shoved the curtain aside, blew through the hallway, and took the stairs two at a time. The glow of the television flickered from the gap beneath the door. She slowly opened it and entered, already knowing what she would find when she turned on the light.

Her grandmother lay on the bed, just as she had before, her head propped on the pillow, her mouth hanging open. The quilt no longer rose and fell with her labored exhalations. Her eyelids were only partially closed, the lower crescents of her irises barely visible.

"No," she sobbed. "Oh, no."

Milana fell to her knees at the bedside, wrapped her arms around the woman who had chosen to be her mother when no one else had wanted the job, and started to cry.

7

Cambridge, Massachusetts

"We've found that common symbology is often used in ancient rock art, even by cultures geographically isolated from one another," Dr. Jack Lucas said. The Harvard professor paced the semicircular stage of the lecture hall, his well-worn cowboy boots echoing from the hollow space underneath it. He wore his dark hair shaggy, a button-down shirt open at the neck, and jeans starting to wear through at the knees. An arrowhead he'd collected from Chaco Canyon hung from a rawhide cord against the tan skin of his exposed chest. In one hand he held a laser pointer, in the other a remote clicker, which he used to control the slides being projected from above the heads of the students seated at the desks ascending the theater, like the bleachers behind home plate. The light shining from behind them made it impossible to discern more than their silhouettes. "As you see here, several different peoples used the common motif of a spiral that starts at the center and expands outward to represent ascension, an inverted U-shape over an object to indicate that it's hidden, and an upside-down figure to show that the subject is deceased."

He switched from one slide to the next, displaying photographs of petroglyphs and pictographs, primitive forms of artwork either etched into or painted onto the walls of remote caves and canyons by long-dead hands to communicate messages or commemorate events of great importance.

"There are countless other examples like these," he continued. "Most of them are fairly intuitive, even to a casual observer — a universal means of communication, if you will — much like curling your index finger to beckon someone closer or holding up your open palm to signal them to stop. These symbols were designed to transcend language barriers, especially in areas where there were multiple overlapping cultures. Directions leading to water and shelter. Comic-like panels memorializing great battles or hunts. Similar maze-like designs that represent the creation myths of otherwise disparate peoples, their emergence into this world from the subterranean world below ours. But what about the designs that aren't so easily interpreted and for which there's no readily apparent explanation for their similarities, especially between societies separated by thousands of miles, or even entire oceans, insurmountable distances in a time before the domestication of horses and the advent of sea travel?"

He clicked again and brought up a slide featuring ten images arranged in two horizontal rows, each containing five pictures labeled by their location of origin. Every single one depicted an anthropomorphic figure with its upper arms and thighs extended laterally from its body, its forearms raised to the sky and its lower legs pointed straight down. Its head and male genitalia were clearly demonstrated, as well as the twin circles on both sides of its body.

"We call this The Squatter Man, for obvious reasons," he said, eliciting a chorus of chuckles from the class. "As you can see, we've discovered his likeness in countries all around the world: Armenia and the United Arab Emirates, the Austrian and Italian Alps, the American Southwest, and even in Guyana and Venezuela, all dating to a time when none of these people could have possibly had physical contact with one another."

A hand shot up into the light and nearly eclipsed the image on the screen.

"Go ahead," Lucas said.

"How does this differ from the archetype of the mother, who's similarly represented in what's considered the 'birthing pose'?"

"Very good question, although in the case of the mother, the answer's entirely intuitive. There's pretty much only one way to get that baby out of there under normal conditions, while The Squatter Man lacks the cultural stylization you'll notice in versions of the mother throughout the world. He utilizes a universal representation, despite the lack of a clear message as to what he represents, and there's no easy explanation for the spheres flanking his thorax or a reason for them to exist in any of them, let alone all."

"Maybe they're like the signs on bathroom doors," someone called from the back, causing the whole theater to erupt with laughter.

Lucas smirked.

"Modesty's largely a construct of modern morality. I'm inclined to think the people who created these designs were more concerned with where their next meal was coming from than who was sitting in the stall next to them."

He clicked the remote and another series of pictures filled the screen, all of them featuring a dark figure with a wide, oval-shaped head and a pair of disproportionately large eyes.

"This recurring motif is referred to as either The Owl Man or The Owl-Eyed Figure, and while one could make a case for the owl representing wisdom or a sixth sense, it's far from a universal interpretation. It's true that owls are indigenous to every continent except Antarctica, but so are countless other avian species, so why this one specifically? Why does this same creation appear in the artwork of aboriginal peoples from North America to the Dominican Republic, and even as far away as Australia?"

The door at the top of the stairs opened, admitting a corridor of light that brightened the entire room. A man with broad shoulders and a crisp suit stood momentarily silhouetted within it. A flash of reflected light from the face of his watch and the door closed once more. The shadows swallowed him whole.

Lucas took a drink from the bottle of water on the lectern and changed the slide. The collection of images on the screen behind him featured faded paintings and weathered carvings that were human in shape and design, if not proportion. Their heads and appendages retained the same scale as the other figures around them, but their bodies had been stretched vertically, as though made of taffy. Their heads were crowned with horns or spikes, their arms extended outward, vertical lines pointing downward from beneath them to indicate upward movement. And at the heart of each of the dark, faceless representations was a white spot where the paint had been chipped away or the rock pecked out.

"This elongated figure is one of the most common motifs across ancient artworks on every continent and among countless primitive societies, and yet it is the commonalities themselves that defy logical explanation. We believe they represent shamans rising from their physical vessels into the celestial or spiritual realm, an out-of-body experience. And while that makes sense from a figurative standpoint, it doesn't mesh with nearly all other aspects of the stone artwork from this period, which is very literal in its interpretation, as I've discovered through my work in the field, translating panels throughout the American Southwest."

"But didn't these people truly believe that their shamans had mystical powers, thus making these designs literal interpretations?" a shadow asked from the third row.

"An excellent observation, but if that were the case, then why do the majority of these panels feature four distinct figures when there was only a single shaman in any given tribe? And what about the disturbed area in the center of their chests, where they've been defaced in a manner otherwise used to show the release of a trapped spirit, most commonly associated with death? From the most literal standpoint, we're looking at figures that so terrified the people of the time that they had to vandalize the artwork in hopes of releasing the evil spirits trapped inside the stone."

Lucas hit the wall switch and turned on the overhead lights. The rumble of voices filled the room, punctuated by the closing of books and the zipping of backpacks. He had to use the microphone to be heard over the din.

"For next class, I want you to find examples of both intuitive and non-intuitive designs common to multiple cultures and write a paragraph of justification for each. I won't be collecting them, but you should be prepared to present them if I call on you."

The man in the suit stepped aside for the mass exodus of students and slowly worked his way down the stairs against the flow of traffic. His bald head was so recently shaved that it reflected the halogen tubes, unlike his eyes, which were dark and flat and fixed intently upon Lucas, who gathered his belongings and packed them into his leather satchel, in case he needed to make a fast getaway.

"That was a fascinating lecture, Dr. Lucas," the man said. He stepped up onto the stage and proffered his hand. "Allow me to introduce myself. My name is Dr. Rutger Bergstrom — M.D. and Ph.D. I'm the executive vice president of research and development for NeXgen Biotechnology and Pharmaceuticals."

Lucas noted the man's manicured nails and expensive cologne as they shook hands. Bergstrom was probably the father of one of his students, although he couldn't recall any of them having that last name. They were only a couple weeks into the summer term, so it was awfully early for this guy to be attempting to influence his kid's grade, but when it came to the level of competition at this school, Lucas had learned early on that there was nothing some parents wouldn't do.

"What can I do for you, Dr. Bergstrom?"

"I'm afraid I'm on a tight schedule, so I'll cut right to the chase. There's a car waiting for us outside. I was hoping you wouldn't mind coming with me."

Lucas slung the strap of his satchel over his shoulder and started toward the stairs.

"These evening lectures always tend to run late," he said. "I'm tired, hungry, and have an early class in the morning. All that aside? I still can't think of a single set of circumstances under which I'd get into a car and go anywhere with someone I've never met."

"Aren't you the least bit curious why I'm here?" He removed a manila folder from inside his suit jacket and held it out for Lucas, who made no move to take it from him. "Trust me, you're going to want to see what's inside."

Lucas met the older man's stare and reluctantly held out his hand.

Bergstrom slapped the folder into his palm, stepped back, and clasped his hands behind his back.

Inside the folder was a single photograph, taken under low-light conditions and featuring a subject dramatically different than Lucas had expected. He tried not to let his surprise show on his face as he studied an ancient petroglyph that had to be at least ten thousand years old. The designs were both familiar and unlike any he'd ever seen before. He suddenly understood exactly why Bergstrom had come to him specifically and heard himself utter words he wouldn't have imagined coming out of his mouth thirty seconds prior.

"So where are we going?"

A TOWN CAR waited outside the anthropology building, its tinted windows reflecting the streetlights along Divinity Avenue. The driver saw them coming, walked around to the back door, and held it open. Lucas ducked his head and followed Bergstrom into the dimly lit interior. There were two seats upholstered with butter-soft black leather and embossed with the stylized X of the NeXgen logo, which he'd seen countless times on TV, generally in conjunction with a list of side effects potentially worse than the symptoms the advertised drug had been designed to alleviate. The heated console between them already held a freshly poured snifter of brandy. Bergstrom removed it as he passed and assumed the seat on the far side.

"Can I offer you a drink?" he asked, swirling the amber liquid.

Lucas settled into the seat and shook his head. He'd never ridden in a chauffeured vehicle and felt hugely uncomfortable. His mother had been a high school teacher, his father an electrician. They'd lived a comfortable life in a modest home on the western slope of the Rockies, in a small town where everyone drove four-wheel-drive vehicles and no one cared that he was of a mutt of mixed Native American, Hispanic, and Caucasian descent. That wasn't to say he hadn't encountered this kind of money since moving to Cambridge, only that he'd maintained a natural degree of separation from it, at least until now.

The vehicle wended through the campus and worked its way down to Broadway, which shot straight as an arrow to the southeast toward the Charles River. Colonial row houses passed on both sides, their small yards illuminated by the upper-story lights of students who'd be studying well into the night.

Bergstrom finished his drink without savoring it, leaned forward, and switched on the overhead light. He nodded for Lucas to take a closer look at the picture he still held in his hands.

"We need to know what that message says," Bergstrom said.

Lucas hesitated before answering.

"It's a warning."

"We figured as much, but we need to know if there's genuinely something to worry about." Bergstrom sighed and settled back into his seat. "Not long after uploading that picture, we received a request for emergency medical evacuation from our research team in the field. As we speak, there's a rapid response team on its way to Alaska. In a matter of hours, those men will land at a remote airstrip above the Arctic Circle, transfer to a helicopter, and fly headlong into a situation about which we know very little, outside of the fact that one of the researchers spiked a fever so high that he had to be immersed in a stream, and they're still having trouble keeping it down. We need to know as much as possible about what our men are getting themselves into before they're exposed to God knows what and they risk bringing it back with them."

"And you think I'll be able to tell you anything from a single petroglyph?"

"Among others," Bergstrom said. He removed another folder from the pocket of the seat in front of him, handed it to Lucas, and waited expectantly. "We might not be experts by any stretch of the imagination, but we recognized from the designs that we weren't dealing with ordinary cave paintings."

Lucas nodded. He'd recognized as much at first sight. He'd spent countless hours hiking through the canyons of the American Southwest, the jungles of Mexico, and the South American Andes, isolated from modern man, hunting for signs of what had happened to the people who'd once lived there, like the Anasazi, who'd simply abandoned the cities they'd built directly into the cliffs. He'd been the first to discover petroglyphs that hadn't been seen by human eyes in hundreds, if not thousands, of years, translated panels that had stymied experts for generations, and immersed himself in the histories of peoples who were nearly as mythical as the deities they worshipped.

The folder was sealed and stamped CONFIDENTIAL. He glanced up at Bergstrom, who gestured for him to proceed, and slit the foil tape with his thumbnail. Inside was a stack of enlarged photographs that were obviously image captures from a video recording, presumably filmed by the researchers who'd first entered what appeared to be a naturally occurring dolomite formation, which, unlike the limestone karst of the southwestern U.S., didn't lend itself to the ready formation of stalactites and stalagmites. The walls were rimed with ice, as though at some point the cave had been filled with water that had subsequently frozen and helped preserve both the skeletal and intact remains featured in several of the pictures. The condition of the mummified corpse reminded him of the Inca mummies that had been discovered high in the mountains of Peru, so well-aged that they appeared to have been shrink-wrapped in their own skin. The characters on the walls, however, were unlike any he'd seen before, and would require more thorough evaluation.

He found other pictures of the panel Bergstrom had originally shown him, only taken from different angles and in such a way as to illustrate that it had been carved not into a wall, but rather onto a flat, circular stone that lay cracked on the ground, just inside the mouth of the cave, as though it had been dislodged from the entrance. The symbols near the top of the design left little doubt as to the message they conveyed, for he'd seen others very much like them at the bases of extremely treacherous trails or in canyons where there wasn't a single drop of water to be found. They were both intuitive and universal, unmistakable in their simplicity, created to be easily interpreted by anyone who might find them, regardless of the language they spoke. The partial counterclockwise spiral meant "turn around." A dot under a half-circle showed that something was "buried" inside, likely the male figure featured prominently in the center.

He'd been carved with great care to demonstrate his elongated torso and demonic, horned head. His heart had been pecked out and his chest and arms superimposed with the thorax and wings of a bat. In their shared belly was a coiled serpent. Twelve inverted figures, all of them with the heads of wolves, surrounded him. Droplets rained from their outstretched arms and legs, ran in ribbons down their bodies, as though bleeding from everywhere at once, as one would expect from a hemorrhagic virus like Ebola: a deadly microscopic organism physically resembling a snake, a virus that had been spread to the human population in the saliva of bats.

"You have to understand that fiction was a foreign concept to our distant ancestors," Lucas said. He stood at the foot of a long maple conference table, a laptop displaying the thumbnail images of the photographs taken inside the cave on a touchscreen monitor in front of him. All he had to do was tap one and it would appear on the screen behind him in the highest possible resolution. "They might have inadvertently fictionalized events as a way of rationalizing them, but the concept of making up stories was outside their realm of experience. All of the petroglyphs we've discovered throughout the world are meant to be interpreted literally, to convey a message of such great importance that considerable time and effort were invested into immortalizing them."

"You're suggesting this bat-man is real?"

The man at the head of the table wore a suit that undoubtedly cost more than Lucas's entire wardrobe and a watch that could have financed any number of tech startups in the basement apartments surrounding MIT, just down the street. Dr. Severn Hodges was the president and CEO of NeXgen, the similarly dressed men flanking him corporate officers representing both the R&D and bioengineering arms of the company, Drs. Rutger Bergstrom and Carter Young, respectively. Beside them, wearing suits, photographic name badges, and looking more than a little nervous, were liaisons from various government agencies: Dr. Angela Ferris, from the Centers for Disease Control and Prevention; Colonel Jackson Xenos, commander of the United States Army Medical Research Institute of Infectious Diseases; Dr. Frank Urban, Secretary for Chemical and Biological Defense at the DOD; and Charles Vickers, the Secretary of the U.S. Department of Homeland Security, none of whom Lucas ever thought he'd meet through the course of his work.

"That's exactly what I'm saying," he said, switching images and zooming in on the figure in question. "The vertically stretched man universally represents a shaman, whether in the act of celestial ascension or merely as a means of delineation. Combining his form with that of a bat implies some sort of amalgamation, like he's absorbed the characteristics of a bat in some way, not to mention the snake in their shared belly, the totality of which is responsible for the bleeding men surrounding him. You don't need extensive experience interpreting indigenous artwork to infer that the shaman might have been afflicted with some sort of hemorrhagic disease. You wouldn't have brought me here if you weren't concerned that was the case."

All eyes turned toward Hodges, who stared Lucas down for several seconds before leaning forward and lacing his fingers on the tabletop.

"Our researchers didn't discover this panel until after they'd already entered the cave," he said. "They speculate it had initially been used to seal the entrance, but fell inward some unknown number of years ago, long after the tunnel leading to it was filled with stones and packed earth. We probably never would have scrutinized the imagery if one of the anthropologists hadn't developed a fever that our site lead described as 'life-threatening.'"

"Why is a company like NeXgen financing an archeological dig in the first place?" Lucas asked.

"Climate change is a very real phenomenon, regardless of whether or not it's anthropogenic in nature. The history of the planet is written in terms of a constantly changing climate from one epoch to the next, from ice ages and droughts to meteorite impacts and volcanic eruptions that fill the sky with so much dust and ash that they block out the sun. It is a system of chaos that always seeks equilibrium: moving entire continents around a molten core, amassing and releasing geothermal pressure, altering wind patterns and oceanic currents, all of which have the cumulative effect of creating a constant state of fluctuation. Nowhere is that more evident than at the poles, where ice packs expand in some areas and contract in others, allowing permafrost that's been frozen for unknown thousands of years to thaw, releasing the anaerobic microbes trapped inside and giving them new breaths of life. That's the challenge the pharmaceutical industry faces on a daily basis, for Lord only knows what kinds of microscopic horrors await us. If we aren't prepared to counteract them, then we could very well be on the brink of the sixth mass extinction."

"Which is why we finance this excavation," Bergstrom said, "and hundreds of others like it, all around the world."

"And why we've done so since we first found Ötzi the Iceman and were able to resurrect the bacteria in his gut. We're talking about an extinct microorganism only somewhat similar to its modern descendants, one that died out through the course of natural selection, yet here it is again, through pure chance. But what if that resurrected species were something other than benign flora? What if it were a bacterium or virus for which we have no cure? Every inch of thawing strata brings us closer to unleashing the next bubonic plague or Spanish flu, diseases responsible for the deaths of millions. And any time we open a cave or unearth a tomb that's been sealed for more than ten thousand years, we run the risk of discovering more than mere pictures on the walls, which is why we need to know what these say. The moment the site manager called for the evacuation of one of her scientists and we recognized the potential significance of the picture you just analyzed, we realized that we could be facing the prospect of having opened Pandora's box and unleashing a pathogen that makes Ebola look like the common cold."

Lucas felt the weight of everyone's stares upon him.

"Translating panels like the ones in these photographs takes time," he said.

"Unfortunately, time is a luxury we don't have," Hodges said. "Our researchers have already been exposed to whatever was in that cave, our rapid response team is currently over the Gulf of Alaska, and we need every bit of information we can get if we hope to contain the threat. We were assured that if anyone could decipher the warnings these people left for whoever discovered the cave, it was you."

Lucas returned his attention to the screen and brought up the panels one by one, in the order they'd been viewed by whoever initially recorded them, as evidenced by the time stamps in the corners.

"If one were to assume the circular stone with the warning had been designed to serve as the final seal at the entrance to the cave, then it stands to reason that anything carved on the inside was meant to be viewed by someone who'd disregarded the warning and entered anyway."

"Like the curse of a mummy's tomb," Vickers said. The tone of the secretary of the DHS's voice was one of disbelief, but Lucas proceeded, undeterred.

"In a sense. Only in this case, these panels tell the tale of the poor souls who'd known they were going to be sealed inside with the infected shaman." He zoomed in on a panel featuring the ghostly outlines of handprints, as though each had been impressed upon the stone in paint and then chiseled away to add permanence. "In the tradition of the Pueblo peoples, the handprint is sacred and serves as a signature of sorts, one often used to mark sacred places so that the gods would know who was responsible for the sacrifices or offerings. These twelve prints likely memorialize the individuals depicted in the next panel, in which they're represented as more hastily carved stick figures with circular heads and eyes, surrounding the elongated shaman with the bat wings. Presumably, the replacement of their human heads with those of wolves in subsequent renderings indicates their state of infection and the strength it would have required to physically restrain the shaman while sealing him inside, knowing that they were going to die, willingly sacrificing themselves so that the rest of the population might survive."

"So the remains of any one of these thirteen individuals could serve as a reservoir for the virus," Colonel Xenos from USAMRIID said.

"If any of the researchers have already contracted it, we have much more immediate concerns," Bergstrom said.

"You're basing all of your assumptions on an interpretation of ancient drawings," Vickers said. "What am I supposed to tell the President? That we're dealing with a potential global pandemic based on a single researcher with a fever and the testimony of a bunch of stick figures?"

"You contracted us for this very reason," Hodges said. "Maybe there's a reason to worry; maybe not. That's why you're all here. I could have easily dismissed this whole thing out of hand on my own, but when it comes to a threat of this nature, we can only guess wrong once. The President understands that. Explain the situation to the National Security Council, determine the appropriate response, and make whatever arrangements you need to make. In the meantime, my team will contain any viral agents and begin implementing countermeasures, just like we've done dozens of times before and will undoubtedly do countless times again."

"We generally have more to go on than this, though."

"And in a matter of hours, you will," Bergstrom said. "Considering the remoteness of the location and the danger posed by a microbe that can raise a man's temperature to the brink of brain damage within a matter of hours, we need to get out ahead of this one."

"And we need to make sure we're the only ones who have it," Urban said. The DoD official cast an imperious eye over the gathering. "With Russia a mere stone's throw away, its military could easily beat us to the site if we hesitate.

"Assuming it's anything at all," Vickers said. "And — no offense intended — we aren't just wasting our time with this cave art nonsense."

Lucas was too busy scrutinizing the final screen-capture to even notice, let alone take offense. It looked at first like a jumble of meaningless lines and characters, but if he were willing to use a little creativity and imagine them being carved by a man in complete darkness, finding his landmarks by feel alone, he could almost envision them forming a coherent image. He let his eyes go out of focus, as though trying to see the 3-D image hidden in a stereogram poster, and visualized an elongated shamanic form rising from a burning butte or mesa and, in the distance, uneven horizontal steppes resembling a city skyline, before which three more shamanic figures stood.

He blinked, and the design returned to a chaos of scratches inflicted upon the stone wall by a man infected with a deadly disease, trapped inside a cave, and subsisting upon the remains of those who'd consigned him to his damnation.

8

Oraibi, Arizona

Robert Sakeva shivered and opened his eyes. The fire had dwindled to little more than glowing embers, crackling deep within the scorched wood, from which a tracery of smoke filtered into a night sky filled with stars, so close they seemed almost within his reach. An unseasonal cold front had descended upon Third Mesa while he slept, causing his breath to plume from his lips and his joints to ache. Old bones like his had not been made for temperatures such as these and protested the mere act of raising his head to survey the living world around him. Red sands spotted with creosote and sage bushes stretched out before him toward the striated buttes lining the horizon. While the outside world had become unrecognizable in his lifetime, this was the same view his ancestors had left for him, and the same view he would leave for future generations, assuming they survived what was to come.

He felt so very, very old, as though time itself had moved on and left him behind. His vision was marred by cataracts, his eyelids fringed with papillomas, his dark eyes wizened by age. He could feel his face hanging from the underlying bones, his long, brittle hair blowing against his cheeks. His skin had become as thin as tissue paper, the vessels beneath it like spider webs. The boy was still somewhere inside him, traveling hand-in-hand with the man. All that was left now was for him to finish the journey they had begun, which, he knew, was almost at an end.

As with every other night, he'd performed his rituals and fallen asleep within the aura of the fire's warmth, as his lineage had done for centuries, standing sentry against the rise of the darkness that had been foretold in prophecies from the lips of Maasaw, the Great Spirit who'd been waiting for his ancestors when they'd emerged from the underworld and the cycle of the Fourth World had begun. Maasaw's warnings had been handed down through countless generations by crazy old women and men, like himself, perhaps a bit muddied by subsequent retellings, but unvarying in meaning. He was one of the last of a dying breed of traditionalists, who lived humble lives defined by simplicity and faith, as their forefathers had promised they would when they'd sealed their covenant with Taiowa, the Creator.

While most of the Hopi people had forsaken their sacred vows and immersed themselves in material ways, his lineage had continued to live in the same adobe home it had occupied for over nine hundred years. When the white men from the agency had stolen their children and shipped them off to schools where they could be steeped in propaganda and purged of their culture, his family had defiantly stood against its fate, until their feet had literally been chopped off for their stubbornness and they could stand no more. And when the federal government had run pipes and conduits to their homes, his father had continued to collect his water from the stream and read by candlelight.

Sakeva had always believed in the old ways, for he had seen with his own eyes the fulfillment of Maasaw's prophecies and watched the neighboring villages suffer from the broken promises they'd made to the Creator. He'd been groomed to sense the dark tide rising, knowing full well that it might not break the horizon in his lifetime, which was growing shorter by the minute. He recalled the question he'd asked his grandfather on this very spot, so many years ago.

"If the darkness never comes, then will you not have wasted your entire life waiting?"

Ahote Sakeva, a man held together by dust and wrinkles, had been alive long enough to have seen four of the nine signs come to fruition: the arrival of the white-skinned men who took what was not theirs and struck down their enemies with thunder; the coming of the wagons with their spinning wheels; the introduction of strange beasts with long horns that would overwhelm the land with their numbers; and the crossing of the desert by snakes of iron in the form of the mighty railroads. This old man who'd borne witness to the beginning of the end had pulled young Robert close and whispered directly into his ear as he gestured toward the vast expanse of land below them.

"The rattlesnake does not need to poke his head from his hole to know if something is out there. He feels the vibrations through the earth and the air, smells his surroundings on his forked tongue. Only when he knows the hawk is not circling overhead does he slither from the ground."

Sakeva hadn't understood the metaphor, at least not way back then, but the conversation had remained with him for more than seventy years, during which time he'd realized that his life was better spent watching for something that never came than being on the front lines when it finally did. And yet with each passing year, he became more and more convinced that it was coming. It was a feeling, one he could not adequately put into words, like the sensation a spider experienced when the shadow of a boot fell upon it. A part of him wondered if such feelings were not simply a part of the life cycle, the unconscious acceptance of his impending death, but deep down he knew he was like the rattlesnake. He was so attuned to the earth that he could sense the vibrations of the coming war, like the footsteps of an army marching in the distance, drawing ever closer with each passing day.

A knot popped in the fire, scattering cinders onto the dirt. He watched them smolder until they turned to ash and danced away on a breeze so sharp it cut through his clothes and burrowed into his bones.

With considerable effort, he struggled to his feet, wrapped the blanket around his torso, and hobbled to the edge of the escarpment. Gravel skittered away from his boots and plummeted down the steep slope. The ground below him sparkled with gemstones. It took him several moments to realize that they were the reflection of the moon from the eyes of so many coyotes, gathered below him as though waiting for him to hurl himself from the precipice and into their jaws.

He shivered and looked to the sky, where artificial stars flashed among the constellations, restlessly circling of the globe. Storm clouds scudded toward him from the northern horizon, blanketing the celestial bodies as they went. Their shadows spread across the desert like an oil spill until darkness engulfed the land, as cold and unfeeling as a burial shroud.

His heart beat faster and he clutched the blanket tighter to keep his hands from trembling.

The Day of Purification would soon arrive.

As one, the coyotes raised their snouts to the heavens and howled, the forlorn sound drifting across the plains.

He gathered his belongings and headed for the trail leading to his home. There was much to do, and, he was afraid, very little time to do it.

SAKEVA BACKED his old Chevy truck up to the front of his house and killed the engine. The taillights painted the adobe red and revealed the stones where the outer layer had crumbled and fallen off. He wished he'd found the time to re-plaster it, but that was neither here nor there. All that mattered now was loading the boxes he'd stashed under the weathered wooden lean-to into the bed without waking anyone. He couldn't stand the prospect of facing his daughter and that disapproving expression of hers. As it was, Millie was convinced he'd gone senile, and she was probably right, but the truth of the matter was that he couldn't remember a time in his life when he'd ever seen things as clearly as he did now.

He climbed out with a crunch of the warped springs under the bench seat and closed the door quietly behind him. All he had to his name was inside those boxes: clothes, dried meats and vegetables, paintbrushes of all shapes and sizes, and crates of paint in buckets and spray cans. Of course, hidden among them were the thousands of dollars his father had tucked away from his settlement with the Indian Claims Commission for the land stolen from his family in the late Forties, money he'd passed down to Sakeva for just this occasion. It seemed fitting that humanity's salvation should come from the very mechanism of its demise.

"So you're just going to sneak off in the middle of the night?" a voice said from behind him. "Without saying a word to any of us?"

Sakeva set down the box, slid it deeper into the rusted bed, and turned to face his daughter. She stood in the front doorway, her thick arms crossed over her ample bosom, her bare feet protruding from beneath her nightgown.

"I was trying not to wake you," he said.

"That old truck of yours sounds like it's trying to rattle itself apart. You probably woke up people all the way over in Winslow."

"I need to leave for a while, Millie, and I don't know how long I'll be gone."

"You think I don't know what you're doing? You should at least tell the council. Maybe they can talk some sense into you."

"What's the point? They broke the covenant a long time ago. They're every bit as white on the inside as any Bahanna you'll ever meet."

"Or maybe they just see how things like electricity and indoor plumbing can make our lives just the tiniest bit better."

"You mean easier," he said. "Life was never meant to be easy. Whether or not we were the ones who spoke the words, our ancestors formed a covenant with Taiowa, and it is our responsibility to live up to our end of the deal. We agreed to walk the straight path, for we all know what awaits us at the end of the crooked one."

"We know nothing of the kind. All we have is a carving on a stupid rock that old men like you treat as though it were inscribed by the hand of God."

Sakeva smiled patiently. There was no debating his daughter when she was in one of her moods. He knew she was only saying such things to hurt him. Like so many of her generation, she'd been raised in the Bahanna's world and hadn't been alive long enough to have seen it as it once was. She simply accepted that the water from the stream had to be boiled and filtered of the pollutants from the coal mine, that there needed to be fences around the fields where their sheep grazed, that she wouldn't be able to survive without the white man's green paper. He wished she could have known the days when everything as far as the eye could see had belonged to the Hopi people, who protected it for the Creator, living simple lives without materialism or greed. Those had been peaceful times, when no man needed a gun or raised a hand against his neighbor, before the covenant was broken and the original council tasted its first dose of power, which the agency doled out, one drop at a time, until it was the only thing that mattered.

From that point on, the reservation had become an ever-shrinking microcosm of the outside world as the council traded away the rights of the tribe for personal gain, leased land that it didn't own to corporations for their exploitation, and allowed the men from the Bureau of Indian Affairs to dictate what they could grow and how many animals they could keep. They'd given everything away until all that was left were the three sacred mesas, a small swatch of land like an island in the vast sea of the Navajo Nation, where they were ruled by a government to which they'd sworn no allegiance, taught a version of history other than their own, and commanded to worship the Bahanna's God. It was no wonder that the prophecies were being fulfilled at such a staggering rate now. The Fourth Cycle was drawing to a close and humanity's days were numbered.

Perhaps this time they'd be found wanting and Taiowa would simply start anew without a dominant species intent on destroying all of the gifts it had been given. Surely the Creator, in his infinite wisdom, had anticipated their folly, and that was why he'd sent Maasaw to wait for Sakeva's ancestors when they emerged from the underworld into the Fourth World, and why the Great Spirit had led them here, into the heart of the unforgiving land, where their faith would be tested on a daily basis, a test they failed time and again.

The old guard had even traveled east in the Fifties to deliver the warnings in the prophecies to the United Nations, but their appeals had fallen upon the deaf ears of men who called the Hopi Way primitive and their beliefs superstitious. Their failing had been their pride, for they should have stayed in the east until the Bahanna listened to them, rather than turning away, more invested in proving they were right than in saving the lives of those who would not survive the end of the cycle. Sakeva hoped they drew immense satisfaction from every prophecy that came to pass from the comfort of their graves.

"Just help an old man load his truck, would you?" he said.

Millie slipped on her shoes and crossed the hardpan to where her father labored with a bucket of paint. She got her hands underneath it and helped him clear the tailgate. When she spoke, it was in a tone of resignation

"So where are you going?"

"Everywhere," he said

"That's not a destination."

"It is if I don't intend to stop for very long. This whole beautiful land awaits me with thousands of miles of open roads—"

"You mean the Bahanna's paved roads?"

"I am certain Taiowa will indulge a humble servant doing his good work."

"Is that how you justify the truck?" she said. "You realize how you sound, don't you?"

Sakeva smiled and embraced her as tightly as he could. She was so much like her mother, whose will had been indomitable and whose tongue had been sharper than a lash. Not a day went by that he didn't miss her and look forward to the time when they would be reunited, a time he could feel fast approaching.

"The world out there is no place for a fossil who knows nothing of its ways," she said.

"It is age that makes the fossil hard, protecting it from the world deteriorating around it."

She rolled her eyes, helped him load the last tub of paint onto the truck, and slammed the tailgate closed.

"If you insist upon this fool's quest, then I have one condition, and it's nonnegotiable."

"I do not need your permission, child."

"You do if you don't want me calling the police and telling them to bring back my ninety-three-year-old father, who has Alzheimer's and will probably kill someone if they don't get him out from behind the wheel."

"You would not dare."

She raised her eyebrows and he read the truth on her face.

"What is your condition?" he asked.

Millie turned without a word and headed back into the house. Several minutes passed in silence. Sakeva grew tired of waiting, started up the truck, and revved the engine a couple of times. His daughter immediately appeared in the rearview mirror. He climbed out and concealed his grin before she could see it.

"Hurry up," she said.

Sakeva thought she was talking to him until she reached behind her, into the dark house, and dragged a shadow out onto the porch. Her grandson — his great-grandson — appeared from the crimson glare, carrying his shoes in one hand and his backpack in the other. His shirt was buttoned wrong and he still had the residue of sleep in his eyes.

"Billy here's agreed to take your little road trip with you," his daughter said. "Someone needs to keep an eye on you and make sure you don't get into any trouble."

Judging by the boy's expression, "agreed" probably wasn't the right term, but Millie never had been one to take "no" for an answer. She'd chosen well, though. Of all his great-grandchildren, Sakeva felt the strongest connection to Billy, who might not have practiced the traditional ways but didn't outright dismiss them, either. While he was only seventeen, he had a man's body honed through years of hard work on the land.

Sakeva experienced a sudden moment of clarity and realized that this was always how it was meant to be.

Billy tossed his backpack into the bed, rubbed his eyes, and slipped on his shoes. He walked around to the passenger-side door and looked at Sakeva through the open window.

"So where are we going?" he asked.

"Everywhere, apparently," Millie said.

Sakeva could still hear her laughing behind them as he hit the clutch, forced the stick into first, and started down the rutted dirt road toward his destiny.

───────

THE OLD CHEVY rocked on its rusted suspension as it navigated roads that would have been paved by now had it not been for the resistance of men like his great-grandfather. Billy recognized the value of tradition and honoring one's ancestors, but surely they could be accomplished without forsaking things like electricity, running water, and the internet, all of which he enjoyed on his trips into Winslow, where he planned to go to college, just as soon as he worked up the courage to break the news to his family. That was part of the reason he'd agreed to come on this road trip in the first place. The other part, of course, being that his grandmother would have made his life a living hell if he hadn't.

"Can I ask where we're really going?" he said.

"As I told your grandmother, we are going everywhere," Sakeva said. He tipped up the brim of his dusty cowboy hat and studied Billy from the corner of his eye. "You and I have embarked upon a mission of great consequence."

"How so?" Billy asked and immediately regretted it.

"The end is at hand and we must lead the chosen to salvation. It is a responsibility our bloodline has willingly borne for countless generations."

Billy didn't know how he was supposed to respond, so he said nothing and hoped that would be the end of the conversation.

"Are you familiar with the concept of the nine worlds?" his great-grandfather asked.

He felt the old man's stare upon him and glanced out the side window, where saguaro cactuses and paloverde shrubs stood apart from the vast stretches of sand. The only thing that could possibly make this experience any more unendurable was a lecture about the old ways, which no one believed were anything more than fairy tales. At least, no one he knew, anyway. There was only one world, and humankind was doing everything in its power to destroy it.

"In the beginning, there was no life," Sakeva said, his eyes growing distant. "There was no time, no shape. No beginning, no end. There was only Taiowa, who created his nephew, Sótuknang, and tasked him with building nine worlds capable of supporting life. The First World was called Tokpela, or 'endless space.' There was only land, water, and air, from which Sótuknang formed Kókyangwúti, the Spider Woman. She, in turn, mixed earth with túchvala — saliva — and gave life to the twins, Pöqánghoya and Palöngawyoha, who were posted at the poles to make sure the planet continued to turn. Meanwhile, Sótuknang created the plants and the trees, the birds and the animals, and gathered the four colors of earth — yellow, red, white, and black — from which to mold the bodies of man and woman under Qoyangnuptu, the deep purple light of dawn. He breathed life into his creations under the yellow light of Síkangnuqa, and, now fully formed, presented the first people to Taiowa under the red light of Tálawva. The Creator was so pleased that he made only one request of them: honor me at all times."

"How very humble," Billy said.

"So these men — our most distant ancestors — set off into the world, singing Taiowa's praises from the highest mountaintops. They lived in harmony with each other and all of the animals and knew neither strife nor sickness, only happiness. At least until Lavaíhoya — the Talker — arrived in the form of Mochni, a mockingbird. He convinced them of the differences between man and the animals and even between the men themselves — their colors, their speech, their beliefs — paving the way for the coming of Káto'ya, the snake with the big head."

"The snake with the big head?"

Sakeva offered a crooked smile.

"His venom caused suspicion among the men, leading to accusations and, ultimately, to warfare. Sótuknang saw all of this and appeared to the chosen — the men and women who'd upheld their vows to Taiowa — and told them to follow a specific cloud by day and the brightest star by night, which led them to the mound of the ant people, who allowed them to live underground while the world was destroyed by fire. Once the surface cooled off, Sótuknang created the Second World, Tokpa, which means 'dark midnight.' He put land where water had been and water where land had been and set the chosen free to populate it once more, only they had learned nothing from their experience. They discovered a lust for material goods and turned their backs on the Creator. Few sang his praises, and those who did were mocked by the wicked among them, which led to so much fighting that Sótuknang was forced to intervene. He again called upon the ant people to save the chosen and commanded Pöqánghoya and Palöngawyoha to leave their posts, causing the earth to roll over and freeze into solid ice.

"While the chosen remained warm and happy with the ant people, Pöqánghoya and Palöngawyoha returned to the poles and the earth once more started to turn, allowing Sótuknang to ready the Third World, known as Kuskurza — an ancient name whose meaning, sadly, has been forgotten. While man lived simply with animals in the First World and built villages and homes in the Second, he multiplied wildly in the Third, building cities and countries, entire civilizations. Man discovered sin and sex, wallowed in war and corruption, and turned his back on Taiowa with such speed and abandon that Sótuknang was caught by surprise. He called upon Spider Woman and implored her to save the few remaining chosen while he destroyed the world with water. 'Find the tall plants with hollow stems,' he told her. 'Cut them down and put the people inside.' And when she'd done as he asked, he sealed her inside with them and unleashed floodwaters upon the entire earth. The chosen floated for countless days and nights, until Spider Woman unsealed them, led them up through the darkness and onto a tiny piece of land, a mountaintop surrounded by infinite seas."

"The Fourth World," Billy said.

"It was known as Túwagachi, or 'world complete,'" Sakeva said. "And in this world of water they built boats from reeds and drifted on the waves until they reached a land ripe with grass and trees and flowers. Here they rested for many years until Spider Woman declared it was time to move on. 'Head north and east,' she said, which they did, paddling on rafts and following a rumbling sound until they reached a sandy shore, where they found Maasaw, the Great Spirit, waiting. He told them the time had come for the four tribes to begin their migrations, gave each of them a stone tablet, and told them to travel north to the verge of the ice, then to the east until they reached the sea, then to the south until they ran out of land, and then to the west until they found the opposite sea, continuing their travels in a spiraling pattern until they reached Túwanasavi, the center of the universe, where life would be hard and they would be forced to sing the songs of Taiowa to remain in his good graces. Some settled in tropical climates where life was too easy, and thus their stone cities decayed and crumbled. Others did not complete all of their migrations before planting roots, so they lost their religious power and standing. The final group persisted and realized the meaning of the migrations, that they needed to place their lives in the hands of Taiowa, to preserve their faith in the Creator who had led them to the Fourth World after they had failed in the previous three. These were our ancestors, the first men molded from the red earth, known to all as the Fire Clan."

"You don't really take all of this literally, do you?" Billy said. "A spider woman and ant people? Twins who control the spin of the earth on its axis? A nephew-deity who creates man only to wipe him out over and over again? A god who's only satisfied when people are actively kissing his ass?"

He regretted the words the moment he'd spoken them. The last thing he wanted to do was hurt his great-grandfather's feelings, but the whole thing was ridiculous.

Sakeva was silent for several moments before resting his hand on Billy's arm. The bones in his fingers felt so light and fragile, like those of a bird.

"You must understand that our history has been passed down through countless generations by word of mouth," he said. "As such, events must be simplified so that they are not lost in the translation, as they say. Fire can be interpreted as the meteor that ended the days of the dinosaurs; ice as the frozen age that allowed our ancestors to cross from one continent to the next; and water as the story of the great flood that appears in countless other religions. These are cataclysmic events that have altered life on this planet, multiple ends of the world from which new worlds have been birthed for the survivors."

"And it's your responsibility to lead the chosen to safety so the world can be destroyed again."

"*Our* responsibility."

Billy glanced away from the window and met his great-grandfather's stare.

"If you're so convinced the Fourth World is ending, how does it happen?"

The old man lowered the brim of his hat and concentrated on the rutted road.

"I do not know, but we will find out soon enough."

9

San Luis Obispo, California

Nicholas Crawford strode down the corridor, his hardhat perched on his head, the attached noise-canceling headphones standing from it like mouse ears. He wore his customary patterned button-down, rolled at the sleeves, precisely one cuff's length below the creases of his elbows; his name badge and dosimeter hanging from a lanyard at breast-pocket level; and khakis that ended right at the top of his work boots.

"Hey, Armando," he said, offering the custodian a firm shake — once, twice — and a clap on the shoulder. "How's that new surf rod treating you? I hope you left some rockfish for the rest of us."

Crawford laughed and continued on his way, leaving the other man to continue buffing the floor. He took immense pride in knowing the names of every one of his employees and remembering something about them or finding a common interest they shared, a way of identifying with each of them on a personal level. It was what made not only him, but the entire Diablo Canyon Power Plant so successful. They were all one great big family, both inside and outside these walls, and had been for nearly thirty years, during which time he'd had the privilege of employing successive genera-tions of families, launching the careers of some of the best and brightest engi-neering minds, and putting more than a thousand kids through college with the scholarships he'd helped establish. Diablo wasn't just a part of the community, it was the foundation of it. Just like he wasn't simply the director of operations and senior nuclear engineer; in many ways, he was the father of this work family, which utilized its combined talents around the clock to produce enough energy for three million fellow Californians.

Sure, it was a thankless job. People took the electricity coursing through their walls for granted, but he wouldn't have had it any other way. He was selfless by nature, the kind of guy who didn't need to be constantly reminded of his value because he could see it in the eyes of his employees and every man and woman he passed on the street. Without him, this plant would never have existed in the first place, let alone provided twelve hundred high-paying jobs, an insane influx of income and tax dollars for a county boasting fewer than three hundred thousand residents, and the carbon emissions-free energy necessary to tackle the impending environmental crisis.

"Tommy," he said. "Tell me that son of yours isn't hoarding all of the coeds at UCD."

Tom Nolan, the chief security guard, glanced up from the bank of monitors before him and offered a wan smile. Behind him, the other guards ran workers through a gamut of radiation detectors, x-ray devices, and hand scanners designed to make sure that everyone who entered and exited the facility was exactly who he or she claimed to be and wasn't attempting to smuggle in anything that might compromise the function of one of the reactors or remove nuclear material. Not that any of Crawford's people would ever think of doing something like that to him.

"The NorCal contingent's waiting in the conference room," the guard said.

"I'm on my way now, Tommy."

"Just Tom is fine."

Crawford cocked his finger like a gun and, with a clicking sound from the corner of his mouth, fired it at the guard.

The head honchos at Northern California Power and Electric had undoubtedly called this impromptu meeting to introduce him to the corporation's new chief nuclear officer. He'd already outlasted a dozen of them and had been through this dog and pony show so many times that he'd learned his role by rote. He'd give the tour, explain how everything worked, and end out at the dry cask storage facility, which was situated on top of a bluff overlooking the Pacific Ocean. Too bad they hadn't come tomorrow, when they would have been able to watch his engineering team place the full cask it was already in the process of loading with spent fuel rods. That would have given them a real thrill.

Crawford opened the door to the conference room and found everyone seated on the opposite side of the long table, like some sort of congressional inquest. All they were missing were their microphones, their aides sitting behind them, and their hands in someone else's pockets. He nearly chuckled out loud at his own wit and stood before his bosses, waiting for them to invite him to take a seat at the lone place that had been set on the near side of the table, reserving his spot using a file folder with his name stenciled across the front.

"Please . . . " Wallace Lowell said, gesturing toward the chair directly opposite him.

Strangely, he didn't rise to shake Crawford's hand, as was their custom going back two decades to when Lowell was promoted to vice president of generation. Even sitting down, the president and chief executive officer of NorCal P&E struck an imposing figure. He wore his hair slicked back, his mustache combed, and the kind of suit that shimmered under the right light.

On his right, in a custom-tailored suit with a blue tie that brought out his eyes, sat Ed Niemann, vice president and chief risk officer; on his left was Jessica Fields, senior vice president and general legal counsel, who couldn't look more like the human version of an owl if she tried. Beside her was Ron Minter, who, until recently, had been Crawford's opposite number at the San Onofre Nuclear Generating Station — SONGS — down the coast in San Clemente. Lord only knew why he was here, or why he seemed to look at everything in the room except for Crawford.

"Let's get right down to business, shall we?" Lowell said. "I trust you know Ed and Jessica."

"Of course," Crawford said. "How's that back of yours feeling by now, Ed? Aces, I hope. And Jessica, tell me you're going to take me up on my offer to join the Diablo softball team."

Niemann grunted and Fields made a noise that might not have been a yes, but it was at least a step in the right direction.

"And surely you and Rod need no introduction," Lowell said.

"Not at all," Crawford said. "Rod and I go back what, fifteen years? How're Sarah and the kids?"

Lowell cut in before Minter could answer.

"As you're aware, we brought Rod into the corporate fold after we closed down SONGS. He's done such an admirable job as our regulatory compliance officer that we've promoted him to chief nuclear officer, in which role he'll effectively become your liaison to both NorCal and the Nuclear Regulatory Commission, not to mention your direct superior."

"That's fantastic," Crawford said, and he meant it. "Congratulations, Rod. I always knew SONGS was just a stumbling block and you were destined for great things."

Minter glanced up at him from beneath his hairy brows and offered a nod and a half-smile. Crawford would have thought the nuclear engineer would be turning cartwheels over his promotion, especially considering it had been on his watch that they had taken the reactors responsible for the production of nearly twenty percent of the power in San Diego County off-line. He could only imagine how terrible it must have been to not only terminate the majority of his staff, but to oversee the slow death of the reactors that he'd tended every day as though they were his own children.

"As you know, the company's been under increasing regulatory pressure," Fields said. "Those of us with more than half a brain understand that there's no cleaner energy than nuclear and that it's the fastest means of achieving our statewide goal of decreasing carbon emissions, but you try convincing the governor of that."

"He has special interests in his ear day and night," Niemann said.

"Not to mention their kickbacks in his pocket."

"And what they want is natural gas."

Crawford laughed.

"Even though natural gas power plants are one of the leading contributors to anthropogenic climate change?" he said.

"He and his cronies just see it as a cheap form of quote-unquote *clean* energy. And one that's not likely to go Fukushima on them."

"They'd have an equally realistic chance of us producing Godzilla," Crawford said. "We've implemented every conceivable safety precaution, from situating the reactors more than fifty feet above the high-water mark of even the largest theoretical tsunami to building them on springs capable of withstanding the worst earthquake mother nature can throw at us. Our potential incidence of a Fukushima-level event is literally one in seven-point-six million reactor years."

"You and I both know that, but try convincing the environmentalists," Fields said. "They hear the word nuclear and imagine three-eyed fish and dead coral reefs. To them, this facility is a ticking time bomb just waiting to go off."

"That's the silliest thing I've ever heard," Crawford said.

"It's all about optics these days. Corporations like ours need to be seen as part of the solution, not part of the problem. And when it comes to nuclear power, the consensus of the general public is that we'd all be better off without it."

Crawford furrowed his brow and looked from one face to the next.

"What are you saying?" he asked.

"We've decided to take Diablo Canyon off-line," Lowell said. "We'll begin preparations now and instigate formal decommissioning to coincide with the end of the regulatory period."

Crawford felt sharp pressure building behind his left eye and pressed the butt of his palm to his temple. The corner of his mouth twitched of its own accord.

"I'm not entirely certain I understand," he said. "We've been producing emissions-free energy for three decades without a single accident."

"That's a credit to your design and leadership," Niemann said.

"As chief nuclear officer and someone who's gone through this exact process before, Rod will be working with you every step of the way to make sure everything goes smoothly," Fields said.

"I don't get it," Crawford said. "We've bowed to every environmental group since our inception. We've added countless redundant safety measures, followed every ridiculous new regulation to the letter of the law, and limited power during operations to make sure the water we return to the ocean is barely warmer than the ambient temperature. Heck, we even built an entire filtration system to make sure not a single minnow was drawn up in our intake. What more can we possibly do?"

"Nothing," Minter said. He raised his head and met Crawford's stare for the first time. "That's the point. Once the tide turns, there's not a goddamn thing you can do to stop it."

Crawford felt like he was going to be sick.

"This can't be happening," he said. "I've been here since Diablo was just a dream. I helped design this site and bring the reactors online. I've personally had a hand in hiring every single employee who's walked through these doors. What am I supposed to tell them?"

"For now, you won't tell them anything," Fields said. "It'll be business as usual until such time as we instruct you to make the announcement. The last thing we need is a mass exodus of personnel on our hands."

"So I'm not supposed to tell the men and women with whom I've worked side-by-side for the last thirty years that they'd better hurry and find new jobs before their income suddenly goes away?"

"Nothing will suddenly go anywhere," Niemann said. "It'll take a full year to decommission Reactor One, and another year after that for Reactor Two. Those who stay on throughout the process will receive five-figure severance packages."

"Which is more than generous on our part," Fields said. "California's an employment-at-will state, which means we can fire anyone and everyone without notice and simply delegate the work to subcontractors who'd probably do it for half the cost."

"What about the city?" Crawford asked. "San Luis Obispo will never recover from the loss of more than a thousand jobs—"

"Enough," Lowell said. "This is not a debate. The decision has already been made. Inside that folder in front of you is your new contract and any number of non-disclosure agreements and liability forms that we're going to need you to fill out and sign before we leave this room."

Crawford braced both hands on the table in an effort to stop the room from spinning. This was his life they were talking about here. He'd been as much a part of the facility as the reactors themselves since he was fresh out of grad school. He'd devoted every moment of every one of the last thirty years to making Diablo an example of what a nuclear power plant was supposed to be. He'd been on call twenty-four hours a day, organized every company event, and even personally covered shifts when necessary. He'd maintained a presence at every picnic, graduation, and sporting event the city put on. He'd attended every birthday party, recital, and bar mitzvah. He was as integral to the lives of his employees as they were. He'd willingly sacrificed everything for NorCal, dedicated every ounce of his being to its success, and now they just wanted to shrug and tell him it'd been a good run? That wasn't how this was going to play out. He wasn't going down without a fight.

"No," Crawford said. He slammed his palms down on the table and shook his head violently back and forth. "I can fix this. You'll see. Just give me a few months to meet with community leaders and environmental interests. I'll get this whole thing straightened out so we can all get back to work."

"There's nothing to straighten out," Lowell said. "This is already a done deal. If you don't want to be a part of it, then we'll find someone who does."

Crawford recoiled and stared at him, incredulous.

"You can't replace me. I've been in charge of operations since before the first fission reaction. I've never been so much as a minute late or called in sick for a single day—"

"Nick," Minter said. He reached across the table and rested his hand on Crawford's. "I know how you feel. This is a hard—"

Crawford jerked his hand away.

"Know how I feel?" He laughed. "You don't have the slightest idea how I feel. You were in charge of SONGS for what, five years before you ran her into the ground?"

Minter tightened his lips across his teeth. He looked at Lowell, and then back at Crawford.

"I went to bat for you, Nick. I really did."

"Enjoy that promotion while it lasts, Rod, because once they close Diablo, you'll be the chief officer of jack squat."

Fields pinched the corner of the folder in front of Crawford and slowly pulled it across the table toward her. He instinctively grabbed it and jerked it out of her grasp, scattering papers everywhere. The senior vice president flinched as if he'd struck her and scooted backward, out of his reach. Lowell and Minter both rose from their seats and stepped in front of her.

"Security!" Lowell shouted.

"I can fix this," Crawford said. He collected as many of the pages as he could, crumpling them as he crammed them back into the folder. "I just need more time."

The door burst open behind him. He turned and saw a trio of security guards entering the conference room.

"Tommy . . . " he said.

The larger man cranked Crawford's wrist behind his back and pinned it between his shoulder blades.

"It's just Tom," he said, directly into Crawford's ear.

The guard spun him around, shoved him into the hallway, and escorted him from the only home he'd ever truly known.

LETICIA SAENZ LEANED over the bathroom sink, closer to the mirror. Several strands of long, dark hair had come untucked from her flowered barrette and clung to the rouge on her cheeks. Her upper lip glistened with mucus and her brown eyes were bloodshot from crying. She carefully wiped away the tears from her lower lids, although she didn't know why she bothered. Her mascara was already ruined. Not that it had ever really looked good in the first place, or at least that's what her mother had said. Her actual words had been "You look like a raccoon in heat," but Leticia had learned long ago to let the old woman's words roll off her back like water from a duck's feathers. Of course, that didn't mean a little support wouldn't have been nice from time to time.

Oh, who was she kidding? Mother was right. No man was ever going to want her, especially not someone as important as Mr. Crawford, who was smart and kind and made her stomach flutter whenever he looked in her direction.

Today was the day, she'd told herself. Not that she hadn't said the same thing countless times before, only to chicken out when the time came to make her move, but today she'd done her hair and makeup, put on her nicest shoes and her favorite floral dress, and spent the entire morning reciting her daily affirmations as Dr. Ridley had taught her so that she'd be good and ready. She'd seen Mr. Crawford striding down the hallway toward her — "like the cock of the walk," as Mother was so fond of saying — and struck the nonchalant pose she'd practiced for hours in front of the mirror, but he hadn't so much as looked in her direction. He'd approached the janitor, engaged the old man with that snappy wit of his, and then walked right past her as though she wasn't even there.

Again.

Sometimes Leticia felt like she was invisible. "You can't allow your sense of self-worth to be defined by other people," Dr. Ridley often said. He didn't understand, though. No matter how she tried to explain it, he couldn't seem to comprehend what it was like to have everyone look through her as though she didn't exist. She'd even caught *him* staring through her on more than one occasion, checking the time on the wall clock or the flashing message light on his phone, although he wasn't nearly as bad as the other engineers in her department. They'd stop talking when she entered the room or pretend not to hear her when she spoke. They wouldn't even look at her when she joined them at their table in the cafeteria, which was why she'd started eating outside in the first place.

She'd been sitting on the bench near the employee entrance, watching the distant ocean through a narrow gap between the rolling hills and taking small nibbles of her sandwich, like polite women were supposed to do, when she'd heard a voice from her left.

"Leticia! How's my favorite Golden Bear?" She'd turned and found Mr. Crawford standing beside the entrance, holding a heavy box. "Mind giving me a hand? I only have two, and they're otherwise occupied at the moment."

He'd wiggled his fingers on the cardboard and laughed at his own joke, an affectation she found strangely endearing.

After carefully resealing her sandwich in its plastic bag, she'd set aside her food and opened the door for him. And, with a wink, he'd disappeared into the facility, leaving her aglow with the knowledge that he'd both remembered her name and the fact that she'd attended UC Berkeley, which Diablo had paid for through its scholarship program for employees' children. She didn't care that he was twenty years her senior. He'd seen her — really seen her — and that was all that mattered.

Four years had passed since then, four long years spent watching him from afar as he walked the hallways of the power plant like he owned the place and commanded the attention of everyone in attendance at company and community functions. She'd even started going to work early so she'd be waiting when he arrived in his shiny blue Dodge Ram and staying late so she could walk out into the parking lot at the same time, hoping upon hope that he'd invite her to join him for dinner, or maybe some of that fancy liquid nitrogen ice cream they served down at The Creamery Marketplace. While he never had, that didn't mean he never would. After all, he'd come to her house every day for a week after Mother's accident in the containment building and he'd smiled at her and called her by name every time.

Such a sweet, sweet man.

It was hard to believe that he was still single, especially with the way he found time in his busy schedule to make sure his yard was tended and his home was clean, what little of it she could see through the inset windows in his front door, anyway. Not that she'd ever found the courage to knock. Life would be so much easier if he'd just invite her over so she could stop walking Mr. Snuffles past his house, praying for him to look outside or check his mail.

Today had been her chance and she'd blown it.

Like always, Mother said. While the voice originated inside Leticia's head, it seemed to echo from the empty stalls behind her.

"Stupid, stupid, stupid," she said, punctuating each word with a tug on her stray bangs.

No, she wasn't stupid; she was a catch. How many times had Father told her so before he'd left? She had a brilliant mind, a loving heart, and a generous soul. And today she was going to make sure Mr. Crawford knew it.

Leticia straightened her lab coat, adjusted her dress, and threw open the bathroom door. She emerged, head held high, into a crowd of people gathered in the hallway. Someone on the other side of them was shouting, his voice echoing from the lobby. She forced her way through the press of bodies and saw Mr. Crawford kicking at the ground, trying to slow his progress as a pair of uniformed guards dragged him toward the main entrance.

"What are they doing?" she asked. "Don't they know who he is?"

She looked from one stunned coworker to the next, but none of them answered. They all just stared through her at the front door, where the guards unceremoniously hauled the man she loved through security and into the parking lot.

The door closed between them, sealing off his cries.

Leticia stood in the corridor until the crowd dispersed and the guards returned to their stations. None of them so much as acknowledged her presence.

CRAWFORD PACED BACK and forth down the hallway between his bedroom and the kitchen like a caged animal. The walls on both sides were lined with framed certificates and placards commemorating his myriad successes on the job. The Dwight D. Eisenhower Distinguished Public Service Award. The Seaborg and Reactor Technology Awards. The American Nuclear Society's Leadership and Meritorious Awards, plus no less than seven citations from its president. He couldn't imagine there was a more storied career than his, let alone one devoted to a single institution. He'd set aside all ambition for the greater good of the community — his community — and what did he have to show for it? He hadn't received a single note of condolence from any of the twelve hundred souls in his employ or the families he'd helped feed and clothe for generations. The company had washed its hands of him, the city had turned its back on him, and there was no one in his life to console him. He'd given them everything and they'd chewed him up and spit him out.

Worse, they'd shown him that his life was meaningless. He'd been as invisible as the little man in the refrigerator who turns on the light when the door opens, the provider of a service people considered a goddamn right. Men and women he'd thought of as family had pretended to like him because he had something they wanted — his knowledge and skills, his jobs and benefits and scholarships for their kids — but they'd never truly cared about him. To them, he was worth less than the skin of a popcorn kernel flossed from between their teeth. He was nothing, no one. The plant would continue to run without him, at least until they struck it dead, like a knight plunging his blade into the heart of a dragon, and then time would pass him by, a relic of a bygone era, when scientists had dreamed of a better future and not the fortunes that could be made by selling their reputations to the highest bidder.

Crawford abruptly stopped and stared at the light overhead, at the clear glass dome, inside of which was a solitary bulb. Its tungsten-alloyed filament shone so brightly that it burned his vision. Without looking away, he knelt, removed his work boot, and stood once more. Current flowed through the fixture with a faint hum. It was the same sound he imagined the blood pulsing through his veins made, if only he could hear it. He cocked his head, listened until he could stand it no more, and then shattered the fixture with his boot.

Tiny shards of glass momentarily filled the air before tinkling to the hard-wood floor.

He ran down the hallway and smashed the next light in the sequence. And the next. He ducked into his study and destroyed first the lamp in the corner, and then the screen of his computer. The globe bulbs over the medicine cabinet in the bathroom burst like tiny balloons. The screen of his alarm clock cracked and darkened. His TV spider-webbed into thousands of dark fissures. He destroyed every object that drew power until he found himself alone in the darkness, doubled over and gasping for breath.

The only illumination was provided by the setting sun, which cast slanted columns of light onto the floor, making the shards of glass sparkle like tiny jewels. He felt pain in the bottom of his foot and looked down to find blood seeping from his sole and smeared crimson footprints positively everywhere. The boot fell from his hand. He stood in the kitchen, acutely aware of the fact that he was completely and utterly alone.

No one had even called to make sure he was okay.

He hung his head so the tears would fall from his eyes rather than run down his cheeks, as the salt burned the tiny nicks and cuts inflicted by the shrapnel of his meltdown.

"What am I supposed to do now?"

His voice sounded strangely hollow in the empty house, as though the sound waves simply died upon contact with the darkness.

The pressure behind his left eye intensified and the corner of his mouth pulled back toward his ear. He felt something akin to a fuse snapping in his head and his hand fell limply to his side before he could raise it to put pressure on his temple. His leg went numb, and he dropped to the floor, tiny bits of glass piercing his hip and shoulder. He tried to cry out for help, but the voice that emerged from his lips was garbled and incoherent.

With the last of his dwindling strength, he dragged himself across the floor, smearing blood from his lacerated palm, only to find his cellphone smashed on the floor at the base of the wall against which he'd hurled it.

Crawford collapsed, shards embedding themselves into his forehead and cheek, and prayed for the stroke to finish the job it had started.

LETICIA PULLED to the curb in front of the white ranch-style house, a pineapple upside-down cake sitting on the passenger's seat beside her. She'd feigned being sick, left work early, and rushed straight home to make it, knowing Mr. Crawford was going to need a little cheering up. With all of the confections and gifts he'd surely be receiving, she'd needed to bring something that really stood out, and her recipe had won a blue ribbon at the California Mid-State Fair. The secret was to melt a little extra butter in a cast-iron skillet before pouring the batter, which was what she'd been doing when she'd heard the telltale whine of an electric wheelchair from the living room.

"Shouldn't you be at work?" Mother asks from the doorway.

"Mr. Crawford was terminated today," Leticia responds, without looking up from the sizzling pan. "I thought maybe —"

"You thought maybe what? You'd show up with a sticky mess and he'd forget all of his troubles and take you to bed?"

"Mother."

"Don't 'Mother' me. That man and everyone else at that infernal plant deserve whatever happens to them."

"You shouldn't say such things," Leticia whispers.

"Why not? It's true. You think I wanted to be in this chair? You think anyone baked me cakes when I fell down those stairs and broke my back?"

"The people there ask after you all the time."

"You know what Proverbs says about liars."

"Lying lips are an abomination to the Lord," Leticia says, hanging her head. "I'm sorry, Mother."

She turns around and Mr. Snuffles immediately jumps up into Mother's lap. The red Havanese props his front paws on her knees and starts yapping. He wears little bows in his long fur, which has been brushed far more recently than his master's graying hair, which she wears in tangles around her fleshy face. The burst vessels in Mother's nose and cheeks make her look like she constantly runs a fever. Her abdominal panniculus folds halfway over her thighs, and her exposed ankles are purple and swollen. The compression fracture in her L4 vertebra impinges upon the nerve roots so much that while she can stand, she detests doing so for any length of time, even if *it means hollering for help to get onto the toilet or into the bath. And with the way she's putting on weight, it's only a matter of time before Leticia won't physically be able to take care of Mother on her own.*

"It's okay, Mr. Snuffles," Mother says, stroking the barking beast's mane. "I won't let her hurt you again."

"One time!" Leticia snapped. "One time I accidentally kicked—"

She clapped her hands over her mouth and looked around to make sure no one had seen her talking to herself. The lights were off inside Mr. Crawford's house, but she'd been sure she'd turned onto his street just in time to catch a flicker from behind the curtains in the great room. She could only imagine that poor man sitting alone in the darkness, reliving the moment those awful people from NorCal had fired him. There was a lot of speculation as to why it had happened, but no one from the corporate office even addressed the situation. All Leticia knew for certain was that Mr. Crawford wouldn't be returning to Diablo and this was her best chance to let him know how she felt.

How long had she been sitting here? It was easier to see from a dark space into a lighter one, which meant that Mr. Crawford could have been watching her from one of the windows and she wouldn't have been able to tell. And if he was, he was probably starting to wonder if there was something wrong with her.

"Oh, God," she whispered.

Leticia's heart raced and her hands trembled. Her first instinct was to put the Camry in gear and drive off, but what if he recognized her car?

She killed the engine before she could change her mind and opened the door, the overhead light spilling out onto the asphalt. The sun was little more than a scarlet stain against the distant horizon. It was obviously later than she thought. What if Mr. Crawford was already in bed? She should have trusted her instincts and baked muffins, which wouldn't have taken nearly as long.

"Stupid, stupid, stupid," she whispered.

Leticia opened the passenger-side door, grabbed the cake, and hurried up the walk. Her pulse was so loud in her ears that she could barely hear the clicking of her heels on the concrete. She stepped up onto the porch and stood there in the shadows for several seconds, mustering the courage to press the bell. It was all she could do not to run away as the chime echoed through the dark house.

She listened for the sound of approaching footsteps, but there was only silence on the other side of the door. Should she ring again? She knocked instead and waited for nearly a full minute before leaning close enough to peek through the inset windows. The entryway and the great room were dark. If she stood on her tiptoes, she could see into the kitchen, where broken glass sparkled on the tiled floor. Had Mr. Crawford dropped a bottle or a plate? Surely he hadn't smashed something in anger. That wouldn't have been like him at all, and she definitely wouldn't have approved of that kind of—

The screen door of the house across the street slammed closed with a sound like a gunshot.

Leticia gasped in surprise and whirled to face the man, who hiked up his plaid shorts to conceal the belly poking out from underneath his polo shirt. He looked right at her as he cleared his throat and lit a cigar.

Had he seen her peeking through the windows?

Leticia panicked. She dropped the cake and scurried back to her car. She was halfway down the street, her tires squealing around the corner, when she realized she'd just thrown away her last opportunity to be with Mr. Crawford.

Tears spilled down her cheeks. She sobbed and drove aimlessly around town until she knew Mother would be asleep. The last thing she wanted was to see that smirk on the old woman's face, the knowing one that told her that no matter how hard she tried to break free, it would always be just the two of them.

10

Brooks Range, Alaska

D r. Riley Middleton opened her eyes and sat up straight in her sleeping bag. A glance at her watch confirmed that her alarm hadn't gone off and it wasn't yet time to spell Montgomery so he could catch some z's while she watched over Edgerton. She'd heard something, though. She was certain of it. Something that almost sounded like—

A scream erupted from somewhere outside her tent, raising the hackles along the backs of her arms and neck. She crawled from her sleeping bag, her pulse so loud in her ears that she could barely hear herself think. The sheer terror of that cry, the unimaginable pain . . .

The campfire flickered through the front wall of her tent. She smelled smoke and heard the crackle of flames, footsteps scuffing the dirt. A dark shape momentarily passed across the light. She reached out and grabbed the inner zipper, surprised to see how badly her hand was shaking.

Every instinct, honed through millions of years of evolution, cried out that something was terribly wrong. It was an irrational feeling, and yet one so insistent that she drew the zipper down one tooth at a time — slowly, silently — and carefully opened the flap just far enough to see the area immediately in front of her tent.

The wind had picked up, causing the flames to flag and the smoke to abruptly change directions. There was no one tending it, and the chairs had toppled and blown up against the stone ring. The approaching storm had swallowed the stars, leaving behind the faintest impression of the moon, a diffuse glow that hardly stained the clouds.

Riley crawled out into the biting cold and surveyed her surroundings. There was no sign of movement, which, for this time of night, wasn't out of the ordinary, and yet somehow only amplified her fear. The doors of the Quonset huts were closed, the windows dark. She looked at Williams's tent, adjacent to her own. She couldn't detect the faint aura of his camp stove, which meant he was either out of fuel oil or hadn't turned in for the night. The larger unit next to his was barely visible beyond it, its yellow walls softly glowing from the heating unit.

A gust of wind kicked up dirt that assailed the tents like sleet. She shielded her eyes against it and rose to her feet, wishing she'd bundled up before braving the elements. A folding chair bounded across the bare earth and struck the building housing their tools with a metallic thud. The flaps of Montgomery's tent waved as she walked past. She was just about to poke her head inside when she saw a silhouette through the fabric of Edgerton's tent. While she should have been relieved, every fiber of her being screamed for her to run in the opposite direction. She was in charge, though. It was her responsibility to watch over these people, and she'd already failed them once. She'd be damned if she let it happen again.

Riley grabbed the flap and ripped it open. Edgerton's sleeping bag was empty, his damp compress cast aside. Dark fluid dripped from the spatters crisscrossing the ceiling and walls, forming a puddle where she'd last seen him. Sadie sat astride Montgomery, her face buried in his neck. For the briefest of moments, Riley thought she'd caught them in an intimate embrace, until Sadie looked over her shoulder, her features shimmering with blood, and revealed the gaping wound in her professor's throat. His mouth hung open and his eyes stared blankly at the ceiling of the tent.

"Oh, God," Riley said. Sadie jumped to her feet and advanced toward Riley, who raised her hands in a placating gesture as she backed away. The grad student's eyes were suffused with so much blood that it was impossible to tell where she was looking. Her bared teeth glistened pink in the dim light, her facial muscles contorting her features into a rictus of rage. "What happened here? Are you all—?"

Sadie lunged at her, striking with open palms, using her fingernails like claws. Riley barely raised her forearms in time to prevent them from raking her face. Her thermal undershirt ripped and her skin tore. She screamed and sprinted from the tent, her only thoughts of distancing herself from the younger woman.

Riley veered for the fire, hoping to use the smoke as a screen. Nothing about the situation made any sense. There was no doubt in her mind that Montgomery was dead, Edgerton was gone, and what she'd seen Sadie doing—

She tripped over something and went down hard, her shoulder absorbing the brunt of the impact. She rolled over and was about to push herself to her feet again when she saw Williams, or at least something that looked like him. The body wore his clothes, but his face was covered with blood and his neck had been attacked with such savagery that she could see the vertebrae inside.

A silhouette appeared behind her through the smoke, which cleared just long enough for her to catch a glimpse of Edgerton — standing on the other side of the fire, bathed in its glow, his irises the same color as the flames — before the smoke swallowed him once more.

"Dale?" she whispered.

Sadie burst from the smoke where he'd been standing a heartbeat prior, planted her foot amid the burning logs, and dove for Riley, who propelled herself to her feet. The grad student clipped her heel, but she managed to stay upright and ran in the opposite direction, heedless of where it might take her. She saw the tent shared by the students, its front flap blowing on the wind. Judson lay on the ground just inside. Nate and Maria crouched over him, blood dripping from their glistening faces. They bared their teeth like animals and collided in their hurry to crawl from the tent.

Riley glanced to either side of her. There was nowhere to hide. The tents had been designed to withstand the elements, not any kind of physical attack, and she was surrounded by miles upon miles of open space, across which she'd be visible at any distance and would undoubtedly freeze to death long before finding shelter.

The Quonset huts!

She turned to her left, but before she'd even taken two strides in that direction, she saw Sadie, the leg of her pants still burning, racing to cut her off.

Riley veered in the opposite direction and realized that it was the last thing in the world she should have done.

The mesa rose ahead of her, a massive stone wall against which she'd find herself trapped. A glance over her shoulder confirmed Nate was gaining on her, while Maria had fanned out to intercept her if she attempted to alter course. The three of them would have her triangulated in a matter of seconds if she didn't find a way—

There!

The framework of the windbreak concealing the excavation materialized from the darkness ahead of her, the tarps flapping on the breeze. If she could reach it and crawl through the tunnel first, she could hide inside the cave, where they wouldn't be able to see any better than she could. It wasn't a solution, but it just might buy her enough time to find one.

She scurried up the rocky slope and dove into the hole, smacking her head on the lip and nearly knocking herself unconscious. Her vision swarmed with stars as she shimmied through the earthen tunnel, tearing the skin from her fingertips and the jeans from her knees as she dragged herself deeper. She heard the clatter of stones, then the sounds of heavy breathing echoing behind her.

What in God's name was happening?

Riley spilled from the tunnel, rolled over the stone that had once sealed it, and scurried away from the hole as fast as she could. She rammed her hand into an unforgiving mound of bones and bit her lip to keep from crying out, but she forced herself to keep going. In her mind, she envisioned the layout of the cave, the wall to her left leading back to the enclosed chamber where the mummified remains lorded over the scattered bones. If she could find it and crawl through the opening, she could hide inside, but if the others figured out where she'd gone and climbed in there with her . . .

She adjusted her course to the right. If she veered too far, she'd wind up trapped in the opposite corner. Her best option was to reach the unexplored honeycomb of passageways in the back and pray that one of them led to safety.

Riley froze.

She'd heard something, something that told her she was out of time. The harsh sounds of breathing carried across the cave, the acoustics making it impossible to divine more than the general direction of their origin. She heard someone scrabble across the rocky ground and crawled away as quickly and quietly as she could, dodging disarticulated remains and breathing through her mouth to minimize the noise, trying desperately to think about anything other than the images of the grad students tearing open her colleagues with their teeth, or the prospect of sharing their fate.

Her shoulder clipped the stone wall. She stifled a gasp of pain. The sounds of pursuit behind her abruptly ceased. Seconds passed in silence as tears trickled down her cheeks. She smoothed her trembling hands across the wall until she found the opening to the crevice with the uncharted tunnels.

Nate and Maria remained silent. They were listening, waiting for her to make a move and betray her location. Their rasping breaths echoed hollowly around her. She heard the fluid in their lungs, felt the sickness positively radiating from them. Maybe if she held still long enough—

She heard someone else coming through the tunnel, smelled burned fabric and scorched skin.

Sadie.

The others were upon the grad student the moment she crawled into the cave. Her scream was cut short by a gurgle and a wet, tearing sound. Blood spattered the ground, so close that Riley could smell it. She heard ripping sounds, clothing and skin alike, and ducked into the passage.

One of her pursuers broke away and scurried toward her, palms slapping the stone floor, bones clattering out of the way, and then stopped. The sounds of breathing were definitely closer, maybe ten feet away. Another surge like that in her direction and whoever it was would be upon her. She couldn't afford to wait any longer.

Riley pressed her shoulder against the wall and used it to guide her. She envisioned the way the crevice bent to the left and how the wall to her right was riddled with orifices, some no more than craters, others barricaded with stacked stones, which had fallen from two of them over time, exposing lava tubes—

Her right hand hit something hard and sent it clattering to the ground.

The pursuit behind her grew frenzied. They knew exactly where she was now, and they were coming fast.

One chance.

She stood up and pawed at the wall, searching for the hole from which the stones had fallen. If she could just find it—

Her fingertips grazed the lip. She grabbed onto it with both hands and pulled herself up, kicking at the wall to propel herself higher, dragging herself over the remaining rocks and clawing at the smooth dolomite to gain traction.

The intonation of the sounds behind her changed as the grad students funneled from the cave into the crevice.

She hit the opposite wall with her heels, braced them against it, and pushed herself all the way into the shaft a split-second before the scurrying sounds stopped directly underneath her. Palms traced the walls outside the lava tube with a sound like whispering, rising higher and higher as whoever was out there stood and inadvertently kicked a stone—

The other grad student attacked before the rock even came to rest. Screams echoed from the confines, but they didn't last long. The sound of blood dripping to the frozen ground did, though. It seemed to go on and on until well after the lone remaining assailant had dropped the body and continued deeper into the earth.

Riley closed her eyes, covered her mouth and nose with both hands, and started to cry.

THE UH-60 BLACK HAWK thundered low across the arctic tundra. The way the frosted earth reflected the rising sun made the entire area appear to burn, which seemed a fitting portent for the day to come. Tyler Cullen knew precisely what was expected of him and what he had to do. His employer's instructions were explicit: contain the situation and make sure not a single viral particle leaves the site. He and his team had performed the same task many times before, from the hot zones in the Rift Valley of Western Africa to the Tumbes region of Peru, and everywhere in between. Every sweaty, mosquito-infested jungle in every godforsaken third-world hellhole. Every reeking swamp and diseased refugee camp. Everywhere God or the universe or whatever you wanted to call it decided to put Darwin's theories to the test, Cullen had been there to thwart His will.

"How far out?" he asked. His voice sounded tinny through the headset, which did little to muffle the roar of the rotors.

"Twenty-eight minutes, sir," the pilot said. He and the copilot were safely sealed in the cockpit, on the other side of an isolation barrier that would protect them from whatever contagion the containment team brought aboard.

Cullen smirked. It'd been a long time since anyone had called him "sir." Not since he wrapped up his tenure at USAMRIID and entered the private sector. There was honor in facing a gruesome, agonizing death for his country, but it was nothing compared to the money he earned doing it for private corporations like NeXgen, which knew how to treat their most valuable resources. He and his men didn't risk their lives subduing hostile actors, securing broad swaths of violent land, and corralling deadly pathogens just so the arrogant pricks from the CDC and WHO could come in after the worst of the danger had been eliminated and start barking commands from the comfort of their fancy tents, nor did they have to justify the means by which they did so. Private companies didn't want to know how they got the job done, only that it was done to their satisfaction.

"Preliminary indications suggest we're dealing with a hemorrhagic virus," he said. "Double check the seals on your suits."

"And pray to God this isn't another Congo," Trevor Ward said.

Cullen glanced back at his teammate, who sat in one of the forward-facing seats in the rear of the chopper, winding a second layer of tape around the seams of his lime-yellow Level A encapsulated Tychem suit. The plastic face shield of Ward's hood hung limply against his chest. Cullen knew exactly what the other man was saying, but they were dealing with a handful of academics, not a terrorist group like the Allied Democratic Front, an Islamic extremist faction known for abducting children and hacking up its adversaries with machetes.

His rapid-response team from USAMRIID had been dispatched to the village of Beni in the Nord Kivu province of the Democratic Republic of the Congo in response to reports of a potential Ebola outbreak, only they hadn't been welcomed as the saviors of the dying people; they'd been attacked from seemingly everywhere at once, by men, women, children, and even the sick they'd been dispatched to quarantine. They'd lost three men in the process, three good men who'd been savagely beaten while trying to secure the site for the doctors who only wanted to save the lives of the villagers. Had Cullen not stepped up and put a decisive end to the conflict, he would have lost his entire team and the afflicted would have escaped the camp and spread the virus throughout the region.

Of course, the doctors he'd prevented from getting slaughtered had lodged a formal complaint and he'd been court-martialed for his efforts, but his men had known what would have happened to all of them had he not done what needed to be done. They'd stood behind him through the entire ordeal, and for saving their lives, he'd earned their loyalty. For its willingness to sacrifice its own men so as not to incur the scorn of the cowardly international community, who valued political correctness and their claim to the moral high ground more than the lives of those protecting them on the front lines, USAMRIID had lost its five best emerging diseases specialists, four to the private sector and one to a gun in the mouth.

"Trust me," Cullen said. "This will be an in-and-out job. As long as everyone sticks to the script, we'll have the site contained in a matter of hours."

He winked at Ward, who was the weak link as far as he was concerned, but that didn't change the fact that they needed him. While Ward might have gone soft since he lost faith in a military that would have willingly consigned him to a violent end, his skills as a diagnostician had saved them on multiple occasions. The other two could be trusted to do exactly what he told them. Rodney Brown, who leaned out the opposite side door, silently taking in the morning sun, kept his thoughts and opinions to himself, while Denny Pritchard sat in the seat across from Ward, bobbing his head to the music playing through the earbuds concealed beneath his headset, like a prize-fighter before a championship bout.

"Do we have any actual intel on this bug?" Brown asked.

"We know next to nothing at this point," Cullen said. "All we have is a single individual exhibiting a high-grade fever."

"Which could just as easily be the result of a ruptured appendix as a viral contagion," Ward said. "Reports of abdominal pain?"

"Negative. At last report, he'd been either unconscious or delirious since his fever spiked."

"What about malaria?" Brown asked. "It's just as likely as a hemorrhagic virus since neither has previously been reported above the Arctic Circle."

"Nothing has," Cullen said. "That's why we're being paid to take this so seriously. For all we know, the site manager's a drama queen and this guy's a pansy with nothing more life-threatening than the common cold."

"There has to be more to it than that," Ward said, looking Cullen dead in the eyes. "What aren't you telling us?"

Cullen held Ward's stare and shrugged. He wasn't about to tell his men about the warning he'd received from his contact at NeXgen. The thought of explaining that a boardroom full of corporate bigwigs feared a hemorrhagic virus based on a professor's interpretation of some cave art was entirely laughable, and yet after being dispatched to contain an outbreak of cholera whose origin could be traced to the tomb of an Egyptian pharaoh, he knew better than to ignore such signs, no matter how absurd they sounded.

"You should be able to see the Brooks Mountains any second now," the pilot said.

"That's our cue," Cullen said. "Hoods on, gentlemen."

He exchanged the cans for a wireless communications device — with a receiver that fit snugly in his ear and a larynx microphone that allowed him to speak, even with the respirator secured over his mouth and nose — donned his helmet, and dialed on the flow of oxygen from the tanks on his back. Ward climbed from his seat, sealed Cullen's hood, and turned around so that the team leader could do the same for him.

The Tyvek fabric utilized a protective polyethylene coating that was impermeable to chemicals and even the most aggressive biological contaminants, in both their naturally occurring and weaponized forms. As long as the suits remained intact, there was zero risk of exposure, although that didn't mean they wouldn't heat up like the ovens in a crematorium. At least this time they didn't have the equatorial temperatures and humidity working against them, too.

"Does everyone understand our directives?" Cullen asked.

"Secure and contain," Pritchard said.

He grabbed a futuristic-looking rifle from the seat beside him, assumed his position in the open doorway beside Brown, and clipped his harness to the frame. Cullen knelt in the opposite opening and did the same, the impelled air from the rotors buffeting him. He watched the mountains grow in the distance from beneath the stub wing, which, like its twin on the other side, was fully loaded with pylons resembling massive torpedoes that contained fuel reserves, decontamination agents, and enough incendiary gel to wipe the entire area from the face of the Earth, should they be left with no alternative.

Ward stepped into position beside him. Cullen sensed the specialist's hesitation and knew what he was going to say, probably even before he did.

"This is my last ride, Ty. Time for me to move on and figure out what comes next."

Cullen merely nodded in response. Ever since Beni, he'd known this was an inevitability. Ward was scared, which potentially made him as dangerous as any enemy combatant. This wasn't a game they were playing; lives hung in the balance and if he didn't have the stomach to do whatever it took, then they were better off without him.

"So be it," Cullen said. "Just don't screw this one up on your way out the door."

He seated the stock of his rifle against his shoulder just in time to see a ring of yellow tents form against the base of a broad mesa.

———————

RILEY TRIED to suppress her terror, to regulate her breathing despite the fact that she'd begun shivering and couldn't stop her nose from running. She had no idea how much time had passed, only that the lone remaining hunter had passed below her twice: once heading deeper into the crevice, then returning to the main cave again. If she was right, Sadie had been killed crawling from the tunnel and Maria was dead on the ground below her, which meant that Nate was still in here with her. Searching for her. She could still hear him, creeping through the darkness.

Surely, he'd eventually give up, but what was she supposed to do when he did. There wasn't the slightest bit of light for her eyes to adjust to. She'd turned around so that she was facing outward, and yet she couldn't see the opposite wall mere feet in front of her face, let alone the route she'd have to take to reach the tunnel—

A scuffing sound from her left. She bit her lip to keep from crying out and scooted deeper into the hole, pulling herself in millimeter increments with her toes, her hands closed so tightly over her nose and mouth that her chattering teeth cut the insides of her cheeks.

Nate's breathing grew more ragged with each pass, the accumulation of fluid in his lungs making it harder and harder for him to exchange air. She smelled fresh blood upon him, the butcher-shop scent of chopped meat, only meat that had gone bad and begun to rot, meat rife with sickness and disease.

The sounds stopped directly below her. The fallen rocks clattered, as though nudged by a toe. A damp palm slapped the wall, traced it back and forth. And then the footsteps resumed, echoing deeper into the darkness. There was now no one between her and freedom, but he was still too close, and she knew she couldn't outrun him. Maybe she could drop down, grab one of the stones, and bludgeon him—

What was wrong with her? She was contemplating beating one of her students to death with a rock, one of the very people who was counting on her to return him safely to civilization at the end of the summer. But this wasn't the Nate she'd gotten to know over the past month. He'd been polite and helpful and one of the most thoughtful young men she'd ever had on one of her digs. She couldn't imagine a situation where he would have raised his voice, let alone violently attacked another human being.

There was definitely something wrong with him. He and Sadie had been the first to turn in for the night, the first to exhibit symptoms. Outside of Edgerton, anyway, whom Riley remembered seeing through the smoke, his eyes reflecting the fire. He hadn't been like the others. There'd been something different about him, something restrained, something that somehow terrified her even more.

Nate's footsteps dissolved into the silence. She didn't know how far the crevice reached, only that it took some amount of time for him to turn around and come back again.

This was her chance.

If she quietly crawled out, crossed the main cave, and found the egress quickly enough, she could beat him to the surface, tear down the chain-link fence holding back the loose talus, and seal him inside. At least until the helicopter arrived and she could get help—

Something moved to her left. The sound was different, stealthier, the patter of palms and knees on the bare stone metered and unhurried. She heard breathing, only it was neither labored nor sickly.

She felt a prickling sensation at the base of her spine and shivered even harder. Her heart beat faster and faster until the urge to make a break for it, to bolt like a rabbit from the brush, was nearly unbearable. She'd never known terror like this, cold and inexplicable, paralyzing.

The figure approached, not merely passing through the darkness, but a part of it, drawing form from it. It paused inside the crevice, seemingly expanded to fill the narrow space, and resumed its advance on two feet.

Riley somehow instinctively knew it was Edgerton, and yet not him at the same time. The heat of sickness radiated from him, while the surrounding air grew even cooler. She buried her face in her hands and prayed he wouldn't notice her, for him to look in any other direction than to his right. The mere thought of him being able to see anything in the utter darkness was absurd, and yet she was certain that he could.

One step at a time, his soft footsteps closed upon her hiding place, her breath too loud in her own ears. He slowed his pace, and she was convinced he'd found her. A scream rose to her lips, and she prepared to lash out at him, to claw out his eyes and fight with everything she had left. She felt him just outside the opening, smelled his fetid breath, and realized that the coming seconds would determine whether she lived or died. Every fiber of her being cried out for her to attack, but she couldn't make her body move. This was where she would die, alone in the darkness, like the ancient men and women whose bones littered the ground, her life serving no other purpose than feeding the insatiable hunger of whatever evil now inhabited Edgerton's skin, the same evil she'd felt, but failed to recognize, the moment she'd first entered the cave.

She heard a whispering sound, like white noise formed from countless voices, all crying out in unison from someplace far away.

Riley bit her lip so hard to keep from screaming that she tasted blood in her mouth.

Edgerton started walking again, that horrible susurration fading away into the mountain, through which she felt faint vibrations. They grew incrementally stronger with every passing second until they merged into an audible sound that reminded her of a heartbeat, only faster, harder.

Riley knew exactly what it was, and with that recognition, forced her body to move. She dragged herself to the edge of the hole and tried to contort her body in such a way that she could lower herself down, but she was trembling too badly. She lost her grip, then her balance, and plummeted toward the ground. The cry she'd hoped to contain burst from her chest when she hit the pile of rocks. She crawled over Maria's body, pushed herself to her feet, and staggered back toward the cave.

A drumroll of footsteps erupted from behind her.

Riley fixed the sound of the helicopter ahead of her, ducked her head, and ran toward it. The walls of the crevice fell away and the ceiling lowered, passing so close to her scalp that she could feel it against her hair. All that mattered now was reaching the surface first.

She tripped on a pile of petrified remains and barely raised her hands in time to keep her face from slamming into the ground. Pushing herself to all fours, she crawled until she found the strength to stand again, ducked her head, and ran for everything she was worth, focused solely on the thunder of rotors, growing louder and louder until she heard it clearly — not passing through stone, but rather through the open air — and slowed just in time to keep from sprinting headlong into the wall. She found the hole with hands shaking so badly she could barely drag herself inside and wriggled toward the freezing air she could feel against her damp cheeks.

The scrabbling sounds behind her grew closer and closer until the roar of the approaching chopper drowned them out.

Riley sobbed and drove herself harder, her palms and knees growing slick with blood, the pain nothing compared to her animalistic desire to survive. The tunnel brightened ahead of her, the light blinding after so long in the darkness. She fought toward it, through it, and tumbled from the tunnel, down the talus slope.

She lunged to her feet and ran toward the massive shape descending from the sky, waving her arms over her head even as the tempestuous winds buffeted her backward. The Black Hawk drew contrast from the red dawn. Its side door was already open, its runners within reach if she could jump high enough.

A man in a yellow isolation suit crouched in the opening, the shield over his face reflecting the sky. He turned toward her and aimed his rifle at her chest.

THE BLACK HAWK hovered at the edge of the camp, rotor wash whipping up a cloud of dust and flattening the surrounding grasses. Cullen took in everything at a glance, from the blood-spattered tents to the body sprawled on the ground beside the guttering fire. It looked more like the aftermath of an animal attack than the epicenter of any outbreak he'd ever seen.

"What the hell happened here?" Brown asked through his earpiece.

That was exactly the question Cullen needed to answer and he was running out of time to do so. The woman who'd emerged from the excavation in the side of the mesa waved her arms over her head and screamed words he couldn't hear over the roar of the blades. Her eyes were wild, her face and clothing covered with blood.

"I don't like this," Ward said. "Something's really wrong here."

Cullen sensed the exact same thing.

"Secure the site," he said. "At all costs."

He aimed squarely at the woman's center mass.

And pulled the trigger.

11

Bethesda, Maryland

Davis knotted his tie and did his best to center it. He looked like a kid pretending to be a grownup. With his hair parted and his face cleanly shaven, he could have passed for a seventeen-year-old getting ready to have his senior picture taken, but he wanted to make a good first impression. He was already preparing to step into a world outside of his experience, one inhabited by microbiologists and geneticists with multiple doctorates and social skills honed through countless hours of eschewing human contact in favor of staring into microscopes. It was no secret that he didn't fit into that world; he just needed to fool the others long enough for them to get to know him.

Again, he was reminded of high school and felt the panic rising inside him, forcing him to close his eyes and focus on regulating his breathing. In, out. In, out. Slowly, patiently. Filling his entire thoracic cavity before expelling every last molecule of air. Repeating the process over and over, clearing his mind of every memory struggling to reach the surface, until he felt that familiar warmth resonating within his core, and counted down from three, just like the therapists had taught him.

"Three . . . two . . . one."

Davis opened his eyes and met his own stare in the mirror, only the reflection was that of a fifteen-year-old version of himself, his face and clothes drenched with blood.

He closed his eyes, balled his fists at his sides, and started the entire process over. Clearing his mind and slowing his breathing until his heart resumed a slow, steady beat that he could feel all the way into his fingertips. When he opened his eyes again, the version of himself in the mirror was every bit as awkward, but a decade older and with tears streaming down his cheeks.

Stress always caused the wall he'd built between his conscious mind and his memories to crumble, no matter how many coping mechanisms he employed. He used every one of the calming techniques he'd been taught, carefully monitored his diet, and didn't consume alcohol or any other substance that might cause even momentary loss of control. The doctors had diagnosed him with post-traumatic stress disorder, but that was like putting a collar on a wolf and calling it a dog. His memories were still strikingly lucid, not mere electrical impulses recalled along well-worn neural tracts from long-term storage in his hippocampus, but transcendental experiences, as though he were transported back in time and into the body of his teenage self so he could relive the tragedy over and over and over again.

When that happened, he could smell the old books on the shelves in the library, the haze of gunpowder hanging in the air, and the scent of freshly spilled blood. He could hear the terrified screams all around him, the heavy tread of combat boots echoing from the hallway, and the thunderous boom of every shotgun blast. If he looked down, he could see the polo shirt and khakis he'd been wearing that day to impress Tammy Simpson, whom he'd intended to ask to the homecoming dance, and would have done so already had he not been such a—

"Coward," he whispered.

Again, the face in the mirror was that of his younger self and he was transported into the halls of Front Range High School, a blue binder and biology book at his side in one hand, gesticulating with the other as he tried to convince Todd Lewis, walking beside him, to go in on a limo with him for the dance. He heard the first shot as clear as day from behind him, but it was so far out of context that his mind interpreted it as someone slamming a locker. The second shot burst Todd's head, stray pellets ricocheting from his skull and ripping through Davis's cheek, shattering his molars.

Time stood still as he stared down at the body of his best friend, unable to rationalize what had happened. The searing pain in his mouth and the warmth pouring down his neck roused him from his stupor. He turned and saw Stephen Leonard Thomas striding down the hall in gray-and-white urban camouflage fatigues and infantry boots, his face painted black, his wild eyes standing out like beacons.

Shuck-shuck.

An empty red shell flipped over his shoulder as he leveled the barrel at Davis's chest—

"Three . . . two . . . one," Davis said, and again found himself in the here and now.

He opened the medicine cabinet and grabbed a prescription bottle. His hands were shaking so badly that the pills rattled like beans inside a maraca. He fumbled with the lid until it popped off, scattering little blue tablets across the countertop. He crammed one into his mouth, swallowed it with water straight from the faucet, and hung his head, letting the tears fall from his eyes.

The propranolol would take at least thirty minutes to work its magic, but the beta blocker would be coursing through his system by the time he met up with Dr. Pennington at the lab. In the meantime, he just needed to concentrate on something he could use to bind himself to the present, something other than the mirror image of the boy who'd left his best friend dying on the floor while he ran for his life, dodging classmates whose pictures he would see in the paper the following day and enlarged on tripods at their memorials, boys and girls for whom he'd lit candles and uttered condolences, while unconsciously celebrating the fact that it had been them and not him. Even then, he'd known that had he run toward the shooter instead of away from him, it likely would have cost him his life, but it just might have saved all of theirs. Instead, he'd hidden underneath a table in the library, listening to the thudding sound of approaching boots and praying for God to take anyone else, everyone else. Just please, God, let him survive.

Davis hurried out of the bathroom before he saw his reflection again. At this point, he simply didn't care how he looked or what anyone else thought of him. All he wanted to do was get out of his own head, to feel the warmth of the sun on his face, to smell the flowers blooming from the vines in the courtyard, and to hear something other than—

The sound of footsteps from the apartment above his transported him right back into the library, where Stephen Leonard Thomas, who'd merely been Steve-from-his-math-class at the time, clomped down the hallway, shouting epithets as he fired off round after round, taking his time to reload each time the breech ran dry.

You can't hide from me! I'll find you wherever you go!

"Three . . . two . . . one," Davis said, only this time it didn't work. He was still underneath the table, broken fragments of teeth on his tongue, blood sluicing from the holes in his cheek and dripping onto the white tiles, his entire body trembling so badly that he lost control of his bladder. Other frightened students stared back at him from beneath the adjacent tables, among them Tammy Simpson, who'd take her own life two years later.

The footsteps stopped just outside the library door and Stephen Leonard Thomas put his black face to the inset window, smearing makeup on the mesh-reinforced glass. Their eyes met across the distance, only in that moment he was Richard Wesley Taylor, the soft tissue beneath his chin lacerated and the crown of his head ruptured where the razor blade had shot straight through it.

"You and I aren't through just yet," he said in an amalgam of both voices. "I'll be seeing you again soon."

Davis snapped out of his trance with the realization that both killers had used the exact same words.

DAVIS FELT as though he'd stepped from the reality he knew into some kind of virtual realm. His was a science conducted on the macroscopic level, in psychiatric and medical suites, while this place was the complete opposite, like a chemistry lab on crack. The walls were all made of glass, allowing him to see scientists in white lab coats working at stations with equipment he didn't recognize and whose functions were beyond his limited comprehension. Everything was clean and sterile; there wasn't so much as a single fingerprint on any of the immaculate surfaces.

"This is the biomedical wing," Dr. Pennington said. "While Project Trident occupies the offices in the north building, it shares the facilities with both governmental and private corporate interests developing genetic treatments for all kinds of inheritable diseases, from muscular sclerosis to sickle cell anemia, not to mention prophylactic medications with both civilian and military applications, although the latter is above my paygrade."

Pennington laughed at his own joke, although Davis wasn't sure if it was because the details really were above his station or because nothing transpired within these walls without his knowledge. He looked from one side of the transparent corridor to the other as he tried to keep up with the scientific director of the NHGRI. The scientists were all focused so intently on their work that they didn't notice the kid in the cheap suit passing through their midst. He didn't belong among them. There was a part of him that was still waiting for the other shoe to drop, for Dr. Hightower to fire him at the end of the tour, after seeing everything he'd be missing.

Pennington stopped outside a lab filled with equipment resembling enormous microwaves networked to copy machines, from the tops of which computer monitors on swiveling armatures jutted.

"This is our sequencing platform," he said. "It took thirteen years and more than a billion dollars to sequence the first human genome, a feat we can now accomplish in just about ten hours and at a cost of a couple grand. Needless to say, we keep these machines running day and night."

Davis felt as though he were supposed to say something, but no words would form. He'd always considered himself to be a bright individual, and yet here he was, out of his depth and drowning in information.

"I can only imagine how overwhelming this all must be for someone with a background in the behavioral sciences." Pennington winked at him and started walking once more. "Sequencing a genome is the easy part. Interpreting it, however, is an entirely different story. It's like trying to decipher an ancient language without a Rosetta Stone. We have what amounts to a story longer than the entire combined works of Stephen King, only with no spaces or repeated words or phrases to help us begin the translation, and all written with only four letters: A, T, C, and G — representing the nucleotides adenosine, thymine, cytosine, and guanine — in seemingly infinite combinations of unknown length, collectively referred to as genes, which essentially form one giant run-on sentence that tells the unique story that is each and every one of us. And a single typo — an A where there should have been a C or a T where there should have been a G — can be responsible for a physical mutation or the genesis of a disease for which we don't have a cure."

They passed laboratories with fume hoods and men wearing goggles, laboring with pipettes over rows of test tubes.

"To add to the challenge," Pennington said, "every cell in the human body contains the same information, only each one interprets the message in an entirely subjective way. The same gene can act differently in various parts of the body or express itself at different developmental stages, which means that not only do we need to isolate that typo, we need to interpret it in the proper context to figure out whether it's responsible for the production of a protein that doesn't function properly or for one that's simply being activated at the wrong time."

"How do you even know where to start?" Davis asked.

"That's the question, isn't it?" They passed a room that looked like an ordinary computer lab with racks of machines resembling small digital safes. "You can't just pick any random starting point in the genome. Considering there are about three million differences between those of any two people, you have to compare hundreds, if not thousands, of individuals against one another to find the points of divergence, then localize them within the experimental group — in this case the genomes collected from mass murderers dating back over two decades, samples gathered in the field and from penitentiaries, from spree killers terminated by law enforcement during the commission of their crimes. We're talking about the Peshawar and Sandy Hook school shootings. The Norway and Paris terrorist attacks. The Las Vegas and Orlando night club massacres. We even have samples collected from historical monsters like Hitler, Stalin, and Mao. For our purposes, we consider all of these individuals to be part of one great big family, which helps narrow our search field so we can more easily find the genetic commonalities between them and their shared points of variance from the normal, unaffected population."

"Enter the Trident Gene," Davis said.

"Precisely." Pennington opened the door at the end of the hallway and led him from the lab wing into the adjacent building, which housed offices with windows bearing the frosted insignias of the entities housed inside. It wasn't hard to identify the one they were looking for by the massive three-pronged trident. Pennington punched in the combination to open the door and preceded Davis into an anteroom that was seamlessly white, from the floor tiles to the leather furniture to the vaulted ceiling. "Of course, that's also what led us to the third mutation, which codes for proteins we believe are responsible for structural development elsewhere within the cerebrum, in much the same way that the second, mutated version produces the anomalies you noticed in the amygdalae and prefrontal cortices."

Pennington passed an unmanned reception desk and led Davis down a short hallway, at the end of which was a conference room with digital picture frames on the walls, each of which displayed a rotating collection of images, and a futuristic table with computer monitors built directly into its surface. There were three stacks of paperwork at the head: a contract, a non-disclosure agreement, and a security clearance application.

"So, you want me to use medical imaging technology to identify the anomalous physical structures produced by the third variant, which should — theoretically, anyway — help us determine the corresponding function," Davis said.

"Think bigger," Pennington said. "We have the technology to change the typos within these genes. Not only can we eliminate the second variant from the gene pool, essentially curing the condition of psychopathy, we can permanently alter the common form of the gene to represent the third variant, should we be able to prove our theory."

"What theory?"

Pennington brought up an image on the main screen at the head of the table, which populated the other monitors as well. Dozens of rows of As, Cs, Ts, and Gs had been arranged into three subsets, the differences between them highlighted in red.

"Let me ask you a question," Pennington said. "What's the opposite of psychopathy?"

"I don't know."

"Come on, Davis. Use that brain of yours. What's the textbook definition of psychopathy?"

"A mental condition characterized by an inability to distinguish right from wrong. A complete lack of remorse or empathy."

"Exactly. And what is empathy?"

"The ability to understand and share the feelings of someone outside of yourself."

"So, would it be unreasonable to consider the opposite of psychopathy to be a condition characterized by an overabundance of empathy, an extreme sensitivity to the thoughts and emotions of others?"

Davis suddenly understood exactly where Pennington was leading him. Project Trident intended to tap into the hidden potential of the human mind.

"You're talking about extra-sensory perception," Davis said.

"That might be a bit of an overstatement, but you have to remember we're not collecting blind samples here. Our database includes billionaires and celebrities, professional athletes and musicians, anybody who thought it might be fun to drop thirty bucks on a DNA kit that would tell them about their ancestry."

Pennington played a series of images featuring faces Davis would have recognized anywhere, men and women who'd distinguished themselves from the ordinary population using talents or gifts others simply didn't possess. He recognized championship racecar drivers with split-second reflexes; hockey goalies who could seemingly see where the puck was going before it left the shooter's stick; Hall-of-Fame quarterbacks and receivers; Academy Award-winning actors and writers; revolutionary artists and inventors; computer and software designers who were now household names; investors responsible for launching some of the biggest companies in the world; astronauts; poker champions; magicians; and even lottery winners.

"You think the third mutation is responsible for their unique abilities," Davis said.

"I think it could very well be the key to unlocking the next phase of human evolution."

12

Detroit, Michigan

Banks groaned and pinched her temples. She'd only planned on closing her eyes long enough to dull her headache, which had instead only intensified while she slept. She sat up, swung her legs over the side of the couch, and hung her head while she struggled to maintain her grasp on consciousness. The bottles of ibuprofen and Jack Daniels were still on the coffee table, right where she'd left them, standing sentry over the case file she'd spread out on it. Forensics had already confirmed that the four most recent sets of eyes belonged to the victims of the string of killings attributed to The Executioner and had matched four of the six sets from the middle cabinet to the '85 murders. While they didn't have DNA samples from the girls killed in '48, Duvall had reached out to authorities in Vermilion Parish, Louisiana to lay the groundwork for acquiring samples from their surviving relatives.

Lord only knew what they hoped to accomplish, though. No matter how long she stared at the details from the various crime scenes, going back three-quarters of a century, she couldn't see the connection. It was almost like three distinct serial murderers with no relation to one another had spontaneously developed identical facets of their MOs and somehow acquired the mementos of their predecessors. Where had those eyes been for the last seventy-some years and how had they come to be in the possession of a man who'd murdered four young girls? Not to mention her partner, whose photograph was among those of the other victims.

She flipped over the picture and was just about to swallow a handful of liquid caps with a swig from the bottle when she noticed the flashing green light on her cell phone, indicating she had unread email. She awakened the screen and saw that the message was from Duvall. The header consisted of two letters that made her pulse race: ID.

Banks tossed back the pills, headed for the kitchen sink, and swallowed them with water from her cupped palm. She opened the message, which read simply: Matthew Avery Marshall. There were two attachments. The first was a copy of an Illinois driver's license with a picture of a man who looked just like any and every other she might pass on the street. There was nothing in his face that so much as hinted at the horrors he was capable of perpetrating upon his victims. No outward sign of anything beyond the standard frustration of a man who'd spent too long in line at the DMV. Something about his eyes bothered her, though. They weren't the same as those of the man who'd looked right at her while slicing her partner's throat, almost as though he'd been an entirely different person.

She closed the image and opened the second file, which contained a summary completely at odds with the profile Behavioral had created for them. Matt, as his friends had called him, had never been arrested or charged with any crime, let alone one of a violent or sexual nature. He'd never even gotten a parking ticket. He'd graduated at the top of his class in high school, earned both his bachelor's and medical degrees from the University of Chicago, and performed his surgical residency at Johns Hopkins. He'd married his high school sweetheart, Emma, who'd given him two children: Marissa and Tobias, aged two and four, respectively. She'd reported him missing nearly a year ago, when he simply walked away from Northwestern Memorial Hospital between scheduled surgeries and never returned. He'd left his BMW in the parking lot, his clothes and wallet in his office, and set off with nothing more than the scrubs on his back. There was no explanation for how he'd ended up in an abandoned building nearly three hundred miles away, in possession of the eyes of sixteen dead girls. Even more inexplicable was the fact that a man with a surgical background could do such a brutal job of excising them, almost as though he'd lost his skills and finesse in the interim.

Banks responded to Duvall with a request for him to look into Marshall's mental health history, his dealings outside of work, and his patients in the days leading up to his disappearance. She was just about to put her phone on the charger and see if a hot shower would at least dull the blasted headache when her phone rang in her hand. She recognized the number and answered on the first ring.

"I just responded to your email. I was hoping—"

"Later," Duvall said. "I need you to come down to Islandview."

"Why are you calling me and not the locals? I'm up to my neck in The Executioner case."

"You're going to want to see this one for yourself."

The way he said it made the hackles rise on the back of her neck.

"Talk to me, Desmond."

He hesitated for several seconds, as though determining whether to say anything over the phone.

"We found another one," he finally said.

"You're sure it's The Executioner's work?"

"Without a doubt."

"How long has she been dead?"

"Six hours. Maybe a little more. She's only now exhibiting fixed rigor."

The world seemed to tilt on an unseen axis.

"That's impossible," Banks said. "I put a bullet through his head."

"Check your email," Duvall said, and hung up without another word.

Banks opened her email just as the message came through. She tapped it and watched the attached image form.

The whooshing sound of blood filled her ears.

She grabbed her jacket and her gun belt from where she'd draped them over the back of the chair and sprinted for the door.

BANKS JOGGED through the alternating red and blue glare cast by the light bars on the cruisers parked against the curb, their sirens silent, a cold rain drumming on their hoods. Her mind was a chaos of warring images. Nothing made sense, least of all the photograph Duvall had sent her. She repeatedly returned to the memory of The Executioner in the split-second before his forehead collapsed from the impact of the bullet. The expression of triumph on his face, his last words echoing in her ears.

This is only the beginning.

She signed the crime scene log, donned paper booties and nitrile gloves, and ducked underneath the yellow police cordon. All of the windows on the main floor had been boarded over and the electricity had been shut off years ago, necessitating the use of portable lights on tripods. Criminalists in white jumpsuits scoured the barren interior, searching for evidence to collect, although they didn't appear to be having any more success than they'd had at the previous crime scenes attributed to The Executioner.

The plaster had been broken from the walls in the living room to reveal horizontal wooden slats, most of which had been smashed to harvest the copper wiring. She could see through the holes and into the kitchen, where the weeds in the backyard had grown through the rubble where the countertops and sink had once been. Ivy ascended the walls toward a hole from which algal growth and rust discolorations formed patterns like green and orange icicles. The top few steps of the staircase leading down into the basement were missing, exposing a pit of darkness. Bright lights spilled onto the hardwood landing of the adjacent flight, halfway up to the second story.

Banks followed the path marked off by the crime scene response team and mounted the stairs, her footsteps thudding hollowly in time with her pulse. The banister had been removed, as had the runner, leaving behind rusted bolts and carpet tacks. She heard voices and caught the occasional flash of a camera. The scent radiating from above her was enough to make her stomach clench, for she'd smelled it a mere twenty-four hours ago, with her partner and his murderer lying at her feet, their blood expanding around them, seeping through the cracks between the floorboards and dripping into the room below. She pressed the back of her wrist against her mouth and nose and mentally prepared herself for the ghastly tableau awaiting her.

As a young girl, she'd dreamed of owning a home just like this one, only she'd never imagined that this was what its future held. Islandview had always been a respectable neighborhood, full of middle-class families and historic homes dating back more than a century, with tree-lined streets, tended lawns, and parks filled with the laughter of children. Or at least that's how it had been twenty-some years ago, before urban blight had spread like a cancer throughout the city.

Abandoned houses now dotted the streets, relics of a bygone era that seemed to crumble before her very eyes, like decayed teeth in an aging smile. The remaining residents pretended not to see them for fear of acknowledging their own slippery financial slopes, influenced by the exodus of manufacturing jobs and plummeting property values.

To its credit, the city raged defiantly against its denouement, but the gentrification efforts were largely confined to the city centers, where millennials sought lifestyles of convenience, within walking distance of pretentious coffee houses and craft breweries, where they could potty their pocket-size dogs on squares of grass the size of doormats and overpay for groceries from trendy corporate outfits claiming to be for fair trade and farmers' rights while abusing the system of wholesale ignorance. And this was the cumulative result: once viable neighborhoods exsanguinating from the death of a thousand cuts, much like the victim in the attic, whose blood darkened the cracked ceiling of the hallway underneath it, the plaster swelling like a hot-water bottle, preparing to burst.

Banks passed the criminalists photographing the stain and climbed into the attic, where the action was. The sloped roof was missing so many boards and shingles that she could see the night sky. The wooden flooring was warped and water-damaged, with rings of mold surrounding sections that hardly appeared capable of supporting the weight of so many investigators, all of whom turned at the sound of her approach. They parted before her, offering her a glimpse of the victim.

The woman rested with her knees underneath her, her forehead against the ground, and her wrists bound behind her back. Her face was concealed by her matted brown hair, which had coagulated in the standing blood. She was completely naked, although it hardly appeared as such with the crimson skein covering every inch of her skin. What little was still intact and not swarming with flies, anyway.

"Walk me through it," she said.

The responding officer stepped forward. He was shorter than she was and filled his uniform as though it had been painted on him. He spoke in a curt manner that suggested past military service.

"My partner and I responded to reports of a ten-forty-five at 9:43 PM. We smelled the victim the moment we entered the premises and immediately realized we were dealing with something other than an animal carcass, so we secured the site and called for support. We've already begun canvassing the neighborhood, but so far no one's seen anyone enter this house in years."

"What do we know about the victim?"

Duvall answered from where he crouched beside the body. He looked as though he hadn't slept at all since she'd last seen him.

"Caucasian female between twenty-five and thirty years of age. No forms of ID or readily identifiable physical characteristics. Her body's still in fixed rigor, although the first stages of livor mortis can be seen where the blood's settled in her forehead and knees, placing her time of death at no longer than eight hours ago."

He raised his eyes to meet hers in an attempt to communicate what they both already knew. Despite the fact that *lingchi*, a Chinese form of ritualistic execution, fit The Executioner's MO, he couldn't possibly have been responsible because she'd already killed him by then.

"Has anyone matching her general description been reported missing?" Banks asked.

"We're looking into that now," the responding officer said.

"What about COD?"

"You want to know if she bled out from her wounds or if the scene was staged," Duvall said.

"Something like that."

"I'm leaning toward acute exsanguination, but I reserve the right to revise my answer pending physical and toxicological evaluation. Even if I'm right, I doubt I'd ever be able to tell you which was the fatal laceration."

"But she was definitely still alive while she was being carved up?"

"Let me show you something." Duvall leaned sideways and shone a penlight through the woman's hair, onto the side of her face. "Judging by the ragged incision marks and the advanced levels of clotting on her eyelids and inside her sockets, I'm confident that not only did he take her eyes first, she was actively fighting for her life while he did so."

His choice of the word "taken" was deliberate and meant to communicate the detail they'd been able to conceal from the press for fear of inspiring a copycat. Outside of those directly involved in the investigation, no one knew The Executioner had excised the eyes of his victims.

She raised the question with her eyebrows. He merely shook his head to signify that they hadn't found them yet.

Footsteps echoed from behind her, approaching rapidly. A criminalist burst into the attic, his face beaded with sweat beneath his Plexiglas visor.

"We found something in the basement," he said. "You're going to want to see this."

Banks brushed past him, took the stairs two at a time, and descended to the main level. A faint light blossomed from the darkness where the stairs to the basement had once been. She sat at the edge of the floor, lowered her legs through the hole, and dropped down onto the rubble.

Something scurried away from her feet, but she didn't so much as glance at it. She was too enrapt by the criminalist standing in front of her, silhouetted by the light he shone onto the wall, where symbols just like those that had been painted on The Executioner's greenhouse lair had been carved into the concrete wall, hieroglyphics she would have recognized anywhere by the horned figures with the elongated bodies.

She watched the light play upon the wall, revealing characters that had been so meticulously carved that it must have taken days, unlike the words hurriedly scratched across them in large letters, words that caused her breath to stale in her chest and the world to fall away.

This is only the beginning.

BANKS HUNG up the phone and barely resisted the urge to punch her monitor in frustration. The agent at the Bureau's Cryptanalysis and Racketeering Records Unit hadn't been nearly as helpful as she'd hoped. While he'd been more than willing to examine the symbols from both crime scenes, she'd been counting on at least some preliminary answers to get her pointed in the right direction, something beyond an "amalgamation of styles ranging from Native American to Sumerian," anyway. She could have figured out that much on her own with a few hours on the internet, but she simply didn't have that kind of time or patience. There were only a handful of people who knew Marshall's final words, all of whom were inside the investigation. If one of her colleagues had been working with The Executioner, then they needed to root him out before another innocent woman died, although she'd personally cleared every single one of them and had a forensics team going back over the greenhouse to make sure there were no audio or video surveillance units.

She spun around in the chair at her desk, watching the walls of her cubicle blur past. There were no pictures of family or loved ones, no photographs of herself with celebrities or politicians or even a dog, nothing at all to suggest that she was anything more than a physical manifestation of her job, outside of a single brass placard engraved with a quote by Sir Arthur Conan Doyle: *Once you eliminate the impossible, whatever remains, no matter how improbable, must be the truth.* The problem was that in this case, there was simply one impossibility she couldn't eliminate, no matter how hard she tried. It was both the only explanation that made any kind of sense and the only one that couldn't possibly be true. She'd killed the man she believed to be The Executioner, but still she could feel it, deep down, as completely and inarguably as the fact that the sun would rise in the east and set in the west . . .

The Executioner was still alive.

And yet she'd seen proof to the contrary with her own eyes, which had witnessed the moment when the bullet fired from her gun met Matthew Avery Marshall's face, like a fastball striking the heart of a catcher's mitt. She could slow down the memory, replay it frame by frame, watching the bridge of his nose turn inside out, his eyes look inward at each other, and the contents of his head explode from the back of his skull.

She shook her head to dispel the image. Despite the conventional wisdom that serial killers worked alone, this one obviously had a partner. The two murderers must have arranged for the sacrifice of the first to free up the second, and she'd be damned if she wasn't going to find the link between them before he killed again.

Banks awakened her computer and initiated a search for experts in deciphering primitive languages, which returned a much longer list than she'd expected. A cursory search of Native American stone art showed a wide range of styles and motifs, most of which appeared fairly basic, almost childlike, except for several from Horseshoe Canyon in Utah. With their horned, elongated figures, they most closely resembled what she'd seen at the crime scenes. They weren't identical by any stretch of the imagination, but they seemed like a good enough place to start.

The photographer credited for the images was a man named Jack Lucas, who turned out to be a professor at Harvard. She dialed the number listed for him. While the phone was ringing, she clicked the link to his email, attached a photo, and sent it to him so he'd have it in front of him when he answered, which, of course, he didn't.

She left a message and was just about to set the handset back in the cradle when the phone rang again. The Caller ID displayed the number of the internal line corresponding to the main switchboard. She answered before the second ring.

"Special Agent Banks? This is Madsen in Public Affairs. I have an officer from Redmond, Washington, who wants to speak with the lead investigator in The Executioner case. Do you have time to take the call?"

"Does he know The Executioner is no longer with us?"

"Yes, but he still insists on talking to you."

"Does he have anything useful?"

"He'll only talk to you," Madsen said. "He sounds kind of skittish, if you ask me."

"Tell him I'll call him back."

"He's already called several times—"

"Then put him through," Banks said. "Let's get this over with."

Madsen clicked off and the phone rang several times through the receiver. Banks answered when she heard the hum of an open line.

"Special Agent Banks," she said. "What can I do for you, Officer. . . ?"

"Detective," he said. "Detective Ron Patrick with the Redmond Police Department, outside of Seattle."

"I was told you have information about a case I'm working."

He cleared his throat, started to speak, and then stopped. The public affairs specialist had been spot-on in her assessment; Banks could positively hear the detective's nerves crackling through the phone.

"Look, detective," she said. "I don't have time to play games—"

"You're investigating the serial killer they call The Executioner, right? The one who kills his victims using medieval forms of torture?" He plowed on before she could answer. "I'm working a case where a stranger kicked in the front door of a private residence and was subsequently shot by the home-owner, who then — for whatever unknown reason — turned his weapon first on his wife, and then on his son. Only his fifteen-year-old daughter survived, and she hasn't spoken since he killed himself right in front of her."

"What does that have to do with me?"

"This girl? She doesn't talk, right? But she draws. She draws a lot. Really detailed, morbid stuff. I'm talking murders. Blood everywhere."

"I'm sure she's been through a traumatic ordeal—"

"She drew a picture of a girl with her head smashed in a homemade vise, another impaled on a spike. One with her skin peeled off—"

"She can find all of those details on the internet. They're readily available just about everywhere you look."

"Believe me, I know. I wouldn't even have considered calling had it not been for the fact that I couldn't find a match for her latest . . . creation." He paused as though consulting the work in question. "It shows a woman on her hands and knees, with chunks of flesh cut off just about everywhere."

Banks abruptly sat up in her chair. The CSRT was still processing the crime scene and they hadn't released any of those details to the press.

"Look," Patrick said. Banks could practically see him pressing the butt of his palm to his forehead. "I know how this sounds. Trust me. I normally don't buy into this kind of thing any more than you do, but there's something about this kid. She's — I don't know — *special*."

"You think she's psychic."

"I don't know what I think. Like you said, she's survived a traumatic ordeal. You know how people who go through that kind of thing can be. They come out of the experience . . . changed."

Banks took a moment to compose her thoughts. She rarely placed the slightest credence in such things, but she could tell that not only did Patrick believe what he was saying, the mere thought of it terrified him.

"What can you tell me about these drawings, detective? Are there any details that might not have appeared on the internet? Something we might have held back from the press?"

"You mean like the eyes?"

Banks couldn't find the voice to reply.

"In all of her pictures," Patrick said, "the victims . . . they don't have eyes."

13

Brooks Range, Alaska

Pritchard heaved the plastic-wrapped body draped over his shoulder into the chopper and shoved it up against the others.

"That accounts for all but four of them," he said.

"Who are we still missing?" Brown asked.

Cullen consulted his tablet, which displayed pictures and biographical data for all of the researchers at the site. The physical damage to the remains had rendered them nearly unidentifiable, especially Dr. Niles Williams, the anthropologist, whose face had been savaged to the bone by what had obviously been teeth. His remains were among those already bagged, tagged, and ready for transport, assuming they ever received confirmation of their destination.

"We're still missing Dale Edgerton, and three of the graduate students: Nate Paulson, Maria Sanchez, and . . . Sadie Rogers," he said.

"They must have gone underground," Ward said. He stood uphill from the camp, near the entrance to the excavation. "We'd still be able to see them if they'd taken off across the open terrain."

"You're certain you cleared both of the Quonset huts?" Cullen said.

Brown drilled him with a stare that showed exactly what he thought of having his skills questioned. Cullen took exception to the challenge and issued one of his own.

"Check them again," he said, climbing up into the chopper, where he began stacking the corpses even tighter to make room for the remaining four.

He'd never seen anything like this in all of his years on the job. Sure, he'd witnessed carnage inflicted by numerous hemorrhagic viruses that made it look like the infected had been turned inside out, but never in conjunction with such extreme levels of violence. Not even in the Congo, where those afflicted with Ebola continued fighting their pointless wars until they could no longer stand. These bodies demonstrated wounds consistent with those he'd expect from teeth and fingernails, the style of fighting borne of desperation and self-preservation, and yet these appeared to have been inflicted in an offensive manner. There was no doubt in his mind that the disease had produced the staggering levels of aggression. It reminded him of how the rabies virus was spread between animals, a means that he'd always been surprised they hadn't encountered with other pathogens, especially with the way these infernal scientists tinkered around in their labs, trying to engineer the deadliest virus, all the while knowing that its sole biological imperative was to reproduce and spread.

"Quonset huts: clear," Brown said through his headset. "Still."

"There's only one place they could have gone," Pritchard said.

Cullen nodded and hopped down. He loathed the prospect of going into that tunnel after them. There were too many variables for which he couldn't account. Even a healthy individual could become dangerously frightened or agitated and panic, inadvertently compromising the integrity of their suits. A single puncture could derail the entire mission, not to mention kill them in the process. He'd seen it happen many times, but never in such a remote location, so far from the nearest emergency medical facility. It was always possible that the missing scientists who'd taken refuge underground were as healthy as the woman, Dr. Riley Middleton — currently strapped to a backboard on the floor inside the opposite door of the Black Hawk, recovering from the effects of the tranquilizer dart with an IV in her arm — but if they were infected, he didn't relish the prospect of combat in such close quarters.

Had it not been imperative to account for all of the researchers, he would have happily sealed them inside the mesa and let them suffocate in the darkness.

"I don't like this," Ward said. "The rocks could tear our suits while we're trying to squeeze through."

"We all have to die sometime," Pritchard said.

"We've never encountered anything like this before. No one has. You saw what they did to each other. This is no mere hemorrhagic virus."

"You're the epidemiologist," Brown said. "What do you think it is?"

"I don't know, but it obviously acts directly upon the central nervous system—"

"It doesn't matter what it is," Cullen said. "We have a job to do and we're damn well going to do it."

He shouldered past Brown and headed straight toward the mesa. Navigating the slope was tricky in the bulky suit, but he made it to the excavation site, where Ward caught up with him at the base of the chain-link fence holding back the loose talus. How easy it would have been simply to cut it and let nature take care of the problem for them.

Ward looked Cullen directly in the eyes and killed his comm link so that no one else would hear him when he spoke.

"We've spent our entire lives preparing for the big one," he said. "You and I both know that what happened here could very well be beyond our ability to contain. If we're dealing with a virus capable of triggering both behavioral and physiological symptoms of this magnitude, and with such a short incubation period, we could be standing at ground zero of an extinction-level event."

Cullen shut off his own mike before replying.

"Then it's a good thing they sent me, because if all we had on the front lines were sniveling worms like you, then we'd all have been wiped out ten times over by now. Now, start crawling or I'll shoot you where you stand." He switched on his comm link and offered the widest smile he could manage. "After you, doctor."

Ward blinked several times in seeming incomprehension before crouching and shining the light mounted to the tactical helmet he wore beneath the hood of his isolation suit into the hole. He slid his tranquilizer rifle into the hole and squirmed in after it. It was all Cullen could do to keep from laughing as he switched on his headlamp and squeezed in behind the epidemiologist's legs.

The passage was even narrower than it had appeared from the outside, forcing him to flatten his face to the ground to compress his hood. He heard the heavy breathing of Brown and Pritchard through his earpiece, the scraping of their toes against the hard earth, and the clatter of their rifles across the bare stone as they slithered through the tunnel behind him. The temperature dropped so quickly that Cullen started shivering, even inside the infernal isolation suit, which had never happened in all of the countless hours he'd worn it.

Ward grunted as he crawled out of the tunnel ahead of Cullen, whose light passed through the orifice and spotlighted the stone that had once sealed it. The ghostly figure carved upon it resembled a spirit attempting to escape eternal damnation.

"I have eyes on Rogers," Ward said.

Cullen climbed out and followed the epidemiologist's headlight to the ground, where a young girl was sprawled on her back, her throat opened, her braided pigtails frozen in the pool of blood beneath her head.

"It looks like she was attacked by wild animals," Pritchard said from behind him.

"Focus on the task at hand," Cullen said.

He knelt and appraised what appeared to be four sets of bloody foot-prints: three leading deeper underground and one heading back toward the surface, which presumably belonged to the woman he'd tranquilized. Of the three sets of tracks, one was significantly smaller, likely female, while the other two featured similar tread — hiking boots of some kind — although one of them was larger and transferred more heavily. He ducked his head and followed them toward the crevice in the rear wall, not caring about the chalk lines he scuffed or the bones he kicked out of his way.

Sanchez's body lay crumpled on the ground inside the narrow passage-way, the surrounding stone decorated with arterial arcs and high-velocity spatters. Cullen stepped over her remains and advanced in a shooter's stance, leading with his air rifle. The Dan-inject darts were loaded with a combina-tion of tiletamine and zolazepam at a dose roughly halfway between what they'd use on a chimpanzee and a gorilla, which would completely incapaci-tate the target for several hours. Unfortunately, it required approximately three minutes to achieve maximum effect. The dose had been too high for someone the size of Middleton, whose blood oxygen saturation and respira-tions had dropped to dangerous levels, but ought to work perfectly for the adult males they were hunting, assuming they hadn't already done each other in.

He sidestepped a pile of rocks and shone his beam into the lava tube from which they'd fallen, but there was no sign of blood transference to suggest their quarry had crawled inside. The two sets of footprints diverged at a fork, where twin fissures descended precipitously into the depths of the formation. The larger set of footprints led to the left and into seemingly impregnable darkness, from which he heard the faint clatter of rocks.

Cullen smiled and readied a second dart.

"Pritchard," he said. "You're with me. Brown and Ward: the two of you take the smaller subject. Edgerton. Assuming you can handle him."

He chuckled and advanced into the darkness, hoping to God that the larger subject, Paulson, had been infected so that he could use whatever means he deemed necessary to subdue him.

WARD FOLLOWED Brown into the depths, alternately walking forward and backward to cover their rear. The footprints grew fainter and fainter until all of the blood had transferred from the tread and they vanished altogether. Something wasn't right; it was an instinctive feeling, one he couldn't entirely rationalize. There was no coherent explanation for what was happening, let alone for the fact that the temperature seemed to drop with every step he took. Every breath came faster and faster until he was on the verge of hyper-ventilating. The urge to turn and run in the opposite direction was over-whelming, so much so that it was all he could do not to abandon Brown to whatever fate awaited them ahead.

The logical part of his brain — the part sharpened by medical school at the Uniformed Services University at Walter Reed and honed to a razor's edge by his training at the CDC's Epidemic Intelligence Service — couldn't make sense of what he'd seen. He'd studied every hemorrhagic virus known to man, from Dengue and Lassa to Ebola and Marburg, and yet this one was completely unlike any of them. Sure, the physical symptoms — fever, hemop-tysis, and periodontal, subconjunctival, and tympanic hemorrhaging — aligned, but there was simply no precedent for the behavioral component.

While a disease like rabies could definitely cause spontaneous and fren-zied episodes of violence, it generally took weeks to reach that stage in humans, at which point the subject already had one foot in the grave. A virulent organism capable of acting so quickly undoubtedly proliferated directly within the CNS and released some combination of proteins respon-sible for impairing the neurotransmission of serotonin, but if the two seem-ingly disparate viral components were somehow working in conjunction, they were potentially dealing with a singular pathogen the likes of which the world had never known, one capable of spreading at an astronomical rate.

If his theory was even partially correct, then the only logical course of action was to incinerate the entire area. The consequences of releasing some-thing this deadly upon an unprepared population would be catastrophic.

"Did you hear that?" Brown asked.

He abruptly stopped in front of Ward, who listened intently to silence marred by the sounds of breathing through his earpiece. There was barely enough room for them to walk single file, their shoulders grazing the stone walls and their hoods rubbing the roof.

"There's someone down there," Brown said.

"Down where?" Ward asked, but the answer became clear when Brown lowered himself to the ground and swung his legs over the edge. A rocky slope descended into darkness so deep that it appeared to have no bottom. A faint scratching noise emanated from somewhere beyond the range of sight. The sound caused the hairs to rise on the backs of his arms.

Brown glanced back at him, his unease apparent on his face, and started down into the earth.

Ward followed, half-scooting, half-sliding, keeping his rifle raised and sighted ahead of him. The temperature plummeted with every vertical foot until he was shaking so badly that he questioned the steadiness of his aim. It was more than just the air around him, though; it was almost as if the coldness radiated from a single source ahead of him, like the frozen heart of a glacier imprisoned within the very darkness itself.

Brown slowed his pace. He could obviously feel it, too.

Ward's headlamp flickered. He tapped the side of his head to stabilize it.

Brown stopped and turned around. The beam from his tactical helmet dimmed and then died altogether.

A rock clattered downhill below them. Ward angled his beam toward the source and caught a fleeting glimpse of a silhouette before the shadows swallowed it once more.

They just needed to get this done and over with so they could get the hell out.

There wasn't enough room to pass Brown, so Ward shone his light in such a way that they could both negotiate the treacherous terrain. Hieroglyphics appeared on the walls; ancient carvings nearly worn smooth by eons of flooding. He recognized vaguely hominid shapes, their heads bristling with spikes, antlers, and horns, surrounded by dead animals hanging by their rear hooves or paws, and even some humans among them. The designs reminded him of the paintings of Hieronymus Bosch, nightmarish visions marking their descent into hell.

Again, he glimpsed the silhouette, its eyes reflecting like those of an animal. By the time he sighted it down the barrel, it had faded back into the darkness. They needed to hurry and close the gap so that one of them could get a clean shot—

Other shapes appeared ahead of him, hunched as though crawling up the fallen rocks, cloaked in the pelts of animals, their naked skin pale and filthy. He nearly fired off a shot in surprise, but they vanished the moment his light hit them, as though they'd never been there at all.

His heart beat faster and faster until the edges of his vision throbbed. He wanted to ask Brown if he'd seen them too, but he couldn't find the voice to form words.

Ward's light flickered again, and, in that fleeting moment, he saw the faces of men and women, their hair matted and tangled, their features dirty, and their eyes milky from lack of sunlight.

And then they were gone.

"Jesus Christ," Brown said. "What the hell was—?"

A dark shape reared up below them, its body seemingly growing to unnatural proportions, its arms extending outward to inhuman lengths.

Brown turned and lunged uphill, just as Ward pulled the air rifle's trigger. The epidemiologist swung the barrel wide to avoid shooting his partner and lost his balance. He tumbled down the rocks and barely regained traction before colliding with a man he recognized as the evolutionary anthropologist, Dale Edgerton, only his eyes appeared to burn with trapped flames.

"What's going on in there?" Cullen shouted through the comm link.

Edgerton reached out and touched Ward's mask with the tip of his index finger. The Plexiglas pitted, then split with an audible *crack*. A fine network of fissures spider-webbed outward toward the edges. Ward rocked back, opened his mouth, and—

He's transported to a world of fire. Sirens echo in his ears. Shadows streak through the surrounding smoke. He catches glimpses of snapping teeth and tearing flesh. Bodies hanging from streetlamps and littering the sidewalks. He sees his own face, blood streaming down his cheeks from the ruptured vessels in his eyes.

—released a scream from deep in his chest. Instinctively, he raised his weapon and pulled the trigger.

The vision dissipated and Edgerton once more stood before him, blinking in confusion as he stared down at the tranquilizer dart protruding from his chest. He closed his fist around it and tried to rip it out, but the tiny internal barbs were firmly hooked into his flesh. His stare rose from the syringe to meet that of the man who'd just shot him.

And in that moment Ward saw not Edgerton, but the darkness inside him, and the destiny that awaited them all.

Ward's beam flickered, capturing Edgerton like the flash from a camera. And then he was gone. Ward caught a fleeting glimpse of the anthropologist tumbling backward down the rugged slope before his light died and the darkness swallowed him whole.

"ANSWER ME, GODDAMN IT!" Cullen shouted.

He was just about to double back and check on Brown and Ward when he heard the drumroll of footsteps, coming in fast.

"Down!" Pritchard shouted.

Cullen dropped and hit the ground right as Pritchard pulled the trigger. A loaded dart screamed past, mere inches above his face, and ricocheted from the rock wall. His light pinned the man sprinting toward them from deeper in the passage, his shirt torn and his chest lacerated, his face a contorted mask of blood-soaked rage.

In one swift motion, Cullen rolled out of the man's path, shouldered his rifle, and pulled the trigger.

The dart struck his assailant squarely in the thigh, the force of the impact causing the man's legs to crumple underneath him.

Cullen lunged to the side as his attacker slid past. He squared himself and dove on top of a man he only peripherally recognized as Nate Paulson. The grad student bucked against him, struggled to pry the tip of the syringe from his quad.

"Help me hold him down!"

He braced his forearm against Paulson's neck to keep away the snapping jaws and used his body weight to immobilize the torso, but with the way the kid thrashed and clawed, Cullen wouldn't be able to hold him down for very long.

Pritchard hurled himself into the fray, grabbing Paulson by the wrists and forcing them to the ground.

"The hell is wrong with him?" he shouted.

Cullen could only look at Paulson, whose eyes bled from the ruptured vessels in the sclera. His broken teeth scratched at Cullen's face shield, freckling it with blood. There was nothing human about the grad student anymore. All that remained was an animal at the mercy of its primitive instincts. He'd witnessed similar behavior in chimpanzees during an outbreak of Ebola in Zaire, which had left the canopy dripping with blood and the forest floor saturated where the brutalized bodies had fallen, but nothing even close to this level of violence in humans.

Ward said something through his earpiece. Cullen tuned him out and focused on keeping Paulson's teeth and fingernails away from his suit.

The sedatives slowly began to take effect. Paulson's strength and ferocity waned, allowing Cullen to gain the leverage he needed to pin down the grad student's hips, and yet Paulson continued to strain against him, snapping with his teeth and spouting gouts of crimson from deep in his chest, until the last of the fight drained from him. His head settled to the ground and his eyes rolled up beneath his lids.

"Christ," Pritchard whispered. "What the hell, man? I mean — Jesus — what the hell was that?"

Cullen pushed himself up and slung his rifle over his shoulder. He checked the integrity of his suit while he watched the subtle rise and fall of Paulson's chest to confirm that the grad student was still alive.

"Get him onto the chopper," he said.

"We should just put him down right here," Pritchard said. "Him and all of the others. Turn this entire area into a smoldering crater."

"We need to know what we're dealing with."

"Turn them all to ashes and we won't be dealing with a mother-loving thing."

Cullen switched off his comm link and rounded on Pritchard. He grabbed handfuls of his subordinate's suit, drove him backward against the wall, and butted his visor against Pritchard's so that their faces were mere inches apart.

"We have our orders."

"You're the one who always says we don't take orders from old men in suits." Pritchard thrust out his jaw and held Cullen's stare. "You know damn well what we need to do here, but I can see those dollar signs in your eyes.

You, of all people, should know better; some things aren't worth any amount of money. You think anything good can come from a bunch of scientists screwing around with this virus?"

"We're not paid to think. We're paid to do what needs to be done."

"Then tell me you can't see exactly what that is."

Cullen bared his teeth in frustration. He hated that Pritchard was right, but he hated having his orders questioned even more. He twisted his grip on Pritchard's suit, tighter and tighter, until he saw the hint of fear form in the other man's eyes.

"Get that body onto the chopper or I'll incinerate you with the rest of this godforsaken hellhole."

Cullen slammed Pritchard against the wall for good measure, turned without another word, and strode back toward the surface. First it was Ward with his whimpering, then Brown with his insolence, and now Pritchard with his defiance. He was going to have to replace the entire lot of them. There was no room in this business for fear, let alone second-guessing a field commander, which was the quickest way to get them all killed.

He switched on his comm and spoke in the calmest tone he could manage.

"Tell me you secured Edgerton."

"Yes, sir," Brown said. "We're heading back toward the Black Hawk now."

"Is he infected?"

"It's hard to tell what he is. He's covered with blood and looks like he's been run through the wringer, and there's something . . . I don't know . . . " Brown hesitated as though preparing to elaborate, but apparently decided against it. "No, sir. I don't believe he is. At least not like the others."

"Then secure him with Middleton and let's get the hell out of here."

"With pleasure."

Cullen again entered the crevice, grabbed Sanchez by the hood of her jacket, and dragged her into the main cave. He dropped her body beside Rogers's and crawled through the tunnel toward the surface. Let the others drag those slabs of meat out of this infernal cave.

"Have we received our orders yet?" he asked.

"We're to head to Fort Wainwright," the pilot responded through his headset. "Our instructions are to transfer our cargo to a waiting plane, which will take you to an undisclosed location in the Rocky Mountains."

Cullen nodded. He knew exactly what that meant. They were going to Riverton, a decommissioned Cold War-era deep underground military base that had been secretly renovated for just this contingency, which meant that they were no longer working exclusively for NeXgen. They were back in the employ of the good old US of A.

"Get that incendiary gel primed and ready for dispersal," he said. "I want us in the air in fifteen minutes and nothing but scorched earth in our wake."

"Yes, sir."

Cullen squeezed from the tunnel and skidded downhill toward the Black Hawk, already picturing the world around him turning to flames.

WARD WANTED nothing to do with this. He should have found the guts to tell Cullen he was quitting a year ago, before the Yellow Fever outbreak in Brazil. Heck, probably even before that. Despite his ballooning bank account, his heart simply wasn't in it anymore. There'd been a time when he'd lived for the adventure, walking the knife's edge between life and death, being airlifted into dangerous situations where he knew neither the language nor what virulent agent awaited him, identifying and containing the disease before it could spread, saving countless lives that would never have the slightest idea of what he'd done for them.

It'd been like being a superhero, but that was a job for a kid in his twenties, not for a thirty-six-year-old man who had only an empty apartment waiting for him back home. Heck, the word itself held no meaning for him. He had no wife to keep his bed warm, no kids to give his life meaning, not even a bloody dog to slobber all over him when he walked through the door. He was a physician, for Christ's sake. He should be wearing tuxedos and going to charity fundraisers, romancing beautiful women, building a life for himself outside of his job.

While he didn't feel as though he'd wasted his life, he'd definitely wasted his youth. So many years . . . gone in the blink of an eye. All he had left to look forward to were divorcees angling to maintain their lush lifestyles, stepkids who made sure he knew he wasn't their real father, and his nightly walks with a dog he could fit in his pocket, just so he could get out of the house and have a few moments to himself.

He hated when this kind of mood settled upon him, but it was far better than facing the reality of the situation. Or the bodies piled on the floor behind him.

The white CDC Hot Zone body bags might have been puncture proof and impervious to fluids, but they did little to conceal the shapes of the corpses inside. He tried not to think about who the dead people were, the suffering their families would endure when they never came home, or the stories that would be fabricated to explain why their bodies were never recovered. That was someone else's problem, though. As far as he was concerned, once he got off this chopper, he was done for good and on the first commercial flight back home. Damn the money and damn NeXgen, Cullen, and the rest of them straight to hell.

Vast swatches of tundra gave way to dense white spruce and paper birch forests. Random houses appeared as if from nowhere before vanishing back into the trees. They had to be nearing Fairbanks, a fact confirmed by the appearance of first dirt, then asphalt roads. The Black Hawk banked to the east and circled around the airfield at Fort Wainwright to conceal their approach.

Ward glanced down at Edgerton for the thousandth time. He didn't like being in such close proximity. There was something wrong with the man, something beyond his presumed infection, the symptoms of which had largely already resolved. He couldn't shake the feeling that Edgerton was watching him, even with the continuous flow of sedatives through the IV in his arm. He'd felt that way ever since dragging the anthropologist's limp body out of the cave, loading it onto the chopper, and strapping it to the back-board on the floor beside him.

The episode in the cave had really done a number on his psyche. No matter how hard he tried not to think about it, he was haunted by the vision of a city in flames and himself bleeding from the eyes. It couldn't possibly have been real, but there was no rational explanation for what Edgerton had done to his visor, either. Cullen might have believed that Ward had cracked it when he fell, but the team leader hadn't been there. Ward knew exactly what had happened. He'd witnessed the Plexiglas splintering apart mere inches from his face. At least the integrity of the suit hadn't been compromised — knock on wood — and the gas mask underneath it had remained sealed over his mouth and nose.

"They've closed off the southern runway and secured a hangar with a little extra privacy," the pilot said. "Your plane's inside and ready to lift off the moment you're on board. No offense, boys, but this is where we wash our hands of you."

The Black Hawk came in low over the Chena River and alighted on a concrete apron outside of a peaked hangar. Matching Hazmat vehicles resem-bling armored firetrucks were parked on either side of a closed garage door easily wide enough to accommodate the wingspan of a 737. Men in isolation suits emerged from the pedestrian entrance to the building, leaned into the rotor wash, and closed the distance at a jog.

Brown slid open the side door, jumped down, and helped transfer the backboards with their drugged researchers to the Hazmat team. Several men carried them into the building, while the rest loaded the body bags onto an electric baggage cart and ushered Ward's team into the hangar. They passed through the doorway and straight into a decontamination corridor, an inflat-able tentlike structure with multiple subdivisions, which, combined, formed a continuous self-contained structure nearly as long as the building was deep.

High-pressure hoses buffeted them through the gross contamination reduction chamber, which was followed in sequence by several wash-and-rinse stations, where the men were alternately sprayed with diluted chlorine bleach and ordinary water. They finished in a wind room where they were dried with fans that felt like turbojet engines, and exited into a makeshift locker room, where new isolation suits awaited them. Ward was just about to change out of his old suit when he noticed something that made his heart stop and his blood run cold.

A single drop of water trickled down his cracked face shield.

On the inside.

The room started to spin around him. His pulse rushed in his ears, and he couldn't seem to make himself breathe.

It was just a single drop. Not even a whole drop, really. A droplet. They'd misted his visor in the field and no water had passed through the cracks, even facing into the hurricane-force gale of the Black Hawk's rotors. Surely the leak must have been caused by the high-pressure hoses and the impelled air blasting right at it, weakening the fissures. That had to be it.

He hurriedly removed his hood, cast it aside, and glanced at the others to make sure none of them had seen, but they were too preoccupied with their own suits to have noticed. The taped seals around Cullen's wrists and Pritchard's boots had peeled off from the pressurized water, which had also torn open the flaps on the back of Brown's suit, exposing his oxygen tanks.

Ward breathed a sigh of relief. It wasn't like he could have potentially inhaled the contagion, anyway. Not with his respirator on. And he hadn't been directly exposed to any bodily fluids, either. As long as the virus hadn't slipped through the cracks and come into contact with the surface of his open eyes, there was zero possibility of exposure. He wasn't about to take any chances, though. He'd start a course of prophylactic antivirals when he got home, just to be sure—

"Ward," Cullen said. "Are you coming or what?"

He jumped at the sound of his commanding officer's voice.

"Yeah," he said, quickly donning his suit and following the others into the hangar.

An olive-green C-130 Hercules filled the vast space. It was a massive transport aircraft with four turbo props, a 132-foot wingspan, and a 400-square-foot cargo hold. The rear ramp was down and the men from the Hazmat team were already transferring the bagged bodies from the sanitized cart.

"I can't do this," Ward whispered.

The others strode straight up the ramp and onto the plane. Ward stopped halfway up and stared into a customized interior unlike any he'd seen before. On one side was a row of seats, on the other a sealed Plexiglas partition with inset vents and negative-pressure environmental control systems designed to make sure there was no cross-contamination of the internal air. Edgerton,

Middleton, and Paulson had been transferred into clear medical isolation transport units reminiscent of escape pods and were already secured inside the chamber next to the one housing the individual containment units for the deceased.

"Get a move on, Ward!" Cullen shouted.

The hangar door started to open, and the engines came to life with a high-pitched whine that metamorphosed into a roar.

"I can't do this," he said, louder this time.

"We need to raise the ramp," a member of the crew called down to him.

"Get on the goddamn plane!" Cullen shouted.

"I'm out, chief," Ward said. "I can't do this anymore."

Cullen drilled him with a laser-like stare, but this time Ward didn't back down. His commanding officer's jaw muscles bulged behind his visor. There was no mistaking how badly Cullen wanted to rip him apart with his bare hands.

"Just let him go," Brown said.

Cullen rounded on him and stabbed a finger into his face.

"You stay out of it. This is between me and Ward."

"My heart's just not in it anymore," Ward said. "I'd be a liability to the team and you know it."

"We're out of time," the crewman waiting at the control console said. "We need to raise the ramp."

Cullen narrowed his eyes and bared his teeth.

"Fine," he said. "Have it your way. You're on your own from here. Just don't come crying to me when the money runs out and you can't find anything else that gets your juices pumping."

There was nothing else to say. Ward backed down the ramp and stepped off onto the concrete. Cullen's eyes didn't leave his until the ramp closed between them, sealing off the cargo hold. The plane rolled out onto the apron and turned toward the runway, where it taxied to the west, accelerated until it reached liftoff speed, and rose into the sky.

Ward walked out onto the tarmac, took off his hood, and breathed in a lungful of the cold air, reveling in the sensation within his chest. Freedom had never felt so good. He slipped out of his suit and, with a smile on his face, headed across the airfield toward Fort Wainwright, where he'd be able to catch a ride to Fairbanks International Airport, his first stop on the road to a new life.

14

Snoqualmie, Washington

Ciara opened her eyes and quickly closed them before she started crying again. This wasn't her home and this wasn't her room. This was a place devoid of hope, where overly solicitous counselors were waiting around every corner with open arms and that scrunched-up expression on their faces, like they wanted to share her pain, to give her a shoulder to cry on, to help lighten her burden, but every evening they clocked out and went back to their cozy little houses, hugged their families a little tighter, and prayed their children never had to suffer the fate of those at work.

Unfortunately, the nights here were no better than the days. Ciara's dreams were filled with ghosts. They overwhelmed her with such powerful emotions that she often woke up with a painful longing in her heart that consciousness only intensified, leaving her to stare at the bare ceiling and walls for as long as she could stomach before subjecting herself to them once more. She'd find herself with her brother, eating breakfast at the kitchen table or sitting on the couch playing Nintendo, only he'd turn to her with a terrified expression on his face and utter his final words — *No, please . . .* — and, with a clap of thunder, his face would vanish. She'd see her mother leaning over her to give her a goodnight kiss, one she was far too old and mature to receive, but her mother's features would abruptly change and suddenly she was yanking Ciara out of bed and dragging her down the hallway, their eyes meeting one last time as her mother shoved her out the window — *Don't make a sound, do you hear me? No matter what you see, don't make a sound.* And she'd see her father, swinging her in circles by her arms in the backyard, getting dizzy and falling to his knees, his laughter metamorphosing into ragged breathing as he propped the shotgun under his chin, looked at her through eyes not his own, and pulled the trigger.

Ciara sat up and swung her legs over the side of the bed. There was nowhere to go, nothing to do, and she couldn't seem to get out of her own head for more than a few seconds at a time. None of her friends from school had come to see her and, knowing their parents, likely never would. Not as long as she was in a place like this, part of the dreaded *system*. Her grandparents had all died years ago and she didn't have any extended family beyond a couple of great aunts and uncles and their children — her parents' cousins — most of whom she'd never even met. This was where damaged children, the kids no one wanted, were taken to be among their kind, outside the sight of a society invested in their well-being and rehabilitation, if only from a distance.

At least the act of drawing helped. She could sit down in front of her sketch pad and next thing she knew, hours had passed without her even once having to think about her situation or the fact that she would soon have to attend a funeral with three closed caskets, stand before enlarged pictures of the only family she'd ever known, and accept the condolences of people she didn't know, assuming anyone even came, considering what had happened. Of course, all of that would have to wait until the autopsies had been completed, the criminal investigation was finished, and the bodies were formally released to her.

The detective, Patrick, had already come to see her several times and seemed to be the only one capable of speaking in a manner she could comprehend. He spoke directly to her, instead of tiptoeing around her feelings, and used blunt words that stung, but somehow cut through the fog of emotions. Miss Amanda stayed with them the whole time, although there was no mistaking how uncomfortable Ciara's artwork made her. She'd been hugely supportive of what she called "emotional catharsis," at least in the beginning, but that support had quickly turned to thinly veiled revulsion, which was probably the only reason she'd mentioned the sketchpad to the detective in the first place. Patrick, on the other hand, hadn't even tried to hide his disgust. Or his fascination. He'd studied each drawing carefully, asked lots of questions, and even taken pictures of them on his cellphone.

The problem was she simply didn't know where the ideas came from, couldn't remember drawing them, and didn't have the slightest clue what they were supposed to mean. These "pieces," as Miss Amanda called them, were so precisely detailed and carefully shaded that they appeared photorealistic. Were it not for the smudged charcoal on the meat of her palm and pinkie, she wouldn't have believed she'd been the one responsible for their creation. That and the subject matter, of course, which she found every bit as frightening as the others did, and yet strangely comforting at the same time.

The feeling reminded her of the time she'd fallen into a cactus patch as a little girl. She'd been running downhill, tripped, and tumbled right into a veritable thicket of prickly pears with pads the size of platters. The sheer agony of those needles piercing every inch of her flesh had been unbearable. She remembered her mother using a pair of eyelash tweezers to pull them out, one by one, each simultaneously producing a soul-deep pain and a sense of relief the moment it was gone. That was how she viewed these pictures, although she tried to do so as seldomly as possible, especially since the last thing she wanted was to see so much blood.

There was a gentle rap at her door. When she didn't immediately respond, it swung slowly inward.

"Good morning, Ciara," Miss Amanda said. She wore her badge clipped to the pocket of her customary flannel shirt and a pair of dress jeans. "How are you feeling this morning?"

Ciara offered a smile that she hoped appeared more genuine than it felt.

"What do you think about having some breakfast and maybe spending some time outside in the garden?"

Ciara recalled the memory of the man who'd looked like one of the body collectors from the medical examiner's office, just standing there in the shadows of the trees, and shook her head.

"I think some fresh air and a little exercise might do you some good."

Ciara shook her head more emphatically.

"Still not up for talking?"

Again, Ciara shook her head. The truth was she was trying, but she couldn't seem to remember how. She'd never had to think about the mechanism of producing speech; it was just something that happened. There seemed to be some sort of short circuit between her brain and her vocal cords. She could clearly hear the words forming in her brain and she could open her mouth and frame them with her lips, but she simply couldn't give them voice, no matter how hard she tried. It was a helpless feeling, one she'd be happy enough to relinquish. The thought of spending additional time in therapy trying to "isolate the psychological and physiological disconnect" made her physically ill.

"Then what do you say to spending the morning in the group room," Miss Amanda said. "You can bring your drawing supplies with you. Just, you know, try to draw something a little more positive, especially around the younger kids. With a gift like yours, you could produce some wonderful pieces we'd be happy to hang on the walls. You and I could even learn how to make those cute driftwood frames and use them to liven up some of the bare spaces. I mean, everyone loves our cartoon characters, but imagine the happiness you could bring to everyone around here with the magic you possess."

Ciara smiled and nodded. It felt good to see Miss Amanda beam in response, unlike the way the older woman looked at her while viewing her drawings. She just hoped she'd be able to create something good this time. If her talent were indeed a gift, then surely she could learn to control it.

Unfortunately, she could already feel that familiar scratching sensation at the back of her brain and feared the images it would conjure.

THE CHARCOAL PENCIL blurred across the page, almost frantic in its movements. It seemed like it had a mind of its own, a magic wand that guided Ciara's movements instead of the other way around. And while her hand worked, her mind simply went away. To where, she couldn't say. It was almost as though she were experiencing jumps in time; one moment she was sitting at the table with a blank sheet of paper before her, and the next she was awakening from what felt like a deep slumber to find herself staring at a drawing that both surprised and terrified her. It wasn't so much the images themselves — although the sheer level of carnage was shocking — as much as the fact that they were there at all.

Before she'd arrived at the group home, she'd never demonstrated anything remotely resembling artistic talent. Sure, she'd been known to doodle from time to time, but this was on a level beyond her wildest aspirations. She wouldn't have been able to trace these pieces from a photograph, let alone shade them with such accuracy, especially not in such a short period of time. And yet if she searched her mind for any sign of where the image had originated — a movie she might have watched, an episode of *Criminal Minds*, a photograph she'd stumbled across on the internet — she could find no recollection of ever having seen it before.

Worse, the rest of the staff were beginning to keep their distance, like there was something wrong with her. In the head. She could see it in the way they looked at her, in the way they spoke to her, and in the physical distance they maintained, constantly gauging and revising, as though trying not to get too close, but not wanting her to know that was what they were doing, either. She'd heard them, though, whispering down the hallway when they thought she was asleep.

Such a fascination with death isn't healthy.

That's just her mind's way of working through her issues. You try living through what she did and see what kind of pictures you draw.

But have you looked at them? I mean, really looked at them? You've seen the news. They're just like—

She doesn't have access to the news. None of these children are exposed to anything that could derail their rehabilitation.

That's the thing, though. She's frightening the other children. They're every bit as fragile as she is. We can't risk compromising their healing by exposing them to . . . this kind of imagery.

We can't isolate her, either. We need to channel her talents into something—

Less repulsive?

I was going to say more productive.

We need to consider the possibility that she's beyond our skills and needs a situation better suited to her advanced needs.

You mean somewhere they'll keep her medicated around the clock? She's a kid who watched her entire family die in front of her less than seventy-two hours ago. Give her time. If she ultimately proves unresponsive to our plan of care, then we can discuss alternative courses of action.

She scares me, though. I hate to even think such a thing about a girl her age, but you've seen the way her eyes roll up in her head while she's—

"—drawing."

Ciara blinked repeatedly and looked up toward the source of the voice.

"I said, that's one badass drawing."

Wes Parker stood before her, the television, which always seemed to be playing one episode of *Sponge-Bob SquarePants* or another, at his back. His blue eyes sought hers and held them as he tucked his long bangs behind his ear, an affectation that made her stomach tingle just a little bit. She couldn't help but blush when he smiled, although her face quickly paled when she glanced down at what she'd drawn.

Ciara recognized Miss Amanda by her eyes, despite the fact that the whites had been shaded black. As had the tears running down her cheeks. Her teeth were bared, her central incisors broken, her face contorted by an expression that could only be described as unadulterated rage. Behind her was the hallway leading to the residential wing, the cartoon characters painted on the walls spattered with dark arcs and covered with handprints. Sparks rained from the shattered lights above her head.

"It's like something from *The Walking Dead*," Wes said.

Ciara smeared the drawing with her palm until Miss Amanda was barely discernible, crumpled it up, and threw it into the trash can beside the snack bar.

"Why'd you do that?" Wes asked. "You should have at least shown it to her first. Of course, she'd have probably blown a gasket and you would have spent the rest of the day bouncing from one counselor's office to the next, but it would have been worth it just to see the look on her face."

Ciara broke eye contact with considerable effort. There was something about this boy that she found simultaneously disarming and unnerving. It was as though he could look inside her and see the darkness she could feel trying to burrow its way out. As irrational as that thought seemed, she couldn't deny the truth of it. She'd recognized it on an instinctive level when she'd first run into him on the day she arrived and every time she'd caught him watching her since.

She wasn't oblivious to the way boys worked. They were at the mercy of their hormones and incapable of thinking about anything other than sex, but there was something different about the way he looked at her . . . a hunger he made no attempt to hide. She had no idea what sequence of events had led him to the Snoqualmie Center for Children and wasn't sure she wanted to know, either.

He settled into the seat across from hers, leaned forward, and cocked his head so that he was looking directly up into her face.

"You really can't talk, can you?" he said. "And here I was on the verge of taking it personally. Tell me I'm right." He laughed. "Or don't."

His smile was so charming that it forced her to question her assessment of him. Maybe he was simply scarred by the experience that had brought him here, just like she was, although there was something about his eyes that reminded her of her father's, not as they'd been throughout her life, but rather as they'd been when he knelt before her and braced his chin on the barrel of the shotgun.

"There's something special about you," he said. "I can tell. You aren't like the others."

Wes placed his hand on hers and traced the back of it with his thumb. She watched its restless movement for several seconds before reaching toward his face. He instinctively recoiled and stared at her for several seconds, but ultimately closed his eyes and trembled ever so slightly as she placed her palm upon it. She felt the heat of his breath on the underside of her wrist, the waxiness of his skin against her fingertips. His eyes remained closed when she removed her hand, leaving behind a charcoal handprint that covered his features, the residue from her fingers forming stripes on his forehead and marring his cheek. He slowly opened his eyes, looked directly into hers, and realized what she'd done.

Ciara had marked him.

In doing so, she'd stripped away all pretense. Just as he'd seen her, she'd seen him.

A spark of fear flickered in his eyes. He abruptly stood, knocked over his chair, and headed for the residential wing without another word, nearly plowing through a group of younger kids settling in to watch TV.

───────

"AND REMEMBER, if at any point you start to feel overwhelmed or uncomfortable, you're free to simply get up and leave," Miss Amanda said. She crouched in front of Ciara and looked her directly in the eyes. "Your well-being is our first and only priority. It's the promise that I, and every other counselor in this facility, have made to you and fully intend to keep. I need you to understand that."

Ciara furrowed her brow. She'd already attended several meetings with Detective Patrick, each of which had been preceded by a similar speech, but this one felt different, somehow more urgent, as though there was something Miss Amanda wasn't telling her. Still, she nodded that she understood. As much as she hated the constant reminders of that night, there were still questions for which she needed answers — chief among them what had transpired between the man who'd broken into their house and her father that had caused him to turn his weapon on his family — and Patrick was the only one who might be able to provide them.

"I envy your strength, Ciara," Miss Amanda said. "Very few people, let alone your age, could handle this situation as well as you have. This is part of the process, though, and the sooner we get through it, the sooner the healing can truly begin. Unfortunately, your process is a lot more complicated than most, but I'll be right by your side the entire time, and if you don't like what anyone in that room has to say, just let me know and I'll drag them out of there by the ear. You have my word."

Ciara smiled at the mental image. There was no doubt in her mind that Miss Amanda was more than capable of following through on her threat. Once more, she nodded and Miss Amanda stood, straightened her ID badge, and opened the door.

The room inside had been designed for supervised visitation with parents who must have done some pretty awful things to have their children taken from them and brought here. There was a laundry basket filled with toys, overstuffed chairs surrounding a TV wired to an X-Box, a pair of couches opposite them, and a circular table all the way in the back, where Patrick and an African American woman Ciara had never seen before sat facing her, slivers of light passing through the closed horizontal blinds behind them. They both rose and straightened their suit jackets when she entered. The woman was barely taller than she was and openly studied her through eyes that betrayed nothing of the thoughts behind them. Patrick offered a smile that looked like the result of abdominal cramping and gestured to the seat opposite him, where her sketch pad rested.

Ciara glanced back at Miss Amanda, who suddenly couldn't meet her stare. She would have willingly brought her artwork with her had anyone asked. Taking it while she was eating — and without asking her permission — was a violation of her trust. This was what Miss Amanda had been holding back from her, and the only reason she would have done so was if the request had been handed down to her from above, through the kinds of formal channels that required stacks of paperwork and careful documentation.

"Please . . . " Patrick said. "Have a seat. This is Special Agent Delilah Banks. She's a federal agent with the FBI out of Detroit."

The woman nodded to Ciara, leaned forward, and laced her fingers on the table. She had white patches on her hands that stood out in stark contrast to her ebon skin and wore her hair like the woman who played Missandei in *Game of Thrones*.

"You're not in any kind of trouble, Ciara," Banks said. "Let me be clear about that up front. And after everything you've been through these past few days, you need to believe me when I say that being here right now is just about the last thing in the world I want to do, but I've come a long way to ask you some questions and I'm going to need you to answer them to the best of your ability. Can you do that for me?"

Ciara's eyes never left the agent's as she pulled back the chair and eased into the seat. Miss Amanda hovered momentarily before assuming the seat beside her.

"Your drawings," Banks said. "I need to know where you get the inspiration for them."

Ciara stared mutely at her. She thought she'd already made it clear that she had no more idea where they came from than anyone else did.

"Allow me to interject," Miss Amanda said. "Ciara suffers from psychogenic mutism, a kind of aphasia known to affect children who've experienced traumatic events."

"My apologies. How about I just run down my list of questions, and you can either nod or shake your head in response? Will that be all right?" She waited for Ciara to nod before proceeding. "The subjects of your drawings . . . have you read about anything like them online? Or maybe in the papers? Did your parents watch the nightly news? Is it possible you might have seen pictures on the broadcasts or overheard the anchors from another room while you were doing something else?"

Ciara shook her head in response to each question as it was asked.

"I want you to think carefully about what Special Agent Banks is asking," Patrick said. "The unconscious mind can pick up on things that the conscious mind doesn't always remember, so I want you to look over the pictures you've drawn and ask yourself if there's any way you might have seen or heard anything even remotely like them."

Ciara nodded and opened the sketchbook. She looked at one page after another, scrutinizing images she knew from a rational perspective that she'd drawn, but to which she felt no emotional connection whatsoever. They were simply pictures of young women dying in the worst possible ways, by means she couldn't have conjured in her most terrifying nightmares. The detail on the faces of the victims was so lifelike that she couldn't bear to look at the bloody sockets where their eyes had been.

She shook her head as she flipped through them. Had she been exposed to horrors like these, even by a TV in another room, she would have remembered. These weren't the kinds of things she was likely to forget, nor the kinds to which her parents would have even inadvertently exposed her. They would have changed the channel long before any of the gruesome details were divulged.

It suddenly hit her that the only reason the FBI agent would have asked such specific questions was if the things she'd drawn had actually happened. This meeting wasn't about her, or even what had happened to her parents . . . it was about her drawings. Somewhere out there was a monster capable of doing such horrible things to women not much older than she was, a monster with whom her subconscious mind was somehow attuned.

She remembered her father's eyes at the moment of his death. Whatever dark sentience had been behind them had recognized her, just as she had recognized it. They were now connected in ways she could neither define nor entirely comprehend.

"This one here," Banks said, placing her hand on the book so Ciara couldn't turn the page again. "This woman appears to have had portions of her skin and the underlying tissue sliced off. Is that how you see it, too?"

Ciara shrugged and averted her eyes. She couldn't bear to look at it.

"Have you ever heard of *lingchi*? Or how about 'the death of a thousand cuts'?"

Ciara shook her head.

"Can you tell me anything about this picture? Anything at all?"

A tear crept from the corner of Ciara's eye at the thought of such a horrible fate befalling someone in real life. She wished to God she *did* know something so that maybe nothing like this would ever happen again.

"It's my understanding that you drew this picture yesterday morning. Is that correct?"

Ciara nodded. She caught Banks glance at Patrick from the corner of her eye.

"Are you one hundred percent certain?"

Again, Ciara nodded. She'd drawn it shortly after waking up for her first full day as a resident at the center. She remembered it clearly, just like she remembered Miss Amanda suggesting she show it to Detective Patrick that afternoon.

Banks's foot tapped restlessly underneath the table, but her hands remained still.

"Have you drawn any pictures since this one?" she asked.

Ciara nodded and flipped the page, relieved that she'd had the foresight to tear out the picture of Miss Amanda she'd drawn this morning. She looked at the next picture for several seconds before turning it around so that it faced the special agent.

———

THE DRAWING DEPICTED a young woman on her knees, her head hanging forward to her chest, her long hair concealing her facial features. Her arms had been raised to her sides, her wrists bound with rope, and the flesh and ribs on her back pried all the way open to form what looked like leathery wings. The floor was covered with standing blood, the concrete wall behind her discolored by water and rust stains. There was a narrow window high on the wall, through which a sliver of the world outside the basement was visible, as though taunting the victim, who'd never be able to reach it.

Banks concentrated on speaking slowly and carefully so as not to frighten Ciara. The woman she'd drawn had been killed in a manner known as "the blood eagle," a ritualistic form of execution practiced by Vikings, one that definitely would have appealed to The Executioner, or whoever had taken up the mantle after his death.

Banks removed her cellphone from the inner pocket of her jacket and held it up for Ciara.

"Do you mind?" she asked.

Ciara shook her head and Banks took several pictures, starting with the entire scene, then zooming in on the salient details, starting with the victim herself and finishing with the view through the ground-level window. Her heart rate accelerated at the prospect of what she might have discovered, assuming, of course, she was willing to believe that this slip of a girl had some sort of psychic connection to the murders.

Banks flipped to the next page in the book, but it was blank. She flicked at the tatters of paper clinging to the spiral binding and glanced up at Ciara.

"What happened to this page?"

Ciara shrugged and maintained eye contact for longer than necessary.

Banks nodded and closed the book.

"Just a few more questions and I'll get out of your hair," she said. "The basement in the last picture. Have you ever seen it before?"

Ciara shook her head.

"What about the view through the window? Is it possible you might have seen it from a window at a friend's house?"

Again, a shake of the head.

Banks forced a smile, reached across the table, and placed her hand on Ciara's. There was something about the young girl's eyes that made her uncomfortable, as though she were both here and somewhere else at the same time, present and absent, full and hollow.

"I'm sorry about what happened to your family," she said. "No one should have to go through something like that."

Ciara nodded and pulled her hand away.

"Unless you have any further questions . . . " the counselor prompted.

Banks had about a million, all fighting to get out, but now was not the time.

She left her card and explicit instructions for someone to call her if Ciara remembered anything important or drew another picture like the others. By the time she retrieved her ID and sidearm from security, she was already planning how to proceed. She was going to have to be careful how she approached this, as she couldn't afford to let the killer slip through her grasp.

Banks opened the images file on her phone and scrolled through the pictures until she found the one of the basement window behind the victim. She zoomed in as far as the resolution would allow, and while the details became pixilated and grainy, she was able to see exactly what she thought she'd seen in person. The brittle branches of a dead juniper shrub partially obscured the view from the ground-level window, but not so much that she couldn't see the peaked roof of the garage across the street or the four numbers mounted below it: 1629.

She was already dialing Duvall's number when Detective Patrick popped the locks of his Crown Victoria with his remote key fob.

"I need you to do me a favor and not ask a lot of questions," she said the moment Duvall picked up.

"And good afternoon to you too, Special Agent Banks."

"Now's not the time, Desmond."

Banks had to cover her free ear as Patrick started the car and pulled away from the group home.

"Sounds like your proposed favor is of the unofficial variety," Duvall said.

"At least for now," Banks said. "Can you help me out or not?"

"Has anyone ever told you 'no' and not ended up doing it anyway?"

Banks allowed herself a half-smile.

"I need you to get me imagery of every house in the Detroit area with the numerical address of one-six-two-nine. Can you do that for me?"

"Without breaking a sweat," he said. "Just give me a few minutes."

She listened to his fingers clatter across the keyboard more than a thousand miles away as lush evergreen forests blurred past through the windows. A drizzle started to fall from the gray sky, forcing Patrick to trigger his windshield wipers.

"You should receive them any second," Duvall said.

"Hold on," Banks said.

She put the call on speaker so she could check her email. The attached file was enormous and took nearly thirty seconds to download. She opened it and scanned through the pictures. Her breath caught in her chest with an audible gasp.

"I take it you found what you were looking for?" Duvall said.

Banks stared at the upper portion of the garage, where the number 1629 was precisely aligned between an attic vent and the peaked roofline.

"Get me an address, imagery, and anything you can find out about the house across the street from the fifth one," she said. "Drop everything else if you have to."

She hung up, speed-dialed her special agent in charge's number, and turned to the detective.

"I need someplace private and access to a computer with a dedicated satellite uplink," she said. "And step on it."

BANKS DIDN'T DARE BLINK for fear she might miss something. The array of monitors at the station in front of her were divided into quadrants, each of which featured a live feed from the cameras mounted to the helmets of the tactical agents. At the moment, she could see little more than disorienting views of the backyards of neighboring houses and the parked cars lining the opposite side of the street, but that was about to change.

She would have killed to be there with the penetration team when they stormed the place. There just hadn't been enough time to get her back to Detroit, at least not before something terrible happened.

It had taken a miracle to convince her special agent in charge to file for a limited search warrant allowing them to surveil the house at 1630 Brace Street, one provided by an *anonymous* call to the FBI tip line. While it hadn't been enough to convince a judge to let them enter the house, it had been more than enough to allow a unit to discreetly cross the front yard and use an articulated camera on a retractable fiberoptic cord to look through the basement window. The agents had captured imagery of wooden posts with ropes attached to them, hieroglyphics carved into the concrete walls, a jar filled with clear fluid, and a single blurry shot of a woman's lower leg protruding from behind a mound of rubble. Within minutes, there'd been a drone with thermal-imaging capabilities overhead, confirming the presence of two distinct heat sources inside the abandoned structure and surveilling the premises until the tactical unit was in position.

"Ready on my mark," the team leader said. His voice boomed from the speakers mounted on the wall above the computer station; Banks had raised the volume as high as it would go to better hear everything that transpired. Every whisper, every breath, every crinkle of the detritus and swish of branches against their Kevlar vests.

Her heart raced and her mouth went dry. She could feel Patrick and the other detectives behind her, watching the monitors over her shoulders. They had a stake in the takedown, too; after all, they'd gone out on a legal limb by calling in the tip.

The views all subtly changed as the agents leaned forward in anticipation or stole a peek at the house. Entire sections of shingles had fallen off and accumulated on the brown lawn amid the clumps of bushy weeds. The windows on the main floor were boarded, the latticework surrounding the porch veined with dead vines, the stairs leading up to it broken and uneven.

"Go," the agent said.

All the quadrants came to life at once. The live feeds tilted from side to side as the agents sprinted toward the house, blowing past shrubs and trees, scaling fences, and crawling across lawns. She heard the thunder of footsteps striking the weathered porch and caught a quick glimpse of the front door, followed by a handheld battering ram, and then the agents were inside, the barrels of their M4 carbines sweeping the dark interior. The back door provided even less resistance for the rear penetration team, who rushed through the barren kitchen and converged upon the living room, where agents in black fatigues were already heading upstairs to secure the second level and flanking the doorway leading to the basement.

Banks found the feed belonging to the lead agent descending the staircase and enlarged it to fill the central screen. The sound of his breathing echoed throughout the room, even louder than her own. Her hands trembled in anticipation.

The agent pressed his back against the wall of the stairwell and crept down sideways, his rifle aimed at the concrete landing, where debris had accumulated from the fallen ceiling, its rotting joists exposed. He glanced back at the agents following him, then back down into the darkness. When he reached the bottom, he crouched and waited for the others to catch up.

"Second floor clear," a voice whispered from the speakers.

"What if we weren't fast enough?" one of the detectives said from behind Banks. "What if he already killed her and snuck out before the SWAT team arrived?"

Banks tuned him out and concentrated on the screen, her throat so parched she couldn't even swallow.

The agent went around the corner, low and fast, his sightline rushing past walls adorned with the same symbols from the previous crime scenes and wooden posts standing from X-shaped supports made from two-by-fours. A woman lay naked on the ground between them, her wrists bound by the ropes tethered to the posts, the skin of her back mercifully still intact. The agent crouched and reached for the side of her neck to check her carotid pulse—

A shout erupted from all of the feeds at once.

The view pivoted toward the pile of rubble in the back corner of the room as a man burst from the darkness, raised a scalpel over his head, and lunged toward the camera in a blur of wild eyes and dreadlocks. The agent grabbed the man's wrist, twisted him around, and disarmed him in a single motion. The blade clattered to the ground as the agent shoved his assailant against the wall, pinning his arms behind his back and the side of his face against the concrete wall. Tattoos covered seemingly every inch of his dark skin.

"Someone grab a screenshot of his face and run it through the NGI," Banks said.

"I'm on it," Patrick said.

The tattooed man dislocated his own shoulder with a sickening crack, shoved against the wall, and knocked the agent back just far enough to land a roundhouse punch with his good arm. The agent dropped to his knees, his view snapping back to the suspect, who quickly picked up his scalpel and raised it between them.

All the live feeds focused on the tattooed man from slightly different angles. He blindly sliced at the air to hold the agents at bay, his dislocated arm flopping at his side. Everyone started shouting at once, their voices forming an incoherent garble from the speaker.

"Don't do this," she whispered.

The tattooed man lunged and slashed, driving back the agents trying to outflank him.

"Drop your weapon!" someone shouted.

"Get down on the ground!" another yelled.

Banks heard their voices as though from a million miles away, the red dots of their laser sights swarming on the man's chest. He turned from one to the next to the next. His posture slumped when the reality of the situation hit him.

There was no way he was getting past all of them.

Banks willed one of her fellow agents to take the shoulder shot. It was the only way to disarm the man without anyone getting killed. She wanted him alive and fully intended to do everything in her power to make him talk.

"Drop the knife!"

"Show us your hands!"

"You don't have the slightest idea what's about to happen, do you?" the tattooed man said. His voice was so deep that it reverberated throughout the room, as though originating from everywhere at once. "You're all dead and you don't even know it."

"This is your last warning!" an agent shouted. "Drop the weapon!"

The tattooed man smiled and twirled the scalpel between his fingers.

"This ends right now!" another agent yelled.

The tattooed man's smile grew even wider. His teeth were long and yellowed, almost skeletal. He seemed to look directly at all of the agents surrounding him at once, their live feeds making it appear as though he were staring right at Banks through the monitors, his irises the color of fire. She recognized his eyes, for she'd seen the exact same ones before putting a bullet between them.

"You're wrong," the tattooed man said. "This is only the beginning."

Banks felt the breath seep from her chest and experienced a sensation of lightheadedness, like she was about to pass out.

The tattooed man's eyes never left hers as he raised the scalpel and thrust it into the side of his neck.

15

The narrow dirt road wended through the Wind River Mountain Range, following a course dictated by hostile topography that seemed to resist their advance every step of the way. Sharp granite escarpments lorded over dense pine forests struggling to cling to their slopes. The occasional glacier materialized in the shaded valleys between sheer peaks, their prehistoric ice the source of the frigid streams trickling down both sides of the continental divide. On the western slope, they worked their way through barren valleys carved by millions of years of erosion, meandered through windswept meadows where only lichen was brave enough to grow from the exposed rocks, and formed crystalline lakes that served as the headwaters for the Green and Wind Rivers, the largest tributaries of the Colorado and Yellowstone Rivers, respectively.

At this elevation, their surroundings looked like the arctic nightmare they'd barely left behind in Alaska. At least to Cullen, who hated geology like this. It was as if nature had grown weary of being nice and thrust giant middle fingers of rock into their faces every time they rounded one of the hairpin turns forming the treacherous ascent. Why anyone would want to build a DUMB — deep underground military base — way up here was beyond him. Sure, there was just about zero chance of anyone even accidentally stumbling upon the turnoff from Highway 131 out of Lander, let alone following the narrow, rutted roads through the rugged foothills to the point where the graders started tending the sixteen-mile gravel road, but had the facility served its intended purpose and protected hundreds of people from a rain of Soviet nukes and shielded them from the fallout, the last thing in the world he would have wanted was to stick his head out of the ground after decades entombed in the earth and see such a barren gray wasteland.

The engine of the camouflaged Oshkosh Defense Global HET — heavy equipment transporter — roared in defiance of the dicey road. The vehicle had been designed to haul tanks, but this one had been modified with an armored trailer nearly identical on the inside to the Hercules carrier they'd boarded in Fairbanks. It was equipped with a retractable corridor that could be extended right up the ramp to avoid moving any of the infected contents through the open air. Edgerton, Middleton, and Paulson were comfortably sedated within their transport pods and attached to monitors that would alert the medical team babysitting them should their conditions suddenly change.

Thanks to the Level A Hazmat suits and the oxygen tanks on their backs, the six-man cab was a lot more cramped, even with only Cullen and the driver — an older man with a vertically creased face who'd introduced himself as Badgett — in front, and Brown and Pritchard in the seats behind them. Badgett had obviously made this drive many times, as he didn't seem the slightest bit worried when the outside tires rode out over the edge of the road, giving Cullen a dizzying view of the stream cutting through the forested bottom of the valley, a quarter of a mile straight down.

"At least it's not an insect-infested African jungle," Pritchard said. "How much longer until we get there?"

"First time at Riverton?" Badgett asked.

"How can you tell?" Cullen said.

"Because you're looking right at it."

Cullen stared out the front windshield as they rounded a bend that offered an unobstructed view of the mountainous face opposite them. A thick mist clung to the canopy of the black forest all the way up to timberline, but if he looked at just the right angle and used a little imagination, he could almost see the course of an invisible road carving through the trees and the faint outline of an artificial cut in the granite slope.

The worsening terrain forced the truck to slow to such an extent that it took a full twenty minutes for them to circumnavigate the valley and weave through the forest. Laser sensors and motion detectors projected from within clumps of scrub oak. Security and thermal-imaging cameras were concealed among the foliage to either side and, if Cullen looked hard enough, he could occasionally see the well-worn paths through the underbrush cut by patrolling sentries.

"This is the lone terrestrial approach to the base," Badgett said. "The only other way of reaching it is by air, but there's nowhere to land on those peaks and the winds up there'll toss around a chopper like a child's toy. You could maybe try parachuting or hiking in from the other side of the mountain, although you wouldn't make it far without triggering one of the motion sensors. Assuming you even knew this place was here to begin with."

He barked a laugh that degenerated into a smoker's cough.

Cullen pressed his visor against the side window, the cold radiating against his cheek, and looked up into the canopy. The branches on both sides of the road had been cultivated in such a way as to form a veritable tunnel of vegetation. He could still see the camouflage netting that provided its framework, effectively making it invisible from the air. The passage had to be at least fifty years old to have bent the old-growth forest to its will.

The rocky earth slowly rose on both sides until they were driving through a trench, the forest floor at the level of the roof of the cab. An earthen maw opened before them and they penetrated the dark heart of the mountain. The ceiling was rounded and formed three-quarters of a circle around the road. Conduits as thick as tree trunks lined the walls. The recessed lighting was staggeringly bright, revealing concrete discolored by water damage and accumulated rubber from the tread of decades' worth of heavy haulers moving back and forth through the tunnel.

The truck's headlights narrowed against a steel wall with an inset mechanical door. An armed guard appeared in front of them as if by magic and waved for them to stop. Another emerged from the guard shack built into the recessed wall and walked circles around the semi with an undercarriage inspection mirror. When he was satisfied, the first guard hit the mechanism to open the door. Red lights flashed as a blast door easily three feet thick slid back into the wall. Once it was clear and the lights stopped flashing, the guards waved the truck through. Cullen watched the flashing lights and closing door in the side mirror until it fell away behind them.

"The military started construction on this place just prior to World War Two," Badgett said. "Back then, the plan had been to build a network of interconnected bases underneath the western states. We're talking thousands of miles of subterranean tunnels connecting military and research facilities throughout Wyoming, Colorado, New Mexico, Arizona, Nevada, California, Kansas, and Oklahoma, with proposed expansions going all the way to D.C., New York, and the Raven Rock and Mount Weather complexes. An entire underground highway system that would allow us to move our arsenal and troops across the country on a moment's notice without the Soviets having the slightest idea what we were doing."

"There are tunnels down here that go all the way to California?" Brown said.

Badgett again cough-laughed.

"This is a military installation, son. Or at least it was. You know the government likes to negotiate construction contracts based not on the quality of the work, but on how much money our fine elected officials can get in kickbacks. There are tunnels down here. I've seen them with my own eyes, but Lord only knows how far they run or where they go. Half of them are buried under millions of tons of rock, while the other half look like it's only a matter of time before they collapse, too. I wouldn't even think about walking through one of them for fear the sound of my breathing would bring the whole mountain down on top of me."

The tunnel opened into an enormous manmade cavern easily the size of three football fields aligned side by side. Fifty-foot-wide stone pillars carved straight from the mountain supported the thirty-foot-tall ceiling. Domed tunnels lined the walls in the far distance. Most of them were sealed, while some contained darkness so deep it swallowed the light before it could penetrate more than a few feet. Yellow arrows had been painted on the ground to guide the truck to its destination.

"The base was overhauled in the Sixties and converted into something of a remote command center crossed with a fallout shelter capable of housing more than a thousand people," Badgett said. "The plan was to have a backup facility capable of handling NORAD's load, should the Soviets turn Cheyenne Mountain to rubble, but with the fall of communism in the Nineties and no real threat looming on the horizon, the powers that be decided to lease this place, and all sorts of other decommissioned bases, to corporations so they could do Lord only knows what away from the prying eyes of the public. Of course, the brass is probably kicking itself for doing so now that the Russians are back, and they brought the Chinese with them."

"So what's in here now?" Brown asked.

Badgett leaned back and winked at him.

"I'm not about to spoil that surprise."

They passed a concrete wall lined with loading docks, only the doors were airtight and looked like they were made from the same material as the blast door at the main entrance. The driver stopped and the screech of brakes echoed throughout the vast space. He jiggled the stick, rammed it into reverse, and started backing up.

Cullen watched the center dock swing into view in the side mirror. The smaller door beside it opened and men wearing yellow Hazmat suits and carrying M4 rifles emerged. One climbed up onto the runner, leaned through the window as Badgett lowered it, and used a portable iris scanner to verify each of their identities.

"Welcome to Riverton," he said. "I hope you took a good long look at the sky, because you won't be seeing it again anytime soon."

Dr. Phil Rankin stood at the Plexiglas observation window, his hands clasped behind his back, watching the chimpanzee inside the negative-pressure observation suite. He glanced up at the monitor, which displayed a running time marking the hours, minutes, and seconds since the injection of the virus, which he'd personally isolated from the remains recovered from the arctic archeological site.

02:34:16.

The primate had initially tolerated the administration quite well, but it had begun showing signs of lethargy at around the ninety-minute mark. Within a matter of minutes, its fever had spiked, its eyes had become glassy, and it had simply taken a seat in the middle of its enclosure, blinked sightlessly at them, and toppled onto its side.

It hadn't moved since.

As Rankin watched, a trickle of blood emerged from the corner of its mouth and dribbled down its chin into its gray muzzle. He'd deliberately selected an older specimen because of its diminished immune system and demonstrably greater susceptibility to infection by hemorrhagic viruses. While younger specimens often took a week or more to exhibit symptoms, the elderly had been known to do so in as little as 48 hours. That this virus had produced them in less than two hours scared the hell out of him. He'd never seen anything this aggressive in his tenure at USAMRIID, during which he'd worked with some of the deadliest pathogens mother nature had ever created, and numerous examples where humankind had improved upon her design, diseases with numbers, letters, and dashes for names that could inadvertently wipe out the planetary population should they ever fall into the wrong hands, and still this one put them to shame.

In his role as chief scientific officer of the National Medical Biodefense Program, it was his responsibility to take everything the mad scientists dreamed up and figure out a way to neutralize it. He'd helped develop antibiotics that could eradicate nearly any bacterial species that could fit inside the human body and reverse engineered the genetic codes of viruses to produce inoculations he prayed they'd never have to use, albeit under controlled conditions and with access to full genomes that had been acquired at a cost of thousands of lives. This one would be his greatest challenge to date. He hadn't felt such exhilaration since leaving the field and moving into the lab.

His role on the global rapid-response team had been exciting but ultimately far too restrictive. His teammates had been decent enough, if somewhat simple. He'd learned a fair amount about exposure patterns and risk-factor analysis from its epidemiologist, but the others might as well have been interchangeable pieces. Ultimately, he'd decided to return to the lab because his commanding officer had started inserting his team into increasingly untenable positions that would have eventually gotten them all killed. Not to mention the fact that he was just about the biggest prick the world had ever known, a fact evidenced by his attempts to derail Rankin's transfer, which had very nearly led to a court-martial.

Rankin looked forward to reacquainting himself with Lieutenant Cullen when he was done here.

His deteriorating relationship with his commanding officer hadn't been his sole reason for leaving the field, though. He'd grown tired of seeing the same diseases over and over without being able to do anything about them. It was always the same situation; only the locations changed, from one mosquito-infested swamp or shantytown on the edge of a godforsaken rainforest to another. And even then, the diseases hadn't been as problematic as the people, who lived in squalor and subsisted on what little they could catch and kill, often consuming dead animals they found on the ground. How many Ebola outbreaks had been started by some idiot who'd eaten an infected monkey that had died and fallen from the trees?

The bottom line was that people were stupid, whether by birth or by choice, especially when it came to religion. They could have easily eradicated Ebola decades ago had these savages allowed them to cremate the bodies of the infected and maybe not cleansed their remains in the same bloody rivers from which they drank, facilitating the mutation of five distinct variants. Any of those strains could easily spawn the one that resisted their established treatments, which, he was beginning to fear, was exactly what they were dealing with here.

Such a short incubation period suggested the symptoms demonstrated at the primary site of infection — or injection, in the case of this chimpanzee — were characteristic of this new disease, in much the same way that the influenza virus entered the system through the respiratory tract and produced coughing, congestion, and a runny nose, often within a single day. Hemorrhagic viruses generally took longer to incubate because they needed time to spread throughout the entire system, inserting their DNA into every cell, slowly overwhelming the immune system with a laundry list of symptoms starting with fever and malaise and culminating with organ failure and exsanguination. A combination of the two was essentially an extinction event waiting to happen.

Rankin watched the chimp's chest as its breathing slowed and grew increasingly labored. Its lips parted and revealed teeth pink with diluted blood. He glanced up at the second monitor, which showed a close-up image of the primate's face, just in time to watch the vessels in its eyes rupture and the sclerae flood with blood.

02:56:53.

"Zoom in on the site of injection," he said.

The camera panned from the animal's ashen face to the shaved swatch on its thigh. The edges of the puncture wound had deteriorated significantly and now showed signs of necrosis, almost as though the virus had been administered through the venomous fang of a pit viper instead of a sterile needle. Blood trickled from the wound, rich and black, a characteristic prodromal symptom and a sign that they were in big trouble.

"Collect a sample of that tissue," he said.

A lab animal technician in a Level A Hazmat suit emerged from the submarine-like hatch at the back of the cage and approached the chimp. He crouched, scraped the wound with a curette, and placed it into a collection tube—

The chimpanzee screeched and swatted it out of his hand. Before the technician recognized what was happening, the beast was upon him, slashing at his suit with its fingernails, snapping at his face with its long canines.

"Get it off me!" he shouted.

Rankin had seen the condition of the human remains upon their arrival, but even knowing what to expect, this level of aggression was beyond his wildest imagination. It was as though the animal had been stripped of all cognitive function and rendered a victim of its own base instincts.

"Magnificent," he whispered.

The back door of the cage burst open and another man rushed in, a five-foot snare pole in one hand and a tranquilizer gun in the other. He raised the weapon and fired. The impact knocked the primate off the technician, who'd gone stark white beneath his visor, which was scratched to hell and spattered with blood. The second man dropped the trank gun, lassoed the chimp's head in the snare, and used both hands to control the animal with the pole. Still, the chimp continued to fight, even as the noose tightened around its neck and the anesthesia slowly took hold.

"Sir," someone said from behind Rankin. "We have the autopsy and lab results you were waiting on."

"Excellent," he said. "Forward them to my email. And let me know the moment our new arrivals have been processed."

"Yes, sir."

Rankin dismissed his subordinate with a faint wave and watched the chimpanzee scratch and claw at the sealed concrete floor until it eventually collapsed, a ribbon of blood unraveling from underneath it and spiraling down the floor drain.

———

CULLEN DONNED a clean pair of black fatigues with the stylized red X of the NeXgen logo on the breast and headed down the corridor to join the others.

He'd spent the last four hours being poked, prodded, and subjected to seemingly every invasive medical test known to man before finally being cleared to take a nice, hot shower. His red and white blood cell counts had been well within the normal range, which made him feel a lot better about letting Ward walk, but that didn't mean his former teammate was in the clear. Cullen had used his connections at NeXgen to track the epidemiologist's movements, and while he hadn't acted quickly enough to prevent Ward from boarding the flight in Fairbanks or transferring in Anchorage, he'd arranged to have men waiting for his old friend when he got off the plane in San Francisco, men who would promptly make him disappear.

No one walked out on Lieutenant Tyler Cullen. No one. A message needed to be sent, one there was no mistaking. His only regret was that he wouldn't be able to deliver it in person.

But that would soon be in the past and Cullen had already moved on to bigger and better things, especially if this disease turned out to be even half as dangerous as the scientists here seemed to think. He hadn't given any thought to the profit potential until Pritchard had accused him of doing so, but he could only imagine how much a novel hemorrhagic virus could fetch on the open market. Once the scientists in this station figured out how it worked and how to counteract it, he'd be free to explore his options. After all, what was the harm in selling a disease for which there was a cure? Obviously, the U.S. military would already have it — thanks to whatever deal it had negotiated with NeXgen — and considering biological weapons were the nukes of the future, every country would need them to maintain the balance of mutually assured destruction. Hell, he'd be doing the entire world a service.

As soon as the brain trust here figured out the source of the immunity shared by Edgerton and Middleton and they handed over the infected bodies from the artic to his team for disposal, maybe he'd take some blood or tissue samples for himself. It's not like he was out in the field, surrounded by doctors and soldiers and watchdogs from the CDC, WHO, Red Cross, and just about every humanitarian agency known to man. He was in an underground lab in the middle of nowhere. A *private* lab. No one would notice a missing finger here or a toe there. A quick *snip-snip* and he'd be able to buy himself an island, maybe even one the size of Manhattan.

Brown and Pritchard were waiting for him in the communal room shared by the non-scientific staff, which consisted of security, custodial, and auxiliary personnel. In all, the facility housed 42 round-the-clock residential employees laboring under two-year contracts. The majority of the dedicated scientific staff worked on projects of such critical importance to NeXgen that they were sequestered from the general population and cut off from all forms of outside communication to eliminate any chance of industrial espionage, but when presented with an opportunity like this one, they were all expected to drop everything and give it their full attention.

Cullen's subordinates rose from their seats when he entered. Neither looked entirely comfortable in his new uniform.

"What are we still doing here?" Brown asked.

"Our contract specifies that we retain custody of any potential reservoirs of contagion until the pathogen, be it viral or bacterial, is officially classified as contained," Cullen said.

"We're in a secure lab hundreds of feet below the most desolate mountain range in the country. How much more contained can it possibly be?"

"Remember Mayibout?"

Brown opened his mouth to object, but no words came out. Of course, he remembered Mayibout. It wasn't the kind of experience that anyone who'd lived through it was likely to forget. Their rapid-response team had been dispatched to the small village in Gabon in response to reports of several inexplicable deaths by what appeared to be exsanguination. Upon arrival, they'd found that 28 individuals, primarily children, had been infected with Ebola after killing and eating a monkey carrying the virus. Ultimately, 24 of them had succumbed to the disease, but the parents had refused to allow Cullen's team to properly dispose of the remains on religious grounds, leading to an altercation that turned ugly in a hurry. Isolation suits had been torn, visors cracked, oxygen tanks ruptured, and bones broken. During the fracas, however, two mothers had deliberately infected themselves from their children's corpses in a primitive attempt at weaponization. They hadn't become symptomatic until after Cullen and his team had incinerated the children's remains and returned to Fort Detrick. By the time USAMRIID was alerted to the resurgence of the virus, a full half of Mayibout's population had been infected. They'd been forced to quarantine nearly a third of the country, close its borders, and work around the clock to contain a pandemic that could have easily gone global.

In the end, more than a hundred succumbed to the virus, and all because a few parents objected to cremating their children. Or perhaps because Cullen and his team hadn't been given the freedom to do what needed to be done. They could have quashed the insurgence and forced the others back into line with as little as a single shot — topple the first domino and the rest will fall — but instead, they'd spent three straight days burning the bodies of men, women, and children who shouldn't have had to die in the first place.

"You mean we're here until they're done with the remains we brought back with us," Pritchard said.

"Not just the remains," Cullen said.

He left the implications unsaid. Brown and Pritchard had been doing this for long enough that they knew exactly what he meant. The survivors were integral to understanding the nature of the contagion, but they could never be allowed to tell anyone of the existence of a facility like Riverton, let alone about the virus and the events that had transpired in Alaska. Edgerton, Paulson, and Middleton were just as dead as the rest of their colleagues.

They just didn't know it yet.

CULLEN TURNED at the sound of footsteps approaching from the outer corridor, coming in fast. A man wearing surgical scrubs pushed through the doorway between Brown and Pritchard, crossed his arms over his chest, and openly appraised the three of them. With his buzz cut, hooded eyes, and protruding jaw, Cullen would have recognized him anywhere.

"I didn't initially believe it when they said you guys collected the remains, but I should have known better," Rankin said. "This one has your stink all over it."

He clapped Pritchard on the shoulder, embraced Brown, and saluted Cullen.

"Major Phil Rankin," Cullen said. "I thought you abandoned us to go into the private sector."

The virologist had been part of his rapid-response team before being seduced by the CDC, despite Cullen's best efforts to intervene. Rankin had something of a sixth sense for viruses and the ability to lay bare their inner workings. He and Ward had made a formidable duo when it came to quickly diagnosing an unknown condition in the field and plotting a plan for containment. Identify, isolate, and terminate with maximum prejudice, as they'd said.

"Surprisingly, they still wanted me, even after the less-than-glowing recommendation from my commanding officer," Rankin said. The tone of his voice suggested he hadn't entirely gotten past the attempted sabotage, but Cullen didn't care any more now than he had then. "It didn't take, though. A guy can only stare at so many samples under a microscope before he starts jonesing for the real thing." He glanced around the room, then back at Cullen. "Where's Ward? I thought he with you guys in Alaska."

"He lost his nerve," Cullen said.

Rankin nodded solemnly. Anyone who'd been a part of a rapid-response team for any length of time recognized that there was no quicker way to get the entire team killed.

"I don't blame him," he said. "Judging by the condition of those bodies, I can only imagine what kind of mess you guys walked into up there."

"You've seen the remains?" Brown said.

"What do you think I've been doing while you guys were sitting around with your thumbs up your asses?" Rankin smirked and gestured for them to follow him. He led them down a sterile white corridor that could have been plucked from any hospital around the world. The closed doors on either side were flanked by golden nameplates and touchscreen computer monitors and surveilled by domed cameras on the ceiling. "I participated in the autopsies of Hays Montgomery and Judson Moore. It was easy enough to confirm that their wounds had been inflicted by fists, fingernails, and teeth, and that they'd both died of their injuries. What's interesting, though, is that the virus transferred from the saliva of the attackers had already begun to replicate within the wounds in the time it took for them to bleed out."

"What are the implications?" Pritchard asked.

"Such an aggressive reaction is exceedingly rare since it involves both suppressing the host's immune system and transcribing the virus's genome into the host cell's DNA, stimulating it to begin mass-producing the virus so it can spread throughout the body. Ordinarily, this is a slow process, as anyone who's ever come down with the flu will tell you, but this bad boy is different. It's almost as though it's able to speed up the rate of infection by instigating death at a cellular level, forcing the host's cells to replicate as fast as possible to compensate for the die-off, which results in spreading the disease at a rate that defies rational explanation."

Rankin guided them into a lounge with a table in the center, a coffee maker and refrigerator in the corner, and couches along the walls. He blew past them on his way to the lone sealed doorway at the back of the room, which opened upon a locker room with Level A Hazmat suits hanging from the walls.

"Whether fortunately or not," he said, "the rapid die-off of cells comes at a steep theoretical price. If my hypothesis is correct and the virus programs every cell it infects to self-destruct as a means of accelerating the course of the infection, once it infiltrates each of the various interconnected systems, the cumulative effect will cause advanced physical deterioration and death at the organismic level, which we're already beginning to see with Patient Gamma—"

"Who?" Cullen asked.

"You know him as Nate Paulson. His hemorrhagic symptoms are progressing at a rate that makes Ebola look like it's not even trying."

"What about the secondary symptoms?" Cullen asked.

"You mean the aggression? We've made considerable headway in that regard, but it'd help if we had some pre-infection lab tests and medical imagery to help corroborate the anomalies we discovered during the autopsies."

"What'd you find?"

The four men donned their protective isolation suits while Rankin explained.

"As you'd expect, the CBC demonstrated diminished levels of red blood cells and platelets from the bleeding and dramatic increases in white blood cells and lymphocytes. We suspect the virus is also responsible for the increase in monocytes — the phagocytic leukocytes that remove injured or dead cells — and their aggregation inside the wounds. Overall, the lab values paint a picture of a hemorrhagic virus not unlike Ebola in its outward expression, but completely unique in its hematological response."

"I don't follow," Pritchard said.

"It's like the virus is attempting to keep the body of its host alive for as long as possible to increase its chances of spreading," Rankin said. "Think of it like a tiny parasitic mosquito that can't survive outside of another organism, one that somehow gets inside of you and breeds until there's an entire swarm. Now, a mosquito can't change its nature; it needs to suck your blood to reproduce, but it knows that if it takes a little at a time, your body will keep making more. As the demand increases, however, the swarm starts taking blood faster than you can replenish it. There's no doubt you'll eventually die from the blood loss, and since these mosquitoes require a host to live, they need a foolproof way to make sure you spread them to someone else before you die, which, I believe, is where the physical changes come into play."

"What physical changes?" Cullen asked.

Rankin raised his face to the retinal scanner and allowed the laser to map the pattern of blood vessels inside his eye. A red light flashed above the sealed door, which opened upon an airlock with chemical showers protruding from the exposed pipes overhead. Once they were all inside and the door was closed behind them, Rankin pressed the button to open the next door in the sequence and admitted them to the inner sanctum. They attached the coiled hoses hanging from the ceiling to their suits and advanced into a laboratory that must have cost a fortune. Every surface was stainless steel, every wall made of spotless Plexiglas, every floor tile polished to such an extent that it reflected the overhead lights.

"We found dramatic increases in the size of the liver, thymus, spleen, and the entire daisy chain of lymph nodes. Stands to reason given the elevated immune response, right? There's also acute inflammation of the brain and spinal cord, which, coupled with the dramatic swelling of the hindbrain — what you'd consider the primitive or animalian brain — causes compression and displacement of the cerebrum. We suspect the combination of the two is responsible for the impairment of higher-order mental capabilities and the transference of situational responses to the autonomic nervous system, whose sole function is the survival of the organism."

"So the infected are at the mercy of their lizard brains."

"That's an oversimplification," Rankin said. "Think of their brains as more like those of higher orders of sharks. The great white's overall structure is similar to ours, only its cerebrum is much smaller and its hindbrain much larger, proportionately. Its hindbrain also houses its brain center, the amygdaloid nucleus, which, much like the amygdalae in our temporal lobes, mediates instinctive fight-or-flight responses. While we might encounter someone we don't immediately recognize in a dark alley and remain wary of the potential threat until we're able to rationalize the situation, a shark's response occurs at a basic, binary level — a yes-no proposition — independent of the learned responses stored in the cerebrum. Every reaction to an unknown situation is determined by instinct alone, attack or flee, with the solitary goal being the survival of the individual."

Rankin led the procession through a maze of laboratories staffed by men in the same yellow suits and attached to similar coiled tubing inside the suites. They passed autopsy rooms, where bodies Cullen only vaguely recognized were at various stages of the process, and labs stocked with microscopes, centrifuges, and all kinds of equipment he'd never seen before. There was a miniature morgue with multiple climate-controlled drawers and an access-restricted door labeled CREMATORIUM.

"Once we're finished with the autopsies, we can begin more thorough dissection to compare and contrast anatomical structures and evaluate brain chemistry," Rankin said. "Meanwhile, we wait on the genomic analysis of the virus, which should be complete any minute now."

"What about the others?" Brown asked.

"You mean the living specimens?" Rankin turned and looked back at him with an expression of confusion. "Were you under the impression I was giving you the grand tour? I'm taking you to them. As long as they're here, they're your responsibility."

The corridor ended at another security door. Rankin again allowed the laser to scan his eye, detached the oxygen, and reattached his suit to the tubing on the other side. This section was different than the last. Gone were the stainless-steel countertops, transparent walls, and clinical sterility of the scientific suites. In their place were enclosures like prison cells, only with Plexiglas windows instead of bars, airtight doors reminiscent of those on a submarine, and self-contained air circulation. Inside were plastic tables and chairs, sloping tiled floors with inset drains, beds with vinyl sheets, and bathrooms with half-walls that offered little in the way of privacy.

Cullen revised his assessment; they were more like cages in a zoo than prison cells, designed to be scoured with chemical solutions and high-pressure hoses.

There were six units on either side, twelve in all, leading to an enclosed surveillance station with its own dedicated air supply, a bank of monitors, and a cabinet containing weaponry the likes of which even Cullen had never seen before. The window of the third unit on the left appeared to have been hurriedly painted a rust color from the inside. It wasn't until he was nearly upon it that he realized it was blood, which preserved smudged handprints and—

Something struck the window from the opposite side.

Cullen inched closer and peered through the streaks—

Another impact.

A hand smeared the blood, just enough to reveal the face of the man inside. Paulson was nearly unrecognizable. His nose was smashed, his front teeth broken at the roots, his lips pulped. Only his eyes stood apart from the mask of blood, his eyes completely lacking humanity.

"Jesus," Brown said.

They passed a pair of empty cells and stopped before the last one on the right. Middleton rested under the covers, her eyes closed, a bedside monitor beside her.

"She still hasn't awakened," Rankin said. "Her vitals are steady and within normal ranges, so it shouldn't be much longer now."

If he said anything else, Cullen didn't hear it. He'd already turned to look through the window of the room opposite hers. Edgerton stood at the inset window, staring straight through him, as though dissecting him like Rankin had the bodies down the hall. A smile crossed the anthropologist's face. His eyes collapsed in upon themselves and became swirling pits of darkness from which not even light could escape. He seemed to simultaneously stretch and expand until he filled the entire window, horns erupting from his forehead—

Cullen whirled and looked at the others, but they appeared oblivious as they continued to talk among themselves, their mouths forming words he couldn't hear over the thunder of his pulse. He again faced Edgerton, who simply stood there, exactly as he had before.

Normal, save for the expression on his face, which caused a shiver to ripple up Cullen's spine.

RILEY FELT as though she were swimming through marshmallow fluff. Her mind was foggy, and every movement seemed slow and deliberate, her arms and legs taking their own sweet time responding to her mental commands. She opened her eyes, but the light was too bright, so she closed them again. Her chest felt heavy, every breath coming slowly, methodically. She smelled chemicals and heard a mechanized thrum reminiscent of an air conditioner.

The last thing she clearly remembered was hiding in the complete and utter darkness, the air so cold she couldn't stop her body from shivering. She recalled covering her mouth and nose to smother the sounds of her breathing and chattering teeth, listening to something stalking her through the rocky fissure, and then the rumble of the helicopter outside. She relived her escape in her mind: tumbling from her hiding place, scurrying through the tunnel, emerging to see the chopper hovering over the camp, a man in a Hazmat suit crouching in its open doorway, his rifle aimed at her chest—

Riley gasped and sat up. The world spun around her as vague shapes resolved from her blurred vision. She pawed at her chest until she felt a surgical dressing where she'd been shot. The tissue surrounding it was swollen, the resultant bruising sensitive to even the slightest touch. Lights flashed from the corner of her eye. It took several seconds to realize that they belonged to the jagged lines streaking across the monitor, the corresponding numeric values, and the muted alarm icon. She pried the gray pulse oximeter from the tip of her index finger, the EKG electrodes from her chest, and the IV from her arm, causing a rivulet of blood to roll down her forearm and onto the covers.

"Try to relax, Dr. Middleton," a voice said. It sounded hollow, as though amplified through a speaker, and seemed to come from all around her at once. "You're safe now."

The room around her slowly came into focus: surgical lights on armatures above her, walls paneled with white laminate material, a shower stall in the corner that appeared to be little more than a cubicle under a square head. The linens covering her felt strangely heavy and appeared almost rubberized. The twin lumps of her feet were silhouetted against a large observation window, on the other side of which stood several men in yellow isolation suits, their faces invisible behind the reflections on their visors.

A single thought cut through the confusion, one so clear and insistent that it dispelled her fugue.

This wasn't a hospital.

And with that realization came a sudden surge of panic. She tried to jump out of bed, but her legs betrayed her and deposited her on the floor, forcing her to drag herself into the corner, away from the unknown men. For the first time, she noticed she was wearing surgical scrubs and realized that someone had changed her while she was unconscious.

"What you're experiencing right now are the residual effects of the anesthesia," the voice said. "You were tranquilized in the field for the safety of the team responsible for your rescue."

Riley traced the contours of the bandage underneath her gown. She remembered trying to pry the syringe from her chest as she stumbled down the talus slope, losing her balance and falling to the hard earth, men in Hazmat suits holding her down and strapping her to a backboard.

"My name is Dr. Phil Rankin," the voice said. "I'm the chief scientific officer of the National Medical Biodefense Program, working in conjunction with the United States Army Medical Research Institute of Infectious Diseases and the Centers for Disease Control and Prevention. You're currently in a secure research and treatment facility outside of Riverton, Wyoming, managed by NeXgen Biotechnology and Pharmaceuticals, who alerted us to the developing situation after you reported Dr. Edgerton's condition and called for evacuation."

"What happened . . . ?" she said, but the words came out garbled, forcing her to start again. "What happened to the others?"

"We can discuss that later, once you're feeling better."

"We'll talk about that now," she said, struggling to her feet on trembling legs.

Riley swayed momentarily before staggering to the inset window. She traced the contours of the door beside it, its edges hermetically sealed. There was no handle on the inside, and it didn't budge when she leaned her shoulder into it.

"How much do you remember about what happened at the camp?" Rankin asked.

She scooted sideways across the Plexiglas until she was face-to-face with the man speaking into the microphone, which projected from the beneath the computer monitor on the other side of the window. She'd never seen him before. She was certain of it. The man next to him, though . . . she'd definitely seen his face . . . down the barrel of his rifle before he shot her in the chest.

"Everyone was sick," she said. She pictured Dale with his pale face, sweat beading on his brow, the same symptoms she'd witnessed with the grad students who'd gone to bed early, Maria and Nate—

She heard a banging sound, like someone hurling himself against a wall, again and again. The men turned around and glanced beyond her range of sight.

"Oh, God," she whispered.

It was all coming back to her now. She saw Sadie straddling Montgomery, her teeth buried in his neck; Williams crumpled on the ground, his face a macerated mess of blood; Maria and Nate, rising from Judson's body and chasing her into the cave. She'd heard them killing each other in the darkness, tearing each other apart with their bare hands and teeth, and she'd felt something moving mere inches away from her, something even more frightening than the infected students hunting her.

Riley looked over the shoulder of the man who'd shot her. On the other side of the hallway stood Dale Edgerton, his hands pressed to the window of his enclosure, his eyes recessed into shadows, his mouth an impassive line. She blinked and his appearance changed. In his place stood the mummified corpse from the cave, desiccated flesh stretched over ancient bone, his parchment skin tattooed by scars from healed lacerations, the skull of a steppe bison concealing his face. His tattered lids parted, revealing eyes the color of fire—

She opened her mouth to scream, but he was again only Dale Edgerton, the same small, petty man she'd found inside the cave, his face crawling with mosquitoes, uttering the same four words, over and over.

All going to die. All going to die. All going to—

"Dr. Middleton?"

Riley shook her head to clear the memory and returned her attention to Rankin.

"I remember waking up to find the students . . . attacking . . . everyone."

"It's our understanding that Dr. Edgerton was the first to become symptomatic," Rankin said. "Is that correct?"

Riley nodded and again glanced across the hall, but Edgerton was no longer standing at the glass.

"Describe for me everything that happened after you called for medical assistance."

"We took turns monitoring his fever. We thought . . . I remember we thought he'd be fine once the helicopter arrived. That if we got him to a hospital . . . "

"What about the others?"

"Maria and Nate retired to their shared tent early that night. I checked on them and could tell . . . they'd cast aside their sleeping bags and were sweating profusely. Niles and I . . . " An image of Williams's defleshed face flashed before her eyes. "We discussed evacuating the entire camp when the rescue team arrived . . . only by then . . . "

Riley closed her eyes to forestall the tears. Now was not the time to fall apart.

"Take your time, Dr. Middleton," Rankin said.

When she opened her eyes again, the tears were gone and she was once more in command of her voice.

"Are Dale and I the only survivors?"

Again, she heard a thumping sound from down the corridor, but Rankin paid it no mind and looked her dead in the eyes when he spoke.

"Yes. None of the others made it."

She nodded and backed away from the Plexiglas. She'd failed them. Maria, Nate, Sadie, Judson. Montgomery and Williams. She'd failed them all.

"What happened to them?" she asked.

"We're still trying to figure out exactly what we're dealing with. We know it's a hemorrhagic virus with a short incubation period, but not a whole lot else at this point. I'm sure that's not much comfort to you right now. You have a lot to process. Unfortunately, we don't have time to let you work through your feelings. We need your help if we're going to make any kind of meaningful breakthrough."

The implications of his words suddenly hit her. She felt the energy drain from her body and had to take a seat at the edge of the bed.

"I'm infected," she said.

"Quite the contrary," Rankin said. "The fact that you never developed symptoms suggests you have an innate immunity. We collected samples of the virus from your skin and the mucous membranes of your mouth and nose, but neither your blood nor your tissue samples show signs of infection. Somehow, your immune system simply destroyed it before it began the process of replication."

"What about Dale? He came down with it and he appears to be okay."

"His is an acquired immunity. He needed to contract the disease for his body to produce the antibodies necessary to fight it off."

"So if we're immune, you can let us out of these cages."

Rankin hesitated before speaking.

"The problem is that while you're demonstrably immune, we have no way of knowing if any of the rest of us are. At least not yet."

"You're telling me we're your prisoners until you figure out what's going on."

"Try not to think of it like that."

"How am I supposed to think of it?"

"You're now an integral part of our team. We need your help figuring out not only what makes this virus tick, but how it can be defeated. You've seen what this thing can do. Imagine what would happen if it were released in a major population center."

"And what happens to Dale and me if you can't?"

She raised her head and met his stare, but he averted his eyes.

"Let's just hope we don't have to plan for that contingency."

Rankin released the button on the microphone with a *click* that reverberated throughout the room. He turned without another word and started down the hallway. The other men followed, minus the man who'd shot her. He stared at her through the observation window for several unendurable seconds, during which time she read the truth in his eyes.

If they couldn't crack the virus's code, then it would fall to him to make sure that neither she nor Edgerton left this place alive.

RANKIN once more stood at the window of the negative-pressure observation suite, only this time the focus of his attention was a subject of a dramatically different nature. The monitor displayed an elapsed time of 02:56:17 since Rich

Hanson, their lead animal handler, had been exposed to the virus through the lacerations inflicted by the claws of the infected chimpanzee. They'd sedated him, exchanged his bloodstained isolation suit for scrubs, and taken great pains to clean and suture his wounds. He now lay strapped to a gurney in the middle of the same room where the primate had died, away from the prying eyes of his coworkers, who would likely find the treatment of one of their own . . . objectionable. He needed to remain down here among the animals, out of sight and out of mind, to eliminate the risk of someone interfering with Rankin's doing what needed to be done. If Hanson were to be housed with the human subjects from Alaska, the other scientists would notice his rapidly deteriorating condition and attempt to arrest the progression of the disease, which, as far as Rankin was concerned, was not part of the plan.

He'd realigned the cameras to provide dedicated imagery of each of Hanson's individual wounds and his entire face, which allowed the AI software to track his eye movements and the nearly undetectable contractions of his facial muscles. His skin had become shockingly pale from the sheer volume of blood he'd lost to his injuries and the samples Rankin had acquired. So far, his temperature was holding steady around 100 degrees as his body ramped up for the fight of its life, one it was most likely destined to lose.

"What do you want me to do if he begins exhibiting symptoms?" Dr. Cynthia Mathers asked.

Rankin watched the physician's reflection in the glass. She stood beside him, her features bathed in the blue glow of the tablet she used to monitor Hanson's vital signs, her isolation suit far too large for her slender frame. As the ranking medical officer at the National Medical Biodefense Program, he'd worked closely with her for the past two years and could count on her discretion, if not her blind loyalty. She was really asking what she was supposed to do when Hanson's suffering became too great; she wanted permission to deliver the cocktail of midazolam, pancuronium bromide, and potassium chloride loaded into the autoinjector attached to his IV line, which would cause respiratory arrest and stop his heart, but Rankin wasn't about to give it. If they were going to defeat this virus, they needed to know absolutely everything about it, and they might never have an opportunity like this one again.

"Nothing," Rankin said. "Let the virus run its course."

16

New York City, New York

Milana watched the men from the funeral home load her grandmother's body into the back of the waiting van. They closed the rear doors with a thudding sound that seemed to drain her of the last of her energy. She collapsed on the stoop and buried her face in her hands. Mrs. Lovato placed her hand on top of Milana's head and gently stroked her hair.

"It's going to be all right," she said.

Milana nodded for the older woman's benefit, but it wasn't going to be.

The engine started and the red glare of taillights stained the night. She raised her head as the van pulled away from the curb, ferrying her *pūridaia* away. She'd never felt such soul-deep loneliness. The one person who'd tethered her to this life was gone, leaving her at the mercy of forces beyond her control. Mrs. Lovato had been kind enough to come over and help her make all of the arrangements she'd never discussed with her grandmother. Who picked up the body and where did they take it? Were both the exterior and interior routes to the collection site unobstructed? Did she have proper identification for both of them? Milana wouldn't have had the slightest idea of where to begin had it not been for her neighbor, who hadn't been able to hide the relief in her voice when she realized she was finally off the hook. That wasn't to say she wasn't a genuinely caring and compassionate woman, only that charity was like taffy in the sense that it could only be stretched so far before the burden became too great.

"Is there anyone I can call for you, honey?"

Milana shook her head. That wasn't entirely true, though; there was still one call that needed to be made, but she was the only one who could make it.

"You know, you're welcome to stay with Raul and me for a few days," Mrs. Lovato said. "I don't like the idea of you going back in there all by yourself. You have so much going on in your life as it is, and you need time to process everything and grieve—"

"Thank you," Milana said. She looked up into the older woman's eyes and gave her hand a gentle squeeze. "I appreciate your offer. More than I could ever hope to express, but I've known this day was coming for a long time. That doesn't make it any easier, you know? It just means . . . we've asked so much of you already and you've done way more — for both of us — than anyone else in your situation would have done. I think . . . I think this is the part I have to handle on my own."

Mrs. Lovato nodded. Her eyes brimmed with tears, one of which broke free and rolled down her cheek.

"The offer stands," she said. "It's been a long time since we've had children around the house. It would be nice to have someone to spoil for a little while."

"Thank you," Milana said.

Mrs. Lovato descended several steps, stopped, and looked back up at her, their faces only inches apart.

"Every time I came over, your grandmother told me how proud of you she was," she said. "How strong you are. But you don't have to be strong all the time."

The older woman cupped Milana's face, leaned in close—

—*the tiny vessels in Mrs. Lovato's eyes rupture and blood replaces her tears. Milana hears sirens and the* whupp-whupp-whupp *of a helicopter as though from a million miles away. She averts her eyes and catches a glimpse of the street below through the window. The asphalt sparkles with broken glass from a car that hopped the curb and hit the stoop of the building across the street. The passengers lay nearby in pools of blood, as though they've been dragged through the shattered windshield and slaughtered right there in the middle of the road*—

—and planted a kiss squarely on her forehead.

Milana gasped and jerked her face from Mrs. Lovato's hands. She staggered backward, frantically looking from one side of the deserted street to the other. There was no one there. No wrecked cars or dead bodies or sirens wailing from the inner city.

"Honey?" Mrs. Lovato said. "Are you all—?"

"I'm fine," Milana said. She took a deep breath and regained her composure. None of what she thought she'd seen had been real. She was simply exhausted from trying to work two jobs on top of going to school and taking care of her grandmother, whose death had simply been the mental straw that broke the camel's back. "I just — I'm fine. Thank you for everything, Mrs. Lovato. I don't know what I would have done without you."

Milana left the older woman staring up at her and ducked inside the townhouse. The tears she thought she'd cried out returned with a vengeance, but she refused to let them break her. Not yet, anyway. She was going to need all of the strength she had left if she was going to do what needed to be done.

She entered her apartment and closed the door. The neon light still glowed in the window. She pulled the cord and welcomed the darkness, which helped conceal the reminders of her grandmother all around her. The decorations on the walls, the furniture, the smells, the memories assailing her from all directions at once.

In that moment, she was simultaneously infinite versions of herself, at every age between the moment she'd been abandoned at her grandmother's house and now. Posing for pictures on first and last days of school, preparing for ballet recitals and school dances, watching her grandmother work through the gap between the velvet curtains, eating those world-famous stuffed peppers, and reliving every conversation, all at once. The years blew past like a draft from another room, and then they were gone, stranding her in a house made hollow by the absence within its walls, haunted by the omnipresent sounds of traffic and car horns as life outside kept going as though nothing had happened.

It took several minutes to find where she'd left her cellphone after making the call to the funeral home. The clock on the wall chimed three times, wrenching her from her thoughts. She had to leave for work in an hour. No one would be able to cover for her now and she couldn't afford to lose this job. A shower would wake her up — not that she would have been able to sleep anyway — and she could make herself a stiff triple-espresso once she got to the shop, but there was something she needed to do first, the one task she'd been dreading more than any other since she'd realized that her grandmother wasn't going to get better.

Milana brushed through the curtains and made her way to the staircase beneath the watchful eyes of long-lost family members she hoped were celebrating the arrival of the woman who'd burned candles for each of them for all these years. She entered her grandmother's room and stared at the empty bed. The covers were rumpled, cast aside by the men who'd collected her body, and the pillow still bore the impression of the back of her head. It smelled of her soap, the stale scents of age, and an undercurrent Milana would never forget for as long as she lived, the indescribable aroma of death that drove home the fact that her grandmother was truly gone.

Your păridaia can no longer protect you.

The bedroom vanished and she was again staring into the face of the old man, his eyelids so thin she could feel his stare upon her, the smell of death amplified tenfold. His cadaver-like fingernails bit into the flesh of her fore-arms and he drew her face to within inches of his own, his breath that of carrion rotting on the side of the road on a late August afternoon.

No one can save you from what is coming.

Milana screamed and returned to the here and now. She was in her grand-mother's bedroom, the tapestries on the walls the same ones she'd first seen upon entering the room, scarves belonging to women in her family dating back hundreds of years, reminders that they were all part of one unique patchwork quilt that would keep her warm when the nights grew cold, which, she could feel, they soon would.

She knelt beside the bed, rummaged underneath it until she found what she was looking for, and pulled it out. The wooden jewelry box was so old that the hinges had turned to rust and the clasp would have broken with the weight of even the smallest lock, but the wood was strong and discolored by the countless hands that had held it. She opened it and smelled her grand-mother again as though she'd just stepped into the room, and then it was gone, never to return.

Milana had always known where her grandmother hid the box and what was inside, and yet it had remained something of an unspoken secret between them. It would be there when she needed it, and not a moment before. Opening it was not so much an admission of weakness as a sign of finality. She'd never had to tell her *pūridaia* that she thought of her as her true mother any more than her grandmother had needed to admit failing Milana's mother, or pay penance by raising her granddaughter as her own child. Theirs had always been a special relationship that required no words, and yet that was exactly what she found waiting for her, on top of the stacks of paper and envelopes, a single sheet of stationary bearing two sentences scrawled in the hand of a woman who barely had the strength to hold the pen.

You must remain strong, Milana. He is afraid of your light and will do every-thing in his power to extinguish it.

Milana reread the message several times before setting it aside. She had no idea what it was supposed to mean, or if it was simply the ramblings of an old woman who knew her time had come. Underneath it was the folder she'd hoped to find, labeled only ROSELLA. Inside were letters her grandmother had saved for the return addresses on the envelopes. She'd catalogued all of them on a sheet of notebook paper, listed by date, so she'd have them should she ever need to track down her wayward daughter, if only to make sure she was still alive. There was a similar list of phone numbers, the most recent of which was from four months ago.

"You can do this," Milana whispered.

She typed the digits into her cellphone and walked aimlessly around the room while she worked up the courage to call the woman who'd never been able to love her. Once she was certain she wouldn't break down into tears at the sound of her mother's voice, she took a deep breath and pressed SEND.

While she listened to the call ring through, she parted the curtains over the window and looked out into the night. The old man was out there, staring up at her from the shadows beneath the tree across the street. He removed his fedora, held it to his chest, and cocked his head to better appraise her from the distance. A horrible smile appeared on his face.

"Mmm . . . hello?"

And then he was gone, as though he'd never been there at all. A mischief of rats scurried over the bags of garbage piled on the curb and funneled through the grate into the sewer.

"Rosella?" Milana asked.

"Who is this?"

"It's me. Milana." She let the curtains fall from her fingers and slumped to the floor. "Sorry to wake you. I just thought you'd want to know that your mother died."

ALL THE TRAVEL had finally caught up with Ward. During the past 48 hours, he'd taken a plane to Cambridge, Massachusetts, where a car had been waiting to drive him to the NeXgen corporate offices for a briefing with no actual substance, before returning to the airport and boarding a plane bound for Fairbanks and the waiting Black Hawk. Not to mention everything that had happened afterward, including the collection of infected bodies that looked like they'd tried to eat each other, the tranquilization and subsequent abduction of the survivors, the incineration of the camp, and the hurried dissolution of his career and professional working relationships. Now here he was at Minneapolis-St. Paul International Airport, a completely different man, in more ways than one.

He knew there was no way Cullen would simply let him walk away. He'd seen the lengths to which his commanding officer had gone to spike Rankin's transfer, including accusations of misconduct, profiteering, and outright treason. And that had been while they were working under the auspices of USAMRIID, which required documentation in triplicate every time a guy so much as thought about breathing. Out here in the real world, without multiple layers of bureaucracy to shield him from Cullen's wrath, he could only imagine how far a man he'd once considered his friend would be willing to go to punish him for abandoning the team.

Of course, this hadn't been a spur-of-the-moment decision. He'd been actively preparing for this eventuality for nearly three years and had plotted several courses of action for when the time came to disappear, depending on where he was when he finally worked up the guts and just how poorly Cullen took the news. Unlike Brown and Pritchard, who'd been living lives of excess with their newfound fortunes, he'd been squirreling his away into offshore real estate investments and accounts under various names and shell companies, all of which were perfectly legal. At least in the Cayman Islands, where he had a beachfront condo and a boat that could take him just about anywhere in the world he wanted to go. Maybe not him specifically, at least so far as the Trevor Ward identity was concerned.

Mr. Ward had booked a flight from Fairbanks to San Francisco, by way of Anchorage, ostensibly to retire to the condo he maintained under his real name in Golden Gate Heights. By the time whoever Cullen had waiting for him at San Francisco International realized he wasn't on the plane and backtracked to Anchorage — where they'd find that Mr. Ward had switched tickets with an Uber driver named Geoff Tilton, whose bank account was currently ten grand richer thanks to one simple electronic transaction — he'd be on the ground in New York City, where he owned an apartment in Midtown. Inside were all of the trappings of his new life, including fake IDs, passports, and bank books belonging to each, all stuffed into a wall safe he could quickly access on his way from LaGuardia to Newark Liberty International, where a flight to Miami was booked under the name Paulo Savino. A single plane ride later and he'd be on Grand Cayman Island with the entire world spread out before him.

"Mr. Tilton?" the check-in agent said. She waved his ticket in front of his face.

"Sorry," he said. "It's been a long couple of days."

Her smile was forced and suggested she neither cared nor appreciated him holding up the boarding process.

Ward was one of the last passengers on the plane, which meant he had to stand in the tunnel seemingly forever and wait until everyone else was seated. He crawled over the people in the aisle and middle seats, stuffed his bag under the chair in front of him, and stared out the porthole window, past the vast expanse of runways, toward where the evergreens serrated the pale blue sky. It must have been the sense of relief flooding through his body, because he'd never been this tired in his entire life. He pulled down the window shade, leaned his head against the wall, and prepared to enjoy the next two-and-a-half hours of blissful sleep.

Everything was falling into place just as he'd planned. By this time tomorrow, he'd finally be free.

He took a deep breath, released it as a long, contented sigh, and closed his eyes. Memories assaulted him from the darkness behind his lids. Edgerton rose before him, his body stretching and expanding as though made of smoke, the anthropologist's eyes dark holes that captured Ward's stare and refused to relinquish it, incapacitating him long enough to extend a single finger, cracking his visor with the merest touch.

Once more, he's transported to a world of fire and ash, where shadows attack each other through the roiling smoke and corpses litter the ground. He sees his own face, blood running down his cheeks like tears —

Ward opened his eyes and choked back the cry that had risen to his lips. His hands shook and he was on the verge of hyperventilating. He took several deep, calming breaths, dialed up the airflow from the overhead nozzle, and tried to get comfortable once more. The physical and mental fatigue had obviously taken their toll, plus these flying germ incubators were always stiflingly hot until they started taxiing. This one especially, although he *had* been north of the Arctic Circle mere hours ago. Going from one temperature extreme to the other in such a short period of time undoubtedly explained the sweat blooming from his brow and causing his shirt to cling to his chest.

MILANA HOVERED at the security perimeter surrounding baggage claim. She probably could have just walked inside, but with as nervous as she felt, security would likely take one good look at her and escort her right out of LaGuardia. The caffeine obviously didn't help. Her hands trembled so badly that she undoubtedly looked like a tweaker in need of a score, but the truth of the matter was that if she sat down for any length of time, she'd simply fall asleep. She couldn't afford to rest now, though, not while there was still so much to do.

She needed to go down to the mortuary and meet with the funeral director so they could determine what to do with her grandmother's body. She'd specifically asked Milana to make sure she was cremated and scatter her ashes with those of her husband, who resided in a bronze urn in her closet-shrine, surrounded by pictures, dried flowers, and candles melted right to the tabletop, but, unfortunately, nothing could ever be easy. Milana had to pick out an urn, decide if she wanted a viewing first, sign all kinds of official government paperwork, and, of course, max out her credit card to cover the expense. At least until she received the life insurance check, the thought of which was probably the only reason she'd been able to convince her mother to drag her weary ass out of bed and head down to McCarron to catch the red eye from Vegas to New York.

On the positive side, Milana's professors had been willing to work with her to make sure she didn't fall too far behind while she was handling her grandmother's affairs. It turned out practicing psychologists could be fairly understanding when it came to things like the death of a loved one, although she was going to have to produce a copy of the death certificate, which the school could keep as far as she was concerned; it wasn't like she had any intention of framing it and hanging it on the wall. In fact, she didn't know what the hell she was going to do from here and she didn't figure the woman who'd be coming down the escalators from the terminal any second now would be much help. Her mother probably just wanted to liquidate the entire estate, take her cut, and go back to doing whatever it was she did, which was why it was a good thing she wasn't the primary beneficiary, although Milana was going to let the lawyer share that little surprise. It was up to her to determine what to do with the money and the townhouse, both of which she would have traded in a heartbeat to talk to her *pūridaia* one last time, if only to ask her what the note she'd found in the chest meant. Who was "he" and what was "extinguish" her light supposed to mean?

Milana watched the bags pass on the distant carousel through a zoetrope of waiting travelers. The lighted sign said they belonged to passengers of flights 1637 from Dallas-Fort Worth, 1274 from Las Vegas, and 2793 from Minneapolis, and yet none of the people fighting for space was her mother. She glanced at the escalator for what had to be the thousandth time, but there was still no sign of her.

"If she missed that flight . . . "

Milana awakened her cellphone and once more confirmed that the flight had landed on time and checked to make sure she didn't have any missed calls or messages. Nothing. She peeked at the suitcase belonging to a man exiting baggage claim through the turnstile beside her and saw the numbers 1637. Maybe the passengers from her mother's flight simply hadn't made it down here yet or, more likely, her mother had stopped in the first duty-free shop she passed, grabbed a bottle of whatever was cheapest, and was currently pounding it down in a bathroom stall. That Milana's mind even went there made her want to cry.

A porter with a rolling dolly passed in front of the rail.

"Excuse me," Milana said. "Do you know if the bags on the carousel are from Vegas?"

"Sorry," he said, and just kept right on going.

Someone bumped her from behind. She braced herself against the railing and flung the spilled coffee from the back of her hand. It was getting more crowded by the second and if she and her mother didn't leave here soon, it would take them an hour to get to the East Side. And the influx of people posed another problem she hadn't considered until that very moment. It had been three years since she'd last seen her mother, and three years was a long time for someone living as hard as her mother was. What if she didn't recognize her? Or worse, what if her mother didn't recognize *her*?

A tear crept from the corner of her eye, but she quickly wiped it away. Not today. If her *pūridaia* wanted her to be strong, then by God, that's what she was going to do.

She finished her coffee, rinsed the travel mug in the drinking fountain, and stuffed it into her backpack. There was no way her mother had missed that flight, not when there was money at stake. She'd be here.

Milana went back to the railing and resumed watching the travelers funneling down the escalators, fanning out around the carousels, and exiting through the automatic doors behind her.

"EXCUSE ME?" The woman's voice sounded like it came from the bottom of a well. "Sir?"

Ward felt the flight attendant nudge his shoulder and opened his eyes. The woman's smile faltered when he looked at her. She glanced down the aisle toward the front of the plane, where the last handful of passengers were squeezing out the front door and the other flight attendants were picking their way through the rows, collecting the trash the slobs had left behind.

"Sorry," he mumbled, dragging his backpack out from beneath the seat in front of him. He hadn't even heard the plane land or the commotion around him as the others fought their way out.

The flight attendant smiled but gave him a wide berth. The others simply watched him from the corners of their eyes as he passed. He must have looked even worse than he felt, which hardly seemed possible given the pounding in his head and the throbbing behind his eyes. So many pressure and altitude changes over such a brief span of time could do that. From sea level to the mountains, the 42nd parallel to the 68th, and back again. He just needed to get moving, flood his system with water and caffeine, and grab something to eat.

Ward nodded to the captain, ducked out the door, and headed up the ramp. A single breath of New York air and he could already feel the exhaust settling into his lungs. He worked through the throng of passengers waiting to board the plane he'd just disembarked and fought his way into the foot traffic in the terminal. Someone rushing in the opposite direction clipped his shoulder and spun him around. The ground tilted and he struggled to regain his balance. He needed to do something about this infernal headache before it got any worse. It was already making him feel sick to his stomach.

He found the nearest restroom, splashed cold water on his face, cupped his hands under the faucet and drank straight from his palms. The cool sensation running down his throat and settling in his belly felt positively divine. He kept drinking until he feared he might vomit, splashed the rapidly warming water onto his face, and leaned onto the sink so he could look at himself in the mirror. His eyes were bloodshot, his skin pale, his lips faintly purple—

His reflection metamorphoses into that of Edgerton, his body stretching upward toward the ceiling and his arms extending outward until his dark form eclipses the entire mirror—

Ward again stared at his own face, water draining from his stubbled jaw line and dampening his shirt. He grabbed a wad of paper towels and dried himself off. Feeling marginally better, he weaved through the men trying to get past him into the restroom and headed for the nearest coffee kiosk. The woman in line ahead of him appeared confused by the process of ordering and asked so many asinine questions that he nearly left, but he eventually got himself a scalding cup of plain old black coffee and a pastry and followed the signs toward baggage claim and ground transportation.

The coffee was too bitter and tasted like fire going down. A single bite of the pastry was all he needed to know that his body simply wasn't having any of it. He must have consumed too much water way too quickly, a theory corroborated by the return of the nausea. All he really needed was to get some fresh air. If he caught a ride quickly enough, he could get into Midtown before the 495 turned into a parking lot. He still had a full four hours before his flight to Miami was scheduled to depart from Newark, which meant that he might even have enough time to grab some antacids and a quick shower before he headed back out.

Ward hiked his backpack higher onto his shoulders, steadied himself, and strode straight toward the escalators at the end of the terminal.

MILANA NEEDN'T HAVE WORRIED about not recognizing her mother, who stood apart from the crowd converging on the carousel like a peacock from a flock of geese. She wore her bottle-blond hair piled high on her head to show off the tattoo on her neck, mirrored sunglasses, stiletto heels, and a yellow floral-patterned sundress with spaghetti straps. Her skin was the color and texture of leather, and she was so thin that the outlines of her sternum and ribs were clearly visible above cleavage she hadn't had the last time she was here. The way she walked, however, with her hips swishing and her delicate right hand raised as though there should have been a cigarette in an old-time holder protruding from it . . . that was all Milana needed to see.

She smiled despite herself and slipped through the gate. A security officer moved to cut her off, but she gestured to her mother, who'd just grabbed a hot-pink suitcase from the conveyor, and he let her pass. Her mother extended the handle and pulled the wheeled bag toward Milana with a clicking of heels so loud that it echoed throughout baggage claim, even over the rumble of warring conversations in any number of languages.

"Rosella?" she said.

Her mother stopped, slid her glasses down to the tip of her nose, and then slid them back up again.

"Look how much you've grown," she said. "You must have all of the boys wrapped around your little finger."

Milana nodded to herself and took the handle of her mother's bag. She'd been full grown the last time her mother was here, too, but now was neither the time nor the place to call her on it.

"How was your flight?" she asked instead.

"Tedious, as I'm sure you must know. How they cram so many people into such a small space and still manage to lift off is beyond me. I've been in clubs with more space between hips."

Milana didn't know how to respond, so she simply wheeled the suitcase through the turnstile and headed for the bus stop, where the M60 would hopefully be waiting to take them to Manhattan.

"Tell me you've already called for an Uber," her mother said. "You know how long it can take to get one heading into the city at this hour."

"Which is why we're taking the bus."

Her mother said something from behind her, but Milana could no longer hear her. The world seemed to slow around her and tilt on an unseen axis. She heard a humming sound, like she'd hit her head. The family walking in front of her veered toward the doors, revealing a man walking straight toward her from the escalators. He wore black sweatpants and a navy-blue hoodie, both of which featured the paw print of a bear with the letters AK in the palm pad. His face was pallid, his mannerisms jerky. He looked up at her from beneath a forehead positively dripping with sweat and his bloodshot eyes met hers—

Everyone around her vanishes. Their conversations abruptly cease and silence settles over the terminal. The humming inside her head grows louder and louder. The tiled floor before her is littered with dead bodies and covered with blood, arcs of which transect the wall to her right and the windows to her left. The cars on the road beyond it are tangled together from a high-speed collision, their windows shattered, their doors standing open. Only the man in the sweat suit remains, his face nearly concealed within the shadows cast by his raised hood. Blood trickles down his cheeks and dribbles from the corners of his mouth when he speaks.

Get out of the city.

His body collapses and his clothes fall to the floor, but before they hit the ground, they metamorphose into ravens that screech and fly straight toward her, their coal-black eyes fixed upon her, their sharp beaks dripping with blood, their clapping wings shedding feathers to the crimson floor.

Milana screams and shields her face—

Once more, the world came to life around her. She opened her eyes to find the man in the sweat suit standing right in front of her, their faces a mere foot apart.

"I said, get out of the way," he said, brushing past her. Heat radiated from him like a furnace. He produced a smell that reminded her of the breath of the old man whose palm she'd read on the night her grandmother died.

Milana couldn't seem to make herself move. Passersby cast sideways glances at her. A child holding his mother's hand started to cry. The clicking of heels ceased behind her. A man in a business suit covered the receiver of his cellphone and swore at her.

She turned around and watched the man in the sweat suit disappear into the crowd, pressed the butts of her palms against her eyes, and desperately tried not to cry. Not in front of her mother. Not ever.

"Are you feeling all right?" her mother asked.

Milana felt her mother's acrylic nails against her cheek and brushed the hand away.

"I'm fine," she said, striking off toward the bus.

But she wasn't. She was the furthest thing in the world from fine.

"YOU'RE NOT GOING to get sick in my car, are you?"

Ward glanced up from his lap. The Uber driver looked back at him from the rearview mirror, his eyes darting back and forth between Ward and the road.

The truth was that he simply didn't know, and he worried about what might come out if he opened his mouth to respond. It felt like bile had crept all the way up into the back of his throat. His head was positively pounding, his forehead dripping with sweat. He rolled down the rear window of the Sonata and leaned his head out into the breeze. The tires made a buzzing sound inside the tunnel, the commercial vehicles in the adjacent lane speeding ahead of them like runaway trains. White-tiled walls with yellow racing stripes blurred past, the recessed lighting producing a strobe effect. Light-dark. Light-dark. He had to close his eyes to keep from hurling onto the cab behind them.

Something was definitely wrong with him. He felt as though he'd sponta-neously come down with a migraine and the stomach flu, and the two maladies seemed to feed one another, intensifying the symptoms. He was certain that some external force was acting upon his head, compressing it like a vise, until at any moment his brains would squeeze out from his ears and nostrils. And the nausea . . . it was more than mere queasiness; it was a sensation akin to acid boiling in his stomach and producing magma that spread through his insides, eating his organs as it went.

A single image cut through the confusion: a droplet of water forming on the inside of his visor and trickling down the cracked Plexiglas.

He sat bolt upright as the car emerged from the tunnel into a brick trench metered by concrete overpasses. Apartment buildings rose against the gray sky, their facades darkened by pollution. The skyscrapers seemed to lean toward one another in an effort to seal off the sunlight.

This couldn't be happening. Not to him. And not this quickly. It had been maybe ten hours, at the very most, since the earliest possible exposure, a quarter of the shortest recorded incubation period for a hemorrhagic virus, and even then the patient had been elderly, not an adult male in solid physical condition. Even if he had somehow contracted the virus, he could undoubtedly still kick it with a course of aggressive antiviral medications, but unless this passed in a hurry, there was no way he was making it to Newark, let alone Miami.

The Sonata pulled to the curb in front of his building to the tune of honking horns.

"Here we are," he said through the back of his hand. He'd drawn the collar of his shirt up over his mouth and nose to keep from breathing the same air. "Out you go."

Ward nodded, opened the door, and fell onto the sidewalk. A woman with a poodle on a purple leash picked up her dog and stepped around him. He was feeling worse by the second. His thoughts were sluggish, his movements almost drunken.

The moment he was clear, the driver sped up sharply, using the sudden surge in momentum to close the door.

Ward pushed himself to his feet, entered the building, and ascended the worn stairs to the second floor. By the time he reached his apartment, he was on the verge of collapse and barely able to make the key work in the lock.

Nightmare scenarios played out in his head. If he was truly infected with whatever virus had infiltrated the arctic camp, then he was in serious trouble, and yet he doubted he'd be able to get himself to the hospital, even if he wanted to.

He leaned against the door, twisted the knob, and toppled into the entryway when it opened. His forehead rebounded from the tile and he tasted blood in his sinuses. It took every last ounce of his strength to drag himself into the living room, where he intended to pass out on the couch, although he never reached it. Vomit rose from his stomach. He choked it back down, spit to get the taste out of his mouth, and dragged the back of his hand across his lips, drawing it away bloody. A drop of crimson fell from his nose and alighted on the ground in front of him.

There was no other option. He needed to call 911 and arrange for emergency medical intervention. Try as he might, though, he couldn't seem to lift his head, let alone raise his arm to reach the cordless phone on the end table. His backpack was nowhere in sight. He must have left it, along with his cellphone, in the Uber.

He saw his reflection on the dusty surface of the TV. There was blood all over his face and his sweatshirt, turning the white paw print design red. The heat in his belly and the smell of the room suggested he'd soiled himself without even knowing it.

The epidemiologist in him ran through everything he knew about the spread of hemorrhagic viruses and the stages of incubation and infection. If he was only now manifesting active symptoms, then surely the headache and nausea he'd experienced on the plane were merely prodromes, in which case he likely hadn't been contagious. Or at least he wouldn't have been if this virus worked by the same mechanism as Ebola. If it were capable of spreading during its incubation period, however, then he could very well have transmitted the disease to any of the thousands of people whose paths he'd crossed in airports from Anchorage to Minneapolis to New York City, passengers both arriving from and departing to any of hundreds of destinations around the world.

He tried to laugh at his own stupidity but produced only a sputtering sound from his chest and had to lean his head to the side to allow the blood to drain out. How ironic was it that the coming pandemic would be caused by, of all people, an epidemiologist? All he could do now was pray that he hadn't been contagious on the flights and hope to God the driver of the Sonata was such a germophobe that he went straight to the hospital for a checkup. Otherwise, a lot of people were going to die.

Just like him.

Ward felt consciousness fading and watched his reflection through unblinking eyes until he sank into the cold, black abyss.

17

Cambridge, Massachusetts

"We've got him," Vickers said. The secretary of the Department of Homeland Security transferred the black-and-white screen grab from his dedicated system to the main monitor for everyone around the conference table to see. The image captured Trevor Ward mid-stride, his face in three-quarter profile beneath the hood of his sweat-shirt. "This was taken in Concourse C of the Anchorage airport last night, at 7:16 PM. We can confirm that Alaska Airlines Flight 197 bound for San Fran-cisco boarded from Concourse A."

"He could have just been killing time," Urban said. The secretary for Chemical and Biological Defense at the DOD ran his fingers through his thin-ning hair. "The airline's records confirm he boarded that flight."

"Or at least someone using his ticket did. He would have gone through TSA screening in Fairbanks, where the airline would have checked him in all the way through to his final destination. He wouldn't have had to show any identification to catch the connecting flight in Anchorage."

"So either he walked out of the airport in Anchorage or he switched tickets with someone else."

"Who was presumably booked on a flight leaving from Concourse C."

"That would explain why he didn't get off the plane in San Francisco."

"Then who did?" Hodges asked.

The president and CEO of NeXgen had been listening to these powerful men struggle to find Ward with growing apprehension. The epidemiologist was a variable for which he couldn't account. Cullen's rapid-response team was not only flying under the radar, but it had also collected a deadly disease, concealed the evidence of the deaths of six researchers under the auspices of the corporation, and abducted three American citizens. While he wasn't worried about the consequences of failing to follow established international protocol for reporting the virus, not with the level of involvement of the federal agencies represented in this conference room, he knew that someone would notice the missing researchers and demand answers he simply wasn't prepared to give, nor would they accept those answers without his being able to produce the bodies, none of which could ever be allowed to leave the Riverton facility.

He could count on the men inside his operation to honor their non-disclosure agreements, though. The personnel at Riverton were loyal to their country, not to mention the almighty dollar, and would do exactly what they were told, no questions asked, as they'd already proven on more than one occasion. If Cullen was right, however, and Ward couldn't be trusted to keep his mouth shut, then someone needed to shut it for him.

The epidemiologist had obviously anticipated their play, though, and the only reason Hodges could think of for such carefully executed defensive maneuvering was if Ward intended to use what he knew about the researchers and the virus against NeXgen, which he simply couldn't allow. An under-the-table cash settlement was one thing, but if Ward took what he knew to the media, the company would be ruined. Hodges would be forced to cut a deal and expose the involvement of the army, DHS, and DOD, a fact that the men in this room understood implicitly, which was why they'd volunteered all of the resources and manpower at their disposal to track down and eliminate the threat.

"Hold on," Vickers said. He pressed his palm over his earpiece to better hear the incoming communication from his team assembled at the St. Elizabeths West Campus in D.C. "Ward purchased a ticket from Fairbanks to San Francisco within minutes of the sale of another ticket from Fairbanks to New York City via Minneapolis, both of which used the same connecting flight to Anchorage. The second ticket was purchased under the name Geoffrey Tilton, who — son of a bitch. He's the Uber driver who picked up Ward at Fort Wainwright."

"We have imagery of Tilton getting off the plane in San Francisco," Urban said.

A new picture appeared on the main screen. Hodges leaned forward and laced his fingers on the tabletop. The man wore a hunting jacket and a baseball cap with a bill that did little to conceal the discomfort on his face. It was the expression of a man who knew he was doing something wrong but was almost in the clear.

"Damn it," he said. "Do we have confirmation that Ward was on the Minneapolis plane?"

"Affirmative," Vickers said. "We have imagery of him preparing to board the flight continuing on to New York City, which landed at LaGuardia less than ninety minutes ago. There's no record of him after that. My team's already scanning the security footage from both inside and outside the airport."

Hodges slammed his fists onto the table in frustration. Silence fell upon the room. All eyes turned toward him.

"Then we've lost him," he said. "He could be anywhere in the world by now."

"Not necessarily," Vickers said. He transferred the image in front of him to the main screen. "This is him inside Terminal One at LaGuardia."

The man on the screen looked nothing like the one who'd boarded the plane in Fairbanks yesterday evening. He wore sweatpants and a hoodie he'd obviously picked up at a gift shop in Anchorage, but the change of clothes was nothing compared to his physical deterioration. His hair was drenched, his gaunt face pale and sweating, his eyes sunken and unfocused. Even his posture was different, as though the mere act of walking was more than he could bear.

Colonel Xenos abruptly sat straight up in his chair. The commander of USAMRIID hadn't spoken since his arrival this morning. He'd seemingly been content to sit back and observe the chaos so as not to embroil himself in anything that might weigh on his conscience.

"We need to find him," he said.

"What do you think we're trying—?" Urban started to say, but Xenos cut him off.

"I mean, right now. We need to find him right this goddamn minute!"

Hodges suddenly felt nauseated. The colonel was right. There was no way around it; Ward was sick, and if he'd somehow been infected with the hemorrhagic virus that they'd thought was securely contained at Riverton . . .

"Get me Bergstrom and Young," he said into the intercom. He needed his heads of R&D and bioengineering if he was going to coordinate a response before events spiraled out of control. And then, as an afterthought: "Send someone from legal, too."

"Check every hospital within two hours of Manhattan," Xenos said into his cellphone. "We need him found and quarantined before—"

"He owns an apartment in Midtown," Vickers said.

"Get me that address," Urban said. "I can have a team anywhere in the city in under ten minutes."

Vickers again covered his ear to better hear his comm link.

"We have satellite confirmation of Ward entering the apartment just over twenty minutes . . . " The secretary's words trailed off. He transferred the aerial photo to the main screen. "Jesus."

Hodges closed his eyes, but the image of the man they were hunting sprawled across the sidewalk outside the open rear door of a sedan remained.

They were in serious trouble.

The door burst open, and Bergstrom rushed inside, panting as though he'd run all the way to the conference room.

"What's going on?" he asked.

"Get ahold of Riverton and have them send us everything they've learned about the virus."

Bergstrom furrowed his brow and opened his mouth, but his question remained unvoiced. The color drained from his face. He ran to one of the dedicated computer stations to access the secure network.

"Get Ferris from the CDC back here and activate every biological defense unit in the city," Xenos said. "We need to seal off and quarantine that entire block."

"We can't do that," Hodges said. "Midtown's right in the heart of New York City. There'll be no way of keeping it under wraps."

"We have an unknown hemorrhagic virus in play and that's your main concern? I've got news for you. This thing appears to have an incubation period measured in hours. If we don't contain it right now, a little negative publicity's going to be the least of our problems."

———

LUCAS PROPPED his laptop on his thighs and settled back into his seat as the train started to roll. He tried to avoid taking the Red Line as much as possible, but it was vastly preferable to sitting in traffic at this time of the morning. Besides, it gave him a chance to track down the pictures he knew had to be here somewhere. The petroglyphs from the Alaskan cave had reminded him of others he'd seen, only he hadn't been able to make the connection at the time. It had taken a sudden jolt of inspiration for his unconscious mind to communicate the answer, although he would have preferred that it had done so a few hours earlier to save him from having to cancel his classes at the last minute. At least he had the car pretty much to himself, save for an elderly woman with a walker at the far end and a couple of businessmen wearing shiny suits and trendy scarves, neither of whom looked away from their phones for longer than it took to make sure they hadn't missed their stop.

"Damn it," he muttered. He removed another USB drive from his leather satchel. "They have to be on one of these."

He'd scanned all of the photographs he'd amassed as a kid and saved them onto these memory sticks so they wouldn't be lost when he went off to college. At the time, he'd listed the contents of each on a piece of paper, but, of course, it hadn't survived the dozens of moves he'd made since then. While the memories seemed clear enough, he needed to see the pictures with his own eyes, especially if he hoped to communicate his theory in such a way that he'd be able to convince the men from last night, who were already more than a little skeptical.

Bergstrom had been on his way into a meeting when Lucas called and initially resistant to the idea of demanding a sit-down with Hodges, and yet Lucas had barely been out the door when Bergstrom had called back and offered to squeeze him in, which told him everything he needed to know. NeXgen had new information about the virus and didn't quite know what to make of it, which meant they were willing to accept help wherever they could get it, even from someone like him. And if that were the case, then they were running out of time.

Lucas scanned through the file names, which, fortunately, he'd had the foresight to list by location, if not by date. He was just about to reach for the next memory stick when he saw the collection he was looking for: Lion Canyon.

The train burst from the darkness and into the artificial light of Park Street Station, where the elderly woman disembarked and a pair of twenty-something women wearing backpacks boarded.

It took seemingly forever for the pictures to load. He remembered the trip to Ute Mountain Tribal Park well. He'd only been sixteen at the time: old enough to know better than to trespass in the sacred canyon without a tribal escort, but young enough not to spare a thought for the consequences of getting caught. He'd spent the better part of his childhood exploring the Canyons of the Ancients from his parents' home in the foothills above Cortez, Colorado, and gotten to be on a first-name basis with the park rangers at Mesa Verde. He could probably still map out the entire network of Anasazi ruins from memory, which was why sneaking into the tribal park had been so exciting.

Mesa Verde had become more of a tourist attraction than a historical site. There were always people walking the trails, climbing over the cliff dwellings, and crawling through the kivas. The spirituality of the ancients, the sacredness of their civilization, and the mystery of why they'd suddenly vanished had been trampled into oblivion beneath the sandals of midwestern families with fish-white legs and Winnebagos, oblivious to the history of the ancients who'd lived behind walls of stacked stone and adobe since long before their European forefathers first set sail for the new world.

Lion Canyon was different because it was on the Ute Reservation, where it was conserved by men and women descended from the land, for whom preserving the history of the early Pueblo peoples was a matter of great consequence. For them, tradition was all that mattered because not only did it remind them of where they'd come from and the sacrifices made along the way, it provided a foundation for everything that was to come, for the past and the future were inextricably linked in much the same way as a tree and its roots, both continually growing and contributing to the perpetuation of the organism, mirror images above and below the dirt of yesterday, the source of infinite possibilities both contributing to and stemming from the trunk that was tomorrow. One could not exist without the other, for to tear down the past was to fell the entire tree.

Thus, the Ute preserved their past, not by opening it to the public to secure government funding, but by hiding it from those who saw it as a novelty, a primitive Disneyland through which to parade their sticky-fingered children, collecting arrowheads that had drawn the sacred blood of the animals that had sustained them and toppling stones that had been stacked so precisely that they'd outlasted the wooden homes of the settlers who'd blown across this land, as transient as tumbleweeds. As such, the Ute Mountain Tribal Park was accessible only by following a maze formed by the Mancos River and its winding tributaries into canyons few modern eyes ever saw, and even fewer were allowed to explore.

Memorialized within its boundaries were hundreds of years of Native American history, dating from the arrival of formerly nomadic people in the fifth century to the region's sudden abandonment in the tenth, a timespan known a world away as the Middle Ages, which encompassed everything from the fall of the Roman empire to the decimation of Europe at the hands of the Black Death. For the Anasazi, it had been a time of rapid advancement as simple basket-makers began building elaborate adobe cities, finally planting firm roots in the sacred land, where their ancient sites had remained untouched since their abandonment.

No one knew exactly why civilizations built upon the Colorado Plateau had been forsaken in favor of dwellings built high on the cliffsides any more than they understood why those seemingly impregnable fortresses had been deserted, along with this once sacred land. Researchers speculated that the root cause was climate change, which was responsible for severe droughts that lasted for years at a time and resulted in centuries of bloody warfare with neighboring tribes over the scant resources shared between them, and yet that didn't explain why entire cities had been hastily abandoned and their entrances barricaded, leaving behind bodies to rot where they'd fallen and entire storerooms filled with grain and supplies that could have lasted several seasons. Taken together, they painted a picture of a people under siege, one that had been slaughtered and driven from its home, one so desperate to hide the truth of what happened that the entire Anasazi population had simply dissolved and filtered into other civilizations as far away as Central America.

Of course, Lucas had figured that if anyone could solve the mystery, it was him. After all, he'd grown up in these canyons and was as much a part of them as anyone else who'd ever lived there, so he'd convinced his friend Bryan to come with him, and together they'd set off into Mancos Canyon with a raft, camping gear, and a camera. They'd been careful not to collect so much as a single shard of pottery in case they got caught and instead used his camera to document every site they visited: Tree House, hidden on a steep canyon wall behind a stand of pine trees; Lion House, with its three-story tower, forty-five rooms, and seven kivas; and Eagle Nest, a cliff dwelling perfectly preserved within an alcove adorned with symbols that could be seen for miles in every direction.

Bryan had only made it as far as the toe-trail, leaving Lucas to explore the ruins on his own. It had felt though he'd traveled back in time. The rooms inside the adobe structure had smelled like another era, one defined by dust and the smoke of long-extinguished campfires. There had still been plaster on the interior walls, although it had deteriorated to the consistency of powder that came away on his fingertips with the slightest touch. He'd crawled through dark chambers inside of which entire families had once lived, the walls now leaning, the logs supporting the roofs nearly petrified. He'd even found a ceremonial kiva so perfectly preserved that the designs painted upon the walls had still been visible.

To this day, he clearly remembered descending the ladder into the pit. While only part of the roof remained, the circular room had contained darkness that resisted the illumination of his flashlight. He'd barely noticed the tombstone-shaped deflector stone, the soot-stained hearth, and the spider web-filled *sipapu*, symbolizing the hole through which their ancestors had emerged into the Fourth World, as his attention had been focused upon pictographs that had defied time and the elements for centuries, primitive artwork that had made the hairs stand on the backs of his arms and the air grow cold around him.

Lucas experienced the same sensation now as he looked at them on his computer screen. While the style of the drawings was markedly different than those the archeologists had found inside the arctic cave, the composition was nearly identical. The pictographs memorialized horned figures stretched in the vertical dimension, the bodies of dead animals and men, and violent battles culminating in the canyon's abandonment. And then there were the pictures he'd taken of piles of coprolite and the bones he'd seen scattered on the floor, nearly the same color as the earth after absorbing its nutrients for hundreds of years.

Something horrible had happened there, something that had led to the hidden city being deserted in such a rush that the residents hadn't even bothered to bury their dead or gather their food stores, an event somehow related to one that had transpired thousands of years earlier and half a world away in Beringia.

An event that was suddenly relevant now.

Lucas could positively feel himself on the verge of making the connection, but he couldn't shake the irrational sensation that he was already too late.

HODGES WATCHED the events playing out on the monitors mounted to the wall with a dawning sense of horror. Each of them showed a different live feed, from the individual cameras on the helmets of the CBRN-clad penetration team inside Ward's apartment complex to the video broadcast from the helicopter circling overhead, which captured Urban's biodefense team hurriedly inflating a mobile decontamination chamber and erecting barricades to hold back the hordes of cable news reporters, their lips framing baseless allegations and speculations designed to draw ratings. They'd been spoon-fed a story about a red team biological preparedness exercise, but if they caught so much as a whiff of the truth, it was all over for Hodges, who'd be sacrificed to the shareholders and tainted for life.

"All teams ready on my mark," Colonel Xenos said. The commander of USAMRIID wore a headset through which he communicated with his rapid-response team and liaised with the unit from the CDC, which had only just arrived on the scene. "Go."

The monitors came to life as men wearing Class A isolation suits and carrying M4 rifles burst from the stairwells and converged upon Ward's apartment, the front door of which had been left open a crack. One of the men nudged it with his boot, revealing linoleum smeared with blood, a trail of which led deeper into the apartment. There was an amoeboid stain in front of the couch where it almost appeared as though someone had bled out, and yet there was no sign of a body.

Hodges's heartbeat pounded in his ears and his mouth grew dry.

The coffee table lay toppled on its side, the TV cracked where the corner had struck it. All of the men suddenly turned toward the hallway leading back to the bedrooms, where a figure stood silhouetted within the darkness, its head lowered and its arms hanging at his sides, swaying ever so slightly as though at the behest of a breeze only it could feel.

"Take him down," Xenos said.

No sooner had the words crossed his lips than the figure on the screen burst into motion, sprinting straight at the cameras. It lunged for the closest one and Hodges caught a fleeting glimpse of a face hardly recognizable as that of Trevor Ward, his eyes wide and filled with blood, his teeth bared, his features contorted into an expression that could only be described as rage.

His forehead struck the soldier's visor and the view tipped toward the ceiling. He ripped off the soldier's helmet, which recorded the floor blurring past as it tumbled down the hallway.

Hodges looked at a different monitor just in time to see Ward bury his face in the man's exposed throat and tear it out with his teeth. He raised his head, blood pouring from his chin, and lunged toward the camera—

The first shot struck Ward squarely in the chest, knocking his torso backward and pinning his legs underneath him. He sputtered, rolled onto his side, and tried to get up. The view constricted until the man wearing the camera stood over him. He sighted his rifle at Ward, who snapped at the open air with his teeth and clawed at the soldier's legs. The second shot took a chunk out of Ward's forehead and spattered the carpet with a fan of blood. His eyes stared sightlessly at the camera and his body lay still.

Silence settled over the conference room, heavy and oppressive. All eyes were on the screen, where a crimson pool expanded on the floor beneath Ward's head.

The blood rushed in Hodges's ears with an audible *thoosh-thoosh-thoosh*.

"Seal the building," Xenos said, his voice flat, affectless.

None of the men on the monitors moved, their cameras focused on the dead man from as many different angles. The personnel gathered on the street outside stared up toward the second-story windows. Even the helicopter appeared to have paused its shark-like circling.

"Seal the goddamn building!" Xenos shouted.

The monitors all came to life at once as the men's training and instincts kicked in and they rushed to contain the situation. Hodges could only stare blankly at the screens, unable to see, let alone process, what he'd just witnessed.

"We need to address the reality of the situation," Vickers said. "If this guy was contagious during the incubation period of the virus, he could have potentially exposed everyone he encountered at the airports in Fairbanks, Anchorage, Minneapolis, and New York City, who could have then taken it with them to any number of destinations all around the world."

"Assuming it's airborne," Urban said. "If it's like any other hemorrhagic virus and only transmissible through direct contact with bodily fluids, then we might have just gotten lucky and ended the threat right here."

"We didn't," Bergstrom said. The head of pharmaceuticals transferred an image to the main screen. It showed a concrete room filled with wire cages stacked on top of each other, from floor to ceiling. Inside of each were chimpanzees repeatedly hurling themselves against the bars until their faces were ruined, their hips and shoulders were broken, their fur was torn, and blood pooled on the floor. "This is live imagery from Riverton. One specimen was directly injected with the virus and taken to a different room for observation.

That minuscule window of exposure resulted in the infection of the entire population in under three hours."

"Jesus," Vickers said. "Nearly a hundred thousand passengers pass through LaGuardia and MSP every day. A single hour of exposure could affect four thousand travelers, who would then infect another hundred-plus on their outgoing flights or the hundreds waiting for their luggage at baggage claim, spreading it to all corners of the city within a matter of hours. By this time tomorrow, we could very well be dealing with a pandemic of Biblical proportions."

"The incubation period of any virus is considerably shorter in primates than in humans," Bergstrom said. "Our team has already sequenced its genome and uploaded it to our system. We have the best virologists and biochemists in the world testing every known anti-viral agent and working on developing one of our own. I've also sent it to both the CDC and the NIH to see what they come up with. It's not time to panic. At least not yet."

The words rang hollow to Hodges, who felt his heart jackhammering in his chest. Regardless of whether they were able to contain the virus, unless he could pull a rabbit out of his hat, this was the end for him.

"Have you made any progress with the two subjects at Riverton who appear to be immune?" he asked.

"We're still trying to isolate the source of the immunity, but these things take time."

"Which is a luxury we don't have."

"What about the guy from yesterday?" Bergstrom said. "The professor from Harvard. He said he's seen designs like those we found in Alaska. If that's the case and there have been indigenous populations that have beaten it, and without the aid of modern medicine—"

"You're grasping at straws," Urban said.

"Without a doubt, but unless you'd rather we sit here with our thumbs up our asses waiting for our guys to pull off a miracle, I say we at least give it a try. If there's an extant population capable of producing antibodies inherited from its ancestors, we need to find it. Comparing its genome with those of the immune at Riverton should tell us exactly how to beat the virus."

"Then find him and bring him here," Hodges said.

"He's already in the building," Bergstrom said.

"What do you mean?" Vickers said.

"He called this morning and demanded another meeting. I figured it couldn't hurt to hear him out."

"Bring him in," Hodges said. "We've got nothing left to lose."

Lucas slung his satchel over his shoulder and hurried to catch up with Bergstrom, who spoke over his shoulder as he led him down the familiar hallway.

"There's a lot going on at the moment, so we're going to need you to be concise and to the point."

Something had changed since last night. Lucas could positively feel it in the air, as though the barometric pressure inside the building had plummeted in his absence, especially in the conference room, which smelled of stale coffee and body odor. The same men were gathered around the table, still wearing the same clothes and looking like they wouldn't be going anywhere soon. A palpable aura of stress crackled from them, suggesting to Lucas that he'd been right to insist upon this meeting. Something terrible was happening, and the mere fact that they were willing to entertain him proved as much. He read the desperation on their faces as he assumed the head of the table and networked his laptop with the system. Gone were the expressions of bemusement and outright contempt. They needed to hear what he had to say, and it frightened him every bit as much as what he believed had happened on the Ute reservation centuries ago.

"It took me a while to track down photographic evidence of where I'd seen similar petroglyphs to those from the cave in Alaska, but I found what I theorize to be a historic analogue from a thousand years ago, roughly eleven millennia after the inhabitation of Beringia." He populated the monitors on the tabletop with images he'd built into a slideshow, which rolled on the screens as he spoke. "These pictures were taken in Lion Canyon in northern Arizona and date to the time of the Anasazi, the native people who abruptly abandoned the region, leaving behind fortified pueblos built into alcoves high up the faces of some of the steepest cliffs, entire cities that could be effectively sealed off by raising ladders and defending treacherous toe trails, as you can clearly see in these first few images."

"Who were they defending themselves from?" Xenos asked.

"That's a question for which there's no definitive answer, I'm afraid. The Anasazi were known as great warriors and there's speculation that they engaged in protracted warfare with just about every other ancient pueblo-era culture, especially the Navajo, who gave the Anasazi their name, which means 'ancient enemy.'"

Lucas caught motion from the corner of his eye and turned to see one of the monitors on the wall, which showed an apartment complex surrounded by personnel in Hazmat suits of both the scientific and tactical variety. Something was transpiring at that very moment, and yet here they were — the secretary of the DHS, the head of biological and chemical defense for the DOD, the commander of the military's institute of infectious diseases, and some of the most powerful men in the bioengineering and pharmaceuticals industries — hanging on his every word while he showed them pictures of structures made from stacked rocks and adobe.

"This site here, with the similar artwork," Hodges said from the head of the table. "What happened to the people who lived there?"

"They simply walked away, leaving behind all of their belongings and, in this case, food stores that could have easily lasted another year, but that's not what you're really asking, is it? You want to know about the bodies."

Lucas skipped ahead in the slideshow to the pictures he'd taken inside the kiva, of the bones scattered across the ground in varying states of articulation, their cortices scarred by teeth marks, and the mounds of coprolite in the corner.

"What can you tell us about them?" Urban asked. "Was there any evidence of disease?"

"There's no way of knowing that without conducting a DNA analysis. There is, however, ample evidence of violence and cannibalism, as demonstrated by the scoring on the bones and the obvious calcific fragments in the fossilized fecal material, which we've found at many sites throughout the American Southwest, dating to the timeframe in question."

Lucas detected several shared glances between the men in the room. He'd hit upon what they wanted to know, although, for the life of him, he couldn't understand why.

"You said the Anasazi left this region," Bergstrom said. "We need you to tell us where they went."

"The prevailing theory is that they filtered into any number of contemporary tribes, only there's no record, either written or of the oral tradition, to confirm as much. All we have are petroglyphs like these that tell a tale of formerly peaceful people who abandoned their pit houses in favor of seemingly unreachable cliff dwellings, and then went to war with everyone and everything around them. It's like the first two acts in a story, but we're missing the ending."

"A story about a vanished people who deserted their civilization at the height of its prowess," Vickers said, "leaving behind artwork and physical remains nearly identical to those discovered above the arctic circle, right down to the same evidence of violence and cannibalism."

"We were hoping you'd be able to help us find any direct descendants, but it doesn't sound like that's something you can do," Bergstrom said. "Is there anything at all you can tell us that might help us track down any of them in a hurry? Any specific tribes the surviving Anasazi might have joined? Any modern cultures that might share their blood?"

The implications smacked Lucas in the face. His interpretation of the petroglyphs inside the arctic cave had been spot-on. There'd been a contagion sealed inside, one that the researchers had contracted and brought back with them, a disease that scared these powerful men so badly that they were willing to listen to him, a pathogen that was responsible for the quarantine of an apartment complex and their staggering interest in evidence of violence and cannibalism in long-gone peoples.

"Cut to the chase," he said. "I can't help you if you don't tell me what's going on."

All eyes turned toward Vickers, who offered a solemn nod. Xenos transferred a live feed to the main screen, which showed men in isolation suits collecting evidence from inside an apartment. Two bodies lay on the floor in the hallway: one of them with his helmet removed and his throat torn out, the other with a posthumous rictus on his bloody face and a crater where his forehead should have been.

Lucas imagined what their remains would look like after being left to rot for a thousand years and realized what these powerful men were trying to convey. They believed that a biological contagion was responsible for the behavioral changes associated with the killings. He brought up the photograph of the message carved into the stone alcove above the abandoned pueblo at Eagle Nest and understood just how right they were.

He transferred the picture to the main screen and translated the symbols for their benefit.

"The ancient Anasazi carved a message in the cliff above the pueblo when they left, a warning written in characters so large they could be seen for miles," he said. "It reads: All dead. Demons — or monsters or witches or something to that effect — in the canyon. Go west if you want to live."

LUCAS EMERGED from Harvard Square Station just like he had most every other day since he'd arrived in Boston, only something was different. The old colonial buildings, redbrick sidewalks, and throngs of students and tourists might have looked the same, but deep down he felt as though nothing would ever be the same again. Not after what he'd seen, what he knew was out there at this very moment. How many people had the man in New York exposed? How fast would the disease spread? If there'd been any real chance of containing it, he never would have set foot inside that conference room, let alone been shown footage of the apartment complex surrounded by emergency personnel or the aftermath of the attack that had happened inside.

He stopped and let the other passengers disgorging from the station pass around him like a stream around a stone. He'd always felt a deep personal connection to the Anasazi, whose very existence was shrouded in mystery. To him, they'd been simultaneously real and imagined, a mystical race that had disappeared as suddenly as it had appeared. Only now, if he was right, he was beginning to understand why. It was as though the curtain had been ripped back to reveal an ancient truth that he'd spent his entire life trying to learn, only to discover that he'd never truly wanted to know it.

In his mind, he saw the two dead men in the apartment — one with a gaping wound in his neck and the other with blood still trickling from between his bared teeth — and a heartbeat later they were lying on the ground inside the kiva in the Ute tribal park, wasting away until all that was left were their disarticulated remains. He envisioned those same bones inside a dark arctic cave, where a lone surviving individual had been forced to feed on those trapped inside with him, if only to survive for one more day. And he thought about the similarities between the primitive artwork etched in the stone in Alaska and painted on the plaster walls at Eagle Nest, shamanic visions immortalizing the warfare that had driven the Anasazi from their seemingly impenetrable cities, abandoning their former lives and never looking back.

Lucas furrowed his brow and turned around. The foot traffic had died down, at least for a few minutes, until the next train arrived. He recognized something his subconscious mind had noticed while he'd been lost in thought. Someone had spray-painted over the red-and-white banner above the glass structure that served as the entrance to the station, but the design was unlike any graffiti he'd seen around town and seemed to speak directly to him. The characters were identical to those he'd deciphered from the rock alcove above Eagle Nest less than an hour ago, words written in a long-dead language.

"Go west if you want to live," he said out loud.

He could no more fathom why they'd been inscribed in an archaic tongue than he could imagine why they'd been painted on a subway sign in one of the busiest parts of the Boston metro area, which only compounded his growing apprehension. He snapped a quick picture on his cellphone and headed across Massachusetts Ave toward campus, where prospective students milled around the arched entryways to the storied university. The day was becoming warmer with each passing minute, although not nearly to the extent that they should be sweating so profusely. Now that he really looked at them, several were strikingly pale and stared at the tour guide through unfocused eyes.

They were sick.

Lucas skirted them and quickened his pace along concrete paths normally packed with students, even during the summer session, and beneath shade trees where kids should have been lounging and studying in the shade. The thought of them holed up in their dorm rooms reminded him of the cliff dwellings on the Ute reservation, where he imagined terrified women and children barricaded in the darkness, trying to keep quiet, while warriors stood sentry over a canyon in the process of being overrun by an enemy that would stop at nothing to slaughter them all. And he saw a petroglyph of an elongated figure with the wings of a bat and a disease in its gut, surrounded by a dozen men and women with the heads of wolves.

By the time he reached his office, an irrational fear had taken hold of him. His conscious mind insisted that he was connecting random dots to form a picture that made no logical sense, and yet the part of him that had always been rooted in the past cried out for him to recognize the truth and head west before it was too late.

He unlocked his door, hit the lights, and took a seat at his desk. The light on his phone flashed to indicate he had unheard messages. He played them on speaker while he logged into a dedicated Reddit group for Southwest archeology and anthropology. Most of the contributors were professionals like himself, while the rest were devoted enthusiasts, mainly retirees, who'd been responsible for some of the most fascinating discoveries throughout the region. He was just about to post the picture of the graffiti at Harvard Square Station when he noticed there was already a thread dedicated to the mysterious appearance of the exact same message all across the southeastern part of the country.

"Hello, Dr. Lucas? My name is Dr. Rutger Bergstrom. I represent NeXgen—"

Lucas deleted the message from the previous evening and concentrated on the images on the screen. The same symbols had been painted on a billboard on I-20 outside of Dallas and again near Shreveport, on the roof of a barn in Littlerock, on a boarded-up gas station near Memphis, on a bridge in downtown Nashville, and on overpasses in Birmingham, Atlanta, and throughout the Carolinas. There were even sightings of graffiti in Independence Square, near the National Mall, and in Times Square. The messages had all appeared within the last few days, as though someone were traveling the major highways, spreading a message few outside of those in his academic circle could read. Several local news stations had even picked up on the story, while conspiracy theorists had latched onto the symbols as a sign of an impending alien invasion.

"I hope this is the right number," a woman's voice said from the speaker. "I'm looking for the Jack Lucas who specializes in Native American artwork. This is Special Agent Delilah Banks with the Detroit Division of the FBI." Lucas turned and looked curiously at the phone while the caller seemed to struggle to find the right words. "I stumbled upon a photograph credited to you while I was researching some designs related to a case I'm working. I'm sending them to your email now. Give me a call as soon as you've had a chance to look at them, okay?"

Lucas wrote down the special agent's number and opened his inbox. Her email was halfway down the page and included several attachments. His breathing accelerated as he opened one photo after another, all of which showed symbols similar to those from the cave in Alaska and the kiva at Eagle Nest. Stretched shamans with horns, claws, and their hearts pecked out. Dead men and animals. Humans with the faces of wolves and blood dripping from their outstretched arms. Only the words were different. They'd been written in such a way that they overlapped, disjointed phrases scrawled over and over and one on top of the other, like chaotic voices all fighting to be heard.

He lives. Time is now. He comes. The end is here. Blood flows. All going to die.

All going to die.

All going to die.

Lucas dialed the number, but the call rang through to voicemail.

"Special Agent Banks? This is Dr. Jack Lucas returning your call. I looked at your pictures . . . " He hesitated, and in that moment reached a decision every bit as irrational as his growing apprehension. If he wanted answers, there was only one place to find them. "Let me give you my cellphone number. I'm going to be heading back west for a while . . . "

18

Binghamton, New York

Sakeva rested his forehead against the passenger window and watched the world blur past. He couldn't remember ever having been this tired, but he didn't want to close his eyes for fear of missing a single second of his travels. His entire life had been spent on the Hopi Reservation, confined by arbitrarily drawn boundaries and unchanging horizons. He loved his land and the sacred mesas, and yet now that he saw the outside world with his own eyes, he wished he'd allowed himself to explore it sooner, to see the sights and hear the sounds he'd denied himself as a traditionalist and caretaker of his people, whether they believed in his mission or not. It was one thing to willingly devote his life to Taiowa's cause when he knew nothing else, while it was another thing entirely to do so when presented with other options.

He was glad Billy had come with him and not just to spell him at the wheel when his body started to fail him. His grandson stared out over the rusted hood of the old Chevy with an expression of wonder on his face, not merely at the enormous houses or the skyscrapers with windows that appeared to burn with the fire of the sun, but at the forests filled with trees that couldn't grow from the red sands back home, at animals that would never tolerate the harsh climate, at lush marshlands and towering blue mountains and lakes and streams and even the ocean, into which they'd watched the sun set from a bluff in Rhode Island, the grainy sensation of salt on their cheeks, the restless waves materializing as if from the horizon itself. If the purification were to commence today, it was that image to which he would cling as the light faded from the world.

It had begun, of course. There was no longer any hope of denying it. He'd seen the dawning sickness in the faces of several people in Times Square during the night, walking dead with bloodshot eyes and foreheads beaded with sweat. He'd always thought that the end would come with a thunderous crash that would shake the earth and raise great clouds of ash and dust, spreading invisible waves of radiation and decimating humanity in the blink of an eye. Only during the dark of night did he consider the possibility that it would arrive in the form of a lingering sickness that promised such suffering, although he supposed humankind deserved no less. They'd strayed from the true path and, in doing so, thumbed their noses at the Creator, who'd already shown he had no qualms about wiping the slate clean and starting over again.

Billy pulled to the side of the highway, offering Sakeva a view of the murky Chenango River through the shimmering leaves of the deciduous trees. The road was gray and ugly, with its fading paint, patchwork pavement, and trash drifting against the concrete barriers. Cars roared past with the buzzing of tires and the cloying scent of exhaust fumes.

The engine made a ticking sound as Billy consulted the New York roadmap.

"We're going to have to make a decision," he said. "We can either head north and hit Syracuse, Rochester, and Buffalo or continue west toward Cleveland and Columbus."

"What do your instincts tell you to do?"

"We need to keep moving or we won't make it to the west coast in time."

Sakeva nodded and placed his callused hand on his grandson's shoulder. He understood the conflicting thoughts that plagued the boy. Not leaving their message meant abandoning all of those people to their fates. It meant choosing some cities over others, essentially determining who lived and who died. It was a tremendous weight to place upon the shoulders of one so young, but Billy needed to learn how to carry it now, for soon Sakeva would be gone and it would be his burden, and his burden alone, to bear.

"If their paths lead to salvation, then they will find our messages along the way," Sakeva said. "They are directions, mere signposts like all of the others along this road, reminders to keep following the path Taiowa has laid out before them."

Billy hit the gas and the truck sped up with a clanking sound. A cloud hung over him, as though Sakeva's answer had only raised more questions, which his great-grandson would undoubtedly ask when he was ready. For now, Sakeva was content to let the boy have his space.

They crossed through Binghamton and merged onto Highway 17, which followed the meandering course of the Susquehanna River through tree-lined trenches that opened upon pastures filled with bluebells and daisies. The clouds overhead were dark and wispy, like smoke hanging just outside of their reach.

"What if there are no chosen people?" Billy asked. "I can see how some people could survive a nuclear war or a natural disaster like an earthquake or a meteor strike. You could probably even make a case for it having been the hand of the Creator that led them to wherever they sheltered, but those people back there in the big cities? I know you saw them, too. They were coming down with something. Maybe even some kind of flu, and you know as well as I do that diseases don't just infect some people. They infect everyone. If we're looking at a disease as deadly as you seem to think, have you considered the possibility that maybe everyone's time is up?"

"Those are your grandmother's words."

"You're probably right, but that doesn't necessarily make them wrong."

Sakeva smiled and reveled in the sensation of the earth racing past beneath his feet.

"What if I told you that every living creature has a role to play in Taiowa's story?"

"I'd ask why the spider's role was to be squashed beneath a heel or a snake's was to be run over crossing the road, why they were fated to die in the most meaningless of ways?"

"Meaning is found in life, not death. What if that spider had just finished laying thousands of eggs that upon hatching would fill the trees with silk and that snake had just devoured the rat that would have spread the plague? Are beauty and sacrifice not the lifeblood of existence? Is not a single smile worth a hundred sunsets? Life will continue long after you and I are gone, as it had for untold years before we arrived. Our purpose is not to be the answer, but rather the question. To make each day a little brighter and leave the world a better place than we found it. That is the true path, which we all must choose to follow, regardless of whether it leads us beneath the shadow of a heel or the tire of a car. Our purpose is to walk that path with our heads held high, hope in our hearts, and belief that our roles, no matter how small, are integral to the grand design."

"Then surely you must see how ridiculous all of this seems," Billy said. "That our purpose is to drive across the entire country, leaving messages no one can read for the survivors of an apocalyptic event that hasn't happened yet, is a delusion of grandeur on an epic scale. None of the people out here believe in Taiowa. I'm not even sure that I do."

"If you do not believe, then why are you here? I freely admit that sometimes your grandmother scares even me, but you could have gotten out of this truck at any stop along the way and found your way home."

Billy said nothing for several minutes. Sakeva was content to watch the cattle grazing lazily in the surrounding fields and the insects popping against the windshield.

"Because I want to believe," he finally said. "Not that people are going to die and we're some sort of saviors of the human race — which sounds stupid when you say it like that — but because there has to be more to life than sitting around in that godforsaken desert, drinking and waiting to die."

A tear crept from the corner of his eye. He tried to wipe it away before Sakeva saw it.

"The Creator only lays out the road before us. You must choose to travel it. You must choose to believe. Our road, the same one upon which generations of our forefathers have traveled, has been paved since long before you and I were born. It is our purpose not just to post the signs and light the way, but to be waiting at the end, for it is not only Taiowa's chosen who will come."

"What do you mean?"

"There can be no light without darkness, no calm without the storm, no peace without war. Others will come, as they always have, and it will be up to us to drive them back into the shadows so that the covenant can be renewed once more."

THE TRUCK CRAWLED through midday traffic in Columbus. Billy tried to focus his attention on the road, despite the cacophony of sights and sounds that overwhelmed him from seemingly everywhere at once. He knew this was a quaint village compared to cities like New York and Boston, both of which they'd hit during the night to avoid this kind of slowdown. A part of him wished he could have witnessed them in all their glory, while the majority was grateful to have been spared the press of bodies and cars around him. He'd always thought he'd make his way to one of the big cities once he broke free of the reservation, but now he understood that he wanted no part of that life, a revelation that made him feel sad and insignificant.

Even a place like this was more than he could handle, with people mere feet to either side of him, looking from their cellphones to the road and back again, cranking harsh music so loud that his seat vibrated, shouting and honking and raising a ruckus that caused the muscles in his neck to tighten. He wanted nothing more than to stomp his foot on the gas and ram the other cars out of his way. The feeling was all-consuming, like the desperation one experienced when sinking under water and watching the surface rise out of reach. He couldn't imagine enduring this sensation all the time, as though his entire existence were an exercise in slowly drowning. Never had he imagined himself missing his home, with its miles upon miles of desolate sands and living conditions completely at odds with what he saw on TV and the internet, but this was way more than he'd bargained for.

"This entire area used to be grasslands filled with crystalline streams flowing beneath the shade of deciduous trees older than time," his great-grandfather said. "I am not speaking of ancient history, mind you, but rather a mere two hundred years ago. The land was lush and ripe for farming thanks to pristine soil preserved beneath mountains of ice, dating to the end of the Third World and the beginning of the Fourth."

"Then why didn't our ancestors settle here instead of in the middle of a desert where next to nothing will grow?" Billy asked.

"Because life would have been too easy, and that was never part of Taiowa's plan, for without struggle there can be no triumph, without suffering there can be no happiness, and without sacrifice there can be no salvation."

"Haven't our people struggled and sacrificed enough for everyone? Everything we ever had has been taken from us — our land, our sovereignty, our pride — and still we cling to the old ways as though by cloaking ourselves in misery we can claim the moral high ground. And yet somehow that's not good enough for your Creator, who's decided to destroy the world so he can start all over again, but this time with even more suffering?"

"Only for the chosen," his grandfather said. "For the rest, the suffering will be brief."

"Then why would anyone want to be chosen?"

"Because every breath is precious, every sunrise a gift, and every life we bring into this world a miracle. Sometimes, we forget this — we get lost on our personal quests for success and material possessions — and need to be reminded."

"There are probably more subtle reminders than wiping us out."

"But none more effective."

A glimmering SUV pulled even with the truck. The woman in the passenger seat leaned her head against the window, which was cracked just far enough to allow the wind to blow her bangs from her sweat-beaded brow. Her glassy eyes seemed to stare right through Billy. There was no doubt in his mind that she was sick, just like so many others they'd seen.

At first, he'd been able to chalk it up to coincidence, but he was beginning to see the shadow of disease on the faces of everyone he passed and couldn't help but wonder when it would come for him. He found himself keeping the window rolled up so as not to breathe the outside air and unconsciously holding his breath until the corners of his vision started to sparkle. Defacing private property and setting up their little scavenger hunt had been fun at first, but now he just wanted to go home.

And suddenly he realized just how right his grandfather was.

"How do you know that this is the end of the Fourth World?" he asked.

"We were given nine signs," his grandfather said, "and eight have already come to pass. The first foretold of the coming of white men who struck down their enemies with thunder, the second of the arrival of spinning wheels filled with voices. The third promised the appearance of strange beasts like bison that would overrun the grazing fields, the fourth of snakes of iron that would cross the land. The fifth envisioned a giant spider web covering the entire world and the sixth rivers of stone that made pictures in the sun. The seventh predicted the sea would turn black and the eighth the coming of long-haired youth to learn our ways and wisdom."

"Half of those could be interpreted in any number of ways," Billy said. "That's the reason so many people believe in prophecies; they're just vague enough that you can make them fit any event. How many have we already seen fail to come to pass in my lifetime alone?"

"That so many exist should tell you something. We've been living in the Fourth World for thousands of years, and yet all nine of the signs can be traced to the last two centuries. The western migration of the white men with their rifles and pioneer families packed into covered wagons. The proliferation of cattle ranches and the coming of the railroads. Telephone wires and power lines. Highways and paved roads that produce mirages under the hot sun. Oil spills and flower children. All of these things have happened exactly as promised."

"What about the ninth sign?"

His great-grandfather closed his eyes and recited the prophecy from memory.

"'You will hear of a dwelling place in the heavens, above the earth, that shall fall with a great crash. It will appear as a blue star. Very soon after this, the ceremonies of my people will cease.' This is the prophecy of the Saquasohuh — the Blue Star Kachina — which signifies the Day of Purification, the world-engulfing cataclysm, is at hand."

"If you're talking about the International Space Station, you've got a good long time to wait considering we learned in school that its orbit will take decades to decay. And besides, isn't that something of a mixed metaphor since kachinas are the spirits of the dead?"

"They are the spirits of all of the invisible forces of life, of which death is only a small part," his grandfather said. "Kachinas represent minerals and plants, animals and human beings, clouds and stars. They appear and disappear through time and space; as the life force of one wanes, another grows stronger. They are the spiritual manifestations of every object in the universe, with which we must either find a way to live in harmony or risk our very survival."

"So the spirit of the space station will be our doom?"

"It was Patung, the squash kachina, who taught us how to plant corn; Toho, the mountain lion kachina, who showed us how to hunt; Honan, the badger kachina, who demonstrated the power of the herbs we use to heal; and Chop, the antelope kachina, who summons rain in response to the ritual of *Chu'tiva*. Is it so hard to believe they could cause a single manmade object to fall from the sky?"

"Is there a kachina that can get us through this infernal traffic?"

His grandfather smiled.

"You mock me, child, but have you not felt them guiding our actions and watching over us throughout our journey? Have we run out of gas or broken down on the side of the road? Have we been arrested for trespassing on private land or for painting our messages on buildings we do not own? Have we even once encountered traffic so bad that we have been forced to stop and delay our mission?"

Billy let it go. He understood how deeply his grandfather believed and how important it was to the old man to pass down his knowledge, but Billy knew it wasn't their ceremonies that brought the rain or caused the days to grow longer in the summer or the crops to ripen in the fields. Such things happened all around the world without other cultures having to dress up in costumes and dance around like fools. How narcissistic was it to think that such a small society living on a tiny patch of nearly uninhabitable land in the middle of nowhere could be responsible for the fate of the world? And yet, he hoped that was the case, because all around him the signs of sickness were appearing with increasing frequency and severity.

He again caught up with the woman in the SUV, who appeared to have grown even paler in the minutes since he'd seen her last.

Whether or not he believed in prophecies or magical spirits was irrelevant. Something terrible was coming and he wanted to be as far away from here as possible when it arrived.

SAKEVA OPENED his eyes and blinked until his mind made sense of his surroundings. He must have fallen asleep without knowing it, although the dream had felt as real as everything transpiring around him now. Perhaps even more so, for in his dream he'd been back on Third Mesa, surveying the vast expanse of desert below him, watching rooster tails of dust rise behind glinting vehicles approaching from the distance, while now he was in a place he'd never seen before, breathing air heavy with pollutants, and staring out upon a world he didn't recognize.

Billy had developed something of a sixth sense for picking the best locations to leave their directions, where the words would be visible from a distance and they weren't likely to encounter any police officers who'd derail their mission for a little harmless vandalism. Sakeva could hear the roar of traffic behind him, although the highway was concealed from view by rows of trees that had grown wild and feral, nearly barring access to the untended turnoff branching from the frontage road. A sign advertising gasoline prices had faded to an indecipherable miasma of pastel colors, its plastic face spider-webbed and pocked with bullet holes.

Sakeva yawned and climbed down onto the cracked asphalt. He had to stomp his boots to get the blood flowing back to his legs and brace his lower back while he stretched out the kinks. It was hard to believe this body had given him nine good decades after all of the abuse he'd given it, going back to a time before places like this one existed, and yet now it was even more of a relic than he was. The hoses had been removed from the pumps, the windows of the little mechanic shop boarded over, and the repair bay sealed behind a padlocked door that would likely never open again.

He heard the clanking sound of the ball bearing inside a can of spray paint and looked up to find Billy standing on the corrugated roof of the old place, painting the last of the symbols over a lighted sign that had faded to such an extent that the original words existed only in memory. From up there, the message could likely be seen for miles above the treetops, for all the good it had done the owners of the station.

"Where are we by now?" Sakeva asked.

Billy swung his legs over the roof, lowered himself until he was hanging by his fingertips, and dropped to the ground.

"Outside of Dayton," he said, brushing off his palms on his thighs. "If we keep heading west on I-Seventy, we'll pass straight through Indianapolis, St. Louis, Kansas City, and Denver."

"Good plan," Sakeva said. "Why don't I take the wheel for a while so you can get some sleep."

"No offense, but the way you drive, we might never get there."

Billy smirked and clapped him on the shoulder.

"Oh, to be young and foolhardy again."

Sakeva wandered around the side of the building, where the underbrush had grown right up against the siding, as though the forest were tasting it before attempting to swallow it whole. He unzipped his jeans and waited for his prostate to ease the pressure on his bladder. Between the constant thrum of traffic and the whine of planes high in the sky, it was no wonder man had been driven mad. It was like nails on a chalkboard to him, a relentless grating that set his back molars on edge. The sounds of nature were suppressed so much that it was hard to believe that anything could live in this—

A twig tumbled through the canopy and alighted near his foot.

He glanced up and saw diamonds of sky between branches overflowing with leaves. And among them, perched perfectly still, were so many ravens that it was a wonder the trees could support their weight. There had to be a hundred of them, all staring down at him through cold black eyes, which reflected a dark sentience that caused the hairs to rise on the backs of his arms and the flow of urine to cease.

Sakeva zipped up and craned his neck to get a better look. The black birds showed neither fear nor curiosity. Much like the symbols painted on the sign overhead, they were a message, one intended specifically for him. If their intention had been to cause him to tuck tail and run, though, they'd failed miserably. He saw them for what they truly were. *Who* they truly were. The enemy had declared himself, which only fortified Sakeva's convictions. Had he harbored a single doubt, it was now gone. The end would soon be at hand and it would fall to him to stand against the rising darkness foretold by the prophecies.

"You do not scare me," he said in the old tongue.

Raucous shrieking sounds erupted from the canopy in response.

Sakeva grabbed a rock and hurled it into their midst.

"Hyaah!"

The ravens burst from their shadowed enclaves and took to the sky, raining leaves and feathers down upon him. He headed around to the front of the building and looked up into a gray sky swirling with shrieking birds.

"Have you ever seen anything like it?" Billy asked.

Sakeva shook his head. His mouth had gone dry and seemingly incapable of forming words. He might have been right about the coming cataclysm, but he'd been dead wrong about one thing: he was scared. No amount of stories or training could have prepared him to stare into the myriad eyes of his adversary. He might once have been strong and virile, but now he was an old man who might turn to dust if anyone looked at him too hard, and Billy was little more than a child. He'd failed in the one task that his ancestors had bequeathed to him. He'd fathered no son and the man who'd knocked up his daughter had been a shiftless drunk who'd abandoned her with a daughter, who, in turn, had left behind her two young boys for her mother to raise in her stead. He'd waited too long to choose his successor and the entire world would pay the price.

"Come on," he said. "We have a long road ahead of us."

They climbed into the old Chevy and headed back toward the highway, leaving the ravens to scatter once more. There was still much ground to cover, and they were nearly out of time.

19

San Luis Obispo, California

Tick-tock.

Crawford awakened to a screaming headache and a humming sound in his ears. He tried to open his eyes. Failed. Tried again, but even the influx of darkness only succeeded in amplifying his pain.

Tick-tock.

His mouth was so dry that he couldn't peel his tongue from his palate, let alone swallow. He was only peripherally aware that there was something really wrong with him, something that transcended the physical pain.

Tick-tock.

He forced himself to open his eyes and bared his teeth against the pain. Shards of glass littered the floor in front of him, the light slanting through the kitchen window causing them to sparkle. The memories came rushing back to him: the shattering bulbs and electrical components, the rage and anguish, the pain and loss of control.

The stroke.

Tick-tock.

Crawford flexed his fingers. He could feel them all working, but those of his right hand, which rested at the very edge of sight, barely moved. His legs seemed more responsive. He could hear them dragging through the glass, although he couldn't see them from where he lay.

Tick-tock.

He cried out as he raised his head from the floor, prying his cheek from the linoleum with a sound like peeling masking tape. It left behind a pattern of blood filled with ground glass, bits of which he could feel embedded in his skin. He tried to push himself up but couldn't seem to make his right arm bear his weight, so he rolled onto his left side and managed to rise to a semi-seated position. Amoeboid patches of blood darkened his khakis. He wore one boot, while the sock on his other foot was crimson and crusted, obviously the source of the smeared footprints everywhere.

Tick-tock.

Crawford cradled his right arm to his chest, grabbed hold of one of the kitchen chairs, and struggled to raise himself from the floor. His right leg felt sluggish, as though it had fallen asleep, but at least it did its job long enough for him to drag his rear end into the chair. Once he'd caught his breath, he stood and leaned against the wall.

Tick-tock.

He grabbed the battery-powered clock and hurled it across the room. It smashed against the counter with a crash of breaking glass and splintering wood. Something snapped inside him. He started to sob, releasing moans that sounded pathetic, even to his own ears. Why in God's name was he still alive? He had prayed to die, a prayer which, like so many others, had fallen on deaf ears. Or perhaps uncaring ones. Everything had been stripped from him and he'd been left with nothing. Less than nothing, in fact.

"At leas' yoof got your healf," he said, his voice slurred.

His sobs abruptly mutated into laughter. Snot ran from his nose and drool drained from the corner of his mouth. He wiped them away with the sleeve of his shirt and prodded his lip, pinched his cheek. It felt like they'd been numbed by a dentist. He vaguely remembered something about the first few hours being critical to making a full recovery from a stroke, but, for the life of him, he couldn't remember how long ago it had happened. It had been dark and now it was light. He probably should have looked at the clock before he smashed it.

Crawford burst out laughing, only this time he couldn't seem to stop. This was all part of some sick joke, wasn't it?

He just needed to generate some forward momentum. Get himself up and moving. Work on his physical recovery and then he could work on getting his job back. Surely, Lowell and the rest of the NorCal contingent would understand why he might have overreacted a little bit. They weren't inhuman monsters. He'd known them all for years, during which time they'd undoubtedly seen how much Diablo meant to him. He'd make them understand he hadn't meant any harm, convince them to take him back. And once he had his foot in the door again, he'd get down to the business of saving the plant. It wasn't like he didn't have all of the right connections to make it happen. He just needed time to work his patented Crawford magic. After all, that was why no one had come to check on him, wasn't it? He'd failed them when

they'd been counting on him the most, but he wasn't about to give up on
them any more than he was certain they were going to give up on him.

Possessed with a new sense of purpose, he limped into the living room.
He had to brace himself against the wall, but as long as he deliberately swung
his right leg and focused on making the floppy foot land flat, it served its
purpose. And now that he really thought about it, the stroke had been a
blessing because he couldn't feel the cuts on his sole. Heck, the doctor
wouldn't even need to use very much anesthetic to suture it up. After all, the
physician's time would be better spent fixing Crawford's brain so he could
get back to doing what he'd always been meant to do.

———————

LETICIA STEPPED CAREFULLY around the creaking floorboards, wincing at every
whisper of her socked feet on the hallway tile. She carried her shoes in one
hand, clutched her purse tightly to her chest with the other, and held her
breath, although she was certain the thudding of her pulse would give her
away.

Cigarette smoke seeped into the hallway from the family room, the
swirling pall flickering like a storm cloud with the light from the television
inside. The curtains were drawn and the lamps switched off, stranding
Mother in darkness as black as her mood. The old woman was waiting for
her, but Leticia couldn't bear the thought of another lecture this morning, not
after screwing up her last chance with Mr. Crawford and spending the rest of
the night crying into her pillow.

She rose to her tiptoes and hurried past—

Mr. Snuffles jumped up onto the back of Mother's plush chair and started
yapping.

"I didn't hear you come in last night," a disembodied voice said.

Leticia hung her head. Her stomach sank as she stepped into the vile-
smelling room. The infernal Havanese just kept barking until Mother pulled
him down into her lap and resumed stroking his fur. She whispered soothing
words to the beast, while on the TV, newscasters spoke in serious voices and
displayed footage of packed emergency rooms.

"I'm sorry, Mother," Leticia said. "Can we please talk about this tonight?
I'm running late for work."

"Are you suggesting that I don't know your schedule or that I'm not
smart enough to read a clock?"

Leticia walked around the empty wheelchair and faced the old woman in
the recliner. Her mother took a drag from her cigarette, the red glow momentarily drawing the countless portraits of Christ and the Virgin of Guadalupe
from the shadows, every inch of plaster between them adorned with wooden

crosses. She stubbed out the butt in the ashtray balanced on her knee and waited for Leticia to look her in the eyes.

"Are you crying?" Mother asked.

Leticia hadn't even felt the tears on her cheeks. She wiped them away with the back of her hand and looked down at her feet.

"I take it things didn't go as planned last night," Mother said. The tone of her voice was cruel, mocking. "He didn't rip off your clothes and ravish—?"

"Mr. Crawford isn't like that, Mother."

"All men are like that!"

Leticia glanced at the altar in the corner, where a framed picture of her father sat among statues of Jesus and his mother, desiccated flowers coated with dust, and candles that hadn't been burned in years. Lord only knew if he was actually dead, but sometimes, like her mother, Leticia hoped he was, if only for not taking her with him.

"Your father was the same way," Mother said. "He took what he wanted and then left us to fend for ourselves."

Leticia remembered a quiet man with sad eyes and a bushy mustache that tickled her nose when he kissed her. He'd worn patterned western shirts with faux pearl buttons, Wrangler jeans, and boots with pointed toes. Oh, and a big gold belt buckle with a cowboy holding the reins of his horse and kneeling before a cross. He hadn't seemed like the kind of man who'd take anything from anyone, let alone—

Crack.

Leticia flinched at the sound. It had come from right behind her.

Mr. Snuffles jumped up and knocked the ashtray to the floor. His shrill yapping echoed from the small room.

"You should consider yourself fortunate to have been spared so much pain," Mother said. "Your precious Mr. Crawford would have abandoned you, too. You know how you can be. It was your neediness that drove away your father in the first place."

"That's not true," Leticia whispered. "Father loved me. He told me so all the time."

Crack.

Leticia turned around. The sound had come from behind the curtains. Something must have struck the window from the other side.

"Sweet Jesus, you've blessed me with an idiot," Mother said, raising her voice so Leticia could hear her over the barking. "If your father had loved you, he never would have left. *I'm* the one who loved you. *I'm* the one who stayed."

Crack.

Leticia whirled and threw open the curtains. Starbursts of blood marked the points of impact, from which cracks radiated outward to the frame. She had to press her forehead against the glass and lean all the way forward to see the dead birds. They were big and black and lying on the ground around Mother's precious rosebushes.

Crack.

Leticia cried out as another raven struck the window right in front of her, a quarter of an inch from her face. The impact staggered her, the fractured glass lacerating her brow. She let the curtains fall from her hands and rushed past her mother toward the hallway.

"Where are you going?" Mother called after her. "We're not finished with this conversation!"

Leticia hopped into her shoes as she breezed through the kitchen and shouldered open the back door. Feathers blew across the lawn and drifted into the gaps between the colorful species of roses, which Mother had planted the day after Father left and spent more time cultivating than the relationship with her own daughter. One of the ravens appeared to have survived the impact. It scratched at the soil with a single clawed foot. Its head was twisted at an unnatural angle, its beak blunted where the tip had snapped off. The poor thing must have broken its neck and yet somehow managed to survive. She felt the weight of its stare upon her and knew what she had to do.

Carefully, she slid her cupped hands underneath it and lifted it from the ground, blood dribbling from its mouth onto her palms. It was so large that she had to cradle it to her bosom like a newborn.

"I'm so sorry," she whispered, stroking the sleek black feathers on the back of its head.

In one swift motion — *crack!* — she finished the job nature had started.

A chorus of shrieking erupted from seemingly all around her at once. Hundreds of ravens were perched on the peaked roof of the storage shed, the fence lining the alley, and the telephone wires running overhead. They all took to the sky at once and swirled overhead, downy feathers falling around her like black snow.

Leticia sensed eyes upon her and turned around. Mother watched her from the other side of the glass, an expression of abject horror on her face.

CRAWFORD PLUCKED his keys from the ring, stumbled down to the garage, and climbed into his truck. Working the pedals with the wrong foot took some practice, but he figured out a system quickly enough and was a pro at it by the time he reached the main roads. With the AC blowing in his face in the California sun shining down on him, he was already starting to feel like his old self. He flashed a crooked grin at himself in the rearview mirror and winked, although it didn't really work.

"I'll haff to work on that."

Crawford released a bout of laughter so loud that the people in the Prius next to him at the light turned to see what was so funny. He cocked his finger, aimed it at the driver, and fired his trademarked weapon with a clicking sound, which hardly produced any drool this time.

"Progress," he said, as the hybrid peeled away with a squeal of rubber.

There were fewer people out and about than usual, especially for a day as nice as this one, although the parking lot at Sierra Vista Regional Medical Center was positively overflowing. A sign stated that the covered structure was at capacity and cars circled the rows like vultures. He ended up a block away and hoofed it across the campus. Granted, he fell more often than he cared to admit, and there'd been one embarrassing stretch where he'd been forced to crawl until he could get his right leg underneath him again, but by the time he reached the ER, he seemed to be getting a hang of this whole walking thing again.

Crawford heard the chaos before he was even within sight of the automatic doors. There were two ambulances in the bay and a third unloading a patient from the middle of the lot. A nurse wearing an N-95 mask was waving them off and shouting something about "going on divert." There was barely enough room to squeeze through the people in the entryway. All of the chairs in the waiting room were full. There were people doubling up and even sitting or lying on the floor. He couldn't even hear himself think over the crying and shouting.

"You all just need to be patient," a harried nurse yelled. She carried a box of surgical masks and appeared to be passing them out to everyone. She did a double take when she saw him. "Registration's right over there. We'll be with you as quickly as—"

A woman grabbed her by the arm and started complaining about already having been there for two hours, but Crawford got the gist of it. He was inching toward the line by the registration window when he caught a glimpse of Jessica Fields, sitting in a chair across the room underneath the TV. The senior VP and general legal counsel was practically unrecognizable in sweats and a T-shirt and with her hair drawn back into a messy ponytail. He smiled and waved, but she didn't seem to notice.

Crawford couldn't believe his luck. She was exactly who he needed to talk to. They could clear up that little misunderstanding from yesterday and lay the groundwork for going to Lowell about his reinstatement. He forgot all about signing in and headed straight for her, the most congenial expression he could muster on his face.

She was surprisingly pale, with bags under her eyes so dark they looked bruised. There was a childlike quality to the way she sat, as though she were frightened and alone, but trying to pretend she wasn't. She would probably be happy just to see a familiar face and have someone to wait with her.

Fields glanced up at him and her eyes widened. There was the recognition he'd been waiting for.

Crawford limped right up to her and proffered his hand. It might not have been the correct one, but it followed orders well enough. She looked first at his hand, and then at his face. She recoiled and sank back into her chair.

"Looks like you could use some cuppany," he said. "Mine if I join you?"

"You need to back away," she said. Her voice was firm but lacked its customary tone of command. If anything, she almost sounded scared, which didn't make the slightest bit of sense. "Right now."

He waved her off.

"Tell me you're not still mad about yesserday. That was just a misunner-standing. I admit I could have hanneled things better, but you know me . . . Diablo's my life. Now that I'ff had a chance to fink about it, I'd like to take you up on your offer to stick awound."

"Wallace!" Fields shouted.

Crawford followed her eyes to the line at the registration desk. Lowell stood near the front. He didn't look a whole lot better than she did.

"Excellent," Crawford said. He tried to clap his hands, but his right one wasn't quite up to the task. "We can all haff a chat and put this nonsense behind us."

Fields looked up at him. Her eyes hardened now that she'd recovered from the surprise of seeing him here.

"What the hell happened to you?" she asked.

"Oh, this?" He fluttered his hand vaguely at his face. "It's nothing. Prob-ably a stroke, I'm finking. Nuffing to worry that pwetty little head of yours about."

"You have glass sticking out of your check."

He touched it and winced at the pain.

"I should really go to the emergency room."

Crawford laughed so loud at the joke that people from all around the waiting room turned to stare at him. He caught the expressions on their faces and couldn't help but take offense. Didn't they know who he was? They were all looking at him like he was a stranger, as though there was something wrong with *him*. How many of them were using insurance that he'd negoti-ated? How many were paying their deductibles with money from timecards that he'd personally approved?

Lowell pushed through the crowd and got right into Crawford's personal space.

"Walk away, Nick."

"I was just talking to—"

"I said, walk away," Lowell said, shoving him in the chest.

Crawford lost his balance and landed squarely on his back. He tried to sit up but couldn't do so with all of the legs around him and without the full use of his right hand. He stared up helplessly from the floor, like a turtle balanced on its shell, and turned away in shame as he had to roll over onto his side, lean against the legs of a woman wearing fuzzy slippers, and use her knees to get up. All while she repeatedly hit him with her purse.

Lowell took a step toward him, like he was going to push him again. Crawford furrowed his brow and met the older man's stare, unable to comprehend the unmistakable hatred he saw there. They were friends. They'd shared meals and attended awards ceremonies and gone to football games together. Heck, they'd even bunked together at a convention in Kansas City. How had he so soon forgotten?

"Wallace . . . " Crawford said.

"Security!" Lowell shouted.

The uniformed guard stationed beside the doors leading into the ER perked up. He stood on his toes to get a better look and started toward them.

Crawford turned in the opposite direction and saw another guard walking toward him from the main entrance. He looked back at Lowell.

"Come on, Wallace. We'ff known each other for decades. Why are you doing this?" He reached for his old friend, who swatted his hand away, so he appealed to Fields. "Jessica, surely you don't think—"

"Is this gentleman bothering you?" the first security guard asked, his hand settling on his gun belt.

"We don't care that he's here at the hospital," Lowell said. "He just needs to be somewhere else."

The security guard turned to Crawford, his eyes affectless above his mask.

"Perhaps I could help you find a seat on the other side of the waiting room, sir."

Crawford looked first at Lowell, then Fields.

"Please . . . " he implored, but the word sounded so feeble coming out of his mouth that he had to avert his eyes.

The guard took him gently by the elbow and guided him away. Crawford jerked his arm free and limped toward the second guard, who waited with one hand on the walkie-talkie clipped to his shoulder and the other on his holster.

Crawford lowered his gaze. He couldn't bear to be around all of these people with their wretched expressions and mocking whispers. This was a nightmare from which he couldn't awaken. With any luck, he was still lying on the floor in his kitchen, waiting to die.

He limped past the second guard and just kept on going. Out through the automatic doors and across the parking lot. Falling and getting right back up again. By the time he reached his truck, his khakis were torn and there were tiny pebbles mixed in with the blood on his skinned knees. He swung his weak leg inside and climbed in after it. His left hand shook too badly to force the key into the ignition from the wrong side of the steering wheel.

An awful braying sound, like that of a dying animal, burst from his chest. He looked up at himself in the mirror through a sheen of tears and realized just how wrong he'd been to come here in the first place. His bosses had walked into that meeting knowing damn well that he wasn't going to take their deal and they were going to have to fire him. There was never any chance of them giving him his job back. And it wasn't like he could simply take it back either, which left him with only one option.

He was just going to have to make them regret their decision.

"You've, um . . . you've got something right here," Lars Andreesen said, gesturing toward the breast pocket of his dress shirt.

Leticia glanced down and was surprised to see a bloodstain on her blouse. There was even a feather stuck to the fabric. She walked calmly to the industrial sink, wet a paper towel, and cleaned it off as best she could.

"I cut my hand," she said, holding up her palm.

No one who saw the tiny laceration where the raven's broken beak had cut her would believe it could have produced so much blood, but none of the other engineers called her on it. They just continued changing into their white, full-body protective suits and donning their gloves and gas masks.

The day ahead promised to be a long one, especially with three engineers from the day staff having called in sick and everyone from the night crew complaining about having their sleep cycles ruined, but they all knew the drill. Once the pressurized-water fuel assemblies they'd removed from the reactor had been in the cooling tank for five years, they needed to be moved to the dry cask storage site on the bluff overlooking the ocean and encased in concrete for the long haul. They'd already finished loading all thirty-two assemblies into the lead-lined transfer cask and replacing them in the tank with another thirty-two straight from the reactor, so surely the rest of the process wouldn't be as traumatic as the others seemed to think it would be.

All they needed to do was remove the transfer cask from the pool, pump out the water and replace it with helium to prevent the fuel rods for corroding, and load it onto the transport vehicle. From there, it was another department's responsibility. Although, technically, the nuclear material sealed inside would remain dangerously radioactive for another ten thousand years, so they couldn't completely wash their hands of it.

Leticia welcomed the distraction. Anything to take her mind off not only last night's catastrophe, but the memory of the way the raven's neck had felt in her hands when she broke it. While it might have sounded like snapping a stick, she'd been able to feel the individual vertebrae separating, the tendons tightening, the muscles constricting, and then the bird's whole body relaxing at once. She'd even seen the light fade from its eyes in the moment of its death, the peace it had experienced when she ended its suffering.

Mercy.

Leticia understood the concept better than most. She'd watched the hospice nurse pump morphine into her dying grandmother's veins and rubbed Simba's tummy while the veterinarian administered the medication that put her cherished tabby to sleep. In both cases, their deaths had been protracted and unbearable for everyone involved. What she'd done for the raven had been better. There'd been no prolonged misery, only a split-second of pain. No wailing for days on end for the good Lord to take it or mewling all night while its bowels flowed like water. That kind of torment was inflicted by the survivors and their selfish need to cling to something that wasn't theirs. She could only pray that the Almighty showed her the same consideration when her time came.

The team of engineers left the staging area and entered the fuel handling building, which resembled an Olympic swimming facility, only with motorized walkways spanning the width of twin fuel pools. Exhausted nuclear fuel assemblies were housed in gridlike holding systems at the bottom, beneath twenty-three feet of circulating water that prevented further fission events and shielded employees from radioisotopic decay. Leticia remained several paces behind the others. They only wanted to talk about how Mr. Crawford had been fired and what it meant for them. Some of them even joked about the way he talked and mimicked his mannerisms.

Their behavior was in poor taste, but she understood that this was how people acted when they were nervous or uncomfortable, as she was now. The stability that Mr. Crawford had always provided was gone, and the man who'd taken his place seemed overwhelmed trying to learn everything there was to know about Diablo. She might even have allowed herself to feel bad for him had he not been the one who'd turned her life upside down. Of course, he did have kind eyes and spoke nice words about Mr. Crawford, so he couldn't have been *all* bad.

She caught up with her colleagues on the nearest walkway, by the controls for the giant winch they would use to raise the transport cask. All of them knew their designated tasks and were prepared to begin when one of the men suddenly fell to his knees and collapsed against the railing. His head and torso passed between the bars. He toppled forward, as though in slow motion, and started to fall—

Andreesen knocked her aside and dove to the platform, wrapping his arms around the other man's waist. Several others joined him. Together, they pulled the limp engineer through the railing and laid him on his back.

Even with his gas mask concealing half of his face, Leticia recognized Paul Spitzer. She remembered thinking the night engineer had looked awfully pale when he arrived, but she'd assumed he'd just slept poorly because of the abrupt transition to working days while they transferred the fuel assemblies to long-term storage. His forehead was beaded with sweat, and his eyes appeared to have sunken into his skull. He barely seemed able to focus—

"Leticia!" Andreesen shouted. "Snap out of it and call an ambulance."

The engineer barked orders at the others, but Leticia didn't hear them. She was already running toward the phone mounted on the wall near the entrance, her movements made sluggish by the baggy white suit.

In her mind, she saw Paul's eyes, and recognized the same combination of fear and understanding that she'd seen in the raven's before she closed her fist around its head.

CRAWFORD HEADED west on Diablo Canyon Road. Green meadows stretched downhill to the rugged cliffs overlooking the vast Pacific Ocean, its relentless waves crashing against stone formations that reminded him of sinking ships. It was a beautiful drive that he'd enjoyed most every day of his professional life, one he realized with great sadness that he was driving for the last time.

He wended through surprisingly empty parking lots and followed the service road down to the jetty, where he parked on a pinnacle of land surrounded on three sides by the sea. To his right, the incoming waves met with the cooled water returning to the ocean from the plant. Uphill, the twin domes of the reactors towered over the roofline of the building housing the turbines. He remembered standing on this very spot so many years ago, fresh out of grad school and wearing a hardhat even though they hadn't even broken ground yet, staring at the pristine site and imagining the buildings that would soon rise from it, buildings they were about to close forever.

This was where he came when he needed someplace to clear his head and think. It was here where he'd come when he'd learned of his father's passing, where he'd sorted through his complicated feelings for the man who'd torn him down at every opportunity, and yet had ultimately prepared him to make Diablo into something truly special. Here where he'd reread the letter from his fiancée announcing that she was leaving him for a man she'd met while he was getting this place off the ground, a man who made her happy in ways that he hadn't been able to, starting with the child already growing inside of her. Here where he'd wallowed in the misery of a cancer diagnosis about which he'd chosen not to burden anyone else, where he'd come after ripping the seat of his pants in front of everyone at the company picnic and after losing the softball championship and after every one of the stupid calamities that seemed to happen to only him. This was his special place, more so than any other, a place where the racket inside his head ceased, if only momentarily.

Crawford did his best thinking down here, which was exactly what he needed to do right now. He was getting stronger by the minute. The feeling was returning to his right arm and leg, which, if the Internet could be trusted, signified that he'd experienced a transient ischemic attack. A mini stroke, not the real deal. The simple blockage of an artery in his brain, the kind that generally cleared on its own within twenty-four hours.

He'd been given a second chance at life, and he intended to take full advantage of it. And now, thanks to his special thinking spot, he finally understood exactly how to do so.

He was going to teach them all a lesson about power.

Each and every one of them.

He was going to show them what nuclear energy could really do.

20

Riverton, Wyoming

"On my mark," Cullen said. He adjusted his grip on the snare pole, braced his feet, and focused solely on the chimpanzee thrashing against the bars of its cage, spattering the visor of his isolation suit with blood. "Now."

Brown threw open the door and Cullen thrust the snare at the primate. It screeched and dodged the retractable noose, parrying with a slash of its nails and grazing the sleeve of his isolation suit. He managed to slip the coil over the beast's head and tighten it around its neck. Its lacerated face and shoulders dripped with blood, strands of which stretched between its wicked teeth as it screamed.

"Ready or not," Cullen said. "Here it comes."

He wrenched the animal from its cage, which only served to feed the chaos around him, the other chimps hurling themselves even more violently against the walls of their cages. The lone remaining animal handler, a mousy-looking guy named West, sidestepped the flailing arms and legs of the creature suspended before him and stabbed it in the hip with a syringe, plunging the sedative into its muscle and ducking out of its reach once more. He wanted nothing to do with those claws, which had shredded his partner's isolation suit and the flesh underneath.

The chimpanzee spun and raked Cullen's visor with its claws. He jerked back his head and held the infernal beast as far away from his body as he could manage. It twisted and flopped as its movements grew increasingly sluggish. Cullen lowered it to the ground and pinned its neck to the floor until it stopped moving altogether and lay motionless, bleeding from count-less self-inflicted wounds.

Pritchard grabbed it by the scruff of its neck and dragged it into the adjacent room, where a dozen contraptions that looked like miniature electric chairs would be used to immobilize the primates so that when they woke up, they wouldn't be able to hurt each other, or themselves.

"We shouldn't be taking this kind of risk," Brown said. He had to shout to be heard over the shrieking. "Why can't we just shoot them with the trank gun?"

"Because the darts are propelled at the same velocity as a slug from a twenty-two and could easily kill them at such close range," West said.

"They could easily kill *us* at such close range."

Judging by West's reaction, Brown had obviously struck a nerve. The scientists needed these infernal primates alive if they were going to study the progression of the disease, but not so badly that they were willing to come down here and tranquilize them for themselves.

"Let's just get this over with," Cullen said. He again raised the snare pole and waited for the others to assume their positions. "Ready on my go."

Each successive sedation and relocation went smoother than the last until, finally, the room fell deathly quiet, save for the patter of blood dripping to the floor. After enduring the frenetic screaming for so long, the silence was almost overwhelming, accentuating Cullen's headache, which had been steadily building for the past few hours. In all his time in the field, he'd never seen anything like this. For the first time in his life, he felt the stirrings of fear, an emotion so unfamiliar that he could only stand there, visually appraising his reflection in the reinforced window, searching for the tear in the crimson-spattered Tyvek fabric he was almost certain had to be there somewhere.

"WE NEED to bring down his core temperature," Dr. Mathers said. "If we allow it to go any higher, we risk permanent brain damage. Or worse."

Rankin watched Hanson's temperature climb on the monitor. He'd been alerted when it passed 104 and it had been nearly 106 by the time he got down here. The loss of cognitive function didn't concern him nearly as much as the animal handler's death, but the virus needed to be allowed to run its course, regardless of the outcome.

"Stick to the plan," he said.

"He's no good to you dead."

"If not mitigating his fever causes him to die before the hemorrhagic and behavioral symptoms develop, then we've learned something of considerable value, don't you think?"

Rankin glanced at the overhead clock displaying the time elapsed since Hanson's exposure. 04:02:51. It wouldn't be long before they knew for sure.

"He's a human being," Mathers said in little more than a whisper. "We should be doing everything in our power to save him, not just standing here watching him suffer. Tell me you can't see how monstrous that is."

Rankin rounded on her, his face contorted into a knot of anger.

"Then save him, doctor."

Mathers averted her eyes. For all her training, she was as helpless as the rest of them. More importantly, she understood that sometimes sacrifices were necessary for the greater good.

"Hanson knew what he was getting himself into," Rankin said. "He accepted the risks when he signed on."

"What if it were you or someone you love in there?" Mathers asked.

"Everything I do is to make sure that it isn't."

Rankin's phone vibrated in the holster on his hip, alerting him to an incoming message. He accessed the nearest terminal and logged into his private account, which displayed a single message from Colonel Xenos, the commander of USAMRIID. It consisted of two words that made the ground fall out from beneath his feet.

CONTAINMENT BREACH.

His pulse accelerated, and he looked up at Hanson's face on the monitor. The man's skin had paled to near translucence and was positively dripping with sweat. His eyes jerked restlessly beneath his closed lids. Suddenly, the information that could be gleaned from his deterioration was of critical importance, assuming they weren't already too late.

"Let me know the moment there's any change in his condition," Rankin said.

He whirled and headed back to the residential wing.

RANKIN EMERGED from the access-controlled doorway across the hallway, revealing a fleeting glimpse of an observation room with a monitor displaying the face of a man Cullen hadn't seen before. Rankin closed the door behind him, sealing off the view once more. His expression suggested that something serious was going down. He caught Cullen looking and beckoned for him to follow.

"I'll catch up with you guys later," Cullen said, heading for the door.

"What's going on?" Brown asked.

Cullen was about to say that he didn't have the slightest idea when it hit him that he did. Rankin wouldn't have involved him unless something had fundamentally altered their situation, and he could only think of one thing that could have done so.

The virus had somehow gotten out.

He blew past Brown without answering and caught up with Rankin at the airlock. The chief scientific officer of the National Medical Defense Program didn't say a word as they immersed themselves in the chemical showers, changed out of their isolation gear, and proceeded into the residential wing. Rankin's office was at the end of the main corridor and housed a conference room with a table that could comfortably seat eight. Three others, none of whom Cullen recognized, were already waiting.

Rankin assumed the head of the table, directly across from the twin video monitors mounted to the opposite wall, above the foot. One screen displayed an aerial view of a city block, while the other showed what almost looked like a mirror image of the table, around which were seated men who needed no introduction.

"Let's get right down to it," Severn Hodges said. The president and CEO of NeXgen sat at the head of the table, thousands of miles away, flanked on his right by Colonel Xenos, commander of USAMRIID, and Charles Vickers, secretary of the DHS, and on his left by Dr. Angela Ferris of the CDC and Dr. Frank Urban, secretary for Chemical and Biological Defense at the DOD. "Colonel?"

"Approximately thirty minutes ago," Xenos said, "a rapid-response team deployed to Midtown Manhattan terminated an epidemiologist contracted by NeXgen to assist in the analysis of the unknown pathogen and the evacuation of the arctic archeological site. At the time of his death, the man officially classified as Patient Zero exhibited advanced primary and secondary symptoms of the virus."

"Ward," Cullen said. His head was really pounding now. "How the hell did he slip through our net?"

"That's neither here nor there," Urban said. "We couldn't have anticipated the virulence of the pathogen. All that matters now is making sure we contain it."

"We've already quarantined his apartment complex and the entire surrounding block," Dr. Farris said. "FEMA's activated its emergency management plan and is preparing to close every bridge and tunnel off the island, but we fear the damage might have already been done."

"Our teams in Fairbanks and Minneapolis have grounded all flights and assigned dedicated units to monitor local hospitals for reports of any of the prodromal symptoms of the active disease," Vickers said. "Plus, we've sequestered everyone known to have come into contact with Patient Zero and are closely watching them for pathogenesis."

"What do you need from us?" Rankin asked.

"Progress," Hodges said. "One can only contain two million people on a twenty-three-square-mile island for so long before panic sets in. We need to know exactly what we're dealing with and how we intend to handle it."

"The President wants answers we don't have," Vickers said. "He's going to have to go on TV and tell the country that not only do we have this situation under control, but we're already implementing a plan for how to take care of those who've contracted the virus."

"What kind of numbers are we looking at?" Rankin asked.

"We hesitate to speculate at this juncture," Urban said. "Projections depend entirely upon which stage in the incubation process the patient becomes contagious and how long the virus remains viable outside of a biological host."

Rankin surveyed the brain trust gathered around his table. While no one spoke, all of them appeared to have paled significantly since the start of the videoconference.

"We need time," he finally said.

"That's the one thing we can't give you," Hodges said. "Anything else is yours for the asking, but we need results and we need them now. Get me a test for antibodies or viral antigens, something proactive that the President can tout on TV. He's already placed the full resources of the CDC and NIH at your disposal. They're being briefed as we speak, and you should expect to hear from them in a matter of minutes." He took a deep breath and nodded to himself. "Now get back to work and find me a goddamn cure."

The CEO of NeXgen ended the call, leaving those gathered at Riverton staring at one blank screen and another that showed a city block in Midtown Manhattan surrounded by streets crawling with men in black tactical CBRN suits.

Rankin's eyes took on a faraway cast.

Even Cullen knew that Hodges was asking for a miracle they simply couldn't deliver in what little time they had. Vaccines took weeks, at a minimum, to develop and had to pass through rigorous testing protocols before being cleared for emergency use. They were dealing with a virus whose incubation time was measured in hours. If it spread even half as quickly through the human population as it had through the chimpanzees in the lab, then they could very well see the first wave of the pandemic hit before the sun set. And by then, it would already be too late.

If it wasn't already.

THE NURSE INSERTED the needle into Riley's arm. A flash of blood entered the plastic casing of the needle, confirming she'd entered the vein. With the click of a button, the spring-loaded needle retracted, leaving only a thin catheter within the vessel. It was delicate work made exceedingly difficult by the isolation suit's thick gloves. Fortunately, the nurse didn't falter until she set down the plastic cap housing the needle, which slid off the small tray and landed on the floor, where it lay for several seconds, unnoticed, until Riley discreetly covered it with her foot.

She watched the stoppered vial fill with her blood. As soon as it was full, the nurse swapped it out for another vial and repeated the process. They'd already taken so much blood that Riley was starting to feel woozy. Lord only knew what they were doing with all of it.

The nurse set aside the filled tube, pulled the catheter, and pressed a folded piece of gauze against Riley's inner elbow.

"Hold this," the nurse said.

Riley knew the drill by now. Both of her arms were bruised from so many trips to the well, but she didn't know how to make them stop, let alone if she even wanted to do so. If her blood held the secret to beating whatever this virus was, then wasn't she obligated to help them? The problem was she feared that if she didn't do so willingly, they'd take it anyway, which would put her in a much less tenable position, one from which she was certain she wouldn't be able to extricate herself.

The nurse replaced the gauze with a bandage and looked around for several seconds, presumably searching for the needle she wasn't sure if she'd put away or not, before bundling her implements into a case containing numerous other blood samples and used needles.

"Thank you for your cooperation," she said, heading for the door, where a man in a matching yellow isolation suit waited to release her. "You need to eat your breakfast."

"So I can have more blood ready for you when you come back?" Riley said.

The nurse turned and looked at her with a blank expression.

"Yes."

And with that, she was gone, leaving the man to reseal the door behind her.

Riley felt the sudden urge to take the tray of food and hurl it across the room, but she knew that would only open the floodgates of emotion she'd had such a difficult time closing in the first place. Crying about her situation was counterproductive. She needed to figure out exactly what was going on if she hoped to gain at least some small amount of control over the situation, and following instructions seemed like the quickest way of doing so.

At least for the time being.

She slid her foot across the tiled floor, to the edge of the bed, and leaned forward as though to scratch an itch. In one swift motion, she palmed the plastic casing with the needle inside and tucked it underneath her covers.

Playing along appeared to be working well enough for Edgerton, although the tactic wasn't at all like him. Riley would have thought he'd be throwing a fit about how everything was her fault, how neither of them would have been in this predicament had it not been for her obviously deficient leadership, and yet, curiously, he remained out of sight. In fact, she'd only seen him twice since awakening in this awful cell.

The truth was she didn't need him to remind her that she was responsible, if not entirely to blame, for getting them into this mess. She definitely could have used a familiar face though, even one as unsympathetic as his, so she didn't feel so utterly alone.

As if sensing her thoughts, Edgerton materialized at the front wall of his cell, his palms splayed upon the glass. He looked exactly the same, and yet entirely different at the same time. It was more than the mere change of clothes. His posture and resting expression appeared just a little off, while his eyes no longer seemed to match his face. There was something about the weight of his stare that made her skin crawl, as though he weren't merely looking at her, but rather through her, inside of her.

In that moment, he was the man she'd seen through the smoke from the campfire, his eyes glowing with flames. And then the image was gone

Riley rose from her bed and walked to the front of her enclosure, until she and Edgerton were separated by only two sheets of reinforced Plexiglas and six feet of hallway.

"How are you holding up?" she asked.

Edgerton cocked his head from one side to the other, like a vulture watching a dying animal, waiting for it to draw its last breath. Goosebumps rose along the backs of her arms, and she realized that this was not the man she'd known for the past five years. This was someone — something — else entirely.

A smile split his face. He appeared to flicker before her, as though an unseen hand flipped the switch of a light that shone only on him. In one heartbeat he was Dale Edgerton as she'd found him inside the cave, his skin pallid, his face crawling with mosquitoes, and in the next he was a figure formed from shadows, his body lithe and sinewy, his eyes fathomless pits of nothingness, the silhouette of his head that of a steppe bison's skull, just like the one worn by the mummified remains they'd discovered in the arctic. And in those fleeting moments, when she saw the true nature of the otherness inside him, she heard voices from a great distance, men and women crying out, their pain and terror so real she felt them as her own. She sensed these people around her, dying in darkness she could feel, if not see—

The vision cleared and Edgerton once more stood before her, a knowing expression on his face. Riley felt weakened by the experience, strangely displaced from the here and now. She'd seen it, whatever *it* might be, and in doing so absolved it of all pretenses.

She shrank away from the glass wall and retreated all the way to her bed, not once taking her eyes off Edgerton, whose smile widened and filled with teeth, making him appear simultaneously wolf-like and cadaverous.

He turned away from the window and made the same whispering sound she'd heard while she was hiding in the cave, one that chilled her to the marrow and caused her to shiver so hard she could barely close her fist around the safety needle. She broke the plastic casing, removed the inch-and-a-half needle, and turned it over and over in her hands as the horrible sound echoed from the depths of the subterranean complex.

CULLEN BARED his teeth and pressed the butt of his palm against his forehead. His headache was growing worse by the second. He'd left the conference room before the meeting was even formally adjourned and headed straight for his room, which was little more than a prison cell with a single bed, a free-standing bureau, and a desk, on top of which sat his duffel bag. He rummaged through the contents until he found a bottle of ibuprofen, dry-swallowed four capsules, and collapsed onto the bed, burying his head in his arms. He just needed a little sleep to take the edge off the pain, especially if he was going to stay focused enough to keep Rankin from pinning this whole nightmare on him. He'd seen the way his former subordinate had looked at him when Colonel Xenos revealed that Ward was Patient Zero, and while he hadn't explicitly stated that it was Cullen who'd allowed him to slip through his grasp, they all knew the truth.

That was the benefit of hindsight. Rankin hadn't been there. None of them had. There'd been no reason to suspect that Ward had been exposed. So he'd cracked his visor. Big deal. They'd tested its integrity in the field and determined that it hadn't been compromised. However Ward had contracted the virus, it was ultimately on him. And, truth be told, it served him right.

When it came time to cast the blame, though, Cullen knew damn well who Rankin would throw under the bus. Instead of letting him off easy when he bailed on the team, Cullen should have put him in the ground, just like he should have done with Ward. He was still imagining all of the ways he could have forced Ward onto the cargo plane at Fort Wainwright — whether with the rest of the team or with the corpses in the back — when sleep claimed him.

Flames crackle from somewhere beyond the range of sight, casting a flickering glow upon stone walls painted with ancient symbols and the gaunt faces of those gathered before him. They crouch on the bare earth, coughing from the haze of smoke and something worse, a sickness that has settled into their lungs, presumably the source of the fear in their eyes. Their bodies are little more than bone and sinew beneath dry skin mottled by dirt and deep purple bruises. Ratty tanned hides do little to stave off the cold, which causes their breath to plume from their lips.

An animal bleats from the darkness outside of the firelight's reach. He feels its terror, for it senses what comes next. Men drag the bison into the cavern by its broad horns, its broken legs trailing its bulk along the smooth stone. The flames reflect from its brown eyes, the black fur around which is matted with tears. It's small for its breed and thin from subsisting on the sparse vegetation it can find beneath the snow and ice, which is likely the only reason the hunters were able to hobble the behemoth.

A hand that is not his own, one with bulging veins and crescents of grime beneath the fingernails, strokes the beast's muzzle and its broad black nose. It shudders and huffs. The men wrench its head backward by the horns, causing it to bleat and thrash. A wicked blade chiseled from stone appears in his hand. He thrusts it into the flesh of the creature's sagging neck and saws back and forth, the bison's beard darkening with blood, until he hits the hidden vessel and warmth gushes over his arm as—

—he advanced through the airlock door, which admitted him into the room where the isolation gear was housed.

The last thing he remembered was passing out in his bed. How in the world had he gotten here?

Cullen felt strangely detached from his body, as though he were merely a spectator watching a stranger climb into one of the baggy yellow suits, seal the bindings, and head toward the sterile wing. He couldn't recall waking up, let alone leaving his room and walking through the maze of corridors.

With an audible crack, the throbbing in his head abruptly diminished. He felt warmth trickle from his nostrils, tasted blood in—

—his mouth as he gnaws the gristle from the bone. What little remains of the carcass rots in the corner. Its hide has been stretched over the rocks while the greasy fat liquefies from its skin. Everything edible has been consumed and the bones have been hollowed of marrow. Even the head has been harvested for its eyes and tongue and the spongy gray meat, leaving the skull to fester among the hooves and tatters of hair.

The meat has not lasted long enough and subsequent forays into the blowing snow have proven futile, for the hunters fear straying very far from the safety of the caves and the wild game has moved on. It is only a matter of time before the people starve. He sees the specter of death in their faces. They come to him, knowing it is his duty to protect them from the darkness and the spirits that haunt it, to beg for mercy from gods who know none. The Creator has abandoned him too, but he must not let the others know, so he communes with the silence in the hope that someone will respond before his people turn on him, a day that is rapidly approaching.

They have failed to keep the covenant and their punishment is to endure unimag-

inable suffering inside this mountain, with only the promise of death awaiting them. They have been forsaken, much like the animals left to starve on the steppes and die of thirst on the banks of the frozen streams. He cries out in anguish, a voice not his own echoing throughout the warrens, where men and women sob from the hunger and the rattling sounds of their children's dying breaths. If the god of all creation will not help, then perhaps he will find another that will.

His eyes fix upon the hollow sockets of the bison's head. He rises from the ground with considerable effort, sways while he summons his failing strength, and walks—

—down the sterile white corridor, the windows of the vacant quarantine rooms passing in his peripheral vision. The thudding of his footsteps echoed from the corridor ahead of him while—

—silence descends upon the cavern. He stands before the gathering of his people, whose eyes are filled with terror at the sight of the horned skull seated upon his head. Sharp protrusions of bone bite into his forehead and cheeks and his neck aches from the weight it now supports, but he feels the beast's power pulsing through his veins and knows this is the way.

The people part before him as he strides through their midst and toward the back of the chamber, where the fire burns and those who feasted upon the dead bats lay on beds of desiccated straw, bleeding out beneath befouled rawhide tatters, tended by women in little better shape than they are. He unsheathes his blade, and they look up at him from—

—behind the Plexiglas barrier stood Dale Edgerton, whose face dissolved before Cullen's very eyes. Flesh and blood gave way to bone, although the skull was in no way human, but rather that of what looked like a steer, with curved horns and a long, jagged snout. And within its hollow sockets were rings that appeared to burn with captured flames, drawing him into them, dragging—

—the cutting edge of the blade across his palm, summoning the flow of blood. He dabs a finger into it and crouches before each of the dying men, one at a time, studying their faces until he finds the one he wants, and then smears crimson on the man's closed eyelids. What he intends to do is sacrilegious, he knows, much like wearing the skull of another form of life, and yet he will do anything to save his people and thumb his nose at a god that would curse them to such a miserable fate when they've already sacrificed everything for him. And for what? The only god he feels in the darkness with them is the god of vultures and crows, flies and worms.

He gestures for the woman to bring the dying man and heads back into his cavern, the flames behind him casting his shadow upon the earthen wall. His body stretches, becoming infinitely taller, the horns upon his head growing to demonic lengths. He raises his arms and watches them wrap all the way around the cave. And beneath the bony snout he feels the stirrings of a—

—smile crossed Edgerton's lips. Cullen heard screams from a great distance, the pained cries of long-dead souls summoning him back to consciousness. In that moment, the man on the other side of the glass was at once the researcher they'd dragged from the bowels of the artic cave and the entity with the bison's skull and the fiery orbs for eyes. He placed his hand against the window and Cullen watched his own rise to meet it. The glass seemed to disappear. He felt the warmth of the other man's palm, the texture of his skin. Something passed between them, something that singed his skin and burned like acid in his veins. He rocked back and opened his mouth to—

—*screams when he awakens on the cold hard ground with the blade pressed against his throat. The dying man's sacrifice will be great, but no less so than the one made by the shaman, for rather than his body, he is offering his soul. He plunges the blade into the man's soft flesh and with a rush of blood*—

Damned Tyler Cullen.

THE MAN in the isolation suit stood with his back to Riley, his hand pressed against Edgerton's window. He hadn't moved in several minutes, not since he'd first screamed. She'd called to him to see if he was all right, but he hadn't so much as looked in her direction.

She climbed from her bed and was halfway to her window when the man suddenly lowered his arm and turned around. The light struck the visor of his isolation suit in such a way that it concealed his face as he approached. It wasn't until he was just on the other side of the glass that the reflection cleared. She recognized him as the man who'd shot her in Alaska, the man who would dispose of her when she was no longer of any use to the scientists here, only something about him had changed.

His irises were no longer dark, but rather reddish orange, like embers on the brink of igniting.

CULLEN STEPS *over the body lying at his feet, the surrounding tiles slick with rich arterial blood. The dead man's head has been rendered a craterous ruin of broken bones and pulped flesh. A siren blares in the distance, loud and forlorn. He raises the M4 rifle in his hands and strafes the window in front of him, on the other side of which stands the woman he's already shot once, but the bullets only pit the reinforced glass. A roar explodes from his chest, and he fires up into the ceiling in frustration. Sparks burst from the ruined lighting and exposed wiring and cascade through the smoke.*

He catches his reflection in the Plexiglas as he approaches, the hood of his isolation suit hanging against his chest, his bare face spattered with blood. His eyes are wide and wild, his shoulders heaving. He grips the handle of the door and starts to turn it.

Riley backs away from the window and screams —

Cullen's vision shattered like the windshield of an automobile. Light shone from the intact overhead bulbs onto the floor, where there was neither blood nor a body. He closed his empty hand and stared at his reflection in the pristine glass. The inside of his visor was freckled with crimson, expiratory spatter from the blood still flowing from his nose and over his lips, despite which the expression of confusion on his face was unmistakable.

It was as though he'd experienced jumps in time, fleeting moments of consciousness interrupted not by dreams, but rather by the memories of something that had burrowed deep inside of him. Something ancient and angry, eternal and corrupt. A source of feelings and thoughts indistinguishable from his own, superseding his own. A sentience that had somehow become a part of him.

Or perhaps it was he who had become a part of it.

Cullen looked through his reflection and his eyes met those of Little Miss Ambition, Dr. Riley Middleton, who stared back at him with open revulsion. An inexplicable hatred boiled inside of him, one fueled by emotions belonging to someone else. He'd wipe that goddamn expression off her face if it was the last thing—

His headache returned with a vengeance, nearly driving him to his knees. It was all he could do to brace himself against the wall until he felt steady enough to return to the residential wing, the cries of long-dead men and women echoing in his ears.

21

Bethesda, Maryland

Davis suddenly found himself with access to so much information that he simply didn't know where to begin. Catalogued within the various databases were countless studies from as many noteworthy institutions, all focused on different aspects of cognition and the expression of emotions related to both empathy and psychopathy. There were biochemical and hematological assays and comparisons, physiological and structural analyses, and psychological and functional imaging case studies for diagnoses ranging from agoraphobia to zoophobia, and everything in between. There were even declassified case files related to the military applications of extrasensory perception, from the CIA's human experimentation in the Sixties and Seventies to the army's investigations of psychic phenomena under the code name Project Stargate.

He leaned back in his chair and rubbed his eyes. The research room reminded him of a high school computer lab on steroids, with parallel rows of tables supporting individual workstations, each with three dedicated monitors. He'd been staring from one to the other to the other and back again for so long that he felt like his head might explode. Previously, he'd begun his research with a clearly defined psychological diagnosis — psychopathy — and had simply looked for any common anomalous structures that could have been responsible for the manifestation of symptoms. Now here he was, starting with an unsubstantiated mental phenomenon few scientists believed existed and trying to correlate it with various medical studies performed on patients expressing the third and least-common variant of the Trident Gene.

Until he isolated the parts of the brain theoretically responsible for its expression, he wouldn't be able to formulate a structural imaging protocol, let alone a functional means of mapping the activation of those structures.

If ever there were a textbook case of impostor syndrome, this was it. Davis was so far out of his depth that it was only a matter of time before he drowned. Heck, he didn't even have the slightest idea what the equipment in the surrounding rooms did, let alone how he was supposed to integrate his results with those of the real scientists running those machines. He was just a grad student who got lucky and stumbled upon a discovery peripherally related to one of enormous significance. This was his big break, though, and he couldn't afford to give in to the fear that had haunted him since the traumatic day that altered the course of his life.

His breathing sped up at the mere thought of it. The familiar panic swelled like a supernova from his core, radiating outward through his body, causing his hands to tremble and the backs of his arms to tingle. He closed his eyes and concentrated on slowing his breathing and his racing thoughts.

"Three . . . two . . . one," he said, and again opened his eyes.

He needed to take a step back and approach this logically. If the opposite of psychopathy was empathy, then he had to start there and winnow the sheer volume of information to a more manageable amount. Studies from several prominent universities and anthropological institutes demonstrated that, unlike psychopathy, empathic responses to different types of stimuli could be graded on a sliding scale, implying that some people were simply wired to be more empathic than others. Those demonstrating the highest levels of empathy had significantly higher levels of oxytocin, the so-called "love hormone" produced in the hypothalamus and stored in the pituitary gland. Considering a recent study had showed a concrete link between elevated levels of oxytocin in the cerebrospinal fluid and in the blood, if he could find individuals with the third Trident variant who'd taken an ELISA test — an enzyme-linked immunosorbent assay designed to measure antibodies in the blood and diagnose conditions like HIV, syphilis, and certain cancers — then he could work backward and see if any of them had been prescribed an MRI of the brain. Even a small subset would be enough to isolate common anomalous structures, which could then be compared against the brain scans of other patients exhibiting the desired Trident traits.

His fingers blurred across the keyboard. Once he figured out how to search the medical database, access the records for the individual patients, and find the corresponding lab test and imaging results, everything fell into place.

Four specific individuals matched his criteria, all of whom demonstrated elevated levels of oxytocin and had received an MRI of the brain within the last five years. Each of the attached reports, as dictated by the reading radiologist, mentioned hypertrophy of the anterior cingulate cortex and the insula — a collar-shaped structure concealed beneath the frontal lobe and a portion of the cerebral cortex hidden within the fissure separating the temporal lobe from the frontal and parietal lobes, respectively — and overdevelopment of the parahippocampal gyrus, the gray matter surrounding the hippocampus, near the brain stem. All three structures played an important role in impulse control, emotion, and the coding and retrieval of long-term memory. While considered incidental findings, when coupled with the obvious thickening of the amygdalae and the increased volume of the middle and orbital gyri of the frontal lobe, they painted a picture of individuals at the opposite end of the physiological spectrum from the psychopaths he'd studied.

Now, all he needed to do was solicit volunteers from the three subsets of the Trident Gene, subject them to standard non-contrast structural MRI imaging, and generate a protocol for functional and tractographic imaging that would allow him to evaluate the white matter tracts between the ventromedial prefrontal cortex and the amygdalae and voilà . . . he'd have a test to establish levels of empathy—

The door opened and Pennington burst into the research suite, an expression of unbridled excitement on his face.

"How close are you to formalizing an imaging protocol for the Trident Gene?" he asked.

"Honestly? A lot closer than I'd expected to be in such a short amount of time." Davis beamed in anticipation of the praise about to be heaped upon him. Maybe he wasn't so far out of his depth after all. "I'd say, given a decent number of volunteers, I could have the foundation of a functional protocol ready to go within a matter of weeks."

"You have four hours," Pennington said. "Grab your stuff. We're leaving."

"With all due respect, it took six months of amassing data and careful observation to formulate my first test for psychopathy and another six to hone it the way I wanted it."

"I'm afraid we just don't have that kind of time," Pennington said, ducking back out of the room.

"Wait," Davis called after him. He gathered his belongings and hurried to catch up with the director of the NHGRI in the hallway. "What's going on?"

"We've been presented with a unique opportunity. We need to get a move on if we want to take advantage of it."

"What are you talking about?"

Pennington blew through the doorway at the end of the corridor and entered the lounge, where several employees Davis had never seen before waited, their travel bags at the ready and cases of equipment stacked by the opposite door.

"Roughly thirty minutes ago, a DNA sequence was uploaded to our system by a pharmaceutical company looking for help qualifying a virus discovered at an archeological site above the Arctic Circle. Its genome is roughly eleven kilobases — eleven thousand base pairs — in length and encodes for three structural and seven non-structural proteins. And it's an eighty-four percent match to the Trident Gene. I followed up to confirm the veracity of the information and queried the nature of the discovery, which, as of this moment, is classified top secret."

"What exactly does that mean?" Davis asked.

One of the other scientists answered. She was tiny, wore her hair in a pixy cut, and spoke in a childlike voice.

"It means that a large portion of the Trident Gene is potentially the residua of an ancient virus that's been incorporated into our genome."

Davis's confusion must have shown on his face.

"There's a virus out there that poses a distinct threat to our national security and they're looking for anyone who can help them figure out how to counteract it," Pennington said. "And at some point in our distant past, our ancestors were able to fend it off. In doing so, that information was encoded into our genome, where it was filed away within the junk, to be slowly corrupted through successive generations of interbreeding. One of our three variants likely contains that information, and considering we're the closest thing the world has to experts on the sequence, it's up to us to figure out how to neutralize the virus."

"But why only four hours?"

"Because that's how long our flight is."

DAVIS HAD NEVER BEEN on a private jet before. He was used to flying near the back of a cramped 737, squashed between passengers unwilling to relinquish so much as a sliver of either armrest, his knees compressed behind the seat in front of him, its headrest lowered into his lap. Never in his wildest dreams would he have imagined himself riding in a swiveling leather seat at a polished maple table, surrounded by some of the country's foremost scientific minds, with the world streaking past below him at over six hundred miles an hour. It was a positively unreal experience made even more unbelievable by the fact that none of them knew their ultimate destination. All they'd been told was that they'd be landing at Riverton Regional Airport in Wyoming, where a vehicle would be waiting to take them to a secure location.

He'd spent the first half of the flight filling out digital paperwork authorizing background checks for various security clearances and forms with legal language so dense he'd given up trying to understand what it said and just signed where the arrows indicated. At least he'd been introduced to his traveling companions, if only in passing.

Outside of Pennington, who was taking a call in the private office behind them, there was Dr. Emily Wilson, the diminutive epigeneticist who reminded him of a dark-haired Tinker Bell; Dr. Wyman Sanders, a clinical geneticist with bushy brown hair and an even bushier mustache; and Dr. Karen Greenwald, a bioinformatician who both looked and carried herself like Davis's sophomore English teacher, the mere thought of whom brought on the panic that always seemed to be lying in wait.

He couldn't afford to let the others witness one of his episodes, so he stared out the window, concentrated on the patchwork quilt of farmland below him, and took one sip of water at a time, all the while counting down from three, over and over, until he regained control of his breathing, or at least well enough that he could return his attention to what amounted to an introductory briefing, the majority of which was targeted at him, although he still had yet to figure out why they even wanted him here.

They'd each been given a digital tablet containing files with names the others could apparently interpret, but just looked like random combinations of numbers and letters to him. Most featured horizontal bands of varying length, which looked like colored barcodes stretched to fill the width of the page. Lines had been drawn between them to indicate matching segments, identified by their numerical positions in the sequence. He did his best to keep up with the conversation as the others compared the virus' genome to those of the three Trident variants, although he struggled to grasp how a virus could essentially change the entire genetic code of its host without causing a constant state of infection.

"Hold up," he said. "If this ancient virus has incorporated its DNA into our genome, why don't we exhibit any symptoms of the disease?"

"Think of these residual viral sequences as battle scars from the fight that defeated the original virus," Emily said. "You have to understand that the function of a gene is not inextricably bound to its structure. Our genes are constantly interacting with our environment and exist in a dynamic state, switching on and off different genetic and biochemical processes, so just because a viral gene codes for a certain protein doesn't mean our bodies can't hijack the production of that protein for entirely different purposes."

"And these viral segments mutate and change from one generation to the next until all that's left is a fraction of the original virus," Karen said. "Plus, they're what we consider mobile retrotransposons, or 'jumping genes,' which means they can alter the function and expression of nearby genes, depending upon their location within the genome. We've already identified residual viral segments that trigger various autoimmune diseases, others that influence the formation of cancers, and even more we believe are responsible for psychological maladies like schizophrenia and bipolar disorder."

"That's not to say that there aren't beneficial human endogenous retroviruses, or HERVs, like those that regulate the expression of healthy genes and mediate cellular differentiation, especially during embryonic development," Sanders said. "And just because a large portion of this extant virus corresponds to a portion of the Trident Gene doesn't necessarily mean the two are more than peripherally related. The mere fact that the Trident Gene incorporates some amount of viral DNA doesn't mean its capable of producing viral symptoms. In fact, it could be that the viral remnant helps augment the physical changes you demonstrated with your work."

Davis closed his eyes and held up his index finger while he composed his thoughts.

"You're telling me these leftover bits of viruses encoded into our genome are not only still active, but they also contribute to our development," he said. "Perhaps even our evolution."

"While that's a bit of an oversimplification, they make up roughly eight percent of our genome and we wouldn't still be passing them through our bloodlines if they weren't doing *something* useful," Karen said. "Nature abhors waste. If there weren't an evolutionary advantage to their perpetuation, they would have faded away long ago. And while they might be considered dormant, thanks to advances in the field of epigenetics we've come to understand that a good number of these gene fragments are still capable of producing viral proteins, but our bodies simply don't allow them to do so."

"Then why keep those fragments at all?"

"Because our bodies still use them *somewhere*, even if it's just within one seemingly insignificant type of cell."

Davis nodded as though he understood, but he obviously wasn't fooling anyone.

"Our genome is composed of somewhere between twenty and twenty-five thousand genes," Emily said. "Think of them like songs on a really long playlist. There are some you don't want to hear, and since your body knows the order they play in, it allows every different type of cell in your body to play the songs it wants and skip the ones it doesn't. That's how epigenetics works. The individual cells choose which songs they want to play, or which genes they want to activate. Now think of those songs' lyrics as instructions describing how to produce the proteins that cause the physical expression that gene, in this case proteins coding for a viral infection. The body detects these proteins, or antigens, and, in response, skips to a different song in the playlist responsible for producing the antibodies required to kill it. That's the gene we're looking for, and we have a pretty good idea of where it might be based on the location of the viral segment within the Trident Gene."

"So where do we start?"

"With the infected," Pennington said. He hung up his phone and returned to his seat at the table. With a click of the remote control, the TV on the wall separating the cabin from the cockpit awakened. He flashed through a series of windows on his laptop and transferred the image on his monitor to the big screen so they could all see. It featured electronic medical records like so many Davis had seen before, only the patients were identified by a series of letters and numbers, rather than by their names. He selected the first in the series — AKHEMVI-G — and scrolled through the lab and pathology tests until he found a JPEG file. A tap of the mouse and an image from a scanning electron microscope filled the screen. "As you can clearly see here, they've been able to isolate the virus—"

"It's hemorrhagic," Sanders said. "Filoviridae. There's no mistaking it."

Pennington paused a beat before answering.

"Yes," he said, "but it's the secondary symptoms that are of greater clinical concern."

"What could be more concerning than bleeding to death?"

Pennington looked at them with an expression Davis couldn't quite interpret and backed out of the virology results. There was an icon on the main medical records page that resembled a quarter of a circle with three concentric rings. A live feed icon. The director clicked it and a window appeared in the middle of the screen. The image inside looked like a slab of poor-quality marble, swirls of pink and brown and red in a visually unappealing pattern. It took his mind several seconds to rationalize that he was looking at a soiled sheet of Plexiglas, on the other side of which was a vaguely human silhouette standing at the very edge of sight. If he looked through the lightest of the streaks, he could almost make out a man with his wet hair plastered to his scalp and his entire face awash in crimson, save for the dark discs of his irises—

The man hurled himself against the reinforced window, causing everyone seated at the table to flinch at once. He pressed his face against the glass, smearing away the dried blood with an application of fresh, and revealing a mess of overlapping lacerations, one of which was so deep it offered a glimpse of the man's molars through his cheek. He turned sharply, as though catching a glimpse of something outside the camera's range, and began slamming himself against the glass, over and over and over, the thudding sound of each impact echoing from the TV.

Davis suddenly realized exactly why Pennington had brought him along. The secondary symptoms included violent outbursts unmitigated by bouts of conscience or thoughts of self-preservation. This man exhibited psychopathy in its purest, most animalistic form. While the others were working on counteracting the virus, they needed Davis's help to visualize the physiological cause of the symptoms, which could mean only one thing.

They intended to put him in a room with that monster.

WITHIN MOMENTS OF LANDING, the plane had taxied into a hangar where they'd quickly deboarded and squeezed into a black GMC Yukon. The driver, who'd introduced himself only as Badgett, had sped off the moment they closed their doors, seemingly speeding up with every passing mile, which only seamed to brighten the sadistic gleam in his eyes. He appeared to take great pleasure in watching their reflections squirm in the rearview mirror as he raced down dirt roads that hardly looked wide enough to keep the SUV from skidding right over the edge and plummeting into the valley below, although his demeanor had changed as they neared their destination and he'd taken on the role of tour guide, detailing the history of the reappropriated deep underground military base with a tone of reverence.

Fortunately, Davis had taken his propranolol just prior to landing, so as long as he focused on his laptop and not how far the tires rode out over the open air, he could stave off the impending panic attack. It helped to know that his role had little to do with the virus itself. His task was more opportunistic in nature. While the others were working with the teams already assembled within the facility — studying the patients' immune responses, the antibodies they produced, and the genes responsible for creating them — he'd be working directly with the patients in hopes of better qualifying the distinctions between the variants of the Trident Gene.

By the time they'd ascended from the canyon into the maze of aspens and pines leading up to the base, he'd already laid the foundation of an imaging protocol designed to evaluate the less common Trident variants and the structures associated with empathy. He'd been surprised to learn that the base had a fully equipped medical imaging suite and a team of technologists who were already building the sequences he would need to evaluate the insulae, anterior cingulate cortices, and the parahippocampal gyri. They'd have to wait until the patients were on the table to experiment with the tractographic sequences highlighting the neural passageways that connected them, but, all in all, they'd be ready to roll not long after he walked through the door. The only thing left for him to do was formulate a series of questions designed to elicit empathic responses on the EEG, and he was pretty sure he could do so on the fly, if he had to. He felt surprisingly confident about the situation, at least until he remembered the bloodied man slamming himself against the wall of his enclosure, and quickly glanced out the window to clear the mental image.

Davis caught a glimpse of earthen walls rising to either side of the vehicle, and then they were speeding through a concrete tunnel toward armed guards waiting to inspect their vehicle. Everything from that moment on was a blur: passing through a blast door that sealed behind them, weaving through an underground parking lot the size of a small city, climbing from the car and following uniformed men in isolation suits into a subterranean base that offered little more than a hint as to its sheer enormity.

They surrendered their personal belongings, which would be sterilized under ultraviolet light and brought to their quarters, and followed a man in a black uniform with the NeXgen corporate logo emblazoned on the breast down a narrow hallway illuminated by bulbs designed to mimic the rays of the sun. He led them into an anteroom with digital portraits displaying the world topside in real-time, like windows, and turned them over to a man who carried himself with an aura of authority.

"Lewis," the man said, proffering his hand to Pennington. "It's been a long time."

"Not long enough, Phil." Pennington smirked and addressed the others. "Allow me to introduce Dr. Phil Rankin, with whom I rubbed elbows on more than one occasion during his tenure at USAMRIID. Believe me when I say we sequenced some nasty bugs for this guy here."

"None as nasty as this one, though," Rankin said. He turned without another word and guided them through an airlock and into a pass through chamber. Biohazard suits and helmets hung from the walls. Fortunately, Davis wasn't nearly as clumsy at donning his protective attire this time. "We're dealing with a unique virus unlike any we've ever faced before."

Rankin opened the next airlock in the series, led the procession into a chemical shower, and then through the final airlock into an industrial corridor.

"What have you learned about it so far?" Sanders asked.

"While it's both structurally and functionally similar to filoviridae like Ebola and Marburg, it produces glycoprotein molecules that bind to and inhibit nicotinic acetylcholine receptors, altering the host's behavior and causing an acute state of agitation, which we believe is how it spreads."

"Like rabies."

"Precisely, although unlike rabies and other hemorrhagic viruses, which are spread through the transmission of infected fluids, this virus can survive outside of a biological host for nearly ninety minutes."

"It can spread via droplet nuclei?" Pennington said.

The others abruptly stopped walking and Davis bumped into Emily from behind.

"What's the significance?" he asked.

"It means the virus can spread like the flu," Karen said.

"Even during its incubation period," Rankin said.

"That can't possibly be right," Sanders said. "We'd be looking at an organism capable of producing a mass-extinction event within a matter of days."

Rankin waited for them to catch up and gestured to the room on the other side of the Plexiglas barrier behind him. The interior walls were lined with wire cages, stacked one on top of the other. Several workers in isolation suits were scouring tufts of hair and spatters of blood from the walls, the floor, and the bars and liners.

"Which is why you're here," he said. "Our team needs all of the help it can get accelerating the process of producing a vaccine."

"You have the virus's genome and access to the antibodies," Emily said. "What do you need us for?"

It was Pennington who answered.

"Everyone with the standard Trident Gene — nearly ninety-eight percent of the population — is incapable of producing that specific antibody. Injecting it directly will provide immediate protection but will last for only so long. And considering the sheer volume of people who would require those injections, there's no way they'd be able to keep up with the demand. They need us to engineer a retroviral vector capable of altering the host's genome to incorporate the segment of the Trident Gene responsible for producing it."

"That could take months," Emily said.

"I'm afraid we don't have that kind of time," Rankin said.

"Then you'd better start talking," Pennington said. "No more of this classified nonsense. If we're going to help, we're going to need to know everything you know."

Rankin met the director's stare and offered a single nod. Without another word, he turned and struck off deeper into the structure. The five of them followed him through an access-controlled doorway and into a corridor Davis immediately recognized from the live feeds in the medical charts. Empty quarantine rooms passed on either side. The room with the blood-smeared viewing window stood out like a rotten tooth in an otherwise pristine smile.

Davis approached it slowly, cautiously, half-expecting the man on the other side to slam himself against the glass, mere inches away. He leaned closer, until his visor pressed against the window, and found a gap in the dried blood that offered a view of the interior. Every surface was smeared with blood. Handprints. Footprints. It was as though the patient had coated his body with it and attempted to paint the cell, but there was no sign of the man himself.

"A team of archeologists discovered a tomb north of the Arctic Circle," Rankin said. "Inside was a mummified corpse, which we believe to be the initial source of the virus. One of the senior researchers, codenamed Alpha, was the first to be infected. Within a matter of hours, he spiked a life-threatening fever, which broke later that evening, but by then, several others had become symptomatic. Six of the nine were killed by the secondary symptoms of the virus—"

"Hold on," Sanders said. His tone was one of incredulity. "You're saying they attacked and killed each other."

Rankin rounded on him and looked him squarely in the eyes.

"With their bare hands and teeth," he said. "We had their bodies transported here, along with the three survivors, whose records you've presumably familiarized yourselves with by now. Of them, only Patient Beta demonstrates an innate immunity. Her body naturally produces the antibodies without succumbing to the antigen first."

He stopped in front of one of the rooms, clasped his wrists behind his back, and looked through the window. Davis had to stand on his toes to see over the others. The woman inside sat on the edge of the bed, her legs drawn up to her chest and tucked underneath her surgical scrub top. Her red hair was tangled, and her skin was so pale that her freckles stood out, even from a distance. She looked up at them through seemingly indifferent blue eyes, then rolled over onto her side and drew the blanket over her head.

"Why is she here and not in a hospital?" Davis asked.

"Just because she's immune doesn't mean she's not infected," Sanders said. "If they're right about the transmissibility of the virus, it would be too big of a risk."

Davis stepped closer to the window and placed his palm against it. The poor woman looked so small and vulnerable. He could only imagine how terrified she must have been.

"Alpha has tolerated the transition significantly better," Rankin said, drawing their attention to the window across the corridor.

A tall, slender man wearing powder-blue scrubs stood at the back of the room, so still that at first Davis didn't even see him. He felt the heat of the man's eyes upon him and looked up to meet the man's stare—

His ears fill with screams and the repeated blats of an alarm Klaxon. He smells smoke. Tastes electricity in the air. Feels sparks raining down upon him. Focuses on a man rushing toward him, blood streaming from his ruined eye. He raises his rifle—

—and quickly averted his gaze.

The man known as Alpha cocked his head, first one way, and then the other. A broad smile appeared on his face and suddenly Davis wanted to be anywhere else in the world. There was something about the man, something cold and predatory, an otherness he recognized from the eyes of Stephen Leonard Thomas as he pressed his black-painted face against the window in the library door and Richard Wesley Taylor in the moments before the razorblade passed through his chin and burst from the top of his head.

Davis closed his eyes and stepped backward, colliding with Emily.

"Three-two-one," he whispered. "Three-two-one. Three . . . two . . . one."

Again, Davis opened his eyes and found Alpha standing at the window, his palms pressed against the glass. He mouthed six words that Davis would have recognized anywhere.

I'll be seeing you again soon.

DAVIS UNCONSCIOUSLY RETREATED a step as the medical staff rolled Patient Gamma into the MRI suite. Granted, the man was heavily sedated and strapped to the table on the other side of the reinforced glass, but Davis could still positively feel the rage radiating from him. The physicians had done their best to treat Gamma's facial wounds, both from the superficial bleeding caused by the hemorrhagic disease and from repeatedly hurling himself against the glass, but with as many as there were, how deeply he'd been cut, and the inability of his blood to clot properly, it looked more like they'd attempted to suture hamburger into a horrific facsimile of a human face. It glistened with salve and the fresh blood seeping from the ruptured capillaries. Only Gamma's eyelids remained reasonably intact. With them closed, he looked like he was wearing those little white goggles people used in tanning beds. His hair stood up where they'd reattached his scalp to his cranium, much of which, they'd been forewarned, was riddled with fractures that would appear on the scan like the shell of a hard-boiled egg dropped from a great height.

"Don't worry," Victor Dupuis said. The MRI technologist assumed his seat at the console and prepared to run the sequences he'd programmed to Davis's precise specifications. "That propofol drip will keep him from hurting himself or anyone else for about ninety minutes, which is more than enough time to run through our entire protocol."

Davis nodded and once more approached the window overlooking the patient suite, although he didn't feel all that much better. He'd seen the remains that had been brought back from the Arctic Circle with the three surviving patients. Never in his life had he imagined that a man could inflict such violent and visceral damage upon another human being. For as little as he wanted to be in the same underground facility as Gamma, he was positively dying to get him inside the magnet to see if he could figure out what had caused the sudden change in behavior.

Ava Calloway, the resident physician assistant, attached her isolation suit to the coil hanging from the ceiling so she could remain with the patient to monitor his condition. She hooked the head of the table to the gantry, aligned the laser sight to Gamma's brow, and fed him into the narrow tube. As his restrained chest, hips, and legs disappeared into the machine, his face appeared on the ancillary monitor displaying the feed from the closed-circuit camera mounted to the helmet-like magnetic coil. While it obscured the better part of his nose and mouth, Davis could still clearly see Gamma's stitched cheeks and closed eyes, the twin bulges of his irises occasionally moving beneath the lids.

The machine ramped up as Dupuis initiated the first sequence, eliciting a cacophony of high-pitched squealing, grinding, and thumping from the adjacent room. Black-and-white images in all three planes formed on the primary monitor. The damage to Gamma's brain was readily apparent. There were countless subdural hemorrhages, as evidenced by the sheer volume of blood between his skull and his brain, compressing and laterally displacing it.

"Poor guy's lucky to be alive with a hematoma that large," Dupuis said.

"I don't think 'lucky' is a word I'd use to describe him," Davis said.

Ava gave Gamma the widest possible berth as she donned a pair of noise-cancelling headphones and took up position beside the non-magnetic vitals monitoring system.

The intonation of the racket changed from one sequence to the next as Dupuis acquired the specific imagery Davis wanted. Countless tiny intracranial hemorrhages appeared on the gradient echo imagery, pinpointing where the virus had caused localized bleeding from the microscopic capillaries in the brain, and while it would only be a matter of time before Gamma literally bled to death within the confines of his own head, they were the least concerning of the physical manifestations of the disease. Davis's original theory had proven correct. The hemorrhaging had caused necrotic lesions to form on the amygdalae, eroding their outer cortices, and bleeding within the gray matter of the middle and orbital gyri of the frontal lobe, effectively drowning the neural pathways. There also appeared to be a significant accumulation of blood in the cisterna magna and the third and fourth ventricles, shunting the former and compartmentalizing the latter, increasingly cutting off the autonomic portion of the brain from its higher-order capabilities.

"Can you run a time-of-flight sequence so we can trace the flow of blood?" Davis asked.

Dupuis skipped ahead to the next sequence and scanned the images, which showed a faint white tracery outlining the brainstem and sporadic dots throughout the cerebrum.

"The increased pressure has blocked the flow of blood beyond the Circle of Willis," the tech said. He started the three-dimensional reconstruction, which demonstrated the carotid arteries, their bifurcations within the neck, and a semicircular connection between them at the base of the skull, but little more than an outline of the peripheral arteries. "The brain isn't receiving oxygen. It's actively dying before our eyes."

"I assume the diffusion tensor imaging shows similar deterioration of the white matter tracts between the brainstem and the cerebrum," Davis said.

He detected movement from the corner of his eye and glanced at Gamma's face on the screen, just in time to see the twin bulges of his irises twitch beneath his closed eyelids.

Dupuis manipulated the scan and post-processed the data until Davis had his answer. Where there should have been bright, wispy lines radiating throughout the brain like the tentacles of an anemone, there were now only a handful of vessels extending beyond the thalamus, which had been effectively isolated from the cerebrum by the hemorrhaging within the third and fourth ventricles.

"The patient has essentially been cut off from all conscious thought," Davis said. "Everything from logic and reasoning to spatiotemporal awareness and voluntary muscle control — everything that makes him human — leaving him at the mercy of his hindbrain. He's bypassed mere psychopathy and undergone a physiological transformation from a normal human being into an animal for whom every unconscious decision, no matter how inconsequential, is a matter of survival. Without the benefit of his higher faculties to mitigate his impulses or rationalize the consequences of his actions, every stimulus now potentially triggers a kill-or-be-killed response that can only end in bloodshed."

"The medical team suspected as much from the autopsies of the others who arrived with him, but the damage to Gamma's brain is considerably more extensive," Dupuis said. "The condition's obviously degenerative."

"It's worse than that," Davis said. "The condition's terminal. Once the nervous tissue dies, there's no hope for recovery. There's no medication capable of reviving dead neurons or a transplant that can replace necrotic tissue. For all intents and purposes, whoever Gamma was before is now dead."

Again, Gamma's irises twitched on the adjacent monitor.

"Then we need to evaluate the full extent of the dead tissue," Dupuis said. "If we can establish a pattern for its progression and severity, then surely we can generate a predictive model for the entire brain, including the cerebrum and hindbrain."

"Which would help us determine how long the virus takes to cause death both at the cerebral and the organismic level."

"Give me a second," Dupuis said. "Surely I can program a sequence to help us map—"

"The patient's blood pressure is rising," Ava said through the speaker, her voice nearly drowned out by thumping of the machinery. "So is his heart rate. We're going to have to cut this short."

"We just need a little more time," Dupuis said. "Can you dial up the propofol?"

"Not without risking respiratory failure. And regardless of whether I have to intubate him or he wakes up on his own, you're out of time."

"I just need five more minutes—"

The monitor alarmed and Gamma's eyes snapped open, blood draining from the corners like tears. His pupils abruptly constricted. He whipped his head from side to side within the coil and thrashed against his bindings.

A red light bloomed inside the suite and a warning siren blared. Ava jumped up, screamed something they couldn't hear, and threw herself on top of Gamma to hold him down. Davis could only watch in horror as Gamma beat his head against the coil, smearing blood everywhere and snapping at the camera like an animal.

A drumroll of footsteps echoed from down the corridor. Half a dozen men in yellow suits shouldered through the doorway and entered the suite. It took all of them to immobilize Gamma while Dupuis remotely moved the table out of the gantry. Gamma kicked and flailed in a desperate attempt to slip his bindings. He freed one of his arms and slashed at everyone within range until Ava was once more able to sedate him.

Davis's heart was beating so hard and fast that it was all he could hear as he watched men and women in blood-spattered isolation suits wheel Gamma out of the room and back to his cage.

22

Snoqualmie, Washington

Banks unconsciously swirled the amber liquid in her glass as she scrutinized the photographs she'd taken of the drawings in Ciara's notebook. She'd poured herself a celebratory glass of bourbon but had yet to bring it to her lips. The way she was feeling, she knew that once she took that first sip, there was no turning back. Absolutely nothing that had transpired within the past few days made the slightest bit of sense. Here she was, sitting in a hotel room a world away from her home, studying photorealistic drawings made by a girl who, in many ways, frightened her nearly as much as the man who, mere hours earlier, had looked straight at her through the cameras of the agents closing in on him and spoken the words that played over and over in her head.

This is only the beginning.

She rose from the table, headed to the bathroom, and dumped her drink down the drain, but then thought better of it and poured herself another. This one she threw back without hesitation and returned to her work with an empty glass and fire in her chest.

"This is crazy," she said out loud.

And it was. There was no doubt about it. The problem was that it was also completely rational at the same time, which only added to her confusion. She didn't have to close her eyes to see the expression on Matthew Avery Marshall's face when she'd put a bullet through it, and she certainly didn't have to concentrate very hard to hear him speak those final words; the man they'd identified as Ephraim Abraham Waller had worn an identical expression and uttered the same epithet before thrusting a scalpel into the side of his tattooed neck. They were two completely different people — two completely different *dead* people — but if someone had wired her to a polygraph machine and asked her whether she believed they were, in fact, one in the same, she didn't know how she'd respond, let alone what the readout would say about her answer.

Ciara had drawn two more pictures, which the counselor had photographed and emailed to Banks, along with a brief note suggesting that she was cautiously optimistic that the girl had gotten the darkness out of her system. The drawings said otherwise to Banks, who recognized them for what they truly were.

She grabbed her phone and noticed that she had a new message. The Harvard professor, Jack Lucas, had called her back, but she'd have to follow up on that later. Right now, she needed to chase this line of thought and see where it led. She dialed Duvall's number and glanced at the clock while it rang through to the forensics specialist's voicemail. 2:38 AM. At least one of them was getting a little sleep.

"I'm sending you a collection of pictures," Banks said. She wanted to describe what she believed they showed, but she couldn't find the words. "Give me a call once you've had a chance to look at them."

She hung up, tossed the phone onto the bed, and returned to her laptop. The drawing on the screen was of a rocky desert landscape from the perspective of a dirt road snaking through brush and cacti toward a broad mesa. Horizontal steppes ascended its face, like an ancient Grecian amphitheater. While the subject matter was dramatically different than Ciara's other pieces, with their visceral and violent imagery, there was no mistaking the connection.

It was a rock quarry.

Banks opened a new window and searched for "New Mexico Quarry Murders 1985." The screen filled with stories about the unsolved killings of the six young women whose bodies had been discovered near the Chino Mine in Santa Clara, New Mexico. She scrolled past the smiling faces of the victims, all of them just entering the prime of their lives. Three brunettes, two blonds, and a redhead. Three sets of blue eyes, two brown, and one hazel. She skimmed through recounts of a town torn apart at the seams, desperate parents and heartbreaking pleas for outside help, and finally the somber resolution provided by photographs of deputy sheriffs picking their way down a talus slope, away from the brown and white Broncos parked at the top of the hill and toward a dark shaft, from inside of which a lone leg protruded. This was the image picked up by the national press, the one that ran in papers from LA to New York, and everywhere in between. One of two, anyway. The other being a snapshot taken at the entrance to the quarry, miles away from where the bodies were found, a picture nearly identical to the drawing from Ciara's notebook.

According to the articles, there'd been one person of interest who'd stood apart from the others, but ultimately no charges had been filed against him. Harold Saltzman, a fifty-eight-year-old crushing foreman, had lived in the same neighborhood as two of the victims and worked at the quarry with the father of a third. The police had tangentially connected him to the remaining three victims through circumstantial evidence so tenuous that they hadn't been able to secure a search warrant and he hadn't stuck around town while they tried to build a case against him. A follow-up piece from two years later relayed the news that Saltzman had died of lung cancer in another state and included the picture from his obituary.

All she needed to see were his eyes.

Banks abruptly stood and paced the small room. Conflicting emotions warred within her. She simultaneously wanted to smash everything she could get her hands on and crawl into bed for the rest of her life. She settled for pouring herself another glass of the Heritage BSB and returning to the table. There was no way she was going to be able to sleep tonight, especially if she was right about the other seemingly random drawing from the sketchbook, so she might as well just give up on the prospect and get back to work.

She opened the file and stared at a drawing of a decrepit house built on blocks. The roof was tin, the walls weathered vertical planks. The porch sagged in the middle, where the uneven steps ascended from the broad lawn. The branches of deciduous trees wrapped around it like arms trying to crush it in a wooden embrace. She could tell by the Spanish moss bearding their boughs that the setting was somewhere down south, a fact confirmed by a quick search of "Henry Laurent Monroe Vermilion Parish."

The images were yellowed and warped; obviously old newspaper clippings scanned into some library's database. The first was of a house identical to the one Ciara had drawn, only there were mounds of dirt in front of it and police officers with heavy burlap uniforms and white gloves dragging bodies out from underneath it. The second showed a severe man with dark hair combed over his head and a thick beard that had gone gray at the chin. He wore a white shirt without a tie and a suit jacket with wide lapels and looked like any other man she'd ever seen from that era, except for his eyes. They were the color of cinders crackling in the charcoaled remnants of a gutted fire, rings of light burning within the shadows cast by his bushy brows.

Banks shivered and had to rub her arms to get the blood flowing.

They were the same eyes as those of Harold Saltzman, Matthew Avery Marshall, and Ephraim Abraham Waller.

Or at least the same dark sentience she recognized behind them.

BANKS SWALLOWED some ibuprofen with as much water as she could stomach. The shower had helped, but she'd be alternating painkillers for the rest of the day if she hoped to get through it. The lack of sleep made her both mentally and physically sluggish, and yet she hadn't been able to turn off her mind long enough to succumb to the exhaustion. She'd finally just given up, put together a few items she intended to use to test Ciara's abilities, and gotten in the car.

Visitation hours at the Snoqualmie Center for Children had yet to begin, so she'd waited in the Ford Expedition she'd signed out of the pool at the Seattle Field Office until the counselor she recognized from the previous day pulled into the parking lot. Talking her into arranging another meeting with the girl hadn't been as easy as she'd hoped, though. To her credit, Amanda Carter was fiercely protective of her charges; however, Banks had been able to see through the woman's bluster to how she really felt: she was terrified of the girl. Maybe not of Ciara herself, per se, but of whatever part of her was responsible for the drawings. It was a feeling with which Banks completely sympathized, and the sole reason she was sitting in the same infernal visitation room, her feet tapping restlessly while she waited for the counselor to fetch the girl from her room.

Ciara tentatively opened the door and peeked around it, admitting the scents of powdered eggs and sausage links from the cafeteria. She entered with her eyes down and her shoulders hunched, as though prepared for the worst.

"Please," Banks said. "Sit down. You're not in trouble or anything. I just want to talk to you for a few minutes. I mean, if that's okay."

The girl nodded, but she approached the table warily. As Amanda had insisted, the door to the room remained cracked just far enough that Banks could see the counselor standing off to the side, ready to barge in if she so much as sensed there was a problem.

"Look, I'll be honest," Banks said. "I don't even know exactly why I'm here, other than the fact that I've seen some things I can't explain, and I simply can't find a way to let it go. I think you know what I mean."

Ciara nodded and eased into the chair across the table from her.

"And if I'm right, you can't explain them either."

The girl shook her head. Her expression was one of profound sadness.

"Did Miss Amanda tell you that you helped save a young woman's life?" Banks cocked her head and tried to meet Ciara's stare, which was nearly concealed behind her bangs. "Because of that picture you drew, we were able to locate the house where she'd been taken and get her out of there before anything really bad happened. She's at the hospital now, safe and unharmed.

Scared to death, I'm sure, but she'll be able to work through it in time. Thanks to you."

A faint smile traced Ciara's lips and a tear crept from the corner of her eye. She hurriedly wiped it away.

"Can you think of any way you might have known what was going to happen to her?" Banks asked. "Maybe she was your friend on Facebook or you followed her on Instagram?"

Ciara shook her head.

"Does the name Hannah Serviess mean anything to you?"

Again, a shake of the head.

"What about Ephraim Waller?"

The girl furrowed her brow, but then shook her head.

"Would it be okay if I showed you some pictures?" Banks asked.

Ciara glanced back at the door, but she relented with a subtle nod.

Banks reached underneath the table and brought out four panels she'd cut from a piece of poster board. She'd printed dozens of photos on the hotel's printer and used them to create police lineups of eight individuals, in two rows of four. The first featured men in their sixties, all with dark hair and various configurations of gray in their beards.

"Do you remember the picture you drew of the house built on blocks?" she asked. "The one surrounded by trees?"

Ciara nodded.

"If you were to imagine that one of these men lived there, which one would it be?"

The girl looked up at her and raised her eyebrows.

Banks smiled.

"I know how that must sound," she said. "Humor me on this one, okay?"

Ciara rolled her eyes and perused the photographs. Her expression faded from bemusement to discomfort as she scrutinized the men. She rubbed her fingertips on the second image in the top row, smearing the ink across the man's face.

Banks struggled to keep her smile from faltering. The girl had chosen Henry Laurent Monroe, the monster who'd murdered six young black girls and buried them under his home. Her hands trembled ever so slightly as she removed the lineup and replaced it with another, but she chalked it up to the copious amounts of caffeine she'd consumed.

"I want you to think about the landscape you drew," she said. "The one with the mountain and the rock quarry. Imagine the kind of person who might spend time there. Maybe he works there or lives nearby. Now, which one of these men might he be?"

Ciara didn't hesitate. She selected the first man on the bottom row, the ink from her fingertips blotting the face of Harold Saltzman, the crushing foreman who'd been the prime suspect in the murders of the women exhumed from the shaft.

"I understand how strange this must seem," Banks said. Her heart was beating at a million miles an hour, but she couldn't afford to show her excitement and risk scaring the young girl. "I just wanted you to get a feel for what I'm trying to do here. The final two examples are less specific. I just want you to look at the faces, okay? No need to imagine where they might live or work or anything like that."

Ciara offered a weak smile, although it was obviously forced. She obviously knew she was being tested and was willing to tolerate it, at least for the time being.

The third display featured eight young women in their early to mid-twenties, all except for one of whom had been chosen at random from the internet. Ciara studied their faces for several seconds before looking up in confusion.

"Do you recognize any of these women?" Banks asked. "Take all the time you need."

She watched the girl's eyes move from one photo to the next, across the top row and then to the bottom, where it lingered on the second picture from the left. Ciara leaned closer, then farther away. Finally, she tapped the picture several times with her index finger.

Banks concentrated on maintaining a neutral expression.

"You've seen this woman before?" she asked.

Ciara opened her mouth, but only a sharp breath emerged. She appeared frustrated, so Banks tried to help her out.

"Do you know who this woman is?"

The girl shook her head.

"But you've seen her before?"

Ciara held her hand horizontally and tipped it from one side to the other.

"You think you've seen her before, but you're not quite sure."

A hesitant nod.

"Have you ever been to Detroit?"

The girl recoiled, seemingly surprised by the question. And then it hit her. Her eyes dampened with tears as she traced the contours of the woman's face with her fingertips.

"This is Hannah Serviess," Banks whispered.

Ciara closed her eyes and hung her head so she could hide behind her hair.

Banks slid the third lineup out from beneath the girl and replaced it with the final one, which displayed eight men, all African American, all heavily tattooed, all with dreadlocks of various lengths, all of them as close to identical as she could find.

The moment Ciara opened her eyes, they immediately widened in terror.

She slapped her hand over the man on the far right of the top row. Ephraim Abraham Waller, who'd intended to kill Hannah in the ritualistic manner of the blood eagle but had opened his own carotid artery instead. Ciara sputtered and gasped in a desperate attempt to speak.

Miss Amanda opened the door wider, prepared to intercede. Banks held up her hand, silently begging for just a few more seconds.

Ciara looked frantically around the room until her eyes settled on Banks's pen. She grabbed it, flipped the lineup over, and wrote the same five words over and over.

This is only the beginning.
This is only the beginning.
This is only the beginning.

She cast aside the pen and started to sob.

Banks rushed to Ciara's side and wrapped her arms around the girl, whose entire body shuddered against her.

"It's okay," she said. "Everything's going to be all right. He can't hurt you. You have my word. He can't hurt anyone now."

Ciara buried her face in Banks's chest and clung to her so tightly that she could barely breathe. And Banks knew, right then and there, that she'd do everything in her power to make sure that nothing happened to this poor child ever again.

———

"There's no one who can take her in?" Banks asked.

"A great aunt and uncle in Maine and one of her mother's cousins in Kansas, but none of them seem thrilled about the prospect," Amanda said.

They stood at the back of the dayroom, watching kids burdened by the weight of the world attempting to find some semblance of normalcy. They all lived in the moment, trying to be happy for the sake of the others while doing everything in their power not to dwell on the fact that they were wards of the state and would likely never have what so many others took for granted. In a lot of ways, their lives mirrored Banks's own childhood. Her father had left while she was still in diapers and her mother had worked two jobs just to keep a roof over their heads. There'd been a lady from social services who'd checked in on her once a month and could have easily removed her from her home for the violation of any number of regulations. Instead, the caseworker had pulled a few strings to get Banks into a program for at-risk youth that had shown her a path she wouldn't have found on her own, one that led to a college education and the Federal Bureau of Investigation.

"Then what happens to her now?" she asked.

"We're still in the process of figuring that out," Amanda said. She rubbed her temples as though to combat a headache. "Once everything's settled, she stands to inherit a fair amount of money from her parents' estate—"

"Which will make her a whole lot more attractive to her relatives."

"Or at least put her in a position of enrolling at a private school somewhere, should that be the route she chooses to take. Once the court appoints an advocate, she'll be able to explore her options."

"What about the talking thing?"

Amanda offered a wan smile and leaned back against the wall, her face pale under the industrial lighting. The younger children were all gathered around a board game on one of the tables, while the older ones were divided into what appeared to be cliques, although of the kind Banks couldn't easily discern. Ciara sat alone on a beanbag in the far corner, her sketchpad propped on her thighs, peeking around it every so often to catch a glimpse of the TV. Banks could only imagine the thoughts going through her head.

"She can continue working with our therapists for as long as she's here. We lack the resources to bring in the kind of specialist she needs, though. And considering her condition's largely psychosomatic, she could very well start talking again at any moment. There's no way of knowing. It's hard to watch. I can see the frustration growing inside her and worry that the harder she fights it, the longer it'll take to break through to the other side."

"And the drawings?"

A cloud settled over the counselor's features. It was obvious she wanted nothing to do with them.

"I guess we'll just have to wait and see."

Amanda's expression abruptly changed. She pushed off from the wall and headed over to the table surrounded by small children, several of whom cheered her arrival.

Banks hung back, uncertain why she was even still here. There were no new developments back home in Detroit and she'd already heard back from the Bureau office in Albuquerque, who'd confirmed that Harold Saltzman had died more than two decades ago and requested that she forward any new evidence to the cold case team they ran in conjunction with the state police. They'd undoubtedly regretted extending the offer when they received a photograph of a pencil drawing and a hurriedly assembled lineup with the smudged face of a dead man.

What more could she possibly do here? It wasn't like she was in a position to take home a damaged teenager who'd just lost her entire family, although the idea of leaving her here didn't sit right with Banks, either. As irrational as it was, she felt an emotional attachment to Ciara, an instinctive protectiveness of the young girl, who just sat there, drawing away, while a long-haired boy Banks hadn't seen enter the room watched her through eyes that didn't even try to hide what he'd do to her if her could get her alone. Banks had known plenty of guys like him through the years. They got what they wanted and then moved on to the next conquest, leaving only pain in their wake, just as her father had.

The boy glanced over at her. She offered a smile meant to convey the message that she could see right through him, but he appeared unfazed by the implied challenge. He simply sank deeper into his seat, blew his hair out of his eyes, and resumed pushing puzzle pieces across the table.

Banks's phone vibrated in its holster on her hip. She glanced at the number and stepped outside of earshot before answering.

"Took you long enough."

"It's not like my plate isn't full enough without you adding to it," Duvall said. "Especially with something like this. How am I even supposed to respond?"

"That's kind of where I'm at, too," Banks said. She leaned against the wall in such a way that she could still see Ciara down the hallway. "None of this makes any sense."

"Unless you're willing to take it all at face value."

"You mean the part about a fifteen-year-old kid drawing historical crime scenes peripherally related to the case we're working now, or the part about her picking killers who've been dead for decades out of a lineup?"

"Either. Both. I don't know. All I can say is that there's another young woman who's alive today because of her."

Ciara flipped the page and started on another picture, her hand blurring across the page.

"She identified Saltzman as the guy who killed those girls in New Mexico," Banks said. "How could she have possibly known when he was hardly mentioned as a person-of-interest in the papers nearly forty years ago?"

"She couldn't have made the connection between the cases without knowing about the eyes we found in The Executioner's possession," Duvall said. "And we're not about to release that information anytime soon, if ever. You're certain you didn't tell her about them?"

Banks thought carefully before responding. She knew the answer was of great consequence.

"No," she finally said. "And even with having depicted his victims with their eyes cut out, I can't believe she would have drawn parallels to two historical serial killers, and certainly not since she only found out yesterday that there was a correlation between her drawings and the actual murders."

"What do you think of her?" Duvall asked. "I mean, what's your gut tell you?"

Banks watched Ciara draw for several seconds, oblivious to everyone and everything around her.

"There's something about her, Desmond," she said. "Something . . .

special. I don't know how to describe it. That's the whole reason I'm still here. I should have been on a plane first thing this morning, but I can't bring myself to leave—"

"You mean you're still there?" Duvall said. "Listen, Banks. The moment you hang up with me, you need to book the next flight back here. While you still can."

The way he said it made the hairs rise on the back of her neck.

"What's going on?"

"I don't know. All I can say is that my counterparts at other labs around the country have called in all available staff and they've been told to be prepared to coordinate real-time responses with the JTTF and the national lab at Quantico."

"Responses to what? Do we have intel about an impending terrorist attack?"

"Not that anyone would tell me, but, if so, I'm guessing the threat's biological in nature. They've already sealed off an entire city block on Manhattan, and while they're calling it a precautionary measure, the fact that they've raised the travel advisory level to orange and activated CDC screening centers in all of the major airports leads me to believe that you're going to have a hell of a time getting home if you don't do so soon. Better get on it."

Duvall ended the call, leaving Banks staring at a blank screen. She opened her browser and glanced at the news section. Several articles featured pictures of a hard cordon enforced by JTTF officers in CBRN suits, beyond which towered an apartment complex surrounded by agents in yellow Class A isolation garb. One of the photographs had captured a blurry image of a gurney being wheeled out the front doors of the complex and into the shadow of the helicopter circling overhead. There wasn't a body bag on it, but rather a clear medical isolation transport capsule.

There were other articles, too, popping up right before her eyes. Overwhelmed hospitals in California and New York. Airport closures in Minnesota and Alaska, where an Air Force Base had already been placed on lockdown. Vague reports of a rash of high fevers caused by a virus rumored to be everything from a novel coronavirus to Ebola to the bubonic plague. Conspiracy theories about government coverups. Travel warnings and official press releases designed to suppress panic without delivering any actual information.

"Jesus," Banks whispered, and speed-dialed the FBI's travel agency.

23

New York City, New York

Milana jogged up the stairs from the subway and merged into the pedestrian traffic on 63rd. She was nearly a block away when she realized she didn't hear the clicking of heels behind her and had to stop and wait for her mother to catch up. Not that she was apparently in any hurry to do so, despite having an extra eleven blocks to walk thanks to the MTA closing down the Q Line, for whatever stupid reason. At least her mother hadn't thrown a fit like some of the other passengers, who'd complained to no end about whatever was going on in Midtown that'd turned the trains going anywhere near the East Side into cattle cars. There was even speculation that it might have something to do with the CDC, which presumably explained the handful of people she'd seen wearing surgical masks.

Rosella hadn't spoken a word since they'd left the lawyer's office downtown, a small blessing for which Milana was exceedingly grateful. While she hadn't been surprised to learn that her *pūridaia* had bundled all of her worldly possessions into a trust that would soon be a hundred grand richer with the life insurance money, her mother had apparently thought she'd be walking out of there with a big fat cashier's check instead of the promise of an eventual $763 a month for the next ten years and a place to live until such time as Milana agreed to sell the townhouse. The will stipulated that the property would be held in her name alone until her 26th birthday, making it impossible for her mother to sell it out from underneath her or browbeat her into liquidating the assets until after she finished grad school.

It'd already been a long day and all she wanted to do was go back to bed. Before her mother had even started her day, Milana had already opened the coffeehouse, attended two classes, met with the professor of the class she was going to miss, and grabbed some supplies to make sandwiches. Of course, her mother had barely picked at hers, but, in her defense, she'd looked like she just crawled out of her own grave, a state of being that hadn't really improved as the day wore on.

They walked together in silence, through streets filling with traffic that would eventually come to a standstill when all of the professionals fought their way back to the suburbs. Milana was still debating the merits of grabbing a couple hours of sleep and trying to squeeze in a few clients as she ascended the steps and entered the townhouse, oblivious to the fact that her mother had stopped on the sidewalk.

"I'm sorry," Rosella said.

Milana turned and looked down at her mother, who wore a relatively conservative charcoal gray suit that accentuated the hint of the tan line on her bosoms. She couldn't help but wonder if Rosella had picked it out for just this occasion, knowing that her mother's death couldn't be very far off.

"For what?" she asked.

Rosella shook her head and started up the stairs. She couldn't seem to raise her eyes to meet her daughter's.

"For everything."

She brushed past Milana, who felt the heat radiating from her. Up close, she could see the sweat beading on her mother's pale face and upper chest.

"Hold up," she said, placing the back of her hand against her mother's cheek. "You're burning up."

"I just need a drink is all," Rosella said. She offered a wan smile. "It's been a rough day."

Milana let her mother into the apartment and followed her to the kitchen. Her grandmother kept a bottle of *pálinka* hidden underneath the sink, which, apparently, her mother already knew. She went straight for it and took a pull from the bottle. Milana grabbed a glass from the cupboard and set it on the table.

"She was my mom," Rosella said. She collapsed into a chair and looked up at her daughter, but she didn't say anything else. She didn't have to; Milana knew how she felt. While her feelings for the woman who'd given her life were complicated, those she had for the woman who'd raised her weren't.

Milana made sandwiches in silence and served her mother on a paper plate so she wouldn't have to do dishes later. Rosella thanked her with a nod, but just stared at the food while she poured herself three fingers of the fruit brandy. She sipped it slowly, her expression unreadable, even to someone as skilled as Milana.

"You ever wake up one day and wonder how you got there?" Rosella asked. "I'm not talking about after a night out on the town. More like, you just wake up one morning and realize that you're not where you're supposed to be, like years have passed and you don't know how. Like, suddenly, everything about you — about the world around you — is somehow, I don't know . . . wrong."

"I remember waking up one morning to find my mother gone," Milana said.

Rosella nodded.

"I won't pretend to know how you feel," she said. "I know I hurt you, but not as much as I would have if you'd stayed with me."

"I guess we'll never know, will we?"

"Your grandmother was a good mother; something I could never be."

"Not that you even tried."

"You don't think I tried?" her mother shouted, slamming her glass on the table. She took a moment to compose herself. "I just wanted you to know that I'm sorry. That's all."

Milana finished her sandwich and dumped the plate in the trash, all without letting her mother see the tears in her eyes.

"I know you're hurting," her mother said. "I'm hurting, too. Maybe between the two of us we can figure out how to get through this."

Milana's first thought was that Rosella was just trying to get her to let her guard down so she could broach the subject of selling the house, but she saw no sign of deception in her mother's face, only deep sadness and age beyond her years.

"I'll set you up in your old room," Milana said. "You know, if you're going to be staying here for a while."

"That's nice of you, but that's your room now. I'll find a hotel. At least until we can clean out your grandmother's room. Maybe that's something I can do. If you think it will help."

Milana found herself hoping that her mother would actually stick around this time, and she hated herself for it.

"We can figure that out later," she said. "Why don't you get some sleep? You look like hot garbage."

"That good, huh? Believe it or not, I probably feel worse than I look."

Milana forced a laugh, but she thought that was highly unlikely. Her mother's eyes were watery and bloodshot, her skin like wax, and her blouse had become nearly transparent with sweat. She couldn't help but wonder if her mother was going through some kind of withdrawal.

Rosella pushed herself up from the table and blew out a long breath that Milana could smell from across the room. It reminded her of her grandmother's, near the end.

Her mother gave her a gentle squeeze on the shoulder and headed out into the parlor. Milana listened to the sluggish footsteps all the way down the hallway and up the stairs before she hopped down from the countertop. She tossed her mother's uneaten sandwich into the empty refrigerator and set her glass in the sink. After momentarily debating taking a swig of the brandy and thinking better of it, she screwed on the cap, crossed the room, and opened the cupboard underneath—

Something screeched and darted back into the corner. She caught twin reflections of eyeshine and a fleshy pink tail and then it was gone, but she could hear it back there, scratching at the wood.

"That's so freaking gross," she said.

She got the broom from the pantry, nudged aside the bottles of cleaner, and jabbed it back into the darkened recesses—

Several rats squealed and poured from the cupboard.

Milana screamed and hopped from one foot to the other as she swatted at the vermin until they vanished from sight, retreating beneath the appliances and into the hollow walls, where she could still hear them, scurrying behind the plaster.

HER MOTHER HAD PASSED out in her old room with the light on. Granted, it was Milana's room now, but she didn't really care; it wasn't like she was ever home long enough to use it, anyway. She was just about to turn off the light when it struck her just how bad her mother looked. Her bangs were plastered to her forehead, her makeup smudged and patchy, her skin nearly as white as the comforter she'd cast aside. The pillow was damp with sweat, and her shoulders hardly rose with her shallow respirations.

Milana didn't know the first thing about treating the symptoms of withdrawal, but she'd seen it enough times on TV to know that the two of them had some rough times ahead, assuming that was even the problem. She didn't know where her mother had been or what she'd been doing there. For all she knew, her mother had brought back a nasty case of malaria from the Amazon jungle or contracted some designer virus while scaling the Great Wall of China. It didn't matter, though; the least she could do was stock up on some soup and crackers to get her through the worst of it.

She leaned over the bed and reached for the blankets to cover up her mother, but the heat radiating from her caused Milana to pull up short. She didn't even need to touch her mother's skin to know that her fever had climbed in just the few minutes since she'd gone upstairs to lie down. What would her grandmother have prescribed? Ginseng and echinacea? Yarrow root and peppermint? She hurried downstairs and threw open the cupboard.

Unfortunately, they were out of just about every ingredient she could boil into tea. At least there was still a handful of ibuprofen in the bottle she kept in her backpack. She grabbed the pills, filled a glass of water, and rushed back upstairs.

"Here." She crouched beside her mother's bed and gently nudged her shoulder. "Take these. You're burning up."

Rosella groaned and rolled onto her back, her mouth hanging open just like Pūridaia's had in the moments after her passing.

Milana set the glass on the nightstand, reached underneath her mother's neck, and raised her head—

A blitzkrieg of images assaults her. The vessels in a pair of eyes rupture, flooding the whites. She smells sickness and, beneath it, the unmistakable stench of death. Hears the wet gasp of a breath being drawn into flooded lungs, a scream she recognizes as her own, and the tinkle of shattering glass. Looks out the window and sees the tree across the street, its branches filled with black birds. They erupt into the night sky, blotting out the stars.

—and dropped her mother's head back onto the pillow.

Rosella grunted and rolled over to help her. She held out her hand, collected the capsules, and stuffed them into her mouth. A single sip of water to wash them down and she was back asleep again.

"Jesus," Milana whispered.

She needed to get out of there, get some fresh air and clear her head. Stock up on enough food to get them through the next few days. Maybe she could even stop by the clinic and see if they'd be willing to help her figure out if her mother was actually sick or just going through withdrawal.

On the off chance that Rosella awakened before she returned, she left a note on the nightstand and set off toward 2nd Ave with the intention of hitting a market on the way to the urgent care clinic on 67th. She'd hoped to take the subway, but with Q Line still out of commission, she was forced to hoof it. Traffic was surprisingly light. There were fewer people on the sidewalks, too, and a good number of them wore the surgical masks they kept around for heavy pollution days, averting their bloodshot eyes as they hurried to get to wherever they were going.

Sirens wailed in the distance, growing louder and louder until an ambulance streaked across 2nd toward New York-Presbyterian, followed in rapid succession by another. A helicopter thundered across the sky overhead, the Channel 4 logo clearly visible on its underside. She looked back down and nearly ran into an elderly woman, who swore at her, bundled up her Chihuahua, and hustled on her way.

Milana had lived in the city her entire life, more than long enough to have forged something of a symbiotic relationship with it. Its pulse mirrored her own, their moods one and the same.

Something was definitely wrong.

She crossed with the light on 74th. A taxi screeched to a halt, mere inches away from her, so close she had to slam her hand on its hood for balance. The driver's face was pale, his eyes red, and the collar of his shirt soaked with sweat. His hand shook when he waved for her to hurry across.

The line at the East Side Grocery was out the door, forcing shoppers to fight their way through the press of bodies just to get out the door with their purchases. A woman tripped and went down, the contents of her bag tumbling across the ground. A man from the line swooped in, presumably to help her, but instead grabbed her other bag and ran before she could get back to her feet.

"Hey!" Milana yelled, although she couldn't hear her own voice over the shouting coming from inside the market. She squeezed past the line, looked through the window, and saw a group of men fighting near the wall of produce, or at least near the empty bins where the produce had once been. "What the hell is going on?"

"Back of the line!" a woman shouted, shoving her. "Wait your turn like everyone else!"

Milana stumbled away from her and quickened her pace along the sidewalk. There were other grocery stores; she'd just hit another one—

A man clipped the curb and went down — hard — right in front of her. He didn't even raise his hands to brace himself. His face rebounded from the pavement with the sound of either a bone or a tooth breaking.

"Are you okay?" she asked. She knelt beside him and reached for his shoulder—

He rolled away before she could touch him and struggled to his feet. A nasty gash on his forehead bled through his eyebrows and soaked into his surgical mask.

"Get away from me!" he shouted, staggering around the corner.

The Gristedes supermarket on the next block up was overflowing with people, too. The automatic doors continually tried to close, despite the masses trapped between them, like a toothless mouth gumming its meal. Two men tried to enter at the same time and started pushing and shouting at each other. Mrs. Lovato appeared between them, struggling to squeeze through with her shopping bags. Milana took her by the arm and guided her from the chaos.

"What in the world is happening here?" Milana asked.

"Haven't you been watching the news?"

"We were at the lawyer's office all morning and my mother's been sick—"

Mrs. Lovato wrenched her arm from Milana's grasp so quickly that she nearly lost her balance.

"Something happened in Midtown," she said. "No one seems to know what, but April Ramirez told me her son Terry was down there earlier and they had entire blocks roped off and police wearing gas masks everywhere. He even saw people from the CDC in those big yellow suits."

"What were they doing?"

"He couldn't tell. It's been all over the news ever since, though. Not that these talking heads actually know anything. Or, if they do, they're not saying. They just keep repeating the same thing over and over: don't go down there unless you absolutely have to. And stay off the roads so they can keep them clear for emergency vehicles."

"How are people supposed to do that with the Q closed down?"

"It's more than just the Q. Every train this side of Ninety-sixth has been shut down and all of the bridges and tunnels off Manhattan are closed. They aren't even running the ferries."

"You don't think terrorists—?"

"Not a chance. I was here on Nine/Eleven. Everyone knew exactly what was happening. This is different. No one seems to know anything, let alone why there are people in biohazard suits all around the city and they aren't letting anyone off the island. All I can say for sure is that every store's run out of masks and the entire city's stocking up on food. If I were you, I'd get in line and grab everything you can afford before it's all gone. Better to be safe than sorry, you know."

Mrs. Lovato left Milana to fend for herself without so much as a backward glance. The older woman pushed through the passengers disgorging from the M15 bus, one of whom, a man wearing a United Cargo uniform, collapsed the moment his feet hit the sidewalk. A woman helped him to the nearest bench, where he rolled onto his side and curled into fetal position.

What if Mrs. Lovato was wrong? What if terrorists had released some sort of biological weapon in Midtown and it was slowly working its way outward through the surrounding two million people, none of whom could leave with every conceivable route off the island closed?

Another helicopter thundered overhead, so low it shook the windows in their panes. The TV above the bar inside the restaurant next to the grocery store showed aerial footage of—

—*a skyscraper she recognizes as the Jacob K. Javits Federal Building by the woven-fabric arrangement of its windows, from which roiling smoke gushes. A haze has settled over Foley Square, where camouflaged military trucks are parked among emergency vehicles, police/rescue armored Humvees, unmarked semi-trailers, and massive white RVs with FEMA markings and telescoping satellite dishes on their roofs. The barricade surrounding the plaza lays in ruin. Figures emerge from the darkness, flickering in the strobe of automatic gunfire*

Milana gasped and once more found herself staring at a street that looked a lot like Lexington on the TV. The few cars in the frame were all emergency vehicles and the only people in sight wore full-body isolation suits. The caption read "Quarantine Underway."

What in God's name was happening to her? Rationally, she understood that such manifestations of the subconscious were her mind's way of dealing with the stress of her classes and her financial situation and the loss of her grandmother, but these visions of death . . . they seemed so real. If only she could talk to her *pūridaia* . . .

Thoughts of her grandmother turned to her mother, who could very well be suffering from whatever had been released in Midtown. Before she even realized what she intended to do, she was sprinting south on 2nd toward where helicopters swirled like so many dragonflies above the buildings in the distance. Another ambulance slewed onto the road and nearly flipped when it hit the curb. The driver righted the vehicle and veered down an alley to circumvent the stopped traffic on 68th.

The line for the urgent care was all the way around the corner. There were so many people trying to get into the walk-in clinic that they had nurses with digital clipboards registering and triaging them right there on the street, all while being shouted at by people desperate to see the doctor, people who looked just like her mother. Rheumy, bloodshot eyes. Heavy perspiration. Damp clothing. All of them stricken by panic, not just because of how ill they felt or how many others with the same symptoms there were, but because the overwhelmed staff didn't seem to have the slightest idea what to do. There were no inpatient beds, no medical specialists, no emergency units to handle the sickest among them. It was an urgent care clinic unaccustomed to treating anything worse than broken bones or the common cold and sending their patients home with a prescription for Tylenol III or Tamiflu. This was beyond their limited capabilities and everyone knew it, which only amplified the growing tension.

A woman in a skirt suit leaned against the wall, retched, and puked onto the sidewalk between her high heels. Milana turned away in disgust, but not before she noticed the reddish streaks in the vomit.

The nearest nurse squeezed the green N95 mask over the bridge of her nose to make sure it was completely sealed, fogging her glasses in the process.

"Everyone!" she yelled. "Please. You have to be patient and wait your turn. We have two physicians, and they can only treat people so fast. If you're unable to wait or feel your condition is emergent, please consider going to Presbyterian—"

"They're turning people away!" a man in a construction vest shouted back at her. "The ER's overflowing. They were setting up tents when I left. Right there in the parking lot. No way I'm paying to see a doctor in a frigging tent."

"And their pharmacy doesn't have enough drugs to fill the prescriptions they're writing," a man in a wool suit said. "Just give us something to take to Duane Reade before they run out of everything, too."

"Our physicians can't prescribe anything without first examining—" the nurse said.

"We all have the same thing!" an older woman screamed. "Just give us the same prescriptions you're giving everyone else."

"It doesn't work that way. Prescribe the wrong drug and we could do more harm than—"

The man in the wool suit attempted to shove past the nurse, knocking her backward against the facade and brushing aside her mask in the process. Her eyes widened in sheer terror. She struggled to reseat her mask over her mouth and nose, her skin paling and tears streaming down her cheeks. She staggered away from the crowd, tripped over her own feet, and fell right in front of Milana, who instinctively reached out for her—

"Don't touch me!" the nurse screamed.

Milana read the fear and hopelessness on the nurse's face. Something was terribly wrong, something far beyond the ability of the medical community to treat and contain.

The nurse cast aside her digital clipboard, pushed herself to her feet, and sprinted right out into the street. An Audi locked up its brakes to keep from hitting her. The taxi behind it managed to swerve and avoid slamming into its fender, but the truck behind it wasn't so lucky and rammed into it from behind, leaving the nurse standing there in shock, her hands clasped over her mask. She quickly snapped out of it, sprinted past the accident, and around the corner, where an old man in an overcoat stood in the shade of a honey locust tree, behind a mound of black trash bags. Even with his face concealed by the brim of his fedora, Milana recognized him immediately.

She sensed more than saw him smile and watched in horror as rats emerged from the garbage and swarmed around his feet. He cocked his head and watched her for several seconds before turning and heading in the opposite direction. His shadow crept up the bricks of the adjacent building, which distorted his outline to such an extent that it almost appeared as though he had the curved horns of an ox.

The rats trailed him around the corner and vanished from sight.

MILANA DUMPED the last of the ice cubes from the freezer into the bathtub and prayed they'd be enough. Her mother's fever had climbed so much while she was gone that it had raised the temperature of the entire bedroom. The tympanic thermometer hadn't been able to settle on a single number, but the readouts all had been somewhere between 104 and 105, which, she'd learned from the frazzled staff at the clinic, meant that the fever needed to be broken, and in a hurry. She rushed to her bedroom and tried to rouse her mother, who didn't so much as open her eyes.

"Come on, mom," she said. "You have to help me."

She tried to lift Rosella, but she wasn't strong enough, so she had to settle for wrapping her mother's arms around her shoulders and trying to roll her out of bed, which only succeeded in depositing both of them in a heap on the floor.

"Help me, dammit!"

Her mother's skin was hot to the touch and slick with sweat. Her legs were like rubber and her head lolled back on her shoulders. Crawling out from underneath her dead weight was nearly as difficult as getting a good grip on her sweaty wrists and dragging her down the hallway to the bath-room. There was no way she could lift her mother into the tub, at least not without climbing in there with her. The cold hit Milana hard enough to make her gasp and rendered her fingers numb within a matter of seconds. And yet somehow, she maneuvered her mother into the frigid water without drowning either of them.

Milana peeled off her mother's drenched clothes and tossed them into the corner.

"It's g-going to b-be all right," she said through chattering teeth, although she wasn't sure which of them she was trying to convince.

She'd tried calling Mrs. Lovato for help, but the older woman hadn't even answered her phone. Not that Milana blamed her after how heavily she'd leaned on her for the last however many months. She just needed someone to point her in the right direction, to reassure her that she was doing the right things, like Mrs. Lovato had during her grandmother's deterioration. Milana couldn't bear to go through this again, especially not if she was dealing with a biological warfare agent and not withdrawal, which suddenly seemed like wishful thinking. The latter she could ride out, but the former? She had no more control over it than any of the overwhelmed medical professionals at the clinics around town.

The voices of the Channel 7 newscasters carried through the floor from the TV downstairs. They tried to sound confident and reassuring, although with reports of a similar sickness trickling in from other parts of the country and no updates on when the bridges and tunnels would be reopened, it was becoming increasingly apparent that none of them had the slightest idea what was going on, either.

The ice cubes made crackling sounds as they melted. Her mother's goose-bumped skin had passed from pale to translucent, revealing the network of green vessels underneath. She shivered uncontrollably and tried to say something through her chattering teeth, but only a staccato whisper passed her bluish lips.

Milana leaned over the tub and briskly rubbed her mother's arms. Rosella opened her eyes just a crack, revealing the lower crescents of her irises through the eye goo woven into her lashes.

"C-c-cold."

A quick check of Rosella's temperature confirmed that her fever had fallen to 102.6, which was still too high, but at least it was no longer life-threatening and allowed her mother to help get herself out of the tub and into a towel. Milana did her best to dry her off and change her into an oversize T-shirt and a pair of sweats. It took several minutes to get her back into bed and situated with her head propped on the pillows. She was shivering so hard that Milana could barely get a couple sips of tea past her lips, hopefully enough to chase the taste of the expired Nyquil hidden at the back of the medicine cabinet from her mouth.

Milana had stopped at easily half a dozen grocery stores and pharmacies on her way home and fought through the packed aisles to find the shelves of medication bare. Not a single bottle of cold medicine, painkiller, or holistic remedy had remained. Several stores had even posted signs outside stating they were sold out of medicine and ice, while others had simply closed and locked the doors.

Milana prayed she didn't come down with the sickness, too. She didn't know what she'd do if she did. There'd be no one to take care of her mother, let alone her. She was scared and alone and had never needed her grand-mother more—

A shrill tone erupted from the lower level, followed a split-second later by another. The same sound echoed from outside her window.

She grabbed a dry bra and a hoodie and changed on her way downstairs. Her cellphone once more blared the unmistakable tone of the emergency broadcast system from where she'd left it on the kitchen table, while her mother's alarmed from her purse. A dialog box had opened on the screen, inside of which was a red warning symbol beside the words EMERGENCY ALERT. Her heart raced as she read the message:

EXTREME THREAT ALERT
CATEGORY: Safety
RESPONSE TYPE: Take Shelter
SEVERITY: Extreme
URGENCY: Take Action Immediately
CERTAINTY: Observed
Emergency Alert in this area. Go indoors immediately and remain inside. Do

not drive. Call 9-1-1 for emergencies only. Follow link for further instructions. NYC_OEM.

Milana clicked the hyperlink and was transported to a FEMA site with drawings demonstrating how to properly put on an isolation mask and goggles, how to correctly wash your hands, how to use cellophane wrap to form an airtight barrier over your windows from the inside and duct tape to seal the seams around your doors. The instructions were to find a room either without or with minimal access to the exterior of the building, seal the windows and doors, and await subsequent communications from the New York City Office of Emergency Management.

"What's happening?" she screamed as a helicopter thundered so low over the rooftops that the cupboard doors and the paintings on the walls rattled.

Milana had to get ahold of herself. She took several deep breaths and focused on the task at hand. If anyone could do this, it was her. She stuffed her phone into her pocket, grabbed a box of Saran Wrap and a roll of masking tape, and hurried back upstairs.

"Is everything . . . okay?" Rosella asked. Her voice was weak and reedy, and she barely seemed to have the strength to keep her eyes open.

"Of course," Milana said, offering the best smile she could muster.

"You're lying." Her mother coughed and her lips darkened with a faint reddish tint. "I can always tell."

"Everything's under control," Milana said. She went straight to the window, pulled the roll of cellophane from the box, and started stretching it from the top of the frame to the bottom. "We just need to stay in this room for a while. No big deal, right? We have tea and Nyquil; we can make a party out of it."

"You remind me so much of her," Rosella said.

"Who?"

"My mother." A contented smile appeared on Rosella's face and her heavy eyelids closed. "She was so . . . strong."

Milana wiped the tears from the corners of her eyes. She was the furthest thing from strong. It was all she could do to get herself out of bed in the morning.

"I was never strong," her mother whispered. "I was always so . . . scared. Of being alone. Of letting my parents down. Of letting *you* down."

Milana stretched the last of the roll over the pane and smoothed her fingertips around the edges of the frame to make sure the seal would stay in place long enough for her to wrap the tape around the circumference. She caught movement from across the street, a shifting of the shadows near the stoop opposite hers, where the streetlight couldn't reach.

"I'm so . . . sorry," her mother said. She appeared to deflate with the words, physically diminishing before Milana's eyes. "I need you to . . . to know that. Please . . . understand that I never . . . never meant to hurt you."

"I know, Mom."

There was nothing Milana could do to stall the tears, which came all at once and in a torrent of emotions. She looked out the window and watched the shadows coalesce into the form of the old man in the overcoat and fedora. He stepped from the darkness, the wrinkles on his face taking on the appearance of melted wax, and tipped his cap. Rats scurried out from beneath the collar of his jacket and crawled over his neck and shoulders—

Milana stumbled away from the window. She barely caught the scream before it burst from her chest. In her mind, she heard her grandmother's voice: *You must remain strong, Milana. He is afraid of your light and will do everything in his power to extinguish it.*

She returned to the window to find the old man staring back up at her. He raised his index finger and pressed it to his lips—

Milana closed the curtains, turned her back on him, and focused on slowing her heart rate. There was no way he could get inside and, even if he did, he'd find her unwilling to play the role of the victim.

She sat down on the edge of the bed and took her mother's hand in her own, as she'd done so many times with her grandmother. Rosella opened her eyes and started to cry. She looked so small and vulnerable, like Milana often felt. Her mother squeezed her hand, softly, and Milana hugged her for the first time in as long as she could remember.

"I'm so sorry," her mother said, her body trembling.

"It's okay," Milana said, stroking her mother's damp hair. "We'll get through this. You and me. Everything's going to be okay."

She leaned back and wiped the tears from her mother's eyes. The muscles in Rosella's face relaxed. Her pupils dilated and the vessels surrounding her irises ruptured, flooding the whites of her eyes with blood.

MILANA'S HEART hitched in her chest. It felt as though the ground had fallen out from beneath her. She'd lost her grandmother, the most important person in her life, and now here she sat, on the verge of finally having a relationship with her mother, only to have it ripped from her grasp.

Her mother's eyes slowly closed, forcing the blood welling against her lower lashes to run down her cheeks. The sound of her breathing grew harsher, louder. Her chest shuddered, and blood burbled up from between her teeth, darkened her lips, and dribbled down her chin.

Milana sobbed and reached for her mother, hoping to draw her into an embrace so she wouldn't die without knowing that despite everything that had happened, all of the years lost, her daughter still loved—

Rosella raised her head and snapped at Milana's hand with her teeth.

"Mom? What are you—?"

Her mother cast aside her covers and pounced to the bed on all fours.

Milana stumbled backward, tripped over her own feet, and landed squarely on her butt in the middle of the room. Rosella dove at her, but Milana dodged to her left. Her mother hit the ground and slid toward the bedroom door, leaving a smear of blood on the hardwood. Milana scrambled to her feet, raised her hands, and backed toward the nightstand underneath the window.

"What's wrong with you?" she cried.

Rosella clawed her way back to her feet and sprinted at Milana, who turned away and ducked at the same moment her mother launched herself into the air. The impact slammed Milana into the nightstand, which broke against her ribs, knocking the wind out of her. Glass shattered above her head and rained down upon her. She rolled onto her side, shards lacerating her forearm. Her chest felt as though it had been locked from the inside and refused to admit air.

She crawled toward the hallway, glanced back, and saw her mother hanging halfway out the broken window, her palms impaled on the jagged glass protruding from the sill. Rosella looked back at her with an expression of unbridled hatred and bared her teeth. She braced her bloody hands against the frame and pushed herself back inside. A piece of glass pierced her chest, slid straight up her neck, over her jaw, and across her cheek. She stood over Milana with rich black blood gushing from her throat and spattering at her feet.

Milana crawled for the door as Rosella fell upon her from behind, pinning her to the ground. A rush of warmth flooded onto her back. Fingernails bit into her shoulders. She dragged herself out from underneath her mother and scurried up against the wall. The pressure in her lungs finally broke and she inhaled a desperate breath with a sound like a scream.

Rosella made no attempt to rise.

"Mom?"

Milana stood and stared down at her mother's body. There was so much blood, more than she'd ever imagined a person could hold. Rosella couldn't possibly still be alive, and yet Milana took her by the hand and tried to pull her to her feet.

"Come on, Mom."

She tugged again, but only succeeded in dragging Rosella's inert form through the blood. Her mother's wet fingers slipped from her grasp, and she staggered backward into the hallway.

A car horn blared outside. She heard a screech of brakes and someone shouting.

"Help me!" Milana screamed.

She sprinted down the hallway, cleared the stairs, and blew through the parlor. She shouldered open the front door of her apartment and burst from the main entrance onto the stoop. The first thing she saw was the tree across the street, its branches burdened by the weight of the sheer number of ravens. They shrieked and burst from their perches, filling the sky.

A silver SUV idled halfway up on the curb in front of it. The vehicle backed down onto the asphalt, its headlights revealing the body it had hit and thrown up against a decorative wrought-iron fence. The man behind the wheel put the car into drive and hit the gas. The tires spun before gaining traction and sending the vehicle flying in the opposite direction.

"Help!" Milana screamed after the driver, who didn't so much as tap his brakes as he squealed around the corner.

She looked across the street. The man who'd been run down by the silver SUV lay crumpled against the fence. She'd barely reached the bottom step when he pushed himself up from the ground. Swayed and dropped to one knee. Tried again. Stepped unsteadily out into the street and turned in her direction. The streetlight shimmered from the blood on his face and in his eyes. He bared his teeth and ran right at her. She spun and raced back up to her porch. Heard him hit the sidewalk and mount the stairs behind hear, coming up way too fast. Threw open the door and barely stepped out of the way in time. The man sailed past her into the foyer. She slammed the front door closed behind her and hurried down the stairs.

The man struck the other side of the door with a resounding thud.

Milana didn't dare look back as she ran down the sidewalk toward the adjacent townhome.

Another crash and a crack of splintering wood behind her.

She screamed and started up the concrete steps.

The man shouldered through the broken door. His head snapped in her direction and his eyes fixed upon her. He jumped over the railing and landed on her grandmother's roses.

"Mrs. Lovato!" Milana screamed.

She hit the front porch and banged on the door as hard as she could. Pressed the doorbell over and over.

The man sprung to his feet, the broken bones in his forearm tenting the skin, and attempted to scale the side of the stoop. Failed. Pushed off and ran around toward the base of the stairs.

"Please!" she screamed. "Open the—"

The door swung inward and Milana shoved past Mr. Lovato, nearly knocking the older man to the ground in the entryway. She whirled, slammed the door, and threw the deadbolt.

"Milana?" he said. The man outside threw himself against the door, rattling it against its hinges. "What's going on?"

He reached for the knob, but Milana pushed him away.

"Call the police!" she screamed.

The man outside slammed against the front door, over and over.

Milana slumped to the ground and started to cry.

24

Detroit, Michigan

Desmond Duvall removed his glasses and rubbed his weary eyes. He hadn't slept for more than a couple hours at a stretch in days and was running on a combination of sugar and caffeine, but he doubted he'd have been able to make sense of any of this under even the most ideal of conditions. He couldn't find a connection between Matthew Avery Marshall and Ephraim Abraham Waller and was starting to think that none could have possibly existed prior to the killings.

Marshall had been raised in a wealthy household and had traveled exclusively with the upper echelon of society, while Waller had been born into poverty and had spent most of his life wallowing in it. He'd served a total of six years in prison for a laundry list of petty crimes, most of them drug related, and hadn't made much of an effort to hold down a job or establish permanent residency between tours through the Wayne County Jail. In fact, he'd been behind bars, where his internet use and outside communications had been closely monitored, until a mere two weeks ago, which left a very small window of opportunity for him to enter the orbit of The Executioner. By then, Marshall had gone entirely off the grid, which meant that the two murderers would have had to meet in person, and likely somewhere in the vicinity of the abandoned brotherhood hall where he'd been holed up.

At least that was someplace to start.

Duvall reseated his glasses and set to work. He'd uploaded pictures of the two men to the facial-recognition database and initiated a search of the surrounding network of streetlight and security cameras, although that part of town wasn't covered nearly as well as he would have liked.

With both perpetrators dead, he should have been able to let the case go, but he couldn't get it out of his head. Maybe it was just his professional curiosity, an innate desire to understand how, out of the billions of interpersonal connections that occurred on a daily basis, two unrelated men could meet and decide to start killing young women together. And yet he knew there was more to it than that. Something about the nature of the killings had been gnawing at him since he'd first discovered the jars of eyes on the shelves in the killer's lair, something he couldn't quite articulate into words, something that had taken on a sense of urgency the moment he opened the file containing the drawings of the house beneath which Henry Laurent Monroe had buried his victims and the stone quarry where Harold Saltzman had hidden his.

The computer alerted him to several matches, each of which showed Waller standing at one intersection or other, either waiting to cross the road or already doing so. There was nothing extraordinary about any of the images, outside of the fact that he appeared to be so high that he looked like a zombie. There were no matches at all for Marshall, which meant Duvall needed to widen his search to the surrounding neighborhoods, which included the house where Waller had been killed.

While the odds of two mass murderers independently developing the same signature were by no means astronomical, the chances of four doing so were. Copycats were common in a field not necessarily renowned for its originality, but most imitated the monsters who stole headlines and inspired movies, not those buried on microfiche. Finding the trophies of the previous killers in the possession of the most recent, however, proved that there was a connection between them, one quite possibly facilitated by a third party who knew where to find the eyes of the previous incarnation's victims and how to get them into the hands of the next generation of killers.

Duvall's computer returned the results of his broadened search, which consisted of a grand total of zero matches. He drained the last of his coffee and hurled the mug across the empty office in frustration.

There had to be something he'd missed.

He opened the case file and pored over the neighborhood canvassing reports. No one had witnessed anything out of the ordinary, specifically no one entering the house where Hannah Serviess had nearly been murdered in the ritualistic manner of the blood eagle. Even the owners of the adjacent houses hadn't so much as suspected that anyone had been inside. The same held true for the house where Donna Hamilton had been found in the attic, exsanguinated from a thousand cuts, although in that area it wasn't quite as surprising.

For seemingly the thousandth time, he studied the photographs taken of the people who'd gathered outside the police cordon to watch the ME's office remove Donna's body from the abandoned house. Killers often returned to the scene of their crimes to observe the investigation and thrill in their proximity to the officers hunting them, but Waller's face wasn't among those of the onlookers.

Duvall suddenly realized that he hadn't examined the photos taken outside the brotherhood hall, where Matthew Avery Marshall had been killed in his twisted inner sanctum, since the discovery of Waller's involvement. If his theory about one Executioner offering himself up so that the other could be free to continue their shared work was true, then surely Waller would have wanted to be there in person to honor his partner's sacrifice.

The enormity of the operation had drawn an impressive crowd, which wasn't all that surprising considering the media presence, the proximity to a busy thoroughfare, and the sheer number of homeless people living in the surrounding vacant lots. Duvall studied their faces, searching for dreadlocks and tattoos. He found numerous topical matches, although none of them turned out to be Waller.

The last few photographs showed Marshall's body being transported out the back door of the building to the ME's waiting van, its headlights partially blinding the camera, its taillights casting a red glow onto the faces of those standing on the other side of the police tape. The third picture had captured the morgue attendants as they were just about to load the gurney into the back. One of them tried to shield the body bag from view while the other discreetly unzipped it and allowed a reporter with a camera to snap a quick picture, for which they'd likely been paid in cash and would have to be dealt with, but Duvall forgot all about it when he recognized the man standing beside the photographer. Ephraim Abraham Waller. He stared down upon the body of his predecessor, his eyes red from the reflection of the flash. By the next image in the series, he was gone.

Duvall returned to the picture of Waller, his eyes rendered a demonic shade of crimson. There was something about his expression that caused the hairs to stand up on the backs of Duvall's arms. Waller didn't appear to be smiling as much as baring his teeth in pain. Duvall zoomed in on his face and saw that he was bleeding from both nostrils, twin shimmering lines. And there was a haziness around his head, like a double exposure, barely discernible from the trees behind him. It almost looked like the crown of an animal's skull had been superimposed over his forehead, one from which long sharp horns forked straight up into the overhanging branches. The longer Duvall looked at it, the clearer it became.

He furrowed his brow, grabbed his jacket, and headed for his car.

"You're lucky you came in tonight," the morgue technician said. She was short and muscular and wore a lab coat over a T-shirt and scrub pants. The lanyard hanging from her neck identified her as Latonya. "His autopsy's scheduled for first thing in the morning. I was just about to start prepping him."

Their footsteps echoed down the corridor, white walls blurring past in his peripheral vision. Duvall couldn't explain why he was here, let alone the seemingly inexplicable rush to view Waller's body. He'd already spent considerable time documenting it at the crime scene, but there'd been something about that picture, something he couldn't quite put his finger on . . .

Latonya stopped before a wide stainless-steel door with a square inset window. She drew it open and revealed a massive freezer. The refrigeration units mounted to the ceiling gusted visible clouds of frigid air, which settled upon racks overflowing with white body bags stuffed with the remains of the unclaimed dead. The carts in the middle of the room were buried beneath the most-recent additions, identified by the numbers scrawled on them in black marker, among them Ephraim Abraham Waller.

The conditions never failed to unnerve Duvall, whose unguarded reaction betrayed him.

"A lot of families can't afford to bury their loved ones," Latonya said. She slid several bags aside and drove the cart with Waller's body out into the hallway. "So they leave them here, knowing that if they wait long enough, the county will eventually have to do it for them. The problem is that we don't have that kind of money either."

Duvall stood over the head of the cart and waited for her to unzip the bag and fold open the flap. Waller's skin tone had faded to an ashen gray, which made his tattoos stand out like newsprint. His eye sockets were recessed, and his hair had the texture of smudge sticks. The wound on his neck was puckered and raw, his bare chest marred by patches of dried blood.

"I don't know what you're hoping to find," Latonya said, "but I'll give you two lovebirds a few minutes alone."

Duvall nodded mutely and listened to the hollow clapping of her footsteps fade. The truth was that he didn't know what he was looking for, either. He remembered crouching over the body in the basement of the abandoned house and staring down at it just as he did now, only the dead man's lifeless eyes had been open and staring back at him. In that moment, with the strobe of camera flashes all around him, he'd felt something stir inside of him, like a parasite awakening from a long period of dormancy. At first, he'd chalked it up to curiosity — How had a man who appeared to have been living on the street even come into contact with Marshall, a former surgeon who'd walked away from a lucrative career and the kind of family every American dreamed of having? — but it had become something more, an obsession that haunted his every waking thought.

"How did you get here?" he whispered.

The picture of Waller standing behind the police tape while the ME's crew wheeled Marshall's body to the van was the only point of convergence that Duvall could find, and even then, one of them had been dead. He recalled the red reflection from Waller's eyes and the ghost image he'd seen, the horns jutting from the killer's skeletal forehead, which was surely only an illusion created by the chiaroscuro of shadow and light.

He brought up the image on his phone and magnified Waller's face until it filled the screen. His bared teeth. The pained expression on his face. The V-shaped horns standing from his head like extensions of his dreadlocks.

Duvall walked around to the side of the cart and looked down upon Waller's—

—*face reflects from a pool of blood on bare stone, limned around the edges by the flickering glow of flames. A pair of stark white eyes stares back at him from beneath a ragged crown of broken bone, from the top of which project long horns ringed with bony protrusions, like those of a gazelle. The face below them is painted black with charcoal, much like the portion of the bare chest visible between the tattered edges of the matted hide draped over his shoulders.*

He raises his stare from his reflection and sees the carcass rotting in the corner, its bones broken and its hooves fringed with fur. Beyond it is a sliver of light from the outside world. A gust of wind causes the flames to flag and momentarily clears the haze of smoke. He stands and walks toward the light, the cold air biting the skin on his face. Snow blows sideways past the mouth of the cave, nearly concealing the figures staggering through the accumulation, dragging their offerings—

Duvall dropped his phone onto the dead man's chest and hurriedly picked it up. His heart pounded and his respirations bordered on hyperventilation. He stumbled backward and collided with the wall.

Waller's body lay cold and lifeless on the stainless-steel cart, and yet Duvall couldn't shake the feeling that his observation was only half true. He felt dizzy and sick to his stomach. Too much caffeine, too little sleep. Or at least that's what he told himself.

A crimson droplet spattered the ground at his feet. Another landed beside it with a soft *plat*.

Duvall dabbed at his nose with his knuckle and drew it away bloody. He leaned back, pinched his nostril, and tasted copper in the back of his throat.

"Are you all right?"

He nearly jumped at the sound of Latonya's voice. She stood on the other side of the cart, looking at him with an expression of concern. He hadn't heard so much as a single footstep.

"Yeah," he said. "I just . . . "

He turned without another word and headed back down the hallway, his mind struggling to rationalize what he'd seen.

"You're welcome," Latonya called after him, but Duvall didn't respond. He was focused solely on his shadow stretching across the white tiles ahead of him.

And the V-shaped horns protruding from it.

———

DROPLETS OF BLOOD pattered the sink. Duvall couldn't seem to make his nose stop bleeding. He'd already plugged it twice, but the tissue had soaked through and had to be replaced. He pinched his nostrils and leaned forward, pressing his forehead against the mirror, hoping to stimulate the formation of clots. His eyes were bloodshot, his skin ashen, and the bags underneath his eyes appeared to have been packed for an extended vacation. He just needed to get some sleep. That was all. He'd been burning the candle at both ends for too long and the consequences had finally caught up with him. He had experienced physical exhaustion plenty of times, although this was the first time that he'd encountered the psychological.

And it scared him

Duvall hesitantly released the pressure on his nostrils and sniffed back a trickle of fluid. Fortunately, the clots held.

"It's about time."

He returned to his bedroom, too tired to change out of his bloodstained shirt, and collapsed onto his bed. Everything would look different after a few hours of sleep and under the light of day. He closed his eyes and welcomed—

—*columns of sunlight pierce the canopy of cypress trees and strike the bayou like spears thrust from the heavens, imbuing the stagnant water with an ethereal green glow. The insects are out in droves, swarming around his face as he forces his way through the underbrush along the muddy bank, careful not to make too much noise.*

Time moves in lurches, slow and then fast. He emerges from the brush and finds himself on the verge of a park, where families wearing clothes like his grandparents might have worn are gathered at the picnic tables in the distance, near the band shell, where a brass quartet plays music he can't hear over the rushing of blood in his ears, a sound he equates with the primordial, much like the swamp itself. His stare latches upon a young girl skipping rope away from the others, her mahogany skin a stark contrast to her white dress, and he knows — right then and there — why he's been led to this place, even though he has no idea where he is or how he got here. He hears her laughter, his heart thumping in time with the sound of her rope striking the bare dirt, and wonders if she can see him, standing there—

—in his walk-in closet as he stuffed a change of clothes, a couple hundred dollars in cash, and the Beretta M9 he kept in a shoebox on the top shelf into an overnight bag. He felt strangely detached, as though he were merely a spectator watching his body head downstairs, without the slightest idea of where he was going or what he intended to do when he got there.

A throbbing sensation took root at the base of his skull with an audible cracking sound he felt as much as heard. He noticed warmth on his lip, tasted blood in—

—his mouth grows dry, his limbs leaden as he checks to make sure that no one's noticed him watching the girl. She cocks her head as though hearing something in the distance, or perhaps like an antelope sensing a lion approaching through the tall grasses of the savanna. She bundles up her rope and runs across the park toward the road. He finds his legs suddenly responsive and follows at a measured pace, the gap widening between them—

—as he walked through the kitchen and grabbed his car keys from the counter beside the microwave. The thudding of his footsteps echoed from the hallway leading to the garage, while the—

—laughter of families and music fades into the background. It's only him and the little girl, who crosses the street and heads downhill through the trees toward a wooden shanty with a tin roof and a screened porch, where an older woman stands, her hair drawn up under a scarf, her hand shielding her eyes from the sun. The child realizes her mother is looking past her, glances back over her shoulder, and for the first time he clearly sees her eyes, a shade of brown the color of freshly turned earth, just like those of the others, whose bodies now rot—

—inside his Ford Explorer. He caught a glimpse of himself in the rearview mirror, his eyes red as though reflecting a camera's flash, from deep within the shadows cast by the ridge of bone above them, only the bases of the saiga's horns visible jutting from his forehead. The engine came to life with a roar, and the brake lights illuminated the rising garage door. He backed out onto the road and drove—

—away from the little house along the dirt road. He keeps the sun to his right so the girl and her mother can see nothing more than his outline until he passes from sight and hears the squeal of the screen door closing behind him. And then he's gone, out of sight and out of mind, a man like any other, taking a leisurely stroll on a fine summer day, the houses shrinking back into the swamp and growing farther apart until one he recognizes appears from the trees. It's built on blocks to spare it from the floods during hurricane season. The wooden slats show signs of wear and patches of rust have set upon the roof near the eaves, but the home itself isn't his ultimate destination.

He rounds the structure and retrieves a hand spade from where he left it on the back porch. Its weight is familiar in his hand, its blade corroded by the elements, its sharp tip crusted with blood and tissue. He lowers himself all the way to the dirt and slithers underneath the porch, into cool darkness that smells pleasantly of kerosene and burned meat, and thinks of those precious brown eyes as he starts to dig another grave, shallow like the others, so that he can just brush aside the top layers of soil and look upon their faces, their hollow sockets packed with soil, their lips withered from teeth that form a twisted a mockery of—

—a smile crossed Duvall's lips as the buzz of tires on asphalt became the sound of distant screams, the pained cries of long-dead girls summoning him back to the here and now. He was only peripherally aware of the city flying past to either side of him as he rocketed down the highway, heading west on I-80, his bag resting on the passenger seat beside him. There were only a handful of other cars on the road, which was a blessing considering he had such a long way to go, and time was already running short. With the coming dawn, the Day of Purification would finally commence.

Duvall furrowed his brow. He'd never heard those words before and didn't know what they meant, but the harder he thought about them, the worse his head hurt, until he could no longer bear the pain and opened his mouth to—

—screams when she awakens and finds herself in a room she's never seen before, but one she knows she'll never leave, one with the furniture shoved against the walls, a tarp on the floor, and a glass jar filled with formaldehyde on the table, next to a row of knives. He chooses the one he wants, holds the girl's head still, and with the very first slice—

—Desmond Duvall was no more.

25

Riverton, Wyoming

"Our greatest fears have just been realized," Rankin said. He stood at the front of the conference room with a remote clicker in his hand and a video screen at his back. "The WHO designation of the disease now formally classified as 'the Bering Virus' has been raised from Phase Five to Phase Six, meaning that a full-fledged global pandemic is officially underway."

A murmur rippled through the specialists seated at the rows of tables in front of Cullen, who leaned against the rear wall, among them and yet completely apart from them. There was no mistaking his role at Riverton. This wasn't the field, where, as an integral member of the team, he was responsible for securing the location, containing every possible threat, and covering the medical team while it worked its magic under the most extreme of conditions. Here, he was merely a part of the support staff, nominally tasked with safeguarding the infected and the physical remains.

"You're suggesting there's been human-to-human spread of the virus?" someone said from up front.

"As of this moment, we've received reports of confirmed cases in Alaska, California, Minnesota, and New York, with more cases being diagnosed with every subsequent update."

Cullen could positively feel the fear radiating from those gathered before him These were men and women unaccustomed to experiencing it through the course of their work in their safe and comfortable labs, far from the front lines. None of them had previously believed that such an aggressive virus could exist in more than theory and yet they'd fooled themselves into thinking that they'd be prepared for the mythical Disease X, should it ever rear its ugly head.

Now, here they were, struggling with the realization that they were no longer dealing in the hypothetical, that they were completely and utterly outmatched, and that they were no longer firmly seated at the top of the metaphorical food chain. He'd seen the proof of that with his own eyes, and not just in the form of the mastication wounds on the bodies he'd transported from the Arctic, but in the viscera removed from them during their autopsies and the copious amounts of blood and tissue they contained.

Rankin clicked through a series of graphs as he spoke.

"As you can see, this virus is more contagious than any we've previously combatted, and its symptoms progress at a seemingly impossible rate. In the case of the chimpanzees, the average incubation period was just under three hours. Taking into account the relative size and mass of a human being and the prodromal phases of other hemorrhagic viruses, we believe the incubation period to be somewhere between eight and ten hours, which meshes with what we know about the initial exposure in the archeological camp, and with the first clinical indications manifesting shortly after exposure. Arresting the fever appears to slow the progression of the disease, but ultimately does little more than forestall the inevitable."

"So if we're receiving reports from hospitals around the country, then these patients have already exposed countless others and the number of cases will grow exponentially," a woman said from somewhere to Cullen's left. "It's too late the flatten the curve and nothing shy of a nationwide shutdown will prevent it from going global."

"If it hasn't already," someone else said.

"We have to assume that's a foregone conclusion," Rankin said. He brought up a map of the continental United States with a timestamp from three hours ago. There were red circles over San Francisco, Minneapolis, and New York City. The second map in the sequence, from two hours ago, showed the same circles, only now they were much larger and superimposed upon numerous smaller circles, which had also popped up in cities across the country, from Los Angeles, San Diego, and Seattle on the west coast to Denver, Kansas City, and Dallas in the central portion to Boston, Washington D.C., and Orlando on the east coast. On the third map, from a mere hour ago, every major city appeared to have been affected. "By the time the average patient is diagnosed, he or she is already contagious, which means that there are countless other individuals out there at this very moment, all of them well on their way to demonstrating hemorrhagic symptoms and exposing everyone with whom they come into contact."

He flipped through a series of slides predicting the spread of the virus by hour, and then by day. The red circles engulfed cities and then states, until the entire country was concealed beneath countless circles of varying diameter, leaving only slivers in the largely uninhabited regions of the great plains unaffected.

"Based on all of our epidemiological models," Rankin said, "we're facing the imminent extinction of our species."

Silence fell upon the room. The only sound Cullen could hear was the rushing of blood in his ears. He rubbed his temples in an effort to combat the worsening headache that was now on the brink of transforming into a full-scale migraine. He closed his eyes and was assaulted by a memory not his own, one so real that—

—he feels the bony protrusions of the bison's skull pressing into his forehead and cheeks, the sharp edges of the chiseled stone blade in his palm, and the warmth of the blood drying on his forearm. The body of the man lays at his feet in an expanding crimson pool that reflects the golden firelight. He sets upon the carcass with the knife and begins cutting off slabs of meat for his people, who back away from the carnage with expressions of terror on their filthy faces—

"What about the secondary symptoms?"

Cullen's eyes snapped open at the sound of the voice, which only intensified his headache. He shielded them from the overhead lighting and swallowed hard to keep from vomiting.

Rankin hesitated before answering.

"That's the real question, isn't it? If our assumption about the nature of these symptoms is correct and the violence, much like we've encountered with rabies, is triggered as a means of spreading the disease, then we could begin seeing the manifestation of behavioral changes at any moment."

"At which point we will lose any and all hope of containing the virus," a woman near the front said.

"Not necessarily," Rankin said. "An MRI scan of Gamma's brain identified acute hemorrhaging and degenerative lesions that we have no doubt will prove fatal. Hence the necessity for such aggressive secondary symptoms to help spread the virus."

"Are you implying that the condition is inherently terminal?"

"We believe the infection will run its course in approximately seventy-two hours — at least in theory, and even then, that timeframe's largely dependent upon individual physiology — which is why we've formally recommended a shelter-in-place order be issued for an indeterminate length of time. If we can limit the spread of the virus to those who've already been infected, then that will at least buy us time to perfect a treatment—"

Cullen abruptly turned and blew through the door. The hallway seemed to tilt from side to side, forcing him to bounce from one wall to the other, shouldering his way down the corridor to his room. He ran straight into the door and struggled to turn the knob with palms that had grown slick with sweat. It was all he could do to close the wooden slab behind him and stagger to his bed. He collapsed on top of the covers, closed his eyes, and—

—finds himself in the quarantine wing, bathed in the red emergency lighting and facing Dr. Middleton through the blood-spattered window. She wears the same expression of revulsion on her face as those who'd gathered around him in the cave while he'd carved the meat from the dead man so that they might live. A curtain of sparks rains down on him, singeing his hair and scalp. He once more meets his reflection in the glass, only this time he's wearing the skull of an extinct bison, his eyes lost to the shadows. The hallway behind him transforms into the corridor from the animal wing with the access-controlled door from which he'd seen Rankin emerge. He opens his mouth as though to speak and a swarm of mosquitoes funnels from between his lips, swirling around his head and crawling all over his flesh. His voice is composed of many and seems to come from everywhere at once.

"Soon."

And with that proclamation, the darkness dragged Cullen into its depths.

DAVIS WALKED out of the meeting feeling as though he'd been kicked in the stomach. His entire family was still out there. His mom and dad. His grandparents. If the virus spread as quickly as Rankin projected, then he might never see them again. He couldn't even remember the last time he'd spoken to them, let alone what he'd said. He'd taken for granted that there would always be a next time. Of all people, he should have known better. There were no guarantees in life, which could irrevocably change from one heartbeat to the next.

He didn't know what kind of signal he could possibly get this far underground or even if he was technically allowed to contact the outside world, but he had to try. The consequences of doing nothing would be more than he could bear. He dealt with the guilt of inaction every day; adding another log to the fire would break him. But even if he somehow convinced his family to walk away from their lives and leave Sacramento, where were they supposed to go?

"Wait up," someone called from behind him.

Davis turned around and saw Pennington, who'd been sitting on the opposite side of the hall during the meeting. The director of the NHGRI fell in stride beside him and held up his tablet so Davis could see it. He could tell he was looking at lab results of some kind, but he didn't have the slightest clue how to interpret them.

"Pretty amazing, right?" Pennington said. He must have recognized the confusion on Davis's face. "This entry here? It shows the least common of the three Trident variants."

"Are those the lab results of the woman in quarantine? Beta?"

"Look at the name on the top. They're yours, dummy."

Davis took the tablet from him so he could better see it.

"Don't you get it?" Pennington said. "You have the third variant, the same as Beta. You can't contract the virus. You're immune."

Davis abruptly stopped walking. He'd been so wrapped up in mentally preparing himself for Gamma's MRI that he'd forgotten all about the blood draw. He was still trying to wrap his head around the news when the implications hit him.

"Does this mean my parents are immune too?"

"There's no way of knowing for sure without testing them, but it's possible."

Davis felt as though a great weight had been lifted—

Emily came around the corner so fast that she nearly bowled them over. Her eyes lit up when she saw them.

"You didn't answer your comm," the diminutive epigeneticist said.

"I was in the meeting," Pennington said. "What's going on? Is everyone all—?"

"We did it."

"You did it?"

"I think so, anyway," Emily said. "We should get Rankin. He's going to want to see this."

She blew past them and headed back down the hallway in the direction from which they'd come. They had to hurry to keep up.

"Talk to me, Emily," Pennington said.

"While the Bering Virus is morphologically distinct from Ebola, its mechanism of infection is surprisingly similar." She spoke over her shoulder as she walked. "It utilizes the phosphatidylserine on its viral envelope to enter the host cell via its T-cell immunoglobulin mucin domain-one receptors."

"In English?" Davis said.

"Viruses require the presence of a specific protein, or receptor, on the surface of a host cell in order to pass through the cellular membrane and begin replication. Almost like a lock for which they have the key. Identifying that receptor is the most important step in neutralizing the effects of the virus. In a nutshell, antibodies gum up the teeth on that key so that it can't turn in the lock by binding to the surface of the virus and preventing it from interacting with the receptor. In this case, that receptor is a protein known as TIM-one, which plays a critical role in regulating immune response to viral intrusion."

"So all you have to do is prevent the virus from binding to the receptor and you've basically rendered it inert," Davis said.

"Exactly," Emily said. "And, thanks to the Bering Virus's similarities to Ebola, the groundwork had pretty much already been laid for us. All we had to do was piggyback on the years of research that had already been conducted and identify the correct antibodies from those we collected from Alpha and Beta. Now we just need to make sure they work like we believe they will, isolate the corresponding sequences of amino acids from the Trident Gene, splice them into a retroviral vector, and voilà . . . we have a therapeutic vaccine that alters the host's genome so that it can produce the antibodies."

Rankin appeared in the doorway to his office, as if materializing from thin air.

"Are you certain it will work?" he asked.

"There's only one way to know for sure," Emily said. She grabbed the two-way radio she'd clipped it to her waistband and brought it to her lips. "Are you guys ready?"

"Champing at the bit down here," Sanders responded.

Emily turned to Rankin.

"Can you log in to the molecular dynamics simulator?"

Rankin ushered them through his office and into a conference room with twin video monitors mounted on the wall above the foot of a long table. They spread out and waited for Rankin to bring up the program on his screen. A computer-generated model of the virus appeared. It looked like an image capture from a scanning electron microscope, only enhanced to allow better visualization. The wormlike organism was long and gray and covered with reddish structures that looked like little trees growing in clumps of three.

"Those protrusions are trimer glycoproteins," Emily said. "They attach to the host cell, bind to the TIM-one receptors, and facilitate entry of the virus."

The image zoomed in on one of the trimers until it filled the entire screen. Each of the three individual glycoproteins looked like a vaguely spherical clump of cottage cheese, only color-coded in pale shades of white, yellow, and gray to tell them apart. Tiny green dots appeared in the countless concavities.

"Simulations like this one allow us to generate a three-dimension model of the glycoproteins so that we can identify every potential binding site, or epitope, to which an antibody can attach," Sanders said from the two-way. "Those are the green dots you see. The right combination of antibodies fit together with the antigen like the pieces of a puzzle. This program's been running through all of the possible combinations of the antibodies we were able to isolate from Alpha and Beta and finally identified one that should theoretically work. Now we just need to run it through the simulator and see what happens."

A collection of squiggly lines appeared on the screen. They looked like red, yellow, blue, and purple tapeworms that folded back upon themselves so many times that they became hopelessly entangled.

"Those ribbons represent the protein structures of the antibodies," Emily said. "By subtracting their mass, we can clearly see where they bind to the epitopes on the viral glycoproteins. And if everything goes as planned, you're about to see those folds align with the green dots, effectively neutralizing the virus."

They all collectively held their breath as the antibody tapeworms wrapped around the viral trimer. Davis watched in awe as all of the green dots winked out of being. The tapeworms abruptly changed into clumplike structures, like those of the glycoproteins, turning the trimer into a big misshapen ball of color.

"It worked," Emily said. She turned around with an expression of unbridled excitement on her face. "It worked!"

Whooping erupted from the two-way. Emily hugged Pennington, who clapped Davis on the shoulder.

"Run through each and every one of those epitopes and make sure they're completely bound," Rankin said. "And then run the simulator again. We can't afford to take any chances."

"We're already on it," Sanders said from the speaker.

"How quickly can you produce an experimental dose?"

"Of just the antibodies?" Emily said. "Maybe a few hours, but we still need to send them to the lab for safety and toxicology before we can even consider administering—"

"Leave that to me," Rankin said.

Davis smiled and watched the three-dimensional model turn triumphantly on the screen.

Maybe there was still hope after all.

———————

Riley pulled up the covers and rolled onto her side so that the security cameras couldn't see what she was doing. She tried to keep the pain from showing on her face as she carefully inserted the needle she'd hidden from the nurse beneath the skin of her upper thigh. She'd already forced the broken bits of the plastic casing down the drain with her feet, a single shard at a time, but she wasn't about to risk allowing her captors to find the closest thing she had to a weapon. While it wasn't much of one, the threat of puncturing their isolation suits ought to do the trick. She could only imagine herself grabbing one of the scientists around the neck, holding this little needle to his back, and demanding her release. The image was almost laughable, especially considering she didn't have the slightest idea where they were holding her or even how to get out of the facility, but there was one thing she knew with complete certainty.

If she didn't find a way to escape, she was going to die here.

The memory of the man standing on the other side of the glass, staring at her from behind his visor, blood pouring from his nose and dripping from his chin, cut through her thoughts. He frightened her on a primal level. There was something predatory in his eyes when he looked at her, something . . . evil.

She left the broad end of the needle protruding from her skin and traced the length of the bulge just underneath the surface. It was nearly undetectable. As long as she kept the blood from soaking through her scrub pants, there was no reason for anyone to look—

The door opened with a hiss of escaping air. She rolled over and instinctively reached beneath her waistband, ready to draw the needle.

A man she'd never seen before entered, pushing a computer cart with one hand and carrying a collapsed tripod in the other. He hung back momentarily, as though considering how best to approach her, before purposefully striding across the room.

Riley sat up and swung her legs over the side of the bed, letting the covers fall aside.

"My name is Davis Patterson," he said. He appeared to be in his early twenties, although with as nervous as he obviously was, he looked even younger. "I was hoping you wouldn't mind if I asked you a few questions. Or rather recorded your responses to a few statements."

He spread the legs of the tripod and set it down in front of her. The rectangular box mounted on top of it resembled a small flatscreen TV, but there was no screen on the face, only a collection of holes into which dozens of electrical cords had been plugged.

"What is this?" she asked. "A lie detector? Do you really think—?"

"Nothing like that," he said. "Although I guess if you really knew what you were doing, maybe you could use it to that effect."

She raised her eyebrows.

"It's an electroencephalogram," he said. "It records and interprets your brainwaves in real-time. I want to use it to help me learn more about you."

"I've already told you people everything I know. What more could I possibly have to offer?"

"These statements aren't necessarily about you, per se; they're designed to elicit emotional responses that can then be translated through the EEG so we can see which parts of your brain are activated."

"First off, what does this have to do with anything going on here?" she said. "And second, why in the world would I want to help you?"

She thought about the needle in her thigh and how close this man would get while hooking her to his machine. Unlike the others, who'd radiated an aura of authority, he seemed overwhelmed by the situation. And he wasn't so physically imposing that she couldn't control him with the tip of a needle pressed to his suit. Maybe this was her opportunity, but to seize it, she was going to have to get him to relax and let down his guard.

"This will only take a few minutes," he said. "And you won't feel a thing. I promise."

She glanced at the electrical cables hanging from the machine and offered a subtle nod.

"Thank you," Davis said. He slid the stool closer and sat within striking distance, their knees practically touching. She flinched when he reached behind him for a fistful of long cotton swabs and a tube of gel adhesive. "I'm not going to hurt you."

The expression on his face was one of genuine concern. It was the first time she'd seen something other than impatience or clinical curiosity in the eyes of anyone who'd entered her room.

"What do you hope to accomplish with this test?" she asked.

"I can't say. Telling you beforehand will skew the results. I don't want you to think about your responses. You know, is this the right answer? Is this what he wants or doesn't want to hear? For this to work, your answers have to remain unguarded. It needs to be a blind study."

"The law of intended consequences," she said. "That's what I call it anyway. When you look for what you expect to find, invariably you'll find it."

Davis appeared momentarily contemplative.

"I like that," he finally said. "And it fits perfectly. If you're not careful, your expectations will shape the outcome."

"That's how it works in archeology." She spoke while he worked, squirting the adhesive onto the swab, rubbing it against the contact points for the electrodes, and then securing them to her scalp. "You have the benefit of history, whereas the people of the era you're investigating are the ones who wrote it. You can't impose what you've learned upon societies that don't have the same benefit of hindsight. If you want to understand the people whose experiences laid the foundation for all of that accumulated knowledge, then you have to look at the puzzle pieces you unearth for what they are and not immediately try to put them together."

"It's the same for psychology." He let her hair fall back over the electrodes he'd placed around the left side of her head and started on the right. "You have to resist forcing the chaos into recognizable patterns when there are so many variables from one individual to the next."

Riley furrowed her brow.

"You're a psychologist?"

"Doctoral candidate, technically," he said.

"What in the world are you doing here?"

"Believe me, I've asked myself that very question." He smiled and for the briefest of seconds she almost forgot about the needle. "I guess you could say I got swept up in the situation and have a chance to take advantage of it." He recoiled as though shocked by his own words. "No, wait. That makes me sound like a total opportunist, although now that I think about it, I guess that's really what I am."

Riley was surprised to find him genuinely dismayed at the prospect.

"What are you hoping to accomplish?" she asked.

"Like I said, I can't—"

"Not specifically. Put all of this aside. What's your ultimate goal?"

"I want to help people," Davis said. He narrowed his eyes and appeared momentarily lost in thought. "That's not entirely true. I want to help people like me. I want to make it so that no one else will ever have to go through what I did."

"And what was that?"

Davis was silent for several seconds, as though trying to determine how much he could say without compromising the results of his experiment. He affixed the last few electrodes to her scalp and turned on the machine to make sure that everything was properly attached.

"Do you remember the school shooting in Sacramento?" he asked.

"You were there?"

"I try not to spend a whole lot of time thinking about it."

Riley nodded and looked at her hands in her lap, the pinkie of her right hand resting on the bulge of the needle, pressing the surgical steel into the raw flesh underneath. She understood what he was saying. Every time she closed her eyes, she saw Sadie tearing out Montgomery's throat with her teeth, heard Nate ripping apart Maria mere inches from where she hid, and saw Edgerton through the smoke, flames burning behind his eyes.

"I'm sorry," she whispered.

He looked up at her and offered a sad smile.

"I'm sorry for what you had to go through, too." He gestured toward the room around them. "What you're going through."

He wasn't like the others, which forced her to look at him in a new light.

"Ask your questions," she said.

He nodded and turned the monitor so that she could see it, a small gesture for which she was exceedingly grateful. The left side of the screen displayed a column of jagged colored sinewaves, as detected by each of the electrodes. The right side was split horizontally. The upper half showed four axial images of her brain, as though from the perspective of someone looking down on it from above, and her brain activity on a color scale ranging from red to green to blue, the patterns shifting and changing even as she thought about them. The image below it was from a camera built into the machine above the wires and showed her pale face and dirty hair, electrical wires standing at odd angles from it. She realized just how small and terrified she looked and choked back the tears before they could rise. No, she would not be the victim.

Not now. Not ever.

A red blob formed over her central brain on the monitor. She had to concentrate on suppressing her anger to make it go away.

"I'm going to make a series of statements," Davis said. "I don't want you to think about them. Just answer 'true' if you think they apply to you or 'false' if they don't, okay?"

She nodded.

"When I encounter someone who is sad about something, I usually end up feeling sad as well," he said.

"True."

Riley unconsciously traced the contours of the needle. She needed everyone to believe she was helpless. It was the only advantage she'd been given.

"It upsets me to hurt someone, even if he or she deserves it."

"True."

She hoped that wasn't the case, though, because she was certain that if she wanted to get out of here alive, then that was exactly what she was going to have to do.

DAVIS PUSHED the EEG cart across the hallway toward Alpha's observation room. Dr. Dale Edgerton stood right on the other side of the wall, his hands pressed against glass. His eyes locked onto those of Davis, who felt fear unlike any he'd experienced since hiding underneath the table in the school library so many years ago. It was an irrational feeling, but one no less debilitating than his racing heartbeat or his trembling hands. He recalled the memory of Alpha mouthing the same words that Stephen Leonard Thomas and Richard Wesley Taylor had spoken just prior to their deaths — *I'll be seeing you again soon* — and abruptly veered toward the residential wing.

Riley had given him plenty of data to analyze, he told himself. He could always conduct his interview with Alpha later. After all, it wasn't like he was going anywhere.

Davis pretended not to feel the heat of Alpha's stare on his back or hear the chorus of whispered voices echoing from behind him as he chickened out and headed toward the security door.

THE FEW MINUTES of sleep Cullen had been able to steal had done nothing to diminish his headache. If anything, it had gotten worse. He'd shoved clumps of tissue up his nose to plug his nostrils and hopefully stop the bleeding, which had turned his pillowcase into something out of a crime scene photo while he slept. Even without a thermometer, he could tell that he had a fever, but he sure as hell wasn't about to tell anyone else. It didn't take a genius to realize that something was physically wrong with him. Despite the normal bloodwork results from his intake exam, he was beginning to wonder if he hadn't been exposed after all and either the virus hadn't triggered a hematological response, or the incompetent staff here had simply missed it. Or maybe his suit had been compromised while restraining the chimpanzees.

He scrubbed the crust of blood from his nostrils, upper lip, and cheek and headed out once more. There was something he was supposed to be doing, he was certain of it, but he couldn't recall what it was. His thoughts had become sluggish and disconnected, like his neurons were attempting to fire through peanut butter. The last thing he clearly remembered was stabbing the dying man in the neck—

Cullen stopped in his tracks. His heavy breathing echoed throughout the empty corridor. He tasted blood leaking down the back of his throat.

No, that wasn't his memory at all. It took several seconds to recall that he'd actually been in a meeting where he'd viewed maps demonstrating just how badly they were all screwed. At least everyone outside of this base. Down here they were—

All going to die. All going to die. All going to die.

Safe. That was how he'd intended to finish that thought, but the word rang hollow in his head. They weren't safe down here. In fact, they were the furthest thing from it.

They just didn't know it yet.

Soon.

That single word, spoken in a voice composed of many, cut through his fugue like a scalpel through gray matter. It was the last thing he remembered hearing before sleep had ushered him into its cold embrace. He recalled seeing the access-controlled door from the animal wing behind him in the reflection, the one from which he'd watched Rankin emerge and had glimpsed a monitor displaying a man's face. And not just any man, either. A *sick* man. That was where he needed to go, but there was another stop he needed to make first.

Cullen changed into an isolation suit — noting that the first one he found in his size had a nearly imperceptible tear in the fabric at the edge of the visor, one he wouldn't have noticed had he not been specifically looking for it — and made his way down the hallway as though in a dream. One moment he was passing through a sterile white corridor and the next an earthen tunnel, beneath fluorescent tubes and then the flicking glow of torches, a ceiling with coiled tubing and then concealed by smoke and shadows. One second the observation room where Gamma lay sedated was there and the next it was a cavern filled with the grimy faces of those who'd chosen starvation over salvation. And then he was standing before Edgerton's chamber, where one heartbeat the anthropologist was leaning against the glass, and the next he was crouching with three other silhouettes over the remains of the dead man.

The blood from Cullen's nose once more overwhelmed the tissue plugs and streamed down his face. He reveled in the sensation, but it wasn't his blood that he craved.

He glanced over his shoulder and saw the woman lying on her side in bed, facing in the opposite direction. There was something about her, an inner radiance he could no more describe than he could explain his burning desire to see it extinguished. He took a step toward her—

Not yet.

The words were spoken in a voice formed of many, each of which seemed to originate from someplace different than the others.

He turned back to Edgerton, only the man standing before him was naked beneath the tattered hides draped over his shoulders, covered with dried blood, and wearing a bison's skull over his face. His eyes were unfathomable pits of darkness. He reared up before Cullen, growing larger and darker by the second until he transformed into a being made of shadow, first on the other side of the glass, and then in the reflection on it.

Cullen simultaneously saw himself wearing the beast's skull on this side and Edgerton standing on the other, but only for the briefest of seconds. The anthropologist collapsed, like a marionette whose strings had been cut, his forehead rebounding from the floor. He made no attempt to rise.

The reflection slowly faded until once more Cullen saw his own face behind the visor, only his eyes had changed. His irises had taken on a golden-orange cast, as though fires burned behind his pupils.

He cocked his head sharply to one side and then the other, eliciting a popping sound each time, and then headed deeper into the structure, toward the surveillance station. The back of the guard's head and shoulders were framed by the bank of monitors. The man abruptly sat up and leaned forward, as though something on one of the cameras had caught his eye.

Cullen knew exactly what that was.

And what he had to do.

"Help!" he shouted, sprinting toward the station. "Something's wrong with Alpha!"

The guard opened the door as if in slow motion. Cullen hit him squarely in the chest and tackled him to the floor. They slid across the tile and struck the desk, knocking off everything that had been sitting on it. A two-way transceiver landed between them, its battery casing popping off. The guard dove for it, but Cullen climbed onto his back and pinned him to the ground. Still, the man reached for his lone lifeline, his splayed fingers brushing the antenna.

Cullen wrapped his arm around the guard's neck and pulled back with every last ounce of strength he possessed. The guard sputtered and gasped, his gloved fingers grasping for the radio until his hand finally lay still.

Several seconds passed in silence.

Cullen relinquished his grip, allowing the guard's face to clatter to the floor. His blood rushed in his ears with a hollow *thoosh-thoosh-thoosh*. He stood, brushed himself off, and found himself looking at the weapons cabinet. Most of the rifles had been retrofitted to fire tranquilizer darts, except for the M4s at the end of the row. He checked to make sure the twenty-round magazine was full, slammed it home once more, and pulled the charging handle.

The time had finally come.

He dragged the guard's body into the corner behind the door and struck off toward the animal wing. He walked past Middleton's room without a second glance.

After all, he'd be back to take care of her soon enough.

RANKIN STUDIED Hanson's face on the overhead monitor. The detail images showed the animal handler's pallor, the sheen of sweat dampening his skin, and the dark circles around his eyes. His mouth hung open and his breathing had become agonal, his chest hitching with every wet gasp. The vitals monitor alarmed as his heart rate rose and his pulse oxygenation plummeted. His temperature had climbed over 106. It was only a matter of time now.

08:36:23.

The conference call with the brain trust back in Cambridge had gone about as Rankin had expected. Hodges and his team had been cautiously optimistic, but they'd made it clear that a simulation was no substitute for the real thing. They needed to know that the antibodies worked on a living organism.

He lowered his stare to the window, through which he could see Hanson strapped to the gurney. If it was proof they wanted, then, by God, that was exactly what they were going to get.

Time was running out. In the most advanced cases, desperate doctors around the country had begun testing an experimental regimen involving a combination of medically induced comas and therapeutic hypothermia to arrest the progression of the virus. So far, the results were encouraging, but there were only so many ICU beds and even fewer physicians qualified to perform the procedure. At least the media had yet to catch wind of the patients who'd already passed the point of no return, as they'd been quietly transferred to military facilities, where they could be effectively sedated and contained, although the powers that be were in no position to handle the anticipated volume. And no one was prepared to deal with any number of civilians suffering at home, unable to forestall the progression of symptoms that could effectively turn them into monsters and major metropolises into hot zones unlike any the world had ever seen.

"His blood pressure's rising," Dr. Mathers said.

"Come on," Rankin whispered.

"Respirations slowing."

"Kill that infernal alarm."

The doctor did as he asked, but the resulting silence was infinitely worse.

Rankin switched to the proper channel on his two-way and brought the microphone to his lips.

"How close are you to having an experimental dose ready?"

"Maybe half an hour," Pennington responded. "At the most."

Rankin glanced at the clock.

08:40:16.

"You have ten minutes."

He switched off the transceiver and returned his attention to the monitor. It was too late for lab testing on human tissue, experimentation on animals, and clinical trials. Either this worked, the President railroaded the FDA, and they went into mass production, or their only option to contain the spread of the virus would fall on the military to quarantine major cities and make sure that no one broke containment, regardless of what transpired on the streets.

The muted alarm icon flashed on the vitals monitor as the sine waves spiked and then abruptly flatlined, at least momentarily. Jagged crests appeared at irregular intervals, growing closer together with each passing second.

Rankin turned to the main screen in time to watch Hanson's eyelids snap open. The vessels burst and flooded the sclera with blood, which welled against his lashes like tears. He sighed and his body appeared to deflate. Expiratory spatter freckled his face.

"Increase sedation," Rankin said.

Hanson arched his back on the gurney. The tendons stood out from the tented flesh of his neck, and he bared his teeth, which were stained pink from his bleeding gums.

"Increase the goddamn sedation!" Rankin shouted.

Mathers dialed up the dosage on her console.

Hanson snapped at the air with his teeth and strained against his bindings, but it was obvious the propofol was already working its magic. His respirations slowed and his movements ceased. Crimson dribbled from the corners of his mouth and rolled down his cheeks.

Rankin glanced at the clock one last time — 08:46:03 — and headed for the exit. He needed that therapeutic injection and he needed it right now. He grabbed the handle and turned—

CULLEN HEARD the click of the disengaging lock and threw his shoulder into the door. The metal slab met with momentary resistance, and then suddenly swung wide open. He caught a glimpse of yellow Tyvek sliding backward across the ground as he ducked into the observation suite and slammed the door behind him.

Surprise and confusion registered on Rankin's face. Cullen jumped on top of him before he could raise his hands to ward off the coming blows and slammed the butt of the M4 against his former subordinate's visor, over and over. The plastic shield fractured, then shattered, as did the bones underneath. And yet Cullen just kept swinging the rifle, flinging arcs of blood into the air until Rankin's body stilled underneath him.

He sat up and wiped the blood from his mask, which only smeared it across the plastic. The thunder of his pulse in his ears was so loud that he didn't hear the woman screaming. At least not at first. He slowly stood and advanced toward her, taking in the room around him in his peripheral vision. The monitors mounted to the wall displayed vital signs and a close-up of the face of the man on the opposite side of the observation window, strapped to a gurney and surrounded by medical equipment.

The woman stopped screaming and lunged for the two-way radio perched on her console, but he was upon her before she could reach it. He twisted her arm behind her back, turned her to face him, and cracked her upside the head with the stock of the rifle. Her eyes rolled up, and she collapsed backward onto her desk. He grabbed her by the front of her isolation suit and looked directly into—

—the face of a woman standing over him, her wide eyes a stark contrast to her filthy face. She claps her hands over her mouth as she watches him feed on the carcass. He peels a strip of meat, its edges crisp with burned skin and hair, and thrusts it toward her. She must eat if she wants to survive. She recoils and curses him.

He turns to those who would live, three men with blood on their faces, flesh in their mouths, and death in their eyes. They turn away, for they know what must be done and, in doing so, willingly accept their damnation. Doubt can spread from one person to the next faster than any disease. Once it takes root, the only way to get rid of it is to carve it out like any other malignancy, and he cannot afford for his flock to doubt his connection to the gods.

He rises from the ground, takes her by the throat—

—and squeezed with all of his might. The woman swatted at his face and chest until eventually her exertions slowed and her arms fell to her sides.

Cullen watched the light fade from her eyes, the muscles in her face relax, and one final exhalation part her lips. He opened his hands and she slid out from beneath him, puddling on the floor at his feet.

The door to the observation chamber was on the far side of the desk. He stepped over the woman's body and, with a spin of the handle and a hiss of pressurized air, entered the secure room, his footsteps echoing hollowly from the concrete walls. The infected man rested on the gurney before him, just as he'd known he would. Cullen didn't question how he'd come to possess this knowledge any more than he questioned the path laid out before him.

He removed the restraints from the man's arms and legs. Tore the straps from his forehead, chest, and hips and ripped the IV out of his arm, spurting fluid onto the floor and summoning a rivulet of blood from the man's inner elbow.

Whispered voices filled his head, speaking in a language he'd never heard and yet somehow instinctively understood. There were so many of them, all crying out at once. He heard their pain, felt their anguish, sensed their desperate desire for release, and realized what he needed to do.

Cullen left the unconscious man in his cage, dragged Rankin's body across the room, and wedged it into the secure door so it wouldn't be able to close. He exited the observation suite and crossed the hall. The chimpanzees' cages were now clean and shiny, their former occupants in the adjacent room. He opened the door and high-pitched screams erupted from everywhere at once. The simians struggled and screeched in a futile attempt to free themselves from the restraining devices, their heads jerking back and forth, blood flinging from their long canines.

He went straight to the nearest one, loosened its collar and the straps binding its wrists just enough to buy him time to get out of there before they slipped their bindings—

"What the hell are you doing?"

Cullen turned at the sound of the voice and found himself staring at Pritchard, who looked from his superior to the chimp wriggling out of the contraption and back again.

"At long last, the Day of Purification is here," Cullen said in a voice no longer his own.

He raised his rifle and fired a single shot through Pritchard's visor, decorating the wall behind him with a Rorschach pattern of blood and gray matter.

Cullen turned his back on Pritchard's body and moved on to the next chimpanzee in line, and the next after that, until the screaming reached a crescendo and the first of the frenzied primates squirmed free.

26

Cambridge, Massachusetts

Lucas drove west through Boston on the Massachusetts Turnpike. He clipped his cellphone to the suction-cup holder on the inside of his windshield and played the live feed from a cable news channel, the voice of the news anchor emerging from the speakers of his F-150.

"... *reports from panicked first responders coming in from as far away as Alaska and the Pacific Northwest* ... "

The old truck had been with him since high school and had more than a hundred thousand miles to show for it, but it got decent enough gas mileage and was a beast on the ice, so he'd never really felt a pressing need to replace it, especially with as little as he drove in the city. It'd been a long time since he'd taken it across the country, though. He wished he'd popped the hood and given everything a once-over, and yet the urge to leave had been so insistent that it had become a biological imperative, an urge he couldn't have resisted for even the hour it would have taken to change the oil and top off the fluids.

"... *details are still scarce, anonymous sources believe we are dealing with a hemorrhagic virus similar to Ebola,*" the newscaster said, cutting through his thoughts. "*Representatives from the CDC can neither confirm nor deny* ... "

A string of headlights appeared on the opposite side of the road. Both lanes were filled with vehicles, one right behind the other, for as far as he could see. A wash of light caught his eye. He turned and saw Fenway lit up and the surrounding rooftops illuminated by massive portable lighting arrays. Emergency vehicles streaked across the Brookline overpass as the caravan in the eastbound lanes emerged from underneath it. A literal army of olive-green military vehicles rumbled past, everything from troop transports to panel trucks, jeeps of all shapes and sizes, and flatbeds loaded with gear strapped down beneath flagging tarps. He knew where they were going even before they sorted like playing cards in anticipation of taking the next offramp.

" . . . the governor of New York has issued a shelter-in-place order for the entire state. The President is expected to deliver an early morning address in response to concerns . . . "

Lucas thought of the prospective students he'd seen gathered outside the university for their campus tour — the sweat blooming from their foreheads and the aura of sickness radiating from them — and wondered if at that very moment their parents were rushing them to one of the many nearby hospitals, which were quite possibly already overflowing and ready to begin spilling over into Fenway Park. And he remembered the images captured inside the apartment in Midtown and realized that not even a National Guard contingent would be enough to protect this city from what was to come. Yet here he was, one of the few people who had the slightest idea what was going on, speeding away in the middle of the night.

What was he supposed to do, though? He wasn't a physician, and he didn't have anything resembling military training. The men back at the NeXgen corporate offices? This was the kind of contingency they were supposed to be able to prevent, but they didn't know how to stop the spread of the virus any more than he did. Maybe less so, in fact, since he at least had historical precedence upon which to draw. It felt as though his entire life had been building to this singular moment, preparing him to understand what they were up against. He'd spent more time among the deserted cliff dwellings than anyone he knew, countless hours combing through the canyons in search of evidence that would explain why such an advanced civilization had first built fortresses high on the cliffsides and then abandoned them altogether.

He had a pretty good idea now, and it scared the living hell out of him.

" . . . seek immediate medical treatment. The offices of emergency management in all fifty states have released detailed plans . . . "

In his mind, he saw men and women stalking the canyons of the Southwest, bleeding from seemingly everywhere at once, hunting and killing everyone and everything, victims of the same mindless rage that had caused an infected man to tear out the throat of a SWAT officer with his teeth. He imagined ancient people high in their fortified cities, watching the valley below in complete silence, holding their breath and praying—

A red wall of taillights materialized as he rounded the bend.

He stomped the brake and slewed sideways onto the shoulder to keep from hitting the car in front of him. Both lanes were clogged with stopped vehicles, maybe three or four deep. Several of the drivers had gotten out and stood in the wash of headlights up ahead. There appeared to have been an accident, but he couldn't see what had happened. Hopefully no one was seriously—

"Somebody call an ambulance!"

Lucas jumped out of his truck and rushed past men and women standing outside their cars, staring up the road toward where a handful of people had gathered around—

"Jesus," he whispered.

He slowed as he neared the front of the traffic jam and looked down upon a body sprawled on the asphalt. The man's arms and legs were broken at unnatural angles, but his head appeared to have taken the brunt of the impact. His face was sickeningly concave, as though it had met directly with the bumper of the SUV beside him, which, judging by the fan of blood covering the hood and the windshield, it probably had.

Sirens wailed and emergency lights materialized in the distance.

"He came out of nowhere," a man wearing a khaki jacket and work boots said. He thrust his hands into the pockets of his jeans and shifted from side to side in uncomfortable, straight-legged movements. "All of a sudden he was just there. I didn't even have time to hit the brakes."

"How could you not see him in the middle of the road?" a woman asked, her voice high and tight.

"He was running right at me. What was I supposed to do?"

"How about not hit him?"

"Screw you. Don't you think I already feel bad enough?"

An ambulance bleated its siren until the cars in the left lane moved just far enough for it to squeeze past along the median. It parked on the far side of the dead man and paramedics disgorged from the front doors. Both wore full-face masks with filtration canisters. One opened the back of the rig while the other knelt beside the victim, his face stark white in the halogen glare.

They knew.

A police cruiser pulled up beside the ambulance and an officer wearing a surgical mask climbed out.

"Everyone back in your cars," he shouted. "Unless you were directly involved or witnessed the accident, you need to clear out."

Lucas looked down at the body one last time and saw not the cratered face, but rather that of the man in Midtown who'd charged into the crossfire of half a dozen SWAT officers.

He walked back to his truck and drove away. A sensation of numbness settled over him. On a primitive level, he understood that bad things were about to happen.

And there was no hope of stopping them.

————

HODGES SAT at the head of the table, struggling to keep up with everything transpiring around him. Events were spiraling out of control faster than anyone could have anticipated. Hospitals in Fairbanks and Anchorage were already overwhelmed with cases. Doctors were inducing medical comas and hypothermia as quickly as possible, but they had only so many ICU beds to work with. The National Guard had been deployed to Seattle, San Francisco, Minneapolis, Boston, and New York City, while military assets had been mobilized in San Diego, Los Angeles, and Washington, D.C. Authorities had begun converting football stadiums, indoor arenas, and convention centers into overflow triage centers run by representatives from the agencies gathered in this room, under the auspices of FEMA. Barricades were being raised on the major thoroughfares servicing the affected cities and remote quarantine stations were being erected in case large segments of the population needed to be isolated from the rest of the country.

The people surrounding him grew increasingly frantic as they coordinated with their various agencies and field teams, their voices like the whine of so many angry mosquitoes. There was no longer any denying that the balance of power in the room had shifted. Worse, they'd gone from needing Hodges to actively blaming him, if only with the accusatory glances from the corners of their eyes. He knew he'd screwed up, as had so many others up and down the chain. It had been like watching dominos fall, with one mistake leading to another and another, until there was nothing anyone could do to stop the inevitable, which played out on all of the monitors mounted on the walls at once.

Helicopters and armadas of drones filled the night sky above the urban sprawl like flies swarming so many corpses, relaying images ripped from Hodges's worst nightmares. An infected man smashed the window of a car and dragged a woman, kicking and screaming, from behind the wheel as police fired on him. Another attacked the patrons funneling out of a closing bar before being gunned down by bystanders. The flaming wreckage of a flight-for-life chopper burned on the rooftop of an emergency center, brought down by the very woman it had been transporting. Neighbors breaking into one another's houses. Pedestrians being run down on sidewalks or hit trying to escape through traffic. Massacres in hospital waiting rooms and parking lots.

And this was only the beginning.

Lord only knew the horrors they'd be facing by the time the President addressed the nation. Cold War-era contingency plans were being activated.

Soldiers were being deployed on American soil for the first time in its storied history. Borders were being closed, flights grounded, ports shuttered. With as rapidly as the situation was unraveling, Hodges had no doubt that when the commander-in-chief finally stepped to the podium, it would be to declare martial law.

"Sir," a voice said from somewhere far away.

Hodges could positively smell himself, the fear leaking from every pore. When he'd put on this suit, he hadn't anticipated wearing it for several days straight, let along dying in it.

"Sir!" Bergstrom shouted.

Hodges blinked repeatedly and looked away from the bank of monitors. His VP of R&D leaned across the table and thrust a stack of printouts into his face.

"Riverton did it," he said. "They're synthesizing the antibodies as we speak and preparing a trial dose of a therapeutic treatment."

Hodges glanced down at the top page, which showed the trimer of a Bering Virus bound by ribbons of antibody proteins. Subsequent pages detailed clusters of epitopes and their contact points with the corresponding antibody binding sites. But even if the experimental therapeutic worked and every pharmaceutical company rushed it into mass production, entire cities would have fallen by the time they began distributing the first doses.

He crumpled the report, shouted at the top of his lungs, and hurled it in frustration.

The room fell silent as the pages fluttered to the floor. All eyes fixed upon him as he sat there, chest heaving, collar biting into his throat, undershirt soaked with sweat.

"It's over," he finally said.

"The hell it is," Xenos said. He abruptly stood, stormed out of the room, and slammed the door behind him.

"We're receiving reports of hospitalizations for life-threatening fevers in Europe and Asia," Ferris said. "I'll forward that file so that maybe they'll have a chance."

The room spun around Hodges as the chaos resumed once more. Acid churned in his stomach, and he felt a sharp pain behind his right eye. How had he gotten here? He remembered himself as he'd been on the first day of medical school: a skinny know-it-all kid possessed by his superior abilities and the knowledge that great things awaited him. As a resident, he'd been so certain that he was going to change the world that he'd told anyone who would listen, from his attending all the way up to the chief of staff. And he'd been right. His company had produced hundreds of vaccines and therapeutics that had saved countless lives and literally changed the face of modern medicine.

How had he fallen so far that his failure to kill one of his own men had resulted in the chaos playing out before him now? He'd reached for divinity and fallen back to earth, and the price of his hubris would be measured in the souls of the dead.

Hodges hadn't changed the world . . .

He'd destroyed it.

TRAFFIC SLOWED near the outskirts of Newton, where National Guardsmen had blocked the left lane with sandbags and were starting on the right. They'd already barricaded the onramp to I-95, which encircled the greater Boston area and could be used to enforce a citywide quarantine.

Lucas's truck crawled across the overpass beneath blinding construction lights and the watchful eyes of uniformed men wearing full-face gas masks, one of whom stepped out into the road behind him and halted the flow of traffic, stranding the remainder of the cars inside the hot zone. He breathed a sigh of relief, but he couldn't afford to celebrate just yet. The closer he got to the population centers in New York and Philly, the worse the roads were going to get, especially once the sun rose and people learned of the nightmare that had unfolded while they slept.

Go west if you want to live.

The words played on a continuous loop inside his head. There'd been sightings of the cryptic symbols in Indiana and Illinois, although they were fewer and farther between, as though whoever was leaving them had realized that time was running short and accelerated his pace. Of course, even if they'd been left as warnings, there were so few people who could read them that it hardly seemed worth the effort.

" . . . *is being enforced in the Twin Cities, with reports of the outbreak coming in from the surrounding suburbs. Authorities fear that any hope of containment has already been lost . . .* "

Houses blew past in the darkness, entire neighborhoods built upon land where once natives had tracked herds of wild game across acres of forests and grasslands stretching from one horizon to the other. Never in their wildest dreams would they have imagined this land being covered with buildings and roads, just as he'd never contemplated what the world would look like after modern civilization collapsed.

Wooden homes would rot, their roofs and fences falling. Trees would lay claim to their remains and weeds would eventually overtake the roads. Dirt would accumulate on the rubble of shopping malls and superstores, creating hills from which thickets would grow. Overpasses would crumble into rivers, rerouting them into unpredictable offshoots that would destroy entire towns in their eternal quest to reach the ocean. When all was said and done, only concrete and stone structures would stand from the vegetation, surrounded by the bones of the dead, leaving future generations of archeologists to piece together a narrative of pain, suffering, and death, much as he did now.

The big picture was starting to come together all around him, like puzzle pieces clicking into place. There were the petroglyphs from inside the cave in Alaska, which told the tale of infected people being sealed inside with the shaman who'd subsisted on their remains, the same designs that he'd seen at countless other indigenous sites throughout the Americas, most notably at Eagle Nest, above which the cliff had been inscribed with the same message that had popped up everywhere, seemingly overnight. And then there were the photographs the special agent in Detroit had sent to him, which featured symbols whose meanings chilled him to his very core. He lives. Time is now. He comes. The end is here. Blood flows.

"All going to die," he said out loud.

It was impossible to study native cultures without delving into their spirituality and beliefs, which infiltrated every aspect of their daily lives. Spirits and the afterlife. Gods and totems. The anthropomorphism of nature and the seasons. And, most importantly, prophecies and portents. Every civilization had them, but what he'd always found so strange about them was how eerily similar they were from one culture to the next.

The Navajo and Hopi tribes, whom many speculate descended from the Anasazi, believed that they were living in the Fourth World and that it was only a matter of time before it ended in cataclysm, a belief that was nearly identical to the myth of the Five Suns perpetuated by the Aztecs and Toltecs, who cut the still-beating hearts from their sacrifices to stave off the end of the world. Nearly every modern religion had its own apocalyptic mythology with nearly identical imagery: a deity arises from the darkness — be it in the form of an animal or a god or the antichrist — signifying that the end of days had arrived and that only the chosen would survive.

A shiver rippled up his spine that had nothing to do with the cool night air blowing through the open window.

It all made sense now. He needed to return to the Canyons of the Ancients, because that's where everything had started, where history still echoed from the stone, memorialized in petroglyphs carved by the hands of long-dead men. The secret to humankind's survival lay in cliff dwellings abandoned by a culture that had endured the nightmare they now faced and then dissolved in the hope that the communal memories of the horrors inflicted upon it would fade away as well.

Lucas glanced at the live newsfeed on his cellphone and realized that he'd be lucky if he made it that far.

HODGES WATCHED the monitors with a growing sense of dread. Roadblocks had been erected at every juncture of I-95 surrounding the city. Drones were being used to police the inner perimeter and the banks of the Charles River. Logan International was effectively closed and the smaller commercial fields within the radius had been commandeered for military use. The Port of Boston set lifeless and empty.

In just under two hours, sleeping citizens would be awakened by the emergency broadcast tone and instructed not to leave their homes under any circumstances. The governor would take over the airwaves and call for a show of unity in the face of this crisis. He'd say something inspiring and heartfelt, something to the effect of "we'll get through this if we all work together," but it would be a lie.

They were all going to die; they just didn't know it yet.

Hodges did, though. He watched that grim reality play out in low-resolution cellphone videos of the infected tearing through the streets and the bodies littering the sidewalks in their wake, in footage of overwhelmed emergency rooms and field triage centers, in recordings of patients who had to be sedated for the protection of those around them and the medical professionals who'd lost their lives learning that lesson. In hysterical social media posts, conspiracy blogs, and reports of 9-1-1 dispatchers unable to keep up with the volume of calls. Local stations broadcast footage of looters smashing the windows of downtown merchants, climbing over the broken glass, and absconding with boxes of shoes, hangers of clothes, and the kinds of wares that only the most opportunistic would risk jail time to steal. Fires burned in vacant lots, abandoned homes, and Dumpsters. A police cruiser had been flipped onto its roof in Hyde Park, the officers inside beaten nearly to death.

He watched it all through the eyes of a penitent, one who knew that his punishment for his pride was to bear witness to the destruction he had wrought. Where once had sat a man who fancied himself a god, there was now only the shell of a human being who understood that he had killed everyone he loved. His wife and his youngest child were asleep in their beds in Back Bay. His middle child was likely only now returning to the dorms after a night of partying and his oldest was probably still wide awake, studying for one test or another. He'd killed them, as surely as if he'd put the barrel of a shotgun to their heads and pulled the trigger. And all of their friends and their families. Everyone.

It didn't matter that NeXgen was sitting on a viable therapeutic treatment or that a vaccine was already in the works. By the time either was released, there'd be no one left to administer the medications, let alone take them. Maybe those like Alpha and Beta — the two-point-two percent blessed with the ability to manufacture the antibodies — would be able to barricade them-selves in their homes and ride out the secondary symptoms of the virus, but with the way he'd seen the infected drag people from moving cars and run them down in bars and convenience stores, he didn't hold out much hope.

A helicopter thupped overhead, causing the ceiling tiles to shake and the monitors to rattle on the walls.

"Time to go," Xenos said, bursting through the office door.

He bundled his laptop into his attaché case and strode back into the hall-way. Vickers pulled off his headset, hurled it across the room in frustration, and stormed out after him. Ferris and Urban each took one last look at the drama unfolding on the screens, then gathered their belongings and left. Hodges followed as though in a trance, his outstretched arms braced against the walls for balance. He knocked expensive paintings and decorations from their hangers as he went, but it didn't matter now. Nothing mattered.

"All over . . . " he whispered.

Bergstrom took him by the arm and hurried toward the staircase to the roof. They ascended in a concrete blur and leaned into the rotor wash of the Black Hawk on the helipad. Xenos was already on board and helping the secretary of the DHS through the side door. Ferris and Urban raised their briefcases to shield their eyes as they closed the distance.

Hodges ducked his head and jogged toward the chopper, his jacket flar-ing. Xenos took him by the wrist and dragged him inside. He tumbled into a rear-facing seat and strapped on his harness with trembling hands. He'd barely seated the headset over his ears when the commander of USAMRIID slid the door closed, barked for the pilot to lift off, and took the seat opposite Hodges, who couldn't hold the older man's stare.

Instead, he looked out through the window as they rose from the roof of the empire he'd built and banked out over the harbor. Police cruisers sped through the neighborhoods below. A pall of smoke hung over Commercial Street, where several cars appeared to be actively burning. They circled around the airport and headed to the southwest, leaving behind a city which, should any of them be fortunate enough to see it again, would never be the same.

LUCAS PUSHED the speedometer up to ninety. The highway patrol undoubtedly had more pressing concerns than giving speeding tickets, and the few cars on the road were going nearly as fast as he was, anyway. He wondered what the drivers knew about the situation or if they were just going about their daily lives, unprepared for what was to come. Or perhaps the brain trust back at NeXgen had the virus contained in the major metropolises and the rest of the population just needed to hunker down and ride it out.

A billboard defaced by hurriedly painted symbols — *Go west if you want to live* — blew past and he realized that there would be no riding it out. The sun had set on the Fourth World.

The truck roared underneath an overpass and emerged on the other side. Deciduous trees lined the highway, an emerald wall glimmering like a snake's scales in the periphery of his headlights. He'd only made this drive once before, although at the time there'd been no real rush and he'd pretty much zoned out the whole way, envisioning his new life at one of the most prestigious universities on the planet. Now, no matter how hard he pushed his pickup, the miles seemed to crawl past.

He'd sped through Massachusetts and the better part of Connecticut. Worcester and Hartford would have appeared normal had he not been specifically looking for the lights of emergency vehicles racing through the dark streets and the flashing red and green navigation lights of helicopters. Once he crossed the New York state line, it was a straight shot through Scranton and Akron into Columbus.

" . . . *overburdened ER doctors are urging all non-emergent patients to either stay home or seek treatment from their primary care physicians to free up beds for the growing numbers of infected . . .* "

A sign announcing he'd entered the town of Brookfield flashed past in his peripheral vision. The red glow of brake lights bloomed from the road ahead, where the offramp wound down into the trees. An Audi appeared to have missed the turnoff and gone straight into the embankment, the Exit 9 sign standing from its shattered windshield. Smoke rose from its crumpled hood, which was buried in dirt and weeds. A semi and several other cars had stopped in the middle of the right lane. The drivers rushed through the glow of their combined headlights and converged upon the wrecked vehicle.

The driver of the Audi crawled out the window and fell to the ground. Lucas could hear her cries even before he pulled to the shoulder. She barely made it to her feet before whoever was in the backseat kicked out the window. A teenage boy crawled through the broken glass and sprinted after the woman.

"Help me!" she screamed.

The woman threw herself into the trucker's arms a heartbeat before the boy overtook her.

Lucas jumped out of his truck and ran to her aid.

The boy buried his face in the woman's neck and tore out a mouthful of flesh, spattering the trucker with arterial blood. He just stood there, crimson draining from his face, as the boy wrenched the woman from his grasp, rounded on him, and lunged—

A crash of gunfire.

The impact lifted the boy from his feet and tossed him into the bushes.

Lucas turned around and saw a patrol officer standing outside the open driver-side door of his cruiser. He wore an expression of shock as he slowly lowered his weapon and crunched across the gravel into the high weeds.

"Jesus," the trucker said. He stumbled backward, tripped over his own feet, and landed on his rear end, still holding his arms away from his body as though to keep them from getting as bloody as the rest of him. "Jesus H. Christ."

Lucas followed the officer to where the boy lay, his heels scraping uselessly at the earth. He couldn't have been more than fourteen or fifteen, and yet he appeared unfazed by the gunshot wound on his shoulder. Struggling to his haunches, he snapped his teeth and swung at them with his good arm.

"Stay down," the officer said. "Please. You don't want to do this."

The boy sprung at him. The cop pulled the trigger and put the kid down. The report rolled through the valley as the officer dropped to his knees in the dirt.

"Get out of here," he whispered.

Lucas placed a tentative hand on his shoulder.

"I said get out of here!" the officer shouted.

Lucas nodded and backed away. There was nothing he could do to help.

His hands shook so badly when he climbed behind the wheel that he could barely turn the key in the ignition. He pulled onto the highway and did his best not to look in the rearview mirror, although the footage playing on his cellphone wasn't much better. It showed an aerial view of a cluster of tents outside the ambulance bay of an emergency room, where bodies littered the ground in the red and blue glow of police lights.

" . . . appears to be attacking and — My God. He's using his teeth . . . "

Numbness spread throughout Lucas's body. He'd seen the aftermath of the shooting inside the infected man's apartment in New York City, but nothing could have prepared him to witness such an attack in person. There'd been a sterile quality to the images that dissipated in real life with the gun smoke in the air and the scent of fresh blood soaking into the earth.

All hope for containing the virus was lost.

The urge to reach his destination overwhelmed him. He needed to get to the Canyons of the Ancients. As irrational as the impulse was, he knew that the secrets they concealed were humanity's only hope for survival.

Lucas pinned the gas and rocketed westward until a wall of brake lights appeared on the horizon. He watched it draw closer, slowing as the scene before him came into focus. Screams rent the night, awful sounds filled with so much pain that he felt it as his own.

A dozen vehicles were angled across the highway beneath an overpass. Several had collided, while the remainder appeared to have tried to skirt the wreckage on the shoulders. Silhouettes climbed on their roofs, shattering windshields and dragging out the passengers, butchering them right there on the hoods of their cars. One of the attackers looked up and Lucas caught a fleeting glimpse of the woman's blood-red eyes. She leaped down to the asphalt and sprinted toward his truck.

He jammed the stick into reverse, backed away as fast as he could, and swung around just in time to avoid hitting the semi bearing down on him from behind. Its brakes screamed and its trailer jackknifed. He threw the transmission into drive and aimed for the shoulder. The F-150 bounced through a drainage ditch and slammed into the mound of dirt on the other side, throwing up a curtain of soil.

Lucas pinned the gas again. The front tires spun until they finally gained traction and launched the truck uphill, through a wall of saplings, and over the sidewalk on the other side. He stomped the brake and cranked the wheel to keep from flying right off the other side of the road. Shadows materialized from the darkness to his right, running right at him. He accelerated in the opposite direction, the screams of the dying echoing from underneath the overpass.

Hand shaking, he swiped away the news footage on his cell phone and programmed his GPS app to reroute him through the countryside.

27

St. Louis, Missouri

B illy woke with a start. For a moment, he didn't know where he was or how he'd gotten there, but his disorientation faded and he recognized his surroundings. Or at least sort of. He'd gone way too long without sleeping, crashed far harder than he'd expected, and had only the vaguest recollection of the tires buzzing on the notches in the shoulder and his grandfather offering to spell him at the wheel. That had been somewhere just outside of Indianapolis, not long after dark. He remembered it specifically because that's where they'd seen all of the military vehicles parked alongside the highway and the helicopters circling Lucas Oil Stadium, its parking lot awash with emergency lights.

He opened the passenger's door and climbed down onto the asphalt. An interstate truck roared past, its slipstream rocking the old Chevy on its creaky suspension. A gentle rain had started to fall, which explained why they were parked underneath an overpass, a curtain of runoff pouring over the sides. His great-grandfather was at the top of the slanted concrete slope, painting his symbols on the vertical embankment, above which swallows nested in the recesses between girders.

"Where are we?" he asked.

Sakeva finished his work, sealed the tub of paint, and started back down the hill. Billy jumped over the flooded gutter and rushed to help the old man before he fell and broke a hip.

"Outside of St. Louis," Sakeva said. "I am glad you were able to get some sleep. I did not mean to wake you."

"I don't know what woke me up, but it wasn't you."

"Bad dreams?"

Billy recalled images of the eyes of ravens reflecting from high up on telephone wires, bodies hanging by their feet from streetlights, and a blood-red sun setting upon a field dotted with furry carcasses, but he shook his head for the old man's benefit.

"I'm fine to drive," he said.

"You were barely asleep for three hours." Sakeva smirked and tossed him the keys. "Oh, to be young again."

Billy climbed behind the wheel and waited for his great-grandfather to load the paint into the bed and get in beside him. He merged onto the highway and headed west, billboards promising gas stations and restaurants appearing with increasing frequency.

"The years pass so quickly that before you know it, they are nearly gone," Sakeva said. "Your body ages and your mind matures, but inside your head you are still the same person you have always been, with the same hopes and dreams. And the same doubts. I remember thinking that by the time I reached my grandfather's age, I would have undergone some sort of magical transformation and gained the wisdom he possessed. What I never realized is that wisdom is merely having the confidence to state belief as fact, the greatest flaw being that you never have it when it is of any use to you. All you can do is pass it on to younger generations who lack the knowledge to appreciate it, thus your entire existence becomes little more than a story."

Billy had never really thought of his great-grandfather as ever having been young like him. Sure, he'd envisioned Sakeva as a much younger version of the man he was now and could almost see him as he'd once been, but Billy had never imagined him as being anything other than an old man on the inside.

"What was your grandfather like?" he asked.

A wistful smile formed on Sakeva's face.

"He was a hard man, one who was old before his time. He lost two children, which was not uncommon in those days, and suffered the loss of his land and livestock and sovereignty, but the worst was when the tribal council turned against him and the other traditionalists and destroyed his way of life. Our way of life. I still remember when he took me into the canyon and explained the Hopi way of life at the foot of the Prophecy Stone, which shows Maasaw leading our ancestors into the Fourth World, where two paths diverge. The first represents the path followed by most of our people, who are depicted holding hands in their commitment to materialism, a path that degenerates into the crooked line of chaos. The second represents the Road of Life, the one Taiowa wants us to walk. There are obstructions on this path, two circles that represent global conflicts, the first of which belongs to the Great War."

"Never heard of it."

"It is called World War One now. Of course, that is not what it was called at the time because there had yet to be a Second World War, which the carving predicted, much like the vertical line after it that prophesied the exodus of the Hopi who had abandoned their faith, like your father and grandfather. There is another circle after that, representing a third war, on the other side of which stands a man in a cornfield, a herald of hope for the Fifth World, and those who follow the true path."

A smudge appeared against the horizon to the southwest, as though the darkness itself were rising from the earth and erasing the stars as it went. Billy caught the first faint whiff of smoke through the cracked window.

"So how does it end?" he asked.

"Perhaps this world will end in sickness—"

"No, I mean the previous worlds ended when Taiowa's nephew, Sótuknang, gathered the survivors and led them to the ant people for protection while he destroyed it."

"Except for the Third World, the fall of which happened so quickly that he was forced to call upon Spider Woman, who sealed the chosen inside hollow reeds to outlast the flooding."

"Right, so what happens now? Will Sótuknang appear and tell us to follow the stars to the ant people? Will Spider Woman descend from some great web in the sky and pack us into airtight containers?"

"Do you remember what I told you about our ancestors?" Sakeva asked.

"They were the first to complete their migrations and settle on the sacred mesas."

"The Fire Clan," Sakeva said. "And after Maasaw welcomed them to Oraibi, he presented them with a stone tablet. On the front he'd inscribed four characters: the *Meha* in the upper left corner symbolizes the four forces of nature in motion, the commencement of the first great war; the sun in the upper right corner represents the rise of the defeated force and the beginning of a second great war; the red symbol in the bottom right corner signifies the final war, the shedding of much blood, and the purification of all living things. Maasaw broke off the bottom left corner to indicate a great division of the people, although the crooked line rising from the fractured stone is the same as that of the first path on the Prophecy Stone, portending a descent into chaos."

"What symbol was in the bottom corner before it was broken off?"

The sky glowed ahead. The aura was much brighter than the light pollution radiating from other cities they'd encountered at night, and more orange than yellow.

"To understand that, you must first decipher the markings on the back," Sakeva said. "The bow at the top left represents the Fire Clan and designates it the caretaker of the Fourth World, which is why the responsibility has been passed down through our family. The V symbol to its right indicates a division of the people and the end of the Fourth World. Like its mirror image on the opposite side, the bottom right corner is missing. The wavy line in the bottom left shows the path we must follow to reach our ultimate destination — embodied by the symbol for brotherhood — and the three people prophesied to help guide our people into the Fifth World. And in the center, larger than all of the other symbols, is the beheaded man, who portends the final purification and the eradication of humankind."

"So what's on the missing corner?" Billy asked.

"Many believe the symbols inscribed upon it signify the destination where the chosen must gather and the route by which they will get there, a literal map to salvation and the entrance to the Fifth World."

"Then we're pretty well screwed without it, don't you think?"

Billy had meant for the words to sound more flippant than they'd come out. His great-grandfather only smiled and rested his hand on Billy's shoulder.

"The missing piece will be returned when it is needed, and not a moment sooner. Before Maasaw vanished into the desert, he told our ancestors that a day would arrive when our people would be overcome by strangers from another land. They would be forced to develop their land and live according to the dictates of a new ruler, one who would treat them like animals and punish them, often for seemingly no reason at all. Maasaw instructed them not to resist, but rather to bide their time and wait for the arrival of the man who would lead them into the Fifth World. He called this man Pahana, the Lost White Brother, and said he would come from the east, bearing the missing corner of the tablet."

"Lost White Brother?"

Sakeva's smile was sad, and when he spoke, it was in a voice that betrayed his years.

"Pahana will deliver us from the evil of this world and help us forge a new brotherhood of man. However, Maasaw warned us that if any member of our tribal council accepted another religion, our final leader must consent to having his head cut off. For only this act will dispel the evil and save our people."

THE MISSISSIPPI RIVER rumbled below the truck, its brown surface flowing deceptively fast. Sakeva remembered the first time he saw it, mere days ago along the Louisiana-Mississippi border. He'd never seen a body of water so imposing, one that marked the beginning of a journey that was now rapidly coming to an end, and not because they'd run out of country, but rather because they'd run out of time, a realization exacerbated by the glow of flames rising from St. Louis, the thunder of helicopters in the sky, and the sirens screaming from everywhere around them at once. He felt it as a sensation that resonated deep in his bones, an overwhelming feeling that caused his breath to catch in his chest and his heart to race when he least expected it. Times like now, when the black shapes of ravens wheeled above the trees on either side of the road, shrieking so loudly that he had to fight the urge to clap his hands over his ears.

Their adversary was growing stronger by the minute. He appeared to be flexing his muscles, as though awakening from a deep slumber, his tendrils of influence spreading across a dying land like ambitious roots laying claim to an unburied corpse, dragging it down into the darkness.

"It is not yet your time," he said in the old tongue.

Billy glanced over from behind the wheel. He obviously felt it, too. The potential in the air, like a gas leak seeping from the ground, just waiting for someone to strike a match.

A caravan of state patrol cruisers streaked past in the opposite lane, going so fast they outraced their flashing lights and sirens. A news van followed, its driver desperately trying to keep up.

The old truck juddered across an overpass, beneath which a pair of fire trucks raced southward on a four-lane highway.

Groves of trees gave way to strip malls and car dealerships, diners and gas stations. Residents had gathered outside of their apartment buildings and stared toward the source of the smoke. Sakeva wanted to shout for them to get in their cars and flee while they still had a chance, but he knew it wouldn't matter. Those who would survive the purification had already been chosen, marked for the trials that lay ahead. He drew a small measure of comfort from the knowledge that the suffering of the rest would be brief.

A shadow darted from the side of the road, hurdled the guardrail, and streaked right at the truck. The headlights illuminated a man—

Thunk!

Blood spattered the windshield, which cracked a split-second later when the man struck it. His body tumbled over the roof of the truck, bounced from the tailgate, and cartwheeled into the red glare of the taillights. Billy stomped the brake and skidded onto the shoulder.

"What was that?" he asked.

The engine ticked as it idled, the unknown man's blood sizzling on the hot hood.

"Wait here," Sakeva said.

He climbed out into the night and walked slowly away from the vehicle, his boots scuffing the asphalt. A crimson smear led to the man crumpled at the edge of the lane. He wore only a pair of boxers, the knobs of his spine protruding from his bare back. The soles of his feet were thick with mud and spiked with broken glass. One hand clawed uselessly at the ground.

"Is he dead?" Billy asked.

Sakeva turned at the sound of his great-grandson's voice. Billy looked so small and scared, reminding Sakeva just how young he truly was.

"Get back in the truck," he said.

"We should call an ambulance—"

"Back in the truck," Sakeva said in a tone that brooked no argument.

A semi rumbled past without even slowing, scattering the trash in the weeds lining the road.

Sakeva waited until he heard Billy's footsteps heading in the opposite direction before walking closer to get a better look at the body. The man wore a mask of blood, the features underneath which were contorted. One blood-filled eye stared up at Sakeva from its fractured socket. A fragment of bone stood from the man's cheek. He opened a mouth filled with broken teeth, issued the wet sound of fluid burbling in his lungs, and snapped at the air.

The earth tilted beneath Sakeva's feet with the recognition of what lay ahead. He remembered the stories his grandfather had told him during those long nights staring out upon the desert in the glow of the fire, waiting and waiting for something they knew would one day come, and felt fear unlike any he'd experienced before.

"The red symbol," he said out loud.

Sakeva felt Billy's eyes upon him in the rearview mirror as he stood over the dying man. Eventually, the man stopped snapping his teeth and his lone functional eye took on a faraway cast. Ravens wheeled silently overhead, black shapes against an even blacker sky. Sakeva stared up at them for several moments before walking back to the truck. He was acutely aware of his age, the brittleness of his bones, the fragility of his very life force, and not for the first time, wondered if he had the strength to do what needed to be done.

"So we're just going to leave him there?" Billy said.

Sakeva climbed up into the seat and looked straight ahead through the spiderwebbed windshield. The dead man's blood traced the network of cracks and pooled against the wiper.

"There is nothing we can do for him."

"But what about his family?"

"If they were with him when he turned, they are already dead," Sakeva said in a voice held together by dust. "Drive."

Billy shifted the truck into gear and accelerated away from the corpse. He was so enrapt by the reflection in the rearview mirror that he nearly side-swiped a speeding minivan.

Sakeva understood the young man's frustration and felt immensely proud of him for it. Leaving a man for the carrion birds flew in the face of everything they believed, but the last thing they wanted to do was touch his remains and they couldn't spare the time to give him a proper burial. Besides, he needed time to think, to figure out what they were supposed to do next.

Time flowed past, as unstoppable as the mighty river behind them, counting down the seconds until the end of the world.

———

HARVESTED FIELDS BLEW past in the darkness, the exposed nutrients in the soil glimmering in the moonlight. Telephone poles paralleled the highway, their bases overgrown with shrubs, their wires burdened by ravens. Billy drove as though in a fog, his thoughts sluggish, his mind wandering between the empty road in front of him and the realization that he'd killed a man. Granted, it hadn't been his fault and surely the police would have understood, but they hadn't even called them. Maybe if they'd done so quickly enough, the man might have survived. He remembered the way the guy had clawed at the pavement, as though trying to drag himself from the road, and closed his eyes to keep the tears from—

An SUV passed him, blaring its horn.

He'd been so distracted that he hadn't even seen its lights bearing down on him in the rearview mirror. He should probably turn over the wheel to his great-grandfather, although the old man didn't appear to be in a much better frame of mind to handle it. Sakeva hadn't spoken a word in hours. His eyes appeared unfocused as he stared at the world rushing to meet them. He occasionally muttered something under his breath in the old language that no one spoke anymore, not even his grandmother, who'd always seemed to be the last of a dying breed, a woman at odds with her surroundings, both the ancient and the modern.

Grasslands stretched to the horizon in all directions, marred only by sporadic clusters of trees, more desolate even than the red sands of home, where at least the occasional striated butte rose from the vast tangles of creosote and sage.

"Not all of the clans were traveling in the same direction when they finished their migrations," Sakeva said. His voice sounded far away, as though spoken from another place and time. "Our ancestors — the Fire Clan — arrived at Third Mesa from Betatakin to the north. The Snake Clan traveled to First Mesa from Hovenweep to the northeast. The Sand Clan came from Homolovi to the south. The Bear Clan left Mesa Verde and the Four Corners region to settle on Second Mesa, bringing with it the three stone tablets handed down by Soqomhonah, its patron deity. Combined, these tablets tell a story much like ours, only with an additional period of darkness, represented on the first tablet by two roads — one black and one red — which merge to form a serpent. A great spirit emerges from its fanged mouth to comfort a bear, above whom hangs a cloud of destruction and rebirth. The second tablet shows a map of Second Mesa and the lands bestowed upon the people by Soqomhonah. The third tells of the coming of Pahana, the Lost White Brother, who will lead us past the serpent and into the Fifth World."

Billy wanted to ask about the additional period of darkness, but he figured that was what his great-grandfather was building up to and allowed him to tell the story in his own way.

"My grandfather believed there was a correlation between the red road of the Bear Clan's tablet and the red symbol of the Fire Clan's, a relationship between the dark days before the arrival of the Bear Clan at Second Mesa and the war that would bring about the end of the Fourth World. Since our family was tasked with preparing for it, we needed to learn everything we could about those dark days, but none of those who migrated from Mesa Verde would speak of them. It was the Diné, he said, who provided the link he sought. They told stories of the Anasazi, the name given to the people who lived in the Four Corners region. It means 'ancient enemy' or 'enemy ancestor,' a collective term for a people at war with everyone around them, a people including the Bear Clan, none of whom were anything resembling warlike, and yet the canyons they'd left behind were filled with proof to the contrary."

"What kind of proof?"

"Fortified cities built high up on the cliffs of mazelike arroyos, where they could be more easily defended. Pueblos capable of housing thousands of people, while only a small fraction of that number reached Second Mesa. They offered no explanation for what had happened to the remainder, although it was rumored that a war had been fought within those canyons, one waged by enemy combatants whose remains had been left for the carrion birds that had made the fortresses their home."

A pair of military helicopters streaked across the sky, their black forms cutting through the night, barely clearing a billboard that would have been perfect for the old man's message, but Billy didn't want to stop and get out of the car. Right now, he just wanted to go home.

"I remember my grandfather telling me a story as a child," Sakeva continued. "One passed down to him by his grandfather, and his before that. A man from the Bear Clan had grown delirious on his deathbed and spoken of the discovery of the tomb of Soqomhonah, the violation of which had caused the spirit of the bear to enter his people, who hunted down and slaughtered the rest. He claimed to have heard the screams of the dying from where he hid with his mother for three full days, suffering through hunger and thirst, all the while knowing that death would soon come for them too. Only when the moon was full did they venture out and discover the red road, paved with the bodies of the dead, whose very skin had turned to blood. They were the ravings of a madman, or so most had assumed, although my grandfather thought better of it. And now, so do I."

Billy was quiet for a long moment.

"What are you trying to say?" he asked.

"I saw the same thing tonight," Sakeva said, his voice barely audible over the hum of their tires. "The man we hit. He ran straight at the truck, as though trying to attack it. I saw it on his face, in his red eyes, right as it happened. And then afterward, while he was lying on the pavement, I recognized the spirit of the bear as he clawed with his nails and snapped with his teeth. I saw the blood on the road and the death in his eyes and I recognized the connection my grandfather had tried to make. The third and final great war will be fought with the very same ancient enemy that nearly wiped out the Bear Clan generations ago."

28

Snoqualmie, Washington

Banks had barely fallen asleep when she was awakened by the first text from the airline letting her know that her flight had been delayed by two hours. The second, informing her of another delay, had come in mere minutes later. By the time she'd received the notice that all flights out of SeaTac had been canceled, she'd already gotten dressed and turned on the TV, which displayed images so unreal they might as well have been filmed on a Hollywood backlot. National Guardsmen barricading highways, men in camouflage gear wielding semiautomatic rifles on the streets, command centers being set up in parking lots full of military vehicles. Stunned anchors talked over chaotic footage of packed ERs, overflow tents set up on hospital lawns, and even a hurriedly erected field triage unit under the lights of Lumen Field. Aerial imagery showed emergency vehicles racing through the darkened streets, intersections where cars with broken windshields had been abandoned, and downtown storefronts from which panicked patrons flooded into the streets.

She dropped her phone when the emergency broadcast tone erupted from her hands. Picking it up, she read the alert but couldn't seem to wrap her head around the words. Shelter in place. Stay off the roads. Find an interior room and seal all exterior windows and doors. Wear masks if you have them.

The alert wouldn't have been sent out this late at night if the situation weren't dire. The authorities would have waited until morning in hopes of preventing a citywide panic, unless they feared the situation would spiral out of control before then.

She switched to the cable news and saw similar scenes unfolding all around the country. Military vehicles on Hollywood Boulevard and Pennsylvania Avenue. Police barricades on Fisherman's Wharf and the Freedom Trail. Medical centers in the parking lots surrounding Mile High Stadium and Ford Field, not far from her house back home. Staging grounds in the parking lots at Disneyland and the Magic Kingdom. Traffic jams on anonymous highways everywhere, the red of taillights stretching into the dark night. The crawl at the bottom of the screen displayed the emergency hotline numbers for every state, in alphabetical order, and listed symptoms requiring urgent medical intervention.

Something big was going down, but unlike the previous scares, there'd been no warning, no reports of strange illnesses from overseas or vague and misleading press releases from the World Health Organization. They were dealing with something they'd never encountered before, something authorities had no idea how to combat. This response was the governmental equivalent of so many chickens running around with their heads cut off, trying to get out ahead of something that was already beyond their ability to contain.

Banks speed-dialed Duvall's number on the off chance he might know something, but her call rang through to voicemail. While she was leaving a message, she received a text from the special agent in charge of the Detroit Division, promising a status update within the hour. She switched back to the local broadcast and recoiled at the panic in the newscaster's voice.

" . . . *live footage flooding in from all around the city. I can't believe what I'm seeing . . .* "

A grainy cellphone video filled the screen. She recognized the red neon sign of the Pike Place Market in the background. Twenty-somethings dressed for a night on the town screamed and ran down the cobblestone street. Silhouettes emerged from the shadows behind them. A woman in a red dress broke a heel and went down. One of the silhouettes dove on top of her, forced her head to the ground, and buried its teeth in her neck.

"Jesus," Banks gasped.

The station cut to a video captured from the balcony of a downtown apartment. Cars on the street below swerved around a man wandering through traffic. An SUV slewed sideways to avoid hitting him, only to be rammed by the car behind it. The man climbed up onto the hood, smashed through the windshield, and dragged the driver out through the broken glass.

Again, the station cut away to aerial footage of a traffic jam on a bridge surrounded by water. All four lanes were closed, two coming out of each of the twin tunnels. The westbound lanes were bereft of cars, which were presumably being prevented from entering the city on the far side. People backed into each other and scraped the sides of their vehicles against the retaining walls in a desperate attempt to get out of the traffic jam. Many fled their cars on foot and ran toward the barricade, where muzzle flare flashed from the rifles of the soldiers manning it. At first Banks thought they were firing on the crowds, until the camera panned and she saw several people breaking windshields, hauling passengers out onto the ground, and tearing them apart with their bare hands.

A sensation of numbness settled over her. She thought of her mother back in Detroit, alone in her old house, and her coworkers, strapping on their side arms and donning their jackets in anticipation of receiving the orders they knew would come within a matter of minutes. With flights grounded and the highways closed to prevent the spread of whatever contagion was affecting the city, there was no way she was getting out of here anytime—

"The kids," she said.

The thought hit her with the force of a physical blow. She got dressed as quickly as she could, grabbed her keys from the nightstand, and sprinted for her car.

AMANDA CARTER ROLLED over and fell to the floor. She recognized her office but couldn't seem to remember why she was here. And when had it gotten dark?

Slowly, the memories came back to her. The headache she'd been battling for most of the day had gotten worse near the end of her shift and she'd decided to lie down, although she hadn't intended to sleep for more than an hour or two. Considering she was the kind of person who'd work through just about any physical malady, her staff must have recognized that she truly needed the rest and left her alone.

What time was it, anyway? It was too dark to see the hands on the wall clock, not that she would have been able to do so from this vantage point anyway.

She wrapped her arms around her chest. Her clothes were damp, her face dripping with sweat. If anything, the nap had only exacerbated her headache. She heard voices from outside her door and tried to sit up, but a wave of nausea rippled up from her gut, forcing her to close her eyes once more.

Something was wrong with her.

With that realization, the residual fog of sleep cleared, and she experienced fear unlike any she'd felt before. She'd stood toe to toe with abusers whose knuckles still bled from beating their children and faced down violent offenders who "weren't about to let their goddamn children be taken from them," and yet never once had she felt like she did now.

Amanda flinched when the shrill tone of the emergency broadcast system blared from her phone. Its screen glowed faintly from the corner of her desk where she'd left it, well outside of her reach. The sound echoed from the hallway, where she envisioned the night crew reading whatever message had just come through.

Blood trickled down the back of her throat. She gagged and rolled onto her stomach to allow it to drain past her lips.

She was in serious trouble.

"Help," she called.

The word emerged as a muffled grunt. She tried again, to no avail. She'd burned through the last of her energy and couldn't even push herself up from the floor.

Amanda felt pressure behind her eyes and warmth on her cheeks. She watched the pool of blood spreading on the tile, mere millimeters from her face, until the darkness swallowed her and she saw no more.

CIARA AWAKENED to a howling sound and sat up in bed, her heart hammering in her chest. For a moment, she was in her bedroom at home, waiting for the thunder of the shotgun blast and for her mother to rush into her room. Her breathing grew faster and faster until she rationalized her surroundings, and her heart once more sank into the pit of her stomach. She was still at the group home, which was only marginally better—

Another howl.

She rose from her bed and drew open the curtains. A canine silhouette crouched among the shadows beneath the trees. With a flash of eyeshine, it darted off through the underbrush. She was still looking for any sign of where the coyote might have gone when the screaming started.

Ciara stared at the sliver of light passing underneath her closed door. The last thing in the world she wanted to do was go out there, but—

The screams grew louder and louder . . . until they abruptly ceased.

She crept across the room and gripped the knob. Listened. She couldn't hear a thing over the rushing of her pulse. Hands trembling, she opened the door a crack and risked a peek.

The hallway was empty.

She cautiously crept into the corridor and headed for the station where the night counselors worked. Several other doors opened, and nervous faces looked out. A little girl with dark hair and a stuffed dog clutched to her chest stepped out in front of her. Ciara pulled the girl behind her as she advanced.

Another scream.

Louder this time. Closer.

She glanced over her shoulder. The other kids hung back, waiting for her to take charge.

The corridor ended at a T-juncture. To the right was the counselors' office; to the left, the hallway lined with classrooms and therapy suites leading to the community room. She padded across the tiled floor, conscious of the sounds of her heavy breathing. Every instinct screamed for her to go back to her room and hide, but she'd be trapped in there with a door that didn't lock and a window that wouldn't open. The only way out behind her was a stairwell that led to an emergency exit, which was locked, twenty-four hours a day, for their protection.

The only way out lay in the direction of the screams.

Something dark and shiny caught her eye from the floor ahead and to her right. It expanded as she neared, until she recognized it as a pool of blood reflecting the overhead lights. Miss Stephanie was sprawled on her chest beside it, her sightless eyes staring at Ciara's legs, her mouth framing the scream that had died on her lips. The scratches on her cheek were deep, but not nearly as deep as the wound on her neck, from which blood still flowed.

Ciara struggled to suppress the rising panic and regulate her breathing. Her mother's words returned, as though whispered into her ear.

Run as far away as you can and hide where no one will ever find you.

First, however, they needed to get out of a locked ward that had been designed to keep them in.

She forced herself to enter the counselors' office. There were two desks, one on either side, and a padlocked cabinet containing medications and supplies against the back wall. She lifted the phone from the cradle and dialed 9-1-1. A computerized voice answered and informed her that due to the high volume of calls they were currently receiving, she was going to have to hold on the line for the first available—

A scream and a thud from somewhere deeper in the building.

The girl with the stuffed dog whimpered. Ciara pressed her index finger to her lips and set down the handset, knowing that when the emergency operator picked up and found the line open, an officer would be dispatched to their location. She could only hope that happened before—

Shouting. A male voice she didn't recognize. She couldn't make out his words, but there was no mistaking his fear.

The crack of gunfire. Again and again.

A scream cut short, its echo reverberating throughout the facility and dissolving into silence.

They needed to keep moving.

Ciara took the girl by the hand and led her down the hallway, following trails of bloody footprints past the doorways to either side, glancing through the inset windows of the offices and classrooms as she passed. She stopped at the threshold of the community room and looked back at the others. There had to be five or six of them now, their eyes wide and staring at her. A small boy started to cry, but Wes placed a hand over his mouth to quiet him. Ciara took a deep, shuddering breath and stepped out into the open, taking in everything around her as fast as she could. There was no one in the corner with the seascape, nor anyone at the tables near the racks of snack foods. The door beyond them was closed and locked, the inset window revealing only a darkened hallway. One of the tables in the middle of the room had been knocked over, the puzzle once on top of it now scattered—

Ciara clapped her hand over her mouth to stifle a gasp. Miss Ruth lay on her back at the base of the couch, her entire face and upper chest covered with blood, a puddle of which pooled beneath her. Footprints led away from her, toward the main entrance, which was exactly where they needed to go. She thought of the gunshots and realized what had happened to the security guard on duty. Would they even be able to get out of the facility if they made it that far?

Footsteps from the corridor ahead.

They were too exposed in here.

Ciara sprinted back toward the residential wing, dragging the little girl behind her and waving for the others to follow. She grabbed the first door-knob she reached. Turned it back and forth. Locked. Dashed across the hall and tried the cafeteria. Again, locked.

Footsteps from behind them, coming fast. The clattering sound of someone bumping a chair in the rec room.

The classroom door wouldn't budge, but the knob to Miss Amanda's office turned easily in her hand. She ushered the others past her and ducked inside. Drew the door closed with a soft *click*. Released the knob and stepped away from the inset window.

Ciara heard footsteps in the hallway. Right outside the door. A shadow eclipsed the elongated rectangle of light on the floor. She saw the fear in the eyes of the other kids, pressed against the walls on either side of the door. Prayed they had the sense to — *Don't make a sound, do you hear me? No matter what you see, don't make a sound* — keep quiet.

A voice from down the hallway. A child's voice.

Ciara felt a sinking sensation.

The light once more spread across the floor and the footsteps resumed outside the door, heading quickly toward the origin of the voice. Ciara threw open the door and shoved the little girl toward the community room. Grabbed Wes by the shirt and pointed in that direction, gestured for him to get the others out of there. She hoped to God he got the message as she turned and ran into the residential wing to help whoever was still back there.

A shrill scream, filled with so much pain it nearly stopped her in her tracks.

She rounded the corner and slipped in Miss Stephanie's blood. The cry suddenly ceased. She pushed herself back up to her feet and saw a hunched form with a flannel shirt and a frayed braid crouching over a pair of bare legs. Its shoulders heaved and it flung an arc of blood across the wall. It glanced over its shoulder.

Miss Amanda's eyes locked onto hers.

Ciara turned and ran, her bare feet slick with blood. She bounced from one wall to the other in a desperate attempt to get away, smearing crimson handprints all over the cartoon characters.

THE EXPEDITION SKIDDED to the curb in front of the Snoqualmie Center for Children. Banks jumped out without bothering to close the door, ran to the main entrance, and pressed the button. The buzzer echoed from inside, but the security guard didn't respond. She could see his station through the glass, the glow of the monitors in the console flickering on the wall behind it. An arterial spatter drained down the surface and pooled on the floor, where an arm protruded from behind the desk. A jerk on the handle confirmed the door was locked. She stepped back, raised her weapon, and fired. Glass rained down on her as she shouldered through the pane and headed for the interior door, only vaguely aware of the screaming from inside. Without slowing, she shot the glass security door and sprinted through the shards cascading over her head.

A group of children rounded the corner, coming straight at her.

"My car's out front!" she shouted. "Get inside and lock the doors!"

Banks didn't see Ciara among them, which meant the girl still had to be somewhere inside. She ran into the community room. Caught a glimpse of the dead counselor from the corner of her eye as she rounded the toppled table and headed for the residential wing.

Ciara slammed into the wall and burst from the hallway in front of her.

"Down!" Banks yelled, aiming past Ciara and at the woman chasing her.

She recognized Amanda Carter, her face and clothes drenched with blood, at the last possible second and fired a shot into the ceiling above the counselor's head, stopping her dead in her tracks.

CIARA SLID past the special agent's legs and turned around. Miss Amanda stood in the mouth of the hallway, the walls marred with bloody handprints, sparks raining from the ruined light fixture. Ciara's heart stopped when she realized that the scene was exactly how she'd drawn it.

The world took on a surreal quality. The golden sparks seemed to hover in midair as a snarl formed on Miss Amanda's face. Banks shouted as though from miles away, her words forming so slowly as to be unintelligible. Miss Amanda's legs tensed, her arms extended, and she lunged—

The bullet punched through her shoulder, spinning her sideways and sending her toppling to the floor. She landed on the opposite shoulder, the report thundering through the corridor. Slowly, she pushed herself up and staggered toward Banks. Her arm hung uselessly at her side and yet still she advanced, gaining speed with every step until she was nearly upon them.

"Stop right there!" Banks shouted. "Don't make me do this!"

Miss Amanda didn't slow down.

The slug punched through her chest and lifted her from her feet, her legs running out from underneath her. She landed on her back and didn't even try to get up.

———

"THE OTHER KIDS should already be in my car," Banks said. "Make sure they're all right. Don't open the door for anyone but me."

She listened to the padding of bare feet retreating behind her as she advanced into the hallway, her pistol pointed down at the body of a woman with whom she'd spent considerable time only the day before. Never in a million years would she have thought that she'd be forced to kill her mere hours later.

The counselor's eyes were flooded with blood, her lips split over broken teeth. There was flesh underneath her fingernails, one of which had torn off. The heat radiating from her was palpable.

Banks covered her mouth and nose as she skirted the body, although she knew she'd undoubtedly already been exposed to the virus, which appeared to be the same thing causing the bloodshed downtown. She passed another dead counselor and continued toward the bedrooms, where most of the doors stood open.

"You're safe," she said. "You can come out now."

The only response was the sound of her sticky soles peeling from the floor. She opened the first door and found a teenage boy lying in bed, his face dripping with sweat, his covers soaked. The smell radiating from him was one of sickness. She was just about to go in after him when she heard a noise from farther down the hall.

Banks led with her pistol, clearing each of the empty bedrooms as quickly as she could. The sound grew louder and more clearly defined. A wet, sucking noise, like someone walking through deep mud. She nudged open the door beside her and saw a young girl lying prone on the floor beside her bed, blood leaking from somewhere underneath her face. Her back rose and fell ever so subtly with each labored breath.

The source of the sound was in the adjacent room, where a boy of about nine or ten sat astride a girl maybe a few years older than he was, her hair splayed on a pillow saturated with blood, spatters of which decorated the wall above her. The little boy glanced back at Banks, the dim light reflecting from his crimson eyes. He jumped from the bed and ran straight at her. She stumbled backward and sighted him down the barrel of her pistol but couldn't bring herself to pull the trigger. From the corner of her eye, she saw the girl in the next room struggling to her feet. Another child emerged from the door at the end of the hallway.

There was nothing Banks could do for them. She ran for the entrance, the sound of footsteps growing louder behind her. The older boy crawled from his room in front of her. She hurdled him and kept going, while the little girl set upon him with her bare hands and teeth. The hallway and community room were a blur. Banks slid on the glass littering the lobby, regained her balance, and jumped through the jagged frame.

"Open the door!"

Ciara's face was framed in the driver-side window. The young girl's eyes darted toward the hallway behind Banks as she disengaged the locks with a *thunk*.

Banks opened the door and climbed up into the seat. Closed it right as the infected children slammed into it, their bloody hands smearing the glass. She hit the gas and sped away from the youth center, watching in the rearview mirror as the children chasing the vehicle faded into the darkness and the rain.

29

New York City, New York

Milana paced back and forth in front of the window with her phone to her ear, waiting for the paramedics and police to arrive. She'd already called 9-1-1 twice and had been in an endless queue for the past half an hour, listening to the wail of sirens in the distance and the same recorded message about the volume of calls and the first available operator being with her soon. She didn't know what else to do, though. Her mother was dead in the house next door, the guy who'd chased her was still out there somewhere, and the Lovatos had been unable to wait up any longer and gone back to bed. While they tried to downplay their condition for her benefit, it was obvious that they were sick. She promised herself she'd check on them, just as soon as the infernal police—

Headlights shot down the street. She heard the squeal of tires, the rumble of an engine, and a silver Honda Civic appeared, going way too fast. A dark form sprinted out into the road in front of it. The driver swerved, narrowly avoided a parked car, and lost control. The Civic hopped the curb, tore through the decorative wrought-iron fence, and hit the stoop of the townhouse across the street, showering the surrounding pavement with shattered glass. The driver struggled against the airbag, but the man he'd nearly hit was already upon him, dragging him out through the broken windshield. Several other figures materialized from the other end of the street and swarmed over the car, pulling a woman from the passenger seat. Her cries echoed into the night, for as long as they lasted.

Milana watched helplessly from across the street. There was nothing she could have done to stop it, was there? Had she run out there to help them, she'd undoubtedly be dead now too. She thought of her mother and the lack of recognition in her eyes as she'd attacked her own daughter.

She heard a moan from somewhere above her and glanced up the dark staircase, toward where Mrs. Lovato and her husband slept.

A helicopter passed over the rooftops, so low that the beating of the rotors was a physical sensation in Milana's chest. A spotlight swept across the street, casting flickering shadows from the violently shaking branches of the trees. The gusts from the rotors buffeted the assailants, who shielded their eyes and looked up into the light. A crackle of gunfire and they dispersed, leaving the lifeless bodies behind on the sidewalk. The beam swung wildly across the fronts of the townhomes, dispelling the shadows. And then the chopper was gone.

Milana stared at the carnage, her shoulders heaving as she tried to catch her breath. What in God's name was happening?

She pulled the curtains closed and hurried upstairs, where she heard more moaning. The master bedroom was behind the first door on her left. She smelled the sickness when she entered, saw the mounds of covers underneath which Mr. Lovato was buried. His wife had cast hers aside and lay on the sheets in a nightgown soaked with sweat. Her face was so pale in what little moonlight passed through the open window that she already looked dead.

Another moan, fainter this time. Mrs. Lovato scrunched up her face and started to cry.

Milana rushed to her side and took the older woman's hand. The skin was so hot it felt like she was holding a cup of coffee.

"I don't . . . " Mrs. Lovato whispered. "It's too soon . . . "

Her heavy lids peeled open, and her eyes met Milana's.

"You're going to be all right," Milana said. "An ambulance should be here any minute."

She knew better, though. The sirens were still far away, presumably near where she'd heard the helicopters restlessly circling.

Mr. Lovato groaned and rolled over. His wife sought his hand and held it. She looked desperately at Milana.

"Take care of him . . . " Tears streamed down her cheeks. "Please . . . "

The tiny veins in her eyes burst and flooded the whites with blood, just like Rosella's had.

Milana looked away and saw the street below. The silver Civic. The bodies sprawled on the broken glass. She dropped Mrs. Lovato's hand and backed away.

Her vision.

She'd seen that exact same moment when the older woman had kissed her on the forehead the night her grandmother had died.

Milana was halfway out the door when Mrs. Lovato blinked, bared her teeth, and rolled over onto her husband, who barely flinched when she cast aside his blankets and bit down on his neck. A rush of crimson flooded onto his pillow.

Milana clapped her hands over her mouth to keep from screaming and ran down the stairs. She heard a thump overhead, followed by footsteps in the hallway. A glance over her shoulder revealed a pair of bare legs at the top of the staircase, coming down in a hurry.

She unlocked the front door with trembling hands and rushed out into the night. No sign of anyone on the street in either direction. She jumped from the porch and hit the ground running, the sound of Mrs. Lovato's footsteps fading behind her.

If the police wouldn't come to her, Milana thought, then she'd just have to go to them.

She ran west toward Central Park, sprinting across intersections without even looking, focused solely on the distant sound of sirens, which grew louder by the second. A yellow cab, its entire passenger side spattered with blood, ran the red light on Park Avenue and nearly hit her. By the time she reached Madison, she could see the lights of the emergency vehicles on Fifth and the helicopters circling the park, their spotlights shining down through the treetops surrounding the Great Lawn.

The second-story window of the building beside her shattered. A man landed on the sidewalk among the shards, staggered to his feet, and took off after Milana, who pushed herself even harder. She saw emergency lights from the corner of her eye, ran right out into the intersection, and stepped into the path of a police cruiser, waving her arms over her head. The officer locked up his brakes and skidded straight at her.

Milana stepped out of the way as the man chasing her reached—

The cruiser struck him and sent him bouncing up over its hood.

"Let me in!" she screamed, tugging at the handle of the passenger door. She recognized the panic on the officer's face, sensed his indecision. "Hurry!"

He hit the automatic lock and Milana climbed in beside him. The man on the hood was already recovering. He slammed his fist down on the windshield. The glass cracked from the bloody impact. He raised his fist again—

"Go!" Milana screamed.

The officer pinned the gas. The man rolled up over the roof, hit the light bar, and tumbled onto the road behind them.

Milana buried her face in her hands and released all of her fear and frustration in a scream.

"WHAT THE HELL are you doing out here?" the officer asked. His nameplate identified him as Baker. He had brown eyes, a sharp nose, and perma-stubble underneath his full-face gasmask. "You're supposed to be locked in your home, where it's safe."

Voices erupted from the radio on the dashboard, countless men and women talking over one another. Dispatchers yelled to be heard over shouts and gunfire. No one seemed to know what was going on, let alone what they were supposed to do about it. Choppers whupped across the sky, their spot-lights crossing the streets and sweeping the sidewalks, chasing silhouettes ahead of them and into the shadows.

"My mom . . . " Milana said. She steeled herself and started again. "My mom got sick and tried . . . to hurt me. But she died, so I went to my neighbor's house. The same thing happened to them."

"The whole city's gone crazy. It's this goddamn virus—" He jerked the wheel to avoid a woman who ran barefoot into the road, her face painted with blood. "Jesus Christ!"

Smoke rose from Rockefeller Center, diffusing the lights from the circling helicopters. Gunfire echoed from seemingly everywhere at once. Orange-and-white-striped sawhorses barred access to the streets entering the diamond district, which glowed with police lights.

"How did this happen?" Milana asked.

"We're trying to piece it together as we go," Baker said. "If anyone knows anything, they're sure as hell not sharing it with us."

Army vehicles blocked off Midtown. Soldiers in isolation gear moved through the haze, their semiautomatic rifles flickering in the distance.

"Where are we going?" she asked.

"All units have been ordered to fall back," he said. A scream blared from the radio, so loud that it degenerated into feedback. "We're setting up block-ades across Manhattan on MLK to the north and Twenty-third to the south. The goal is to hold the line long enough to set up quarantine centers at City College and Federal Plaza."

Milana recalled her vision of the fallen barricade, flames rising from the Federal Building, and flashes of discharge through the smoke. The ground seemed to tilt underneath her as though she were traveling through a carnival tunnel. She closed her eyes and concentrated on steadying herself.

"What about everyone between Twenty-third and MLK?" she asked, opening her eyes.

"They're the army's responsibility now. Times Square's a freaking war zone, Hell's Kitchen is literally on fire, and Central Park's crawling with infected people. Hopefully, everyone else is doing a better job of following instructions and staying in their homes than you."

The Flatiron Building rose ahead of them, its narrow face awash with alternating red and blue lights. The street in front of it was blocked by police cruisers, lined bumper-to-bumper. Officers wearing full riot gear and gas masks leaned over the hoods and roofs, their weapons aimed at Madison Square Park.

Baker slowed as they neared. An officer directed him to turn onto Twenty-third and park right in the middle of Broadway. Milana heard gunfire behind her as she got out of the cruiser and looked back in time to see a man fall in the street. Several people ran past him and charged the barricade. Shots rang out from behind the wall of vehicles, and they all went down.

She hurried to catch up with Baker, who was already halfway across the plaza. Flatbed trucks burdened by mountains of sandbags were parked where planters and tables had once been. Workers in hardhats and gas masks unloaded them as quickly as they could and started bolstering the blockade.

Baker vanished into a crowd of officers for several minutes before jogging back to her.

"We're running buses back and forth from the Federal Building," he said. "There's one loading on the other side of the Flatiron now. You'll be safe there. I promise."

Milana read the belief and determination on his face and prayed he was right, but the vision . . .

Was there more to it than that? Was it a premonition? She thought of her mother's death and the sounds of shattering glass and shrieking ravens, of Mrs. Lovato's eyes filling with blood and the car crashing on the street below. Just as she'd seen them in her mind. Was the vision of the Federal Building in flames a warning?

She hugged the officer before he could protest and hurried through the bedlam toward Fifth, where a city bus waited. The driver wore combat fatigues and looked more than a little nervous. Milana stared up at him through the open accordion doors but couldn't seem to make herself take the first step.

"In or out, kid," he said. "We've got to get moving."

She heard screams and gunfire and glanced over her shoulder toward where a group of officers dragged a sobbing woman over the hood of a cruiser and fired at the shadows pursuing her.

"Last chance," the driver said.

Milana stepped up onto the bus and grabbed the poles for balance as the vehicle lurched forward. Shell-shocked faces stared through her as she worked her way down the aisle and took a seat near the back.

The driver's wide eyes shifted restlessly from one side of the street to the other. Someone near the front of the bus started to cry. A man in a suit jacket complained to anyone who would listen about his cellphone not having a signal. The teenager in the seat in front of her said she'd heard that the

Chinese had released a bioweapon designed to turn them all into zombies, while the man across the aisle argued that the virus was part of the globalist agenda to depopulate the world.

Milana could see the sickness in their faces, the fear and the denial and all of the warring emotions playing out upon them. An ambulance soared past, its flashing lights casting a red pall over the passengers — *whose mouths open into soundless screams. Chunks of burning debris rain down upon them from the roiling smoke. Their hair catches fire, and their skin begins to blister and burn —* before vanishing down Fourteenth toward Union Square Park.

"Let me off," she whispered.

Her heart was pounding and suddenly she couldn't seem to breathe. She looked around in a panic. Buildings blurred past on either side, blotting out the sky. There was no one on the sidewalks, no signs of life whatsoever. The bus slowed as it neared Ninth and prepared to turn—

Milana jumped up from her seat and hit the "STOP" button on the grab bar.

"Let me off!"

She nearly fell as she fought her way toward the door.

"Are you crazy?" the driver shouted.

Milana pressed up against the doors and banged on them until they opened. She tumbled out onto the asphalt and drew a lungful of fresh air. Tears of relief blurred her vision as she watched the bus round the corner, leaving her in a cloud of exhaust.

Milana stood and stared down Fifth Avenue, through the branches of the trees lining the sidewalks, toward the entrance to Washington Square Park. She walked toward it as though in a fugue, crossed the road against the light, and passed right underneath the arch. Smoke clung to the canopy, through which a cold wind blew, rattling the leaves and casting strange shadows onto the paving stones. Trash accumulated against the bodies surrounding the fountain.

It was just like her dream, only this time she couldn't wake up.

MILANA DIDN'T HAVE the slightest idea what she was supposed to do next. She'd freaked out and jumped off the bus in the middle of an area where she hardly knew a soul. Meanwhile, the rest of the passengers were likely already reaching the quarantine center at Federal Plaza, where they might or might not be safe, based upon a vision she'd experienced while looking through the window of a restaurant. The whole thing seemed ridiculous, with the notable exception that several of her other visions had already come to pass. And if this one was no different, then what kind of person did that make her, abandoning so many innocent people to their fates without even trying to convince them to come with her? If they died, were their deaths not at least partially her fault?

She heard gunfire from somewhere to the east, over toward Broadway. A single thought pushed its way to the forefront of her mind: she needed to get off the street. If she could just find a room on the upper floor of a nearby building, she could lock herself inside and ride out this nightmare, assuming, of course, that none of the other residents turned violent, like her mother and Mrs. Lovato had.

A silhouette raced through the deep shadows beneath the trees to the southeast. She headed in the opposite direction, toward Waverly Place. The Washington Square Hotel was diagonally across the intersection. She still had a couple hundred dollars available on her credit card. It was like the universe was guiding her to safety. And all because she'd read the signs, like her grandmother had told her.

Milana ran across the street, the black awning of the hotel with its big white letters calling to her. She grabbed the handle on the gold-framed door and pulled, but it didn't budge. Again and again she tried, but to no avail. She pressed her face against the inset glass and peered inside. The lobby was dark, although not to such an extent that she couldn't see a figure moving through the hallway beside the ornate staircase.

"Let me in!" she called, banging on the door. "Please! I can pay!"

She glanced nervously over her shoulder to make sure the noise hadn't attracted any unwanted attention. When she looked back, the figure was rushing toward her. She felt a swell of relief, which dissipated when she realized that whoever it was wasn't slowing. A woman took form from the darkness, her bared teeth a stark contrast to her bloody face. She ran face-first into the door, her nose breaking with a burst of scarlet that drained down the glass as she tried to scratch and claw her way through it.

Milana staggered backward, the terror rising inside her as a scream she barely choked back down.

The woman pounded on the door with both fists, over and over, until her flesh split and blood smeared the glass.

Milana turned and ran to the west, trying desperately to formulate a plan to reach safety. Maybe if she found a police station or a firehouse. Another hotel or a restaurant. Anyplace where she could lock herself away from everyone and pray she didn't get sick.

Her eyes filled with tears as she hit Sixth Avenue. To her left was a bank, across from which were a gift shop, a nail salon, and a church. On the other side of the intersection were a diner, a spa, and a dental office, and immediately to her right—

A sign hung from the upright post of the streetlight, a blue metal placard featuring a stylized P made from curved arrows pointing in opposite directions. She heard her grandmother's voice in her head.

You must heed the signs, child, for you are the only one who can read them. The path to salvation leads through darkness.

Milana stared at the sign, her heart pounding, her shoulders rising and falling as she tried not to hyperventilate. The P symbolized the PATH train, which ran underneath the Hudson River. A PATH through the darkness to salvation, or, in this case, New Jersey. It was her way off Manhattan, but surely it had been shut down like every other subway line.

She ran to Ninth Street Station and saw the rolling gate had been lowered, just as she'd expected, only someone had managed to bend the bottom bar, wedge a car jack underneath it, and raise the metal curtain just far enough to squeeze through. She looked from the narrow gap to the darkened entryway leading down to the platform. Was she really considering doing this? The tunnel was just over three miles long. An hour's walk. Maybe forty minutes at a jog, assuming she was even able to get in there in the first place. And then what? Climb onto the platform at the Hoboken Transit Terminal and magically find herself safe and sound?

Milana switched on her cellphone's flashlight. Her charge was at 63%, which dropped to 62% as she watched. If the light didn't drain the battery faster than one percent per minute—

More gunshots. Closer this time. The thunder of rotors grew louder by the second.

"Tell me this is what I'm supposed to do," she whispered.

Only silence answered.

Milana lowered herself to her chest and shone her beam underneath the bent gate but could barely see the top of the staircase around the corner. She listened for any sound to betray the presence of someone inside. Nothing. She slithered through the gap, jumped to her feet, and aimed her beam down into the darkness. No sign of movement. She descended one flight, rounded a bend, and then crept down another. A winding tunnel with tiled walls guided her to a long staircase, at the bottom of which was a row of turnstiles. She swung her legs over and made her way to a platform beneath an arched metal roof, the support pillars casting long shadows into the impregnable darkness. Her light revealed a sign labeled "DOWNTOWN TO HOBOKEN AND JOURNAL SQ." She stood beneath it and stared down at the tracks for several seconds, listening for any sounds from the tunnels.

"Just over three miles," she whispered. "You can do this."

She hopped down and started into a tunnel so narrow that if a train came through, there would be no hope of getting out of its way. The third rail ran along the wall, so she stayed between the tracks and started off at a jog. Her hands shook so badly that she could barely hold her phone, the beam from which swung ahead of her like the glow of a lantern, alternately highlighting one filthy concrete wall and then the other, the tracks appearing to tilt as though on an invisible fulcrum. She focused on detecting any sound that might have been masked by the clapping echoes of her footsteps, the intonation of which subtly changed as she neared Christopher Street Station, the last stop on this side of the river.

Milana slowed and listened, her pulse rushing in her ears. She heard a scuttling sound, followed by squeaking noises that she immediately recognized.

Rats.

She emerged from the tunnel and swept her light across a platform nearly identical to the one she'd left mere blocks ago. A hairy rodent scurried away from her light, casting a giant hunched shadow onto one of the pillars—

A scuffing sound from deeper in the tunnel.

Milana whirled and shone her beam at a man she could have sworn hadn't been there a second ago. He wore an old-fashioned suit and a fedora, which he removed from his head and lowered to his side. His elongated shadow made it appear as though he were holding the skull of a muskox by one of its curved horns. A smile filled with long, yellowed teeth materialized on his face. Even with the rats crawling all over him, gnawing at his exposed skin, she recognized him as the man whose palm she'd read on the night her *pūridaia* had died.

Her heavy breathing echoed from the empty station. She tried to steady herself so he wouldn't see how badly she was shaking.

"You never told me my future," he said.

She recalled images of teeth tearing flesh. Burning buildings turned to rubble. Ashes falling from the sky. A tall man with the horns of a bull.

The old man started to laugh.

He'd known all along.

"You're all going to die!" he shouted, his voice echoing from the tunnel.

The instinctive urge to get away from him overwhelmed her.

Milana screamed and ran straight at him. Shoved him squarely in the chest. Caught a flash of surprise on his face as he toppled backward into the shadows. Heard the cracking sounds of bones breaking when he hit the ground. And just kept on running.

"Come back here!" he shrieked in a voice quivering with rage and pain. "You can't get away from me! No matter where you go, I will find you! Only next time you won't recognize me until I'm bathing in your blood!"

His voice faded behind her as she sprinted away from the station, nearly outracing her light into the darkness, on the path to salvation.

30

San Luis Obispo, California

Crawford sat on top of the bluff, listening to the breakers crash against the rocks below him. The sunset had been one of the most magnificent he'd ever seen, but it paled in comparison to the rise of the full moon, its light shimmering on the waves rolling restlessly toward him. He wished he hadn't gone to the emergency room and exposed himself to whatever nasty disease everyone there had, especially since he hadn't really needed to be there in the first place. His right side had practically returned to normal again, but now he had the mother of all headaches and had to be running a fever, if the sweating was any indication. He didn't suppose any of that mattered now, though.

It was time.

He rose from the rocks, brushed off his khakis, and headed back toward the path. This end of the Pecho Coast Trail was little more than a narrow strip of dirt running along the lip of the aptly named Rattlesnake Canyon, although darkness had chased the feisty buggers back into their dens. He occasionally stumbled over his right foot on the uneven earth, but it otherwise supported his weight and performed like it was supposed to. Clenching his right hand at his side, over and over, only seemed to make it stronger. He was as ready as he was going to get.

He'd parked his truck among the trees near the trailhead. He started the engine and listened to it rumble for several minutes before putting it into gear and following the winding dirt road back to the highway. The Diablo Canyon

Power Plant was another five miles up the coastline. He savored every second of the drive.

The employee parking lots were surprisingly empty. Second shift was nearly halfway through its workday and yet it looked like the majority had already called it a night. He pulled right into his customary spot and just sat there, giving security plenty of time to identify his vehicle and report it to whomever was in charge, presumably Minter, which was undoubtedly the whole reason the former head honcho at San Onofre had been promoted in the first place.

Crawford remembered how his good buddy Ron hadn't been able to meet his stare. It was precisely that empathy he needed to exploit.

He climbed out, donned his jacket despite the lingering heat, and walked toward the main entrance. Once inside, he ducked into the restroom and cleaned himself up, starting with scrubbing the blood from his face, which angered the bits of glass he was forced to pluck from his skin, but the bleeding stopped quickly enough. By the time he was reasonably presentable — or at least as presentable as he was going to get — and left the restroom, Minter was waiting for him, the security guards paying extra-special attention from their posts.

"You shouldn't be here, Nick," Minter said.

Crawford nodded solemnly and tried to look contrite.

"I said a lot of things I shouldn't have, Ron. Things I've since come to regret. We've known each other for a lot of years. You were in my shoes when they decommissioned SONGS and knew better than anyone else what I was going through. I know you did your best to protect me, to help set things up so that I'd be able to go out on the closest possible thing to my own terms, and what did I do? I insulted you and threw your kindness right back in your face. And for that I owe you my sincerest apologies."

He thrust out his right hand, which held steady and strong. After only a minor hesitation, Minter grasped it and gave it a firm shake.

"What, uh . . . what happened to your face?" he asked.

"I had a mild stroke. A TIA, they call it. Fell right onto the lightbulb I was changing at the time." Crawford smiled sadly. "Nothing like a brush with mortality to put things in perspective."

"You should probably be at home recuperating, don't you think?"

"I've been resting all day. Doctor's orders. Speaking of which, I saw Wallace and Jessica at the ER. Neither of them looked very good. I don't suppose you've heard how they're doing?"

"Not a word," Minter said. "I assume they have what everyone else has. One of our day engineers was taken to the hospital by ambulance and most of second shift called off. I'm paying time and a half for volunteers from first shift, but I can't imagine they'll stick around for third."

"I'd offer to help, but . . . you know." Crawford averted his eyes. "I just want to gather my belongings and put this unfortunate episode behind me. If that's okay with you, I mean."

"I'll need to run it past Lowell. You know, after everything that went down earlier."

"Of course," Crawford said. "I completely understand."

He took a seat in one of the chairs and did his best to look pathetic, like a man embarrassed to be seen in his own skin, while he waited for Minter to use the phone at the main security desk to contact the president and CEO of NorCal P&E. This was the greatest window of vulnerability in Crawford's plan. The way Lowell had looked earlier in the day, he'd likely gone back to his hotel and crashed, assuming he hadn't been admitted to the hospital. Either way, he probably wasn't in a position to answer his cellphone.

It was a huge gamble, but one Crawford needed to take.

Several minutes passed as Minter repeatedly tried to raise his boss on the phone. When he finally gave up, he spoke softly to Tommy Nolan. The chief security guard's replacement must have called off, forcing him to work a double shift.

Crawford tried not to smile. Everything was going better than he could have hoped.

Tommy glanced at Crawford from the corner of his eye and offered a reluctant nod.

Crawford rose tentatively and held his breath until Minter beckoned him closer.

"No one's answering their phones tonight," he said. "I don't figure there's any real harm in letting you grab your belongings, though. They are yours, after all. You just have to promise me you won't mention a word of what we discussed yesterday to anyone in the building. Am I clear?"

"Crystal," Crawford said. "Mum's the word."

Minter led him through security to where Tommy waited on the far side of the metal detector with a blank expression on his face and a stack of boxes, folded flat. Crawford accepted them with a nod and followed the usurper down the hall.

"No offense," Minter said, "but when everyone started calling off, I worried that you might have had something to do with it."

"I assure you, Ron, the last thing in the world I'd want to do is jeopardize Diablo—"

"Relax, Nick. Pretty much everyone I know seems to be coming down with something. Ordinarily I'm as healthy as an ox, but even I'm starting to feel a little under the weather. I wouldn't say you look a whole lot better. And have you seen all of that craziness on the news?"

They turned into Crawford's office, where Minter had already commandeered his desk.

"I hope you know that this isn't what I wanted," Minter said.

Crawford merely nodded as he opened the boxes and folded the flaps into place. The knickknacks from his desk had been moved to the visitor's chair. He packaged them all together and set them aside.

"Do you mind . . . ?" he asked, gesturing to the desk chair.

Minter shook his head and moved it aside so Crawford could set about removing the framed degrees and awards from the wall. It was an act of finality, and yet one that didn't hurt nearly as badly as he'd expected, especially considering what he was about to do.

He fumbled the stack of frames and dropped them to the ground with a crash. Wood snapped and glass shattered. He gasped in horror, clapped his hands over his mouth, and fell to the ground to pick up the broken pieces of his life.

Minter knelt beside him and carefully began separating the ruined frames from the few that remained intact.

Crawford saw exactly what he'd hoped to see: a triangular piece of glass roughly eight inches long. He pried it from the frame, curled it into his grasp, and stepped behind Minter, as though heading for the trash can. Then stopped. He wrapped his arm around the usurper's neck and jammed the sharp tip into the side of his throat, just deep enough to summon blood.

"Jesus, Nick. What the hell are you—?"

"You're going to call security and tell them you need a few more boxes."

"You don't really want me to call security, do you? You know what they'll do—"

"Stand up slowly and don't make any sudden moves."

"If that's really what you want."

"Oh, it's definitely what I want."

Together they stood, slowly and cautiously. Minter pressed the button on the phone that connected him directly to the security desk.

"Would you mind bringing a few more boxes down to my office?" He pressed the button to terminate the connection and held up his hands. "There . . . I did as you asked. Now, what do you say about getting that glass away from my neck?"

"Okay," Crawford said.

He raised the sharp tip from his old friend's neck.

And slammed it down again.

SCREECH!

Leticia sideswiped an SUV parked against the curb on the narrow residential street. She jerked the wheel to the left, overcorrecting and nearly colliding with the Prius driving in the other direction. With a halfhearted wave of apology, she glanced out the passenger-side window to gauge the extent of the damage to the car she'd hit, but her side mirror was no longer there. Going back and leaving a note would be the right thing to do. Unfortunately, with as awful as she felt right now, if she didn't hurry home and climb into bed, she'd probably throw up all over her car.

Her head ached so badly that she could hardly keep her eyes open. The glow of the streetlights felt like needles stabbing straight through her pupils and into her brain. She was sweating so profusely that her clothes were positively drenched, yet dialing up the air conditioning only seemed to make her shiver harder. Maybe if she rolled down the window and leaned her head—

Screech!

She spun the wheel and barely missed the fender of the pickup parked on the opposite side of the road. Her Camry hit the curb and bounded into the front yard of the corner lot. She swerved to avoid the stop sign and launched her vehicle onto the cross street, the tires screaming as she narrowly avoided hitting another parked car. Heart hammering in her chest, she straightened out and headed in the right direction, something underneath her car dragging on the asphalt with a metallic scraping sound.

Curse Paul Spitzer and the sickness he'd brought with him. He knew better than to come to work when he wasn't feeling well. Diablo had strict rules in place so that this kind of thing didn't happen. Better one engineer call off and inconvenience the others than risk passing around a nasty virus that left them short-staffed tending a reactor that could literally melt down and make this entire part of the state uninhabitable for generations.

Leticia turned into her driveway going way too fast. She slammed the brakes just in time to avoid hitting the garage. Mother would be furious about the skid marks on the concrete, but that was a problem for another day. Right now, the only thing that mattered was swallowing a fistful of Advil and crawling under the covers.

Thunk.

A raven landed on the Camry's hood, right in front of her. It scrabbled to maintain its footing, its talons scratching the protective coating. Its eyes never left hers.

She killed the engine, popped the door, and promptly fell to the ground. The raven flapped down onto the lawn and hopped toward her. Even more of the giant black birds lined the roof of the garage, every single one of them silently staring down at her.

Leticia used the rear tire to pull herself to her feet. Leaning against the Camry for support, she headed for the front door of her house. The passenger's side of her car was one big dent, from bumper to fender, the paint scraped to the bare metal. She had a hunch that the cars she'd hit were in much worse shape than she'd initially thought.

"Stupid, stupid, stupid," she whispered.

She stopped at the foot of the stoop when she saw all of the ravens clamoring on the overhang above her head. Their talons raked the gutter, which crumpled beneath their combined weight. She took a single step toward them—

They erupted from the roof and descended upon her, their wings beating against one another's, their beaks and claws grabbing at her hair.

Leticia screamed, swatted at her head, and staggered around the side of the house. She opened the gate. Fell. Crawled along the paving stones and onto the lawn. Even more of the great black birds flapped down from the telephone wires, tearing little bits of scalp and hair from her head and flesh from her arms. She couldn't see where she was going until it was too late. A sob wrenched loose from her chest as she thrust her hands into the rosebushes.

The attack ended as suddenly as it had begun.

Leticia brushed her sweat-matted hair from her eyes and looked over her shoulder. Hundreds of ravens stood in the grass or leered down at her from the roof of the house and the storage shed. The frenzied avian cries gave way to the scratching of talons on shingles. Feathers decorated the rosebushes like ornaments on a Christmas tree. Everything else in the yard was either dead, dying from lack of water, or overrun with weeds. Except for these roses with their blood-red blossoms, the only things in this entire godforsaken world that her mother cared for.

The carcasses of the ravens from this morning were gone, the ground smoothed over where they'd fallen on the rich soil that Mother had carted around the side of the house in the days before Father had left. Leticia had thought they were going to plant a garden together as a family. She'd hoped that sharing an activity would help put an end to the constant fighting. Not that she ever got to find out. Her father had split in the middle of the night and her mother had vanished inside of herself, leaving Leticia to take care of both of them. Making their meals. Washing their clothes. Walking to and from school. Accepting charity wherever she could find it. All while Mother worked down at the plant or knelt out here on the ground, tending to her roses as though they were the only things that mattered.

Leticia hated them. Hated everything about them. They were a reminder of the worst time of her life, one that had followed her through school and into her adult life, such as it was. She was a thirty-year-old woman living with her mother because no one else would have her.

Because no one else could even see her.

She turned around and found black eyes focused on her from seemingly everywhere at once. Not looking *past* her. Not looking *through* her. They were looking *at* her.

The ravens *saw* her.

A lifetime of suppressed anger boiled inside of her. How was it that such simple creatures could see her when no one else on the planet even tried? Her father had left her, her coworkers ignored her, and her own mother despised her. It wasn't fair. Nothing in this stupid, stupid, stupid life was fair.

Leticia screamed and grabbed the nearest rosebush. Thorns bit into her palms as she tugged the roots from the ground and cast the plant aside. She did the same thing to the adjacent bush, sweat pouring down her face and blood dripping from her hands, the birds egging her on with their frenetic shrieks. Something snapped inside her, and her vision turned red. She broke branches and kicked dirt and filled the air with leaves until the rosebushes were no more. Finally, she collapsed to her hands and knees, chest heaving, unable to catch her breath. Tears flowed freely, stinging the tiny cuts on her face. She released a pathetic moan and—

Something metallic caught her eye. She brushed aside the soil and revealed a belt buckle. The gold was green with verdigris, but she would have recognized it anywhere. She traced her fingertip over the design.

A cowboy holding his horse's reins and kneeling before a cross.

Leticia stood on trembling legs. She swayed momentarily, then strode purposefully toward the shed. The sea of ravens parted before her and closed in her wake. She threw open the door, grabbed a shovel, and headed straight back toward the upturned rosebushes.

A cacophony of avian screams rent the night as she attacked the soil, throwing it in every direction until she exposed the crescents of a buried ribcage and the crown of a skull.

Leticia fell to her knees.

Her father hadn't left.

He'd been here all along.

The sound of the television called to her from the open window of her mother's bedroom. She picked up the shovel, hefted its weight, and headed for the back door. The knob turned easily in her dirty hand. Her muddy shoes left tracks on the kitchen tile and the living room carpet. Canned laughter echoed from down the hallway, where the glow of the TV illuminated her mother's open doorway. She found Mother asleep in her bed, her covers cast aside and her pale face glistening with sweat. The old woman didn't open her eyes until Mr. Snuffles jumped onto her chest, bared his teeth, and started barking.

Leticia stepped up onto the bed and raised the shovel.

CRAWFORD WRAPPED his handkerchief around his palm to slow the bleeding and provide a little more protection from the sharp edges of the glass, which had cut a lot deeper than he'd expected. He pressed his back to the wall beside the closed door and waited, listening to the blood drip with a metronomic *plat . . . plat . . . plat . . .*

If ever there'd been a time to stop this, he'd passed it long ago.

Footsteps echoed from the hallway. The moment whoever was out there opened the door, he'd see the arterial spatters decorating the desk and the walls and realize what was happening. Crawford needed to make his move before the newcomer could react.

A tiny voice screamed from somewhere deep inside him. He balled his free hand into a fist and pounded it against his forehead until it shut up and he could hear again. Of course, he'd only made his headache worse in the process.

The footsteps stopped. A perfunctory knock and the click of a hand settling onto the knob. The door opened inward, as if in slow motion. Crawford pushed off the wall and raised the wicked shard. A man emerged from behind the door, his face in profile, a stack of flattened boxes held out before him. Tommy. His eyes widened, an expression of shock formed on his face, and his body tensed with instinctive recognition.

Crawford slammed the sharp glass into the side of the security guard's neck before he could react. Jerked it back out, releasing a rush of blood. Brought it back down, again and again.

Tommy turned. Raised one hand to ward off the blows and used the other to shove Crawford away from him. Grabbed his throat and made a move toward the hallway.

Crawford couldn't allow him to get there.

He jumped onto the security guard's back and rode him to the ground, his arm moving like a piston as he repeatedly stabbed Tommy until he stopped moving. Crawford crawled off him and stood over his lifeless body, which was surrounded by so much blood that it had been a wonder it had all fit inside of him in the first place.

"Sorry, Tommy," he said. "Wait. My apologies. Sorry, *Tom.*"

Crawford grabbed the security guard by his ankles and dragged him behind the desk, where Minter's body was already crammed into the hollow. He figured it would take maybe twenty minutes for the other guards to wonder what was taking him so long and perhaps thirty for them to realize that something was wrong and come looking for him, so he needed to hurry and hope to God no one was watching the cameras too closely.

He retrieved his briefcase from the closet, dumped out the contents, and replaced them with Tommy's pistol: a Glock 22 with a magazine holding twenty-two .40-caliber Smith & Wesson rounds. There were advantages to being a hands-on boss, one of them being that he knew how to use it. He'd personally requisitioned fifty of them — after extensive testing on the firing range with the sales rep, of course — to replace their aging supply of Colt M1911 revolvers.

Crawford wiped his boots on Tommy's slacks, grabbed his briefcase, and did his best not to step in any more blood on his way out of the office. He walked purposefully and without looking back, navigating the hallways without allowing his face to appear on any of the cameras. He knew exactly where each and every one of them was, as he'd worked closely with the initial design team to situate them in such a way as to maximize coverage and minimize expense. By the time he reached the fuel handling building, he'd appeared on exactly two of them for fewer than five seconds total.

He headed straight for the spent fuel pools. If everything had gone according to the plan he'd implemented just prior to being so unceremoniously fired, thirty-two pressurized-water fuel assemblies would have been packed into a transfer cask and loaded into a specially designed vertical transporter to be driven to the storage site the following morning. More importantly, thirty-two fresh assemblies would have been added to the pool. It was a slow process that took two full days and required his entire engineering staff, a labor-intensive task that could only be accomplished without incurring extensive overtime by overloading the day staff and running on a skeletal crew at night until the job was complete, which meant that right now the few engineers on the clock were monitoring the reactor and only coming down here to log the temperature, flow rate, and radiation readings once an hour, on the hour.

A glance at the gold watch he'd received for twenty-five years of service confirmed that he had nearly half an hour before that happened and another fifteen minutes before security gave Tommy a second thought.

Plenty of time.

Crawford set aside his briefcase, changed into a white radiation suit with protective gloves and full-face gasmask, and walked out onto the fuel handling platform, an elevated steel walkway spanning the width of the pool that could be moved from one end to the other with the push of a button. He drove it to the far end and parked it about three feet from the railing, which left just enough room to align the boom and lower it through the water until it latched onto the handle of one of the spent fuel assemblies. The hydraulic winch whined and raised it to the surface. Each assembly contained roughly two hundred individual fuel rods: thirteen-foot-long, half-inch-wide zirconium-alloy tubes packed with thimble-sized pellets of enriched uranium-235.

The moment the assembly breached the surface, he ran around to the other side and carefully extracted a dozen rods, one at a time, and set them on the ground. His nerves crackled like downed power lines as he glanced from the entryway to the fuel rods and back again, removing the caps and the springs and dumping the uranium pellets at his feet. He tried not to look at his watch as he repeated the process until he had a decent pile. The heat radiating from them was like a campfire. He slid the empty rods back into the assembly, ran around to the crane, and lowered it back into its slot at the bottom of the pool. Grabbed his briefcase, withdrew the pistol, and shoveled the pellets inside, filling it to the point that he could barely close it. He ditched the suit, stuffed the gun underneath his waistband, and hefted the case.

The walk to the front door was the longest he'd ever made. He passed his office without slowing and headed straight for security. There was no way he was getting through there without setting off the radiation detectors, so he was just going to have to improvise.

A mountain of a man named Bruce Rush was waiting for him. He'd been a promising high school football player who might have gone on to do great things on the gridiron had he not blown out his knee, but Crawford had been right there to give him a job so that he could support his pregnant girlfriend.

"Bruce!" Crawford said. "How's my favorite tailback?"

"Running on fumes, Mr. C."

Crawford laughed at the play on words. Judging by the expression on the security guard's face, however, it hadn't been deliberate.

He surveyed the scene before him. There was only one other guard manning the desk. The third must have been making his rounds. Crawford slowed as he reached the security cordon. Any closer and he'd set off the radiation detector.

Rush glanced around the corner, into the empty hallway. He was looking for Tommy, who should have been there to escort Crawford from the building. Confusion registered on Rush's face a heartbeat before Crawford drew his pistol and put a bullet right between the guard's eyes.

Crawford pivoted toward the other security guard and shot him before he could draw his weapon, knocking him to the ground behind the desk.

Footsteps from his left, coming in fast.

A clap of gunfire and a bullet screamed past his ear. He ducked, aimed, and put two shots through the security guard's chest, dropping him right there in the hallway.

Crawford shoved the scalding barrel down the back of his pants, lifted his briefcase, and headed for his truck. There were two more security guards at the inner gate, controlling vehicular access to the facility, and four more manning the dry cask storage facility, all of whom were armed with Colt M4 carbines capable of turning him into Swiss cheese. He needed to be long gone by the time they figured out why the main desk wasn't answering when they checked in on their prearranged schedule.

He left the alarms from the radiation and metal detectors blaring and cut straight across the parking lot to his truck. A glance over his shoulder confirmed that the outer perimeter guards were still in the security shack. He set the briefcase in the bed, climbed into the driver's seat, and drove away at a steady pace, his heart pounding right through his ribcage. Once the twin domes of the reactors vanished from his rearview mirror, he pinned the gas and accelerated away from Diablo, whooping and punching the roof of the cab.

LETICIA HUNG her head and let the freezing water run over her hands, momentarily assuaging the stinging and flushing the residual dirt and thorns from the myriad lacerations. Diffuse blood swirled around the drain. No matter how hard she scrubbed, she couldn't seem to get it out of the wrinkles in her knuckles or from underneath her nails. She splashed her face but couldn't bring herself to look in the mirror for fear of what she'd see.

At least the cold dulled her headache and reduced the throbbing in the corners of her vision. Throwing up had helped, but she'd missed the toilet and the smell was making her stomach churn again. She needed to figure out what she was going to do now. The thought of spending another second inside this awful house with her mother was more than she could bear, although it wasn't like she had anywhere else to go.

She pushed off from the sink and entered Mother's room. The flickering light from the TV made the blood spatters glisten as they dribbled down the wall and behind the headboard. She averted her eyes from the body in the bed and instead found herself looking at the shovel she'd cast aside. Tangles of human and canine hair clung to the sharp sides, and a black puddle had soaked into the surrounding carpet. She turned away and retched, but this time nothing came up.

"What have I done?" she whispered.

The only answer came in the form of talons clattering on the roof.

Leticia headed down the hallway toward the living room. What was she supposed to do now? Surely the police would understand. She'd just drive down to the station and explain what had happened.

They'll lock you up and throw away the key, Mother said.

Leticia turned around, but no one was there.

"Leave me alone!" she shouted.

You'll always be alone. Who in their right mind would want someone like you?

Leticia thought of Mr. Crawford. He'd know what to do. If anyone could help her figure a way out of this mess, it was him.

She threw open the front door and stumbled onto the porch. Her keys were still in her pocket, and while her Camry had seen better days, it started on the first try. She rolled down the windows, cranked up the air conditioning, and headed north toward her destination.

The streets were even emptier than they'd been half an hour ago. Porches remained dark and lifeless. There were no couples strolling on the sidewalks. No joggers or dog walkers or pizza delivery drivers. It was as though the entire town had collectively decided to hide from her.

Why would they hide from you when they don't even know you exist?

Leticia turned onto Mr. Crawford's street and nearly hit a sedan parked diagonally across the street. The driver had run into a parked vehicle and fled the scene of the accident, if the open driver-side door was any indication. Unless that was him lying on the lawn, but she didn't even want to turn her head to get a better look for fear the motion would cause the acid roiling in her gut to come up. Her headache intensified by the second and the streetlights burned her eyes. The surge of adrenaline that had slowed the progression of her symptoms had obviously run its course.

Maybe she'd feel better if she just closed her eyes for a few seconds—

Leticia woke up when her front tires hit the curb. She caught a glimpse of Mr. Crawford's house from the corner of her eye as she careened across his front lawn. Her bumper struck the post holding up his awning and the whole thing collapsed onto her hood. She spilled out onto the ground and struggled to get to her feet. There was no way she was reaching the front door now. Fortunately, the garage door stood wide open, although her heart dropped when she noticed that the fancy blue pickup truck wasn't parked inside. Presumably, he'd be back at any moment and would be happy to find his favorite Golden Bear waiting for him.

She was only peripherally aware of stumbling into the garage and falling through the door. Her forehead bounced from the floor, jarring her back to consciousness, or at least granting her enough presence of mind to crawl away from the shattered glass prodding her chest. It was all over the floor underneath the light fixtures, and even worse in the kitchen, where a pattern of dried blood decorated the floor. Smeared footprints led away from it, deeper into the house. She followed them down a hallway that seemed to rotate around her like a rolling barrel. By the time she reached the room at the end, she'd vomited the last of her bile and couldn't tell whether the dampness on her cheeks was from tears or mucus.

With the last of her failing strength, she dragged herself onto Mr. Crawford's bed. Ensconced in his scent, she finally allowed herself to close her eyes.

CRAWFORD HIT the 101 South toward Shell Beach just as a single police cruiser streaked down the offramp and sped onto Avila Beach Drive toward Diablo, its light bar flashing. Surely the bodies of his former coworkers had been discovered by now and the police would be looking for him, so where were all of the rest of them? Where were the roadblocks and the choppers? What, did they have better things to do? Was he not worth their effort?

Granted, it would take time for the investigators to discover that he'd accessed the fuel handling building and review the security footage to discover the true nature of his crime, one far more ambitious than the murder of a handful of employees, but once they did, they'd come for him with everything they had. He'd be persona non grata, numero uno on the FBI's wish list, and the skies would fill with helicopters searching for him. Nicholas James Crawford, the man who'd outsmarted them all. And once the heat died down, he'd return and make them all rue the day they attempted to take Diablo from him.

Oh, yes. He'd make them all rue it.

The pellets in his case? They might not have been worthy of the reactor, but that didn't mean they were useless. They were once solid chunks of uranium enriched until their concentration of U-235 — the isotope capable of sustaining the fission reaction they needed to produce the heat that drove the turbines — was between two and five percent. The majority of the U-235 burned off during use, leaving behind U-238, the stable, naturally occurring form mined from the earth. Plus residual amounts of U-235 and plutonium-239, a radioactive isotope formed by the uranium's decay. And while there might not be very much of it, that plutonium was highly enriched and could be reprocessed into a cake of concentrated fissionable material using the Purex process. The combination of the residual U-235 and reclaimed Pu-289 contained within his briefcase likely wouldn't end up being more than a few pounds, but that was enough, in the right hands, to produce a nuclear weapon with a ten-kiloton yield. A tiny fraction of the destructive power contained within the average bomb in the military's arsenal, to be sure, and yet nearly that of the Little Boy atomic bomb dropped on Hiroshima.

His homemade device, when it was complete, would turn San Luis Obispo into a crater, incinerate everything surrounding it, and irradiate people as far away as Santa Barbara.

He smiled at the thought. His satisfaction quickly turned to exhaustion. The day's events had exacted a steep toll from a body that wasn't nearly as resilient as it had once been, especially considering he'd awakened that morning suffering from the aftereffects of a mini stroke. He hadn't had a thing to eat, and his headache was getting worse by the second.

Crawford rolled down the window to get some air. He was sweating like he was in a sauna and couldn't seem to take a deep breath. His stomach roiled, and for a second, he thought he was going to vomit all over the dashboard. He needed to get off the main roads, maybe find someplace to lie low for a while, if only to get a few hours of sleep.

Yeah, a little shuteye would do him some good, allow him to wake up feeling reinvigorated. After all, he had his work cut out for him if he was going to collect all of the supplies he needed and find a place where he'd be able to work uninterrupted—

Sharp pain behind his forehead. He closed his eyes and pinched his temples. Let go of the wheel and nearly went off the side of the road. Gravel pinged from the undercarriage. He barely pulled back onto the asphalt before hitting the guardrail.

The ground tilted underneath him. There was stomach acid everywhere before he even sensed his gorge rising. It stung the back of the hand he'd used to carry the briefcase stuffed with radioactive material, the skin of which was lobster red and looked like he'd microwaved it.

Another wave of vomit rippled up from his gut.

He took the nearest exit. There were only two options: drive into Santa Maria and risk stumbling upon the police or head east on Highway 166 into the national forest. He chose the latter and ascended into rolling hills blanketed with wild grasses and clumps of pine trees and paloverdes.

The horizon teetered and his vision blurred. He recognized that he was in big trouble and looked for a place to pull over. The highway appeared in random snippets as his eyes closed of their own volition. He aimed for a widening on the shoulder—

The truck bounded from the road, tore through a barbed-wire fence, and slammed into the hillside.

Crawford's forehead struck the steering wheel—

Darkness.

31

Riverton, Wyoming

"What was that?" Pennington asked.

Time stood still as everyone looked through the inset window, toward the source of the thunderous boom they'd heard from down the hall where the chimpanzees were housed.

Davis knew exactly what had caused it. His mouth had gone dry, and his breathing bordered on hyperventilation. In his mind, he was again fifteen and standing not in a high-tech lab, surrounded by stainless-steel instrumentation, but rather in the hallway of his old high school, his best friend lying dead at his feet.

"Some kind of explosion?" Emily said.

"We should check and see if everyone's—"

"Gunshot," Davis whispered.

"This is a highly sensitive lab full of scientists," Pennington said. "There's no way—"

"Trust me." Years might have passed, yet Davis still couldn't close his eyes and try to sleep without hearing it. "I know that sound. We need to get out of here while we still can."

"And just what do you think is going to happen?" Emily asked.

Davis glanced back at the others. He knew how he must have looked; he could feel his entire body tightening with panic, his fight-or-flight instincts on a hair-wire trigger.

"I don't know, but—"

"Nothing's going to happen to any of us," Pennington said. "This has to be one of the most secure installations on the face of the planet. There'd be alarms going off left and right if there were any kind of threat."

"And besides . . . " Emily said, holding up a vial of the antibodies they'd synthesized from Beta's blood. "Don't you think we should take this baby out for a spin and see what she can do?"

Karen and Sanders had already gone back to the residential wing to requisition all of the equipment and animals they would need to ramp up production, assuming, of course, that their treatment worked on the infected simians and Rankin was able to convince the President to greenlight the project.

"I'm telling you . . . " Davis started to say, but his words trailed off.

He cocked his head and heard the shrieks of chimpanzees in the far distance. And closer, footsteps. Just around the corner. Slow and methodical.

His heart was beating so hard and fast that his vision pulsed.

Dear Lord, please . . . not again.

"Had something gone wrong, the emergency systems would have kicked in and the labs would have gone on lockdown," Pennington said. "If it'll make you feel better, I'll go down the hall and see if I can figure out what's going on."

He opened the door and stepped out into the corridor. Davis hurried to catch up with him and took him by the arm.

"Get back in the lab," he said.

Pennington shrugged out of his grasp and headed in the direction from which they'd heard the lone gunshot. The sound of footsteps grew louder and faster. Running toward them.

A man wearing powder blue scrubs came around the corner so fast that he slid across the hallway and slammed into the wall. He pushed himself up and looked right at them. Blood trickled down his cheeks from his crimson eyes. He bared his teeth and lunged into a full sprint.

"Oh, God," Pennington said.

He turned and ran for the lab. The man was upon him before he took his second step, driving him to the floor and clipping Davis across the backs of the legs, sending him sprawling. By the time he rolled over, the man had already torn Pennington's suit and was trying to fight through his arms to get at his throat. Pennington screamed and the inside of his mask freckled with blood.

"Lewis!" Emily shouted.

The attacker turned toward the sound of her voice. She tried to slam the door closed, but the man was too fast. He thrust his hand between the frame and the door, wrenched it open, and dove on top of her, knocking her over the counter with a crash of falling equipment and breaking glass. She pulled herself back up and looked at Davis through the window.

"Help—!"

The man rose behind her and dragged her down once more. One final scream and she was gone.

Davis scrabbled away from Pennington's body and used the wall as leverage to get to his feet. He backed away, hoping to God that either the man didn't notice or had forgotten that he was there. Just like he had all those years before, a coward slinking away from danger, looking for someplace to hide. But what could he possibly do—?

The overhead lights died with a thud. Davis took advantage of the darkness and ran in the opposite direction. Klaxons blared and the emergency lights kicked on a split-second later, casting a red glare over the corridor.

Davis heard the lab door burst open behind him, but he didn't dare look back. He just fixed his eyes on the access-controlled door ahead of him and pushed himself even harder, the reflective silver surface drawing closer and closer. He pulled up short and looked up into the laser scanner, suppressing his terror just long enough for the security system to recognize the pattern of vessels on his retina.

The man bore down on him in the reflection on the opening door.

Davis turned sideways and slipped through, hitting the button to close the door behind him.

The man dove through the gap and caught Davis by the leg. He issued a hideous scream as the door bit down on his thorax, the hydraulic motor trying to force it closed.

Davis tugged his leg free and ran. He could still hear the man behind him, clawing at the stainless steel in an effort to pull himself through, as he raced past the quarantine rooms and headed for the security station. Blew through the door. Slammed it shut behind him. Tripped over something and went down hard. Looked back—

The dead security guard stared blankly at him through bulging eyes. His lips had a faint bluish cast and his tongue protruded from between his lips.

Davis struggled to his feet, kicking aside everything that had fallen from the desk in what appeared to have been a ferocious struggle. There was a broken two-way radio under the desk. He picked it up—

Thud.

The door shuddered in its frame. He peeked through the window in time to watch the man get a running start and hurl himself against the door again.

Thud.

Davis caught movement from the corner of his eye and turned to face the bank of closed-circuit monitors.

"Oh my God," he whispered.

CULLEN STOOD IN THE AIRLOCK, listening to the siren and the chimpanzees throwing themselves against the door, over and over. They knew he was in here and they were willing to bludgeon themselves to death to get at him. He needed them good and ready to come barreling in here at full speed if he was going to make his plan work.

He swung his rifle over his back, grabbed the pipes feeding the chemical showers, and hauled himself up to the ceiling. His right leg was just long enough to reach the button. The primates flooded through the opening door and ran headlong into the opposite egress, where they fell upon each other in the chaos.

Cullen swung the other way and kicked the button to open the door to the residential wing. The chimps saw him this time and jumped up and down, reaching for him with their long arms and screaming from their bloody muzzles.

"What the hell . . . ?" someone said from the changing room on the other side.

Brown looked up and met Cullen's stare. He detected a flash of recognition in the eyes of his subordinate, who suddenly understood just how much trouble he was in. Brown lunged for the button to close the door between them, but the chimps swarmed over him before he reached it, slashing at his isolation suit, biting his exposed flesh.

A woman screamed from the inner hallway.

The primates leaped from on top of Brown and chased her around the corner, screeching and slapping their palms on the floor as they went. Cullen stood over his old friend, who tried to drag himself away with trembling hands, leaving a smeared trail of blood behind him.

"Where do you think you're going?" Cullen asked. He kicked Brown in the ribs, rolled him over onto his back. "I thought you'd be happy to see me."

Brown tried to speak but only blood spluttered from his mouth. Cullen got the gist of it from his expression, though. He lowered the barrel of his rifle and ended Rodney Brown.

Screams and shouts, punctuated by the hoots and cries of primates, filled the air.

The world around Cullen slowed as he strode out into the residential wing. Men and women emerged from their rooms to see what was causing the commotion, only to be overwhelmed and dragged to the ground by beasts half their size, but several orders of magnitude stronger. He followed at a distance, cleaning up the mess the chimps left behind with a stomp on the head or a bullet through the brainpan. Any time one of the creatures turned at the sound of discharge, he riddled its chest with bullets. Bodies lay everywhere, human and simian alike. The floors and walls ran with blood.

Reality shifted as he walked down the corridor. One moment he was in a white hallway filled with the remains of his colleagues, the next he was in a cave surrounded by the filthy bodies of those who'd been sealed inside with him, who'd held him down while the rest of his tribe rolled the stone into place, stranding them in darkness. All because they feared him and the covenant he'd made with the gods of darkness when he'd partaken of the infected human flesh, because they blamed him for the sickness and the resultant bloodshed that had nearly eradicated them all, when in truth he had spared them by leading them through the snow and into the underworld, where those hunting them would never find them. Where they'd rewarded his sacrifice by entombing him beneath the earth.

Never again.

Cullen roared like an animal and shot everyone and everything that moved. Bullets tore through the flesh of humans and chimpanzees alike, spreading carnage before him, unfurling a red carpet of blood.

The final shot echoed away into the depths of the structure. He stood still and listened to the silence between the shrill bleats of the Klaxon. There were no more screams or whimpers, no more hoots or shrieks, no more begging or pleading or calling out to a God who'd turned away when they'd needed Him most. Only the soft patter of blood dripping from the walls and ceiling.

Cullen smiled and headed back toward the secure labs. There was still one more stop he needed to make, one he'd been looking forward to more than any other. And then he would be free to revel in the chaos of the end of the Fourth World.

DAVIS SAT ON THE FLOOR, rocking back and forth, the blaring siren on the brink of driving him mad. This was his worst nightmare. Not only had he watched Emily and Pennington die before his very eyes, he'd witnessed the slaughter of everyone else in the facility on the security camera feeds. The rampage of the infected chimpanzees had been so brutal that he'd been unable to look away, and yet somehow the man walking calmly down the hallway behind them, shooting everyone in his path, had been infinitely worse.

"Three . . . two . . . one," he whispered.

Cullen was still out there, walking from one monitor to the next in the red glare of the emergency lights, making his way toward the lab wing. It was the same measured stride that Steven Leonard Thomas had exhibited so many years ago, the thudding of his heavy footfalls providing a soundtrack for the man's advance. How many times during the intervening years had Davis imagined things playing out differently? He'd always told himself that if he were given a chance to relive that nightmare, he'd do everything differently, and yet here he was again, watching helplessly as the man who'd killed everyone in the residential wing passed through the airlock and headed in his direction.

A loud *thud* directly above his head. Davis flinched and drew his legs tighter against his chest, prayed the monster that had chased him in here couldn't see him. He focused solely on the security monitors and not the faint reflection of the man's bloody face, pressed against the window, superimposed over the live feeds.

"Three-two-one. Three-two-one."

Gamma battled through the sedation and thrashed against his restraints as though sensing there was something going on outside his observation room. Alpha lay on the floor, barely within range of the camera, so still that Davis feared he was dead. And then there was Beta, Riley Middleton, who stood at the back of the room, never once looking away from the window, her right hand restlessly rubbing her thigh.

Cullen passed through the final security door and entered the hallway between the observation rooms. If Davis had stood up, he would have been looking right at him, a mere fifty feet away and closing. The infected man who'd killed Emily and Pennington lunged at Cullen, who calmly raised his rifle and brought the butt down on the man's forehead with a loud *crack*, knocking him to the ground. He did the same thing, again and again, until he was soaked with blood and there was nothing left of the infected man's skull.

Davis glanced up at the rack of weapons, then back at the man on the screen, who couldn't possibly know that he was in here. He could grab one of the rifles, throw open the door, and just start firing. Cullen would never know what hit him.

It was his only chance.

Davis scrambled across the room and was just about to reach for one of the rifles when he heard footsteps, right on the other side of the door. He panicked and climbed up on top of the dead guard. Pressed his back against the wall—

The door swung inward and stopped scant inches from his visor. He held his breath so as not to make a sound. Cullen cast his rifle to the ground and grabbed another one.

Davis's stomach sank. His cowardice had cost him his only chance, and now—

The door slammed against the body beneath him, forcing him to turn his face aside. The footsteps headed away from him, into the hallway.

Cullen stopped outside of Riley's room, aimed straight at her through the glass, and started firing.

RILEY FLINCHED as the bullets struck the reinforced glass, although they barely pitted it.

Cullen roared in frustration and strafed the ceiling above his head, shattering the tiles and light fixtures. A rain of dust and sparks cascaded down upon him, and she saw him as he truly was: a dark form limned by the crimson glare, the horns of a steppe bison jutting from his head, the same hideous visage she'd seen superimposed upon Edgerton not so very long ago. This was what they'd released from inside the tomb in the arctic. There'd been more than a virus trapped inside that cave. There'd been something worse, something undeniably evil.

She'd sensed it growing inside Cullen, witnessed it taking root as flames in his irises, and he, in turn, had watched recognition dawn in her eyes. In that moment, she'd known that he would come for her. It was the whole reason she'd hidden the needle under her skin, but now that she saw him with his head exposed and his isolation gear ruined, she realized that the threat of puncturing his suit would do her no good. He was twice her size and armed with a semiautomatic rifle, while all she had was a sharpened piece of metal that wasn't even two inches long.

Cullen smiled. He must have seen the spark of hope fade from her eyes. She heard the squeal of the handle and felt the change of pressure in the room. He stepped to the side and opened the door with a hiss of escaping air. She reached underneath her waistband, pinched the broken hub of the needle, and withdrew it from her thigh.

He stepped inside, slung his rifle over his shoulder, and removed his gloves. When he spoke, it was in a voice formed of many, all of different tone and pitch, as though countless people lived inside of him.

"You can see me, can't you?"

Riley retreated a step and ran into the wall. She wanted to ask him what he meant, but she already knew. He wasn't asking if she could see the man advancing upon her with murderous intent in his eyes; he was asking if she could see the evil sentience inside of him.

"Stay back," she said.

He took another step, and another.

"Don't be afraid. This has always been your destiny, as it has always been mine."

He stopped just outside her reach. She made a fist, adjusted the needle, and gripped it solidly between her thumb and forefinger.

"Don't come any closer!" she screamed.

His smile grew even broader, and his face took on a skeletal cast, as though his true mummified form were fighting to break through.

"The sun will set on the world again, only this time it will rise upon a land of darkness, and humanity will be no more."

He took another step and reached for her throat—

Riley jabbed the needle straight into his eye. Felt warmth on her fingers. The soft give of the orb rupturing.

Cullen struck her squarely in the face and sent her careening to the floor. She glanced up and saw the hatred in his good eye, the needle standing from the other as he tried to pinch it between his large fingers. She scrambled to her feet and ran past him, straight out into the hallway, where she got behind the door and pushed it closed.

He shouted and charged at her.

DAVIS STEPPED over the security guard's body and grabbed the closest rifle on the rack, one that looked almost like a paintball gun, which he'd used in his early teens, before the mere sight of one would have triggered a panic attack. At least he knew how to use it, if only the basics like how to switch off the safety and pull the trigger. It trembled in his hands as he strode out into the open, leaving behind the protection of the security office.

Riley braced herself against the door to her room and started to turn the handle—

Impact from the other side knocked her backward, the door flying open and slamming against the wall. She raised her hands and stumbled away.

Cullen emerged from the observation room, his hand clasped over his eye, blood sluicing between his fingers.

"Please," Riley sobbed. "You don't have to do this."

He roared like an animal, reached over his shoulder, and grabbed his rifle.

She frantically looked both ways, not knowing which direction to go. Her eyes locked onto Davis's and she ran toward him.

"Shoot him!" she screamed.

Davis thumbed off the safety, seated the stock against his shoulder, and aimed over her head as she slid to the ground.

Cullen bore down on him like a charging bull, raising his rifle as he neared. Davis squeezed the trigger in a blind panic. Saw the much larger man's chest buck with the impact of the tranquilizer syringe and his face twist in pain.

Davis pulled the trigger again.

Click.

His heart dropped into his stomach. He raised the useless air gun to shield himself, hitting the barrel of Cullen's rifle right as he pulled the trigger, causing the shot to sail wide. The thunderous report so close to Davis's ear was deafening.

Cullen hit him squarely in the chest and drove him to the ground. Davis's breath exploded from his lungs as he slid across the polished tile beneath the other man's weight. His head rebounded from the wall and sparks filled his vision. He tried to get his arms between them, but he was physically outmatched. Cullen tore off Davis's hood, gripped his face with one hand, and pressed his head into the floor. He caught a glimpse of Cullen's eyes and recognized the darkness within them, the same darkness he'd seen in the eyes of Steven Leonard Thomas and Richard Wesley Taylor.

Davis heard a metallic clatter over the humming in his ears and realized what was about to happen. He swatted at Cullen's rifle in a desperate attempt to keep him from bringing it to bear—

Crack!

Cullen grunted and loosened his grip, if only incrementally. Davis grabbed the smoldering barrel and shouted in pain. Forced himself to hold on so that Cullen couldn't get it close to his body, but the larger man pulled the trigger anyway. Bullets ricocheted first from the floor, then from the wall beside Davis's head.

Crack!

Cullen's grip went slack. He collapsed onto Davis, who jerked his head away and squirmed out from underneath his assailant, his eyes watering and blood streaming from his nose. He looked back in time to see Riley slam the butt of the tranquilizer gun into the back of Cullen's head one more time with a sickening *crack!*

Davis scrambled to his feet and took her by the hand.

"We need to get out of here."

The air rifle fell from her grasp and clattered to the floor. Bloody tatters of scalp and hair clung to the stock. She stared down at Cullen with an expression of shock.

"Come on," Davis said. He gave her a tug to get her feet moving. "We have to find help."

CULLEN OPENED HIS EYES, but the pain forced them closed again. He tried to reach for the source, only his hand wouldn't respond. There was blood in his mouth. Worse, he could feel it dribbling down his cheek and pooling against the side of his nose. The pressure of the syringe pinned under his chest metamorphosed into warmth that spread outward through his limbs.

The echoing sounds of footsteps and voices carried down the hallway. If he didn't get up quickly, his prey would escape. The consequences of allowing them to do so, he feared, would be catastrophic.

He fought through the agony and opened his eyes. Got his arms underneath him and pushed himself up to all fours, blood dripping from his chin and pattering the tile. The ground canted beneath him, and the periphery of his vision darkened as the anesthesia took effect. He rose to his feet and stared down the hallway. The man who'd shot him pulled Middleton through the security door, which whispered closed behind them.

Cullen made a sound like a dying animal and staggered after them. The world became liquid and the corridor spun. He raised the M4 and fired. The bullets embedded themselves in the stainless steel.

He dropped to his knees and let the rifle fall from his hands. His head felt too heavy for his neck to support, his arms like lead at his side. He toppled forward, his eyes rolling up into his skull.

The darkness claimed him before he hit the ground.

32

Ridgefield, Connecticut

Lucas sped through the dark countryside, nearly outracing his headlights. He felt the pressure of time bearing down on him. The last thing he wanted to do was hit Pittsburgh after dawn, which was looking more and more like a real possibility. Maybe he could find a way around it, but unless he wanted to spend his entire life trying to navigate these infernal two-lane highways in the middle of nowhere, he was eventually going to have to run the gamut of Columbus, Cincinnati, Indianapolis, Louisville, Nashville, and St. Louis, and if things were as out of control as he suspected . . .

What had he been thinking? Driving off in the middle of the night on some harebrained scheme to discover the secrets to surviving the pandemic. Only the most narcissistic anthropologist could possibly believe that he'd be able to stroll into two hundred thousand square acres of steep canyons, sprawling mesas, and primitive buildings and walk back out with the knowledge of how the Anasazi had withstood the virus. And yet that was exactly what he expected to do.

As irrational as it sounded, he couldn't shake the certainty that if he didn't do so, all hope would be lost. It was a physical sensation that tightened his chest and made it hard to breathe, a nervousness that settled into the base of his spine, a desperation that caused him to drive a whole lot faster than he should have been going on these back roads.

He nearly missed the sign announcing that he'd entered New York. According to his GPS, if he kept heading west on Highway 35, he'd run into the Saw Mill River Parkway, which would take him south through a handful of small towns and across the Hudson north of White Plains, allowing him to skirt Newark. It wasn't a perfect plan by any stretch of the imagination and would cost him an additional hour, but it meant that Allentown was the largest city he'd have to pass through until he reached Columbus.

The occasional siren called from the distance and from time to time he heard the whupping of helicopters. Headlights appeared every few minutes, traveling in the opposite direction, their drivers switching off their high beams at the last possible second. Only once did he pass a car in his lane. It almost felt as though he were in a different world, where the things he'd seen could never have happened, and yet the emergency broadcast tone blaring from his cellphone reminded him of just how real those events had been.

His screen lit up, displaying a message he read in intermittent glances from the corner of his eye as he navigated the narrow road beneath the over-hanging trees. People in his area were instructed to wear personal protective equipment and lock themselves in their homes. Family members developing fevers needed to be isolated as quickly as possible to prevent the spread of an unknown virus. Stay inside, stay off the roads, and await further instructions.

Maybe there was hope after all. If the residents of isolated towns like the ones surrounding him followed directions, then maybe they'd never be exposed. Perhaps the powers that be had acted fast enough and by quaranti-ning the larger cities, they'd been able to contain the virus. Of course, if there was one thing he'd learned about human nature in all of his studies, it was that if there was a way to screw up even the best-laid plans, humankind would find a way to do so.

"In one thousand feet, take a left onto the I-Six-eighty-four South/Saw Mill River Parkway onramp," the computerized voice said from his phone.

Lucas followed the directions and merged onto a four-lane highway that allowed him to push the speedometer even higher. The flashing lights of helicopters appeared against the horizon, where New York City lurked beneath the urban glow. Even driving in its general direction made him nervous, but Manhattan had been entirely cut off from the surrounding boroughs within hours of the infected man being killed. White Plains was maybe fifteen miles from the heart of the Bronx, but as long as the authorities were doing their jobs and people prone to panic were only now awakening to the squeal of the emergency tone from their phones, he ought to be just fine.

Pleasantville remained dark, save for the lighted signs of the gas stations and twenty-four-hour establishments. Exit signs appeared and buildings passed through the trees with increasing regularity.

"In two thousand feet, stay right to merge onto I-Two-eighty-seven West."

Signs announcing the Tappan Zee Bridge blew past. Once he reached the other side and made it through the suburban sprawl, it was smooth sailing straight through to Allentown.

Lucas inhaled his first full breath since leaving his townhouse and allowed himself to relax, if only by degree. He could do this. Everything was playing out just like he needed it to.

The truck hit the bridge and sped out over the black river. White towers and suspender cables rose ahead of him. A car materialized as if from nowhere — no taillights, no warning — just a sedan resting diagonally across the highway on its roof. He slammed on his brakes and skidded to a halt. There were several more abandoned vehicles on the other side of it, their doors standing open, interior lights revealing bloodstained dashboards sparkling with broken glass.

Golden lights flickered in the distance. He heard the rapid reports and recognized them for what they were.

Discharge from the barrels of so many automatic rifles.

LUCAS SAT in the idling truck, staring at the flickering lights as he tried to figure out what to do. If he turned back now, he'd lose at least another hour backtracking to I-84 and heading south into New York City was out of the question. He should have known there would have been a roadblock—

A man shouted, his voice degenerating into a scream.

Lucas couldn't just drive away now, not if people out here needed his help. He pressed the gas and drove slowly around the overturned car and between the abandoned vehicles. A barricade had been raised at the toll station, where the mountain of sandbags had collapsed on one side, near the guardrail. There were a dozen or so cars parked in between, their headlights shining upon the abandoned fortification. One of them had tried to run the blockade and sat buried in ruptured bags and loose sand, the Humvee parked on the other side knocked sideways from the impact. The golden bursts of discharge had to be a good half a mile past it.

Another scream and one of the flickering lights extinguished.

Lucas hit the gas and accelerated into the breakdown lane. The concrete barrier scraped through the paint on the driver's side, while the parked cars crumpled his side walls on the other. Their windows had been broken and their interiors decorated with crimson spatters. His bumper hit the open door of one of the vehicles, folding it forward and snapping it off. He bore down on the fallen barricade as though he were four-wheeling in the mountains back home, climbing over the toppled bags like so many rocks. His hood bounced, his tires spun for traction, and then, with a sudden lurch, he was over and bounding down onto the asphalt, where bodies lay on the ground, covered with blood. The majority wore civilian clothes, among them a woman and a child.

He sped toward the strobing gunfire, the reports loud enough that he could hear them even over the roar of the engine. Bodies passed in his peripheral vision, sprawled right in the middle of the road. He dodged a man wearing camo fatigues and had to swerve to keep from hitting a woman in a hospital gown. Another man in a windbreaker, a woman wearing denim and cowboy boots. There was blood everywhere, so fresh it reflected his headlights as though from puddles after a rainstorm.

More and more men and women passed, their hospital gowns fluttering in his slipstream, the pale flesh of their naked backsides visible, the entry wounds on their chests as clear as the blood in their eyes. One of them was still alive, a man dragging himself across the bridge with one hand, barely able to raise his head. A woman appeared in the far lane, crouching near the guardrail, the river flowing past on the other side of her. He caught a fleeting glimpse of her raising her bloody face from the throat of a soldier, his rifle resting near his outstretched hand, and then she was gone.

Figures appeared at the farthest reaches of his headlights, running in the same direction he was driving. Flaring gowns and pale bare legs. Several turned and sprinted straight toward his truck. He jerked the wheel to avoid the first, but the second met with his bumper and went under, thumping from the undercarriage and rolling out into the red glow of his taillights.

Lucas could clearly see the men with the automatic rifles now, firing behind them to hold off their pursuit, driving a few terrified civilians ahead of them like cattle. He honked to clear the way but succeeded only in drawing attention to himself. The faces of the men and women in matching gowns lit up in his beams mere seconds before impacting his hood. He slowed as he neared the survivors and rolled down his passenger window.

"Get in!" he shouted.

One of the soldiers stopped and sprayed bullets at the shadows gaining ground behind them, while the other helped load a man and two women into the bed of the truck. He climbed in behind them, took up post at the tailgate, and covered his partner.

"Go!" the first soldier shouted, jumping over the side as Lucas hit the gas. He banged on the rear window until Lucas slid it open. "What the hell are you doing?"

"Saving your skin!"

Asphalt blurred toward him in the headlights. The silhouette of a hillside crowned with trees and houses rose from the distant horizon.

"Slow down!" the soldier shouted.

"Why the hell would I want to do that?"

The answer became clear to Lucas a split-second later as dozens more people appeared, maybe a quarter of a mile ahead and closing fast. He hit the brakes and skidded to a halt, the distant figures gaining contrast as they passed from the glow of one streetlight to the next. Even from this distance, he could tell they were all wearing hospital gowns.

"We just need to buy more time," the solder said. His eyes were wide, his features dotted with blood. His nameplate identified him as Daniels. "A chopper's already on its way for emergency evac."

"How much time?"

"As much time as you can give us. We've got hospitals on both sides of the river overflowing with the infected and we're caught right in the middle."

Lucas put the truck into reverse as the figures rushing toward them closed on their position and gave it just enough gas to maintain their distance. Daniels rose to a crouch, braced his rifle on the roof above Lucas's head, and fired into the crowd to slow its progress.

Red and green lights emerged from the darkness, coming in low across the water.

Lucas gave the engine a little more gas and accelerated away from their pursuit. He watched his side mirror for the first sign of the infected people coming from the opposite direction, the white towers rising behind him, the lights growing brighter and brighter until—

Shadows appeared at the edge of sight, maybe five of them in all. He applied the brakes and coasted to a stop. If he absolutely had to, he could run right over them, but the idea of doing so made him sick to his stomach. Regardless of their condition, they were human beings—

Dozens of people raced into his headlights, closing the distance at a dead sprint.

He heard the rumble of rotors and glanced out his side window. A Black Hawk rose over the rail and settled onto the bridge behind them. Wind battered his passengers, whipping their hair and clothing.

"Come on!" the second soldier shouted. He lowered the tailgate and helped the passengers down. "Hurry!"

They ducked their heads against the furious gale and ran straight toward the side door of the chopper, which slid open as they neared. A man in camouflage fatigues jumped down to the asphalt and guided them into their seats.

"The hell are you waiting for?" Daniels shouted.

Lucas looked through the windshield. The infected patients were maybe fifty feet out and closing faster than he'd expected. Gunfire crackled from behind him. The soldier from inside the chopper was firing in the opposite direction. Lucas couldn't abandon his truck or he'd never make it home, but if he didn't . . .

Daniels opened the driver-side door, dragged him out, and shoved him toward the waiting helicopter, firing behind him the entire way.

The rotor wash buffeted them, forcing Lucas to lower his head and shield his eyes. Someone shouted at him, but he couldn't make out the words over the roar. A tug at his arm, urging him faster. He saw the landing gear and glanced up in time to climb into the chopper. Turned and offered his arm to Daniels, who hopped up beside him and started shooting as shadows rushed around the sides of the truck.

"All clear!" he shouted.

The Black Hawk lifted off and started to bank around—

A man in a hospital gown, his face twisted with rage and covered with blood, jumped up and grabbed hold of the landing gear. He reached for Lucas's feet, but Daniels was faster. A single shot to the forehead and the man plummeted to the bridge, where the others swarmed over him and tore him apart.

Daniels slid the door closed, right in Lucas's face. He stumbled backward and collapsed into the waiting seat.

A projectile streaked away from the stub wing with a high-pitched scream and hit the bridge. Massive sections of asphalt and concrete bucked upward through a cloud of smoke and then crumbled into the river, taking Lucas's truck, and all hope of reaching the Canyons of the Ancients, with it.

———

THE BLACK HAWK followed the Hudson all the way down to Upper Bay. Lucas watched Manhattan pass through the window, the skyscrapers obscured by a haze of smoke. Emergency lights flashed from seemingly everywhere at once, the skyline alive with helicopters shining their spotlights onto the streets.

The chopper banked west at the Statue of Liberty and headed toward New Jersey. Lucas had to shout to be heard over the rotors.

"Where are we going?"

"Newark," Daniels yelled. "Liberty International Airport. USNORTH-COM's deployed the First Brigade Combat Team, Third Infantry Division to bolster National Guard and civilian efforts on the ground. They're already fortifying the perimeter and establishing operational command."

"Operational command?"

"We have to assume that New York City is lost. We have no way of knowing how many people are currently or will become infected, but we have to be prepared to defend ourselves from potentially millions of those things, all rushing our barricades at once, trying to get off Manhattan."

Lucas tried to suppress the mental image the soldier's words conjured.

He'd assumed the roadblocks and barricades would contain the virus, but how do you prevent entire populations from violently breaking through? How do you stop them from crossing the rivers and taking the back roads? How do you withstand a frontal assault when you're overwhelmed by sheer numbers?

The airport came into view straight ahead, lit up like the midday sun shone down on it. It was shaped like a human kidney, with the only roads entering the complex passing through a narrowing built over a stream reminiscent of a moat. At its core, the air traffic control tower lorded over a massive hotel surrounded by parking lots filled with military vehicles. Several sections had been cleared to create landing pads for helicopters coming and going with such regularity that teams had been stationed at each to expedite the process of loading and unloading passengers and gear. Networks of buildings and elevated roads connected three semicircular terminals, each of which branched into three long walkways leading to circular gates capable of serving numerous planes, although only a few were actively in use for olive green military transport planes. The runways behind them were hemmed in by the moat and fortified by a series of security fences.

The chopper settled to the ground, hurling dust in every direction. A man in a helmet and flight gear opened the side door. Lucas climbed out, ducked against the wind, and ran to keep up with Daniels and the others. They crossed Tower Road and headed for a building labeled Terminal B.

"This is where we part ways," Daniels said. He proffered his hand to Lucas. "Thanks for getting us out of that mess back there. It took some serious guts to drive in there like that."

Lucas nodded and shook the soldier's hand.

"What happens from here?" he asked.

"For me? A quick debrief and rapid redeployment. For you? I don't know, but those guys right over there will take care of you."

Lucas tracked Daniels's gaze toward a checkpoint at the entrance to the terminal.

"Good luck," Daniels said. He jogged off toward another soldier, who appeared to be handing out orders from a digital clipboard.

Lucas followed the other shell-shocked civilians to the intake station, where they stated their biographical information, answered a series of personal and medical questions, and submitted to fingerprinting and a blood draw.

"What's that for?" the woman in front of him asked.

"We need to determine who's been infected," the soldier said, capping a vacutainer filled with her blood.

"What happens if we test positive?"

The soldier didn't reply. He simply handed her a surgical mask and ushered her down the concrete corridor toward the elevators.

"Next."

Lucas sat down and offered his arm.

"Please don't think me ungrateful," he said, "but I really have to get back on the road."

"You aren't going anywhere anytime soon."

"I don't think you understand. I need to go—"

"No, I don't think *you* understand," the soldier said. His nameplate read: Fanning. "Do you have any idea how many people would kill to be in your position? They're out there with no one standing between them and the infected, while you're safe inside this fortress with food and electricity, surrounded by eight thousand of the most highly trained soldiers in the entire world. This place can accommodate only so many people. You should thank your lucky stars that you get to be one of them."

Fanning drew a vial of blood and handed it to his partner. He pressed a cotton swab on the puncture wound and folded Lucas's arm to hold it in place.

"Please hear me out," Lucas said. "I was called in to NeXgen corporate headquarters to consult with representatives from the CDC, DHS, DOD, and USAMRIID when this virus was first identified. It's imperative that I reach Colorado so I can continue my research—"

"No one's going anywhere."

"If you could just allow me to contact Colonel Xenos or Secretary Vickers—"

"Good luck getting ahold of either of those guys on the Nightwatch plane."

"The what?"

"The National Emergency Airborne Command Post. You think the President's just sitting in the oval office with his thumb up his ass? He and his brain trust are on their way to meet up with Northern Command at NORAD."

"I need to try," Lucas said.

Fanning's features softened.

"Look, man. I get it. We all want to do our part to help, but you have to understand that this thing's already out of our control. All we can do now is hunker down and pray."

His words were still ringing in Lucas's ears as he rode the elevator up into the chaos in the terminal, worked his way to the window of the nearest gate, and stared out across the empty runways toward the distant lights of Manhattan. He imagined those skyscrapers as fortifications and the streets between them as canyons and realized that no amount of prayers — or even the entire Third Infantry — would be enough to stop what was coming.

33

Washington, D.C.

Hodges hopped down to the tarmac, shielded his eyes from the blowing grit, and ran toward the waiting Boeing E-4B. The turbine engines of the modified 747 started to whine the moment he hit the boarding ramp. He followed Vickers and Xenos up the staircase to the main deck, through the galley and the National Command Authority suite, and into a conference room where six men were already seated at the table, at the foot of which was a video monitor displaying live footage from across the country. Seated at the head was John Mayweather, the President of the United States. To his left were Nathan Waters, the Secretary of Defense; Sharon Poole, the President's personal secretary; and Dr. Timothy Morton, Director of the National Institute of Infectious Diseases. To his right sat General Wilson Geathers, Chairman of the Joint Chiefs of Staff, and three empty chairs, which Vickers, Xenos, and Urban assumed, leaving Hodges, Bergstrom, and Ferris to stand.

"Tell me you have something useful," Mayweather said.

"Mr. President," Vickers said. "This is Dr. Severn Hodges, CEO of NeXgen Biotech. His team at Riverton has developed a cure—"

"A therapeutic treatment," Hodges corrected. "It's an injection of antibodies that attach to the binding sites on the virus, rendering it inert."

"That's great news," the President said. "When can we have it ready for mass production?"

"So far, my team has only generated a small trial dose. We're still waiting for confirmation of its efficacy."

"We should have the results any minute now," Xenos said.

"Say it works just like it's supposed to," the President said. "How long before we can have it in the hands of emergency personnel?"

"Barring any red tape, the first packaged doses could be ready within a matter of weeks," Hodges said, "with wider distribution ramped up in under two months—"

"Did you say months?" the Chairman of the Joint Chiefs of Staff asked. "That's simply not going to work. With such a short incubation period, even conservative computer models suggest nearly a third of the population will be infected within the next forty-eight hours. That's more than a hundred million people, and if the virus runs its course as quickly as we've been seeing, nothing shy of total isolation will protect the rest."

"I want to know how in God's name this thing caught us with our pants down," the Secretary of Defense said.

"It's unlike any virus we've ever faced," Ferris said. "While it's structurally similar to other hemorrhagic viruses, the hematologic component seems to act primarily on the small vessels, compromising the integrity of the structures in the brain and altering the behavior of the infected."

"We know all of this," the President said. "What the general's asking is why we aren't hitting this thing with all of the Ebola vaccines we spent billions of dollars developing."

"Because we haven't been granted the authority to begin prescribing—"

"You want authority? How's this? If there's even the slightest chance that it might work, you have my approval, as the goddamn President of the United States of America, to try anything and everything you think might have a chance of saving lives and ending this nightmare."

"It would be irresponsible to blindly prescribe drugs without testing them first. We could easily end up killing more people than we save."

"I don't know if you've seen the news," the Chairman of the Joint Chiefs of Staff said, "but people are already dying. Or worse."

"It's the 'or worse' that concerns me," the President said. "Sheltering in place might be effective against other airborne diseases, but not one that can literally break down your door."

"We believe the life cycle of the virus to be approximately seventy-two hours," Ferris said. "That means we can outlast it—"

"Is that the official position of the CDC? That we should do nothing?"

"That's not at all what I'm proposing; that's our worst-case scenario. We can try whatever existing drugs and antiviral therapeutics you want, but it's important to bear in mind that if we keep our heads about us, this virus will essentially burn itself out."

"Which has to be how we, as a species, beat it in our distant past," Hodges said.

"I get that this is some ancient virus that somehow survived in the arctic," the President said. "What I don't understand is how it got from there to the heart of Manhattan."

Hodges couldn't bring himself to look at the President when he spoke.

"One of our field agents broke protocol," he heard himself say, as though from far away.

The conference room fell deathly silent.

"One of *your* field agents," the President said.

"NeXgen has a contract with the Department of Defense to help monitor and contain emerging viruses all over the world—"

"And you did a real bang-up job, didn't you?" The President's lips writhed over his bared teeth. He took a deep breath to compose himself. "Check in with your people. Get me confirmation that your treatment works, and then send out that data to every pharmaceutical and biotechnology company in the world. I don't care how much money you lose sharing that information. I want those antibodies put into mass production right now. Am I clear?"

Hodges nodded and allowed Ferris to guide him from the conference room by his elbow. The moment they were out of earshot, she rounded on him and pointed her finger into his face.

"All of these people we're about to murder by stabbing them with experimental inoculations?" she said. "Their deaths are on you."

Add them to the list, he wanted to say, but instead he just nodded and followed her into a narrow corridor that led to the briefing room, at the front of which were three monitors displaying the live feeds from major cable news networks. A dozen or so people he'd never seen before were seated in the blue chairs facing them, all of them shouting over one another as they coordinated with their various departments and agencies on their cellphones.

Hodges took a seat beside Bergstrom in the back row, dialed Rankin's direct line at Riverton, and listened to it ring through to voicemail. He buried his face in his hands and tried not to let the others see him cry.

———————

HODGES PINCHED HIS TEMPLES. The pressure behind his eyes was as unrelenting as the cacophony around him. Everyone in the briefing room was shouting, and yet not a single word separated from the din. There was a constant rumble of voices from the other side of the wall behind him, where the battle staff coordinated with the men in the conference room and the power structure on the ground below. Pressurized air hissed, wind sheared, and engines roared. Worse, he couldn't stop his inner voice from screaming.

He was cracking and he knew it. His gut boiled with caffeine and stomach acid. He couldn't remember the last time he'd eaten, and he hadn't slept in at least forty-eight hours, prior to which he'd been in control of every aspect of his existence. Now, the world was spiraling down the drain and it was all because his field team in the arctic had screwed up and allowed one of its own to unleash this nightmare—

"Sir," Bergstrom shouted, nudging his shoulder. "I can't access the mainframe at Riverton."

Hodges stared at his VP of R&D, whose formerly polished head had darkened with stubble. He couldn't seem to grasp the insinuation.

"What does that mean?" he finally asked.

"It could be something as simple as a networking issue or a power outage, causing backup power to be diverted to critical functions, but coupled with the fact that we can't seem to get ahold of anyone . . . "

He let the implications hang between them.

"You think something's happened?"

"Look at everything going on out there and tell me the thought hasn't crossed your mind," Bergstrom said. He inclined his chin toward the plasma screens at the front of the room. "We just have to have faith that the lab is secure and that our team is following protocol. The problem is that we don't have access to any of their data to know the precise combination of antibodies in their therapeutic treatment or the results of any subsequent testing."

Hodges knew exactly what that meant. The President had asked him to do one thing, and he couldn't even do that. Not that it wasn't already too late, anyway.

He could see it in the faces of the high-ranking officials seated around him, men and women who'd been unceremoniously dragged from their beds and summoned from facilities all around the country. Their eyes were bloodshot, their brows beaded with sweat. How many of them had passed through commercial airports or flown on choppers piloted by men who'd done the same? How many had been unknowingly exposed to the very virus they'd been assembled to combat?

Hodges tugged at his collar and dialed up the airflow. He glanced out the window, through the mesh shielding designed to protect the plane from an electromagnetic pulse, and down upon sparkling lights and vast swatches of darkness. They were heading west, but that was about all he could tell. There were any number of potential destinations in that direction, from Peterson Air Force Base in Colorado to Camp Pendleton in California. Or they could simply be planning to keep flying indefinitely. There was an entire second flight crew upstairs, sleeping in their bunks, preparing to tag in when the first team needed to sleep. The idea of being trapped up here at 35,000 feet without knowing what was happening to his wife and children was his definition of hell, which, he supposed, was no less than he deserved.

How had it all gone so wrong?

That was of no consequence now. The only thing that mattered was fixing this mess and he'd be damned if that wasn't exactly what he was going to do.

Hodges gathered his strength, thrust out his chin, and dialed Rankin's number, letting the call ring and ring and ring . . . .

34

Riverton, Wyoming

Riley heard a ringing sound beneath the blaring Klaxon. She passed a window spattered with crimson and a dead man on the floor where he'd bled out. Davis stopped and stood over the body, his face so pale that she feared he was going into shock.

"They're all dead," he whispered. "Every single one of them."

She took him by the shoulders and stared right into his eyes.

"We're still alive, though. And I need your help to get us out of here. I don't know how long that tranquilizer is going to last, but I don't want to be here when it wears off."

Davis nodded, took a deep breath, and pressed on. The ringing sound grew louder as they neared the end of the hallway. It took Riley a moment to realize that it was coming from underneath the body wedged in the doorway of an access-controlled lab. She rolled it over and saw a face she would have recognized anywhere, or at least what was left of it. It was the first she'd seen upon waking in this horrible place.

"Rankin," she said.

The man's lone remaining eye was glazed over, his forehead a crumpled mess of plastic shards, bone fragments, and tissue. The ringing originated from inside his isolation suit. She pulled off his hood and reached inside. The antenna of a satellite phone protruded from a holster on his hip. She pulled it out and held it up for Davis.

"You have to answer. We can't let anyone know that I'm out of my cage."

Davis took the phone from her and recoiled at the sight of the blood that transferred onto his glove. He pressed the button to answer and put the call on speaker.

"Hello?"

Static crackled from the open line, but the caller didn't immediately respond.

"Hello?" he said again.

"Put Rankin on the phone," the caller said.

"I can't," Davis said. "He's dead."

Again, static buzzed between the repeated wails of the Klaxon.

"Who is this?" the caller asked.

"Davis Patterson."

"Who?"

"Davis Patterson. I'm with the team from the NIH. Who is this?"

"Severn Hodges, president of NeXgen. We've been trying to get ahold of anyone in that facility for the last half an hour. What in the name of God is going on?"

"I don't know," Davis said. "One second I'm standing in the lab with my colleagues and the next I'm being chased by a man who just killed my friends with his bare hands. By the time we escaped from the quarantine wing—"

"We?"

Davis glanced at Riley.

"Another scientist and me."

"Are you telling me that you're the only ones still alive?"

The panic in the man's voice was palpable.

"Yes," Davis said. "Everyone else is dead."

A long silence followed. Riley thought for a moment that Hodges must have hung up, but he eventually spoke in a tone of resignation.

"We're unable to access the system there remotely. I need you to bring it back online."

"I don't know the first thing about computers," Davis said. "I wouldn't know where to begin."

"You said you were with the group from the NIH. That's Lewis Pennington's team, correct?" Hodges plowed ahead without waiting for an answer. "I need you to collect the tablet we assigned to him and everything you can find related to his therapeutic treatment — samples, printouts, cultures, anything at all — and get to the surface. The Wyoming Air National Guard has already dispatched a helicopter, but there's nowhere for it to land up there, so they're going to have to extract you in a harness."

"Surely there's still a car here," Davis said. "We can just drive down—"

"There's no time. We need the data on that tablet, and we need it right now. It's no exaggeration to say that millions of lives are in your hands."

Riley closed her eyes. She understood what that meant. The virus they'd discovered in the arctic had somehow been released. She remembered how quickly it had spread through her camp and the violence that had erupted in its wake.

"Call me the moment you have everything we need," Hodges said. "The chopper will be there in under thirty minutes. I need you to be ready and waiting when it arrives."

Hodges ended the call, leaving Riley and Davis staring at the silent phone.

DAVIS STEPPED over Pennington's body and entered the lab, where Emily's legs protruded from behind the central workstation amid a pattern of broken glass. The tablet had to be in here somewhere. He'd watched Pennington flip through the files while waiting for the others to synthesize a trial dose, which was contained in the unlabeled vial he found lying on the floor near Emily's hand. He tried not to look at her face as he retrieved it.

Her hood had been torn off during the attack. He used it like a shopping bag to collect everything that looked even remotely important, including Pennington's tablet, which he found buried beneath a stack of printouts. They needed to get the research it contained into the hands of someone who knew what to do with it, or everyone in this facility would have died for nothing. Millions of others would die, as well. His mom and dad, his grandparents, everyone he'd ever known. All of them would die if he didn't find the courage to do what needed to be done.

Riley stood outside the lab, staring down the hallway toward the security door barring access to the quarantine rooms. Cullen was on the other side, and it was only a matter of time before the tranquilizer wore off.

"Dale's still down there," she said. Davis was about to ask who she meant, but then it hit him. Alpha. "We can't just leave him."

Davis thought about the images he'd seen on the security monitors while he was hiding in the office. Alpha had been lying on the floor of his enclosure, unmoving, the entire time.

"He didn't make it."

"It was my job to keep him safe," Riley said, tears streaming down her cheeks.

"It's not your fault," Davis said. "None of this is."

"Maybe not, but it was my responsibility."

"The only thing that matters now is getting this information out of here so that people might survive."

Riley wiped the tears from her eyes and nodded.

"Then let's get the hell out of here before that guy wakes up," Davis said, grabbing the hood and hurrying back toward the residential wing.

Riley walked silently beside him, stepping over and around bodies, her bare feet leaving bloody prints behind her. Davis left her to her thoughts. She'd been a prisoner here, caged like a lab animal, until the moment the man with the gun had come to kill her, the same man he'd watched butcher all of these people on the live security feeds. Davis couldn't imagine what had triggered Cullen to pick up a weapon and slaughter his coworkers, but he'd seen something in Cullen's eyes as the larger man tried to crush his skull with his bare hands, the same thing he'd seen in Alpha's eyes when he mouthed the words that Stephen Leonard Thomas and Richard Wesley Taylor had spoken in the moments before their deaths.

I'll be seeing you again soon.

Davis realized in that moment that no matter how hard he looked for the physiological source of their psychopathy, he would never be able to find it. There was something wrong with them that transcended biology and genetics, something dark and insidious that lived deep inside them, something unspeakably evil.

He and Riley passed through the airlock and picked their way through the hellish corridor on the other side. The walls were painted with so much blood that they took on a black cast under the red glow of the emergency lights. There were bodies everywhere. Most bore savage wounds inflicted by the teeth and claws of the chimpanzees, while other victims had been shot in the back as they were trying to flee. Davis found the first simian carcass, its cranium ruptured where a bullet had exited, near where Karen and Sanders had fallen.

The door at the end of the hallway led to a room he vaguely recognized from his initial processing. He stepped over the body of one of the outer perimeter guards, who must have heard the gunfire and come running. Riley extricated the man's semiautomatic rifle from underneath him.

"Just in case," she said, wiping her hand on her scrub pants and leaving a bloody smear.

The door on the opposite side of the room led to a hallway that opened onto the truck docks, where Davis breathed his first breath of fresh air in what felt like forever. Their footsteps echoed from the cavernous space as they followed the arrows painted on the smooth concrete, past enormous columns chiseled from the bedrock and tunnels leading deeper into the earth. The massive blast door stood open and the security office sat empty, the guards drawn to the massacre by the siren Davis could still hear blaring from the depths of the mountain.

They emerged beneath a dark sky blanketed by low-lying cloud cover. The shadows beneath the surrounding pine trees were as thick as tar. A frigid wind screamed through the canyon. There was no sign of the approaching helicopter.

Printed in Great Britain
by Amazon